The Ninth Circle

A CAPTAIN CAL WINTER THRILLER

THE NINTH CIRCLE

DOMINIC ADLER

LUME BOOKS

LUME BOOKS

First published in 2020 by Lume Books
30 Great Guildford Street,
Borough, SE1 0HS

ISBN 978-1-83901-235-8

Typeset using Atomik ePublisher from Easypress Technologies

www.lumebooks.co.uk

O creatures foolish, how great is that ignorance that harms you!
(Dante's Inferno, Canto VII: Fourth Circle)

Table of Contents

PROLOGUE

The Ukraine / Belarus border - January 2008

I'd never liked the word *assassin*. I was a soldier once, and killing was soldier's work. That's what I told myself in the small hours, when Conscience made an occasional visit. And when I looked up assassin in the dictionary, it said:

Assassin (Noun)
A person who murders an important person for political or religious reasons

That ruled me out by a country mile. And despite being good at the job, proficiency at killing was a shallow skill-set. And it had got me into nothing but trouble. So I should have been interested when Harry told me that this job was meant to be different. He assured me that it was a sign of my progress, that I was being trusted with 'this level of work.'

The client, Harry said, wanted the target *spoken* to. The target had been made a final offer of employment and needed reminding that a decision was required. Then, if he declined, I was to revert to type. All very well, but I was a wet-worker, not a careers advisor. The client, it turned out, was an American who spoke completely in euphemisms. Threats were *proposals* and kills were *outcomes*. Maybe he was an MBA graduate who'd wandered into the wrong profession by accident. I reckoned that as long as the end of the job involved *fiscal delivery*, then I'd be happy.

They gave me a codename, NEOPHYTE. I didn't think much of it at the time, just reckoned it was more CIA skulduggery, the sort we'd all gotten used to over the past few years.

When I got my arse in gear and did a recce, I found the target depressingly mindful of his personal security. He took different routes to work every morning and home every night, driving the now-familiar Mercedes, sagging on its suspension under armour plating. He lived a half-hour drive from the barracks near Stara Vyzhivka, which had heavy security on account of him being a colonel in the *HUR*, Ukrainian military intelligence. Built like a truck, the target looked a proper handful and carried a big pistol in a shoulder holster. Occasionally a steroid-raddled bodyguard drove him home, when the Colonel was too drunk to get his car keys in the door of the Merc.

One of my plans involved door-stepping him at home, another involved grabbing him on the way home from work. The last and most tempting involved just killing him and lying to the client about what really happened. Sadly, I didn't have a three-sided coin to toss. Having to find a venue for an afternoon of threats, followed by potential body shifting, was opening up a whole new vista of operational dilemmas.

I'd been in Ukraine for a fortnight, spending the first snowbound week at an agricultural engineering fair. I'd learnt a lot about tractors in-between sloping off to research the Colonel's routine. Then I'd hooked up with a pretty working girl in Kovel and hired her for three times the going rate. Within two days I'd moved into her apartment and began paying her rent. Ludmilla only gently taxed my wallet, grateful for my vanilla sexual tastes and good personal hygiene. She was also a reasonable cook, had a CD library full of vintage Acid Jazz and liked playing chess.

At the end of the second week I parked at a road junction near the target's office, the heater in my hired VW struggling against the brutal weather. The Colonel's office was in an isolated army base, a low-rise cluster of boxy concrete buildings half-buried in snow. I shivered, pretending to read *Newsweek*, the passport in my pocket showing me as a Canadian plant salesman called Brent Oliver. With the passport I got a wad of cash, an Amex card and my choice of things that go bang. I chose a suppressed Ruger .22 Hunter pistol for close work and an M14 SOPMOD rifle with a folding stock for anything else. The weapons had been delivered to my hotel during my first week in Ukraine, by a young American woman who looked like she baked Girl Scout cookies for a living. The guns were on the back seat, covered with a blanket.

As usual, the target drove past me at speed, into the woods and turning right. It was getting dark, the windscreen of my VW strafed by snow flurries. Helpfully, the Colonel's car weaved about, suggesting he'd enjoyed the statutory local Friday afternoon vodka or two. And I meant bottles, not glasses. Back at the barracks, the great-coated soldier on the gate went back to reading the newspaper in his heated guard booth, the glowing amber tip of a cigarette marking his position. I followed the grimy Mercedes, the snow-storm obscuring the tail lights as it bumped along the rutted local roads. Either side of us was endless pine forest. Brake lights glaring, the Mercedes fish-tailed on the icy road. I saw something dart in front of us – a deer, jerkily bouncing into the trees. As per my training I didn't hit the brake, just steered into the skid to correct my course.

Too late.

Pushing my backside into the seat, I anticipated the collision and air-bag deployment. My VW slid into the rear of the Mercedes with a grinding crunch, both vehicles sliding into a shallow ditch at the side of the road. A fat white globe exploded in my face as I scrabbled for my seatbelt. Rolling my shoulders, I pushed the airbag away. I grabbed the M14 from the rear foot well as the Mercedes' door swung open and the target's Sasquatch-sized bodyguard squeezed himself out.

This wasn't part of the plan. I'd not spotted him when the Colonel had left the barracks. I rolled out of the car into the ditch and crawled towards the Mercedes, catching my breath as snow worked its way into my clothes.

"Sir?" said a gruff voice.

"Help!" I shouted in Russian, readying my rifle, "I'm hurt!"

"Fuck you! You drive like an idiot," the bodyguard yelled.

I looked to my right. The driver's door opened and the target fell out into the ditch. His name was Colonel Vasilly Petrovych. He wore a grey military parka with a fur-lined hood over his grey-green uniform. And he was drunk, lying on his back and gazing up at the sky. "Colonel!" shouted the bodyguard, now out of sight and to my left. I peered over the top of the ditch to see him walking towards me, pistol drawn.

My cold weather clothing made me feel lagged like a boiler. I rolled towards the edge of the ditch, rifle cradled in my arms. Crouching, I elevated the weapon, firing as soon as I saw the bodyguard. The snow-smothered forest swallowed the noise of the M14, the 7.62 round tearing through his chin and palate, exiting his head just behind his left ear. He staggered for a moment then fell backwards into the snow. "Stop!" said another voice.

Then I heard the crack and pop of gunfire behind me.

Oh shit. I flinched as incoming rounds whistled through the branches near my head, felt my arse twitch the way it always does on a two-way range. Looking back down the road, another grimy Mercedes saloon had stopped twenty-five metres behind us. Two big men wearing grey winter uniforms crouched behind the engine block, pistols aimed at me. The target never had a back-up car before. It couldn't be an ambush: if they were expecting me then presumably the Colonel would be less refreshed. It was more likely bad luck. I'd picked up two more HRU officers on their way home from work.

My luck is often like that.

Behind me the Colonel was trying to get up, wondering what was going on. His fur *ushanka* fell off, and he pawed at it in that comedy-irritated way drunk people do. Breathless, I rested the M14 on its bipod on the edge of the ditch, lined up the car in my Trijicon sights. My finger, frost-numbed, squeezed the trigger. The first round hit the front passenger window, splintering it, the second gouging a hole in the chassis above the wheel arch. The Ukrainian officers ducked back down as I peppered the front of the car with bullets, 7.62 rounds slicing through the Mercedes like paper. Superior firepower builds confidence, and my arse twitched slightly less.

I was sliding another magazine into the M14 when Colonel Petrovych leapt on my back, knocking me into the butt plate of the rifle and gashing open my forehead. I rolled into the snow, the big Ukrainian pummelling me with meaty fists and growling like a forest animal. Back up the road I heard more shouting. I scrambled from underneath Petrovych and hit him in the nose with a palm-heel strike, breaking it with an audible crack. He lurched backwards, grunting and spitting blood.

We both looked at my rifle, more pistol shots popping in around us. Snow fell like an icy white curtain, our cars barely visible. Petrovych darted forward, fast for such a big man. I pivoted to my right and brought my booted foot up into his groin. Eyes bulging, he fell. Grabbing the back of his head with both hands, I rammed his face into my knee until he fell back into the bloody snow.

The first HRU officer broke cover, boots sliding on ice, pistol pushed in front of him. He fired, the bullet hitting my padded jacket and passing through the sleeve. I let the bolt slide forward on the M14 and squeezed the trigger, the round slamming into his guts. Disembowelled, He staggered to the edge of the ditch. I fired two more shots into his head and fell, panting, as his carcass tumbled past me. Glistening, brain-speckled viscera splashed on my collar and face. "Dmitri," called a voice.

Holding my rifle clear of the snow, I scurried along the ditch towards the Colonel's Mercedes. The last HRU man hopped down, pistol held ready as he looked at his dead colleague then the semi-conscious Colonel. He glanced up, like a hunted deer that could smell me on the wind. Our eyes met. He was no more than ten metres away. "No," he hissed. His voice was urgent and high-pitched. He tossed the pistol to the ground and put his hands in the air. I shouldered the M14, the HRU officer's forehead lined up on the stadia marks of the telescopic sight. Breathing out smoothly, I squeezed the trigger with the pad of my finger. The recoil from the rifle bit into my shoulder.

He wouldn't have felt a thing.

Dragging the bodies of the bodyguard and the two HRU interlopers back to the second Mercedes, I reversed into the trees. By the time I'd covered the front of the vehicle with branches and foliage, the snow was already beginning to conceal my handiwork. Colonel Petrovych was still unconscious: I duct-taped his mouth and cuffed his hands behind his back. He was a tight fit in the hatchback of the VW but it would have to do. My muscles burned from hauling the bodies through the snow, sweat itching at the back of my neck.

Leaving the Colonel's car in the ditch, I gunned the engine of the VW, along a forest trail, snow chains chewing at ice and rocks. I hit the M19 motorway and headed north, towards the border with Belarus. Two hours later I was digging in a lonely forest, icy sweat rolling down my flanks. My shovel chipped away at the frozen earth like a toothpick against rock. Behind me the car rattled unhappily, headlights illuminating the grave as I reached for the thermos flask. It was made up of fifty per cent sweet black coffee and fifty per cent cheap vodka. Snow tickled my nose as I finished it. It was thirsty work.

The snowfall got heavier as I opened the boot. Colonel Petrovych lay curled in a ball, bloody spittle dribbling down his chin. I ripped off the length of duct-tape covering his mouth. "I told them I wasn't interested!" he spat, soberer than he had any right to be, "fucking Americans!"

"I'm meant to give you a last chance," I said. "Do you want to change your mind and come across?" There. I'd said it.

Mission accomplished.

"You've figured out my answer," he replied, nodding at the grave. "Why didn't you make me dig that?"

"What sort of bastard makes a man dig his own grave?" I replied.

Petrovych looked me in the eye. His face was the colour of dirty snow. "I need to make my confession."

"Do I look like a priest, Colonel?"

"You're drunk enough," he coughed, although it might have been a laugh, "and so am I."

I crouched down by the intelligence officer, shivering now I'd stopped digging. I found my spare flask and let the Colonel gulp vodka-laced coffee. Then I held a *Sobranie* to his lips and let him have a drag. "I'm trying to give up," I said.

Colonel Petrovych had some stuff he wanted to get off his chest before he died. Mainly about times like this, when he was the guy with some poor bastard trussed-up in the boot of his car. He confessed the number of times he'd cheated on his wife, his regrets that his kids hated him and how he'd wished he'd been a footballer instead. "Are you done, Colonel?" I said gently, glancing at my watch.

"I think so," he mumbled, "you know what this is about?"

I was stumped by the question. "No, I'm just the messenger. Apparently you know the score if you want to accept the American's offer."

"Anti-ballistic missiles," he laughed. "The bastard Yankees want to build missile defence bases here, satellite-guided. We've already got their secret prisons full of Arabs. I helped accomplish that, and this is the thanks I get." He spat noisily into the snow.

I shrugged. Lie with dogs and you get fleas, as my old man used to say. He used to sell used quality cars in South London, so he knew what he was talking about.

"I am now, for my sins, working in strategic missile intelligence," the Colonel explained. "I am not a great strategist and I know fuck-all about missiles."

"Sounds just like the army," I said.

"Exactly so, but I have the ear of the minister, he is my cousin. Your American friends want me to sell my country out, pay me to manipulate my cousin. Persuade him that their missiles are a good thing for Ukraine. They can fuck off, I am tired of their secrets. This day would come, whatever I decided."

"So? Everybody wants to build missiles, right? That's the sort of shit that got Saddam into trouble."

"Saddam didn't have missiles," the Colonel glowered. He'd told me what this was about now, tainted me with the curse of cognisance. We both knew it. He gave a tight smile, his bloodshot eyes boring into mine.

"Okay," I said softly, easing him out of the car and helping shuffle to the graveside, ankles duct-taped, "I was there, in Iraq. I was a soldier. I know Saddam didn't have any bloody missiles."

Colonel Petrovych sagged to his knees when we reached the grave, snow spattering his face. His uniform jacket flapped open in the wind, rows of medals mocking me. I've got a couple of gongs myself. I wouldn't wear them anymore. I helped him to the edge, felt him tremble through his thick winter uniform. "Get on with it, then," he said, chin jutting as he readied himself.

I nodded and reached for the pistol. The Ruger was tucked in the back of my jeans, but had worked its way inside my long-johns. I'd been too cold to notice. "Close your fucking eyes," I said.

"No," he replied.

I shot the Colonel twice, once in the heart and once in the forehead. Eyes wide open, he tumbled helpfully into his grave. The client was specific that he wanted Petrovych to disappear if he refused to come across, never be found. I didn't know why, and I didn't want to either.

There'd been no need for a suppressor out here, in the forest. I found myself thinking how quiet pistol shots sound in the snow. Grunting and swearing, I filled the grave, picked up my spent brass, pocketed it and threw the shovel in the boot. Fresh snow continued to fall and would cover up my work by morning, but it would melt eventually. I guessed wild animals would pick the Colonel's bones clean when he defrosted in the spring. Then maybe one day somebody would find some scraps of uniform, maybe a medal or two.

Heading west, I drove hard all night. I was picked up by a dour American on the Polish side of the border the next morning. He relieved me of my hire car and weapons, booking me into a cheap hotel so I could shower and change. Twenty-four hours later I was in Prague, being debriefed by my American contact. He was called Ryan, and we discussed the quality of my work over *pivo* in some rough-around-the-edges Great Western. My pay, which was good, was wired into my Swiss bank account via the usual financial ping-pong route between far-flung foreign banks. "That was good work Cal, thanks," said the American, switching on a thousand kilowatt smile.

"No problem," I mumbled, throwing a vodka chaser down my throat and ordering another. "Assets and support in-country was good."

"We try our best, buddy," said Ryan, using the false bonhomie non-field men use with creatures like me. He looked around the room and tried to relax. Ryan had a soft, friendly face, an expensive Rohan outdoor jacket and clean hiking shoes. He looked like a standard-issue American tourist, a guide-book for Prague lying on the bar in front of him. I was expecting a gnarly fucker with a Texan accent, salt-and-pepper crew-cut and Lee Marvin eyes, like you see in the movies. Funny, how life lets you down like that.

"Well, I'll be off," I said.

Ryan was OK as far as spooks go, but I had stuff to do in London. The American nodded. "Sure, Cal. But there are just a couple of things I need to ask, if that's OK?"

I poured the vodka into my remaining beer and drank it, swirling it around like mouthwash. All I wanted was a hot shower, a hooker and twelve hours sleep. "Sure."

Ryan nodded at the girl behind the bar and more vodka appeared. It would have been rude not to drink it. "So, Cal?" he said, ordering a diet soda, "did our *associate* say anything?"

"Plenty," I shrugged. I wasn't going to tell him that I didn't exactly make their offer to the target the way they planned.

Ryan pulled a face, his eyes over my shoulder towards the door. "Such as? Just to see if there's an intel opportunity?"

I glanced over at the door too. Another standard-issue American tourist sat at a table, except this one was bulkier with a high-and-tight haircut. He was trying not to look at me, and kept glancing at a bag on the seat next to him. "Funnily enough, he thought you were screwing his country over" I sighed, "he regretted that his family hated him, that he spent so much time at work. He wanted to be a footballer. Just the usual sort of shit you get off your chest when you're in the boot of a car in the middle of a forest waiting to be executed by a drunken Englishman."

"Nothing else?" Ryan asked.

"No Mister Ryan."

"Are you sure about that?"

I stared into my drink, "why not put me in an orange boiler suit and wire my fucking nuts to the mains? See if I'm lying?"

"OK, no need to get bent outta shape," said the American softly, "we'll be in touch." He got up and left the bar, looking just a bit embarrassed. He left the money for the drinks on the side, like I was a hooker.

Which, I guess, I was.

ONE

Six years later - Mayfair, London, United Kingdom

I stepped out of the black cab, careful not to plant my spit-polished brogues in the slush. Peeling off some banknotes for the driver, I strode across Berkeley Square. The shops were January-empty, the sky low and grey. The sports station on the cab radio had excitedly reported an Extreme Weather Warning; sub-zero temperatures and a major snow dump. My phone bleeped. I answered, clamping it to the side of my head as I narrowed my eyes against the sleet. "Are you there yet?" said Harry, my handler, over the phone.

"Yes, I'm meeting the Russian" I replied. I'd worked in Russia for The Firm, spoke the language and liked the people. Russians enjoyed a drink and there wasn't too much bullshit when you did business with them, as long as you knew the rules. Oh, and the paranoia and conspiracy theories too. They loved those. Anyhow, for all its faults, The Firm tried it's best to hammer roundish pegs into roundish holes. It's more profitable that way.

"I'm letting you negotiate the fee," said Harry, "don't undersell yourself, or us." He had a gravelly West Country accent and sounded like a pirate. He'd certainly had me walking the plank often enough.

I didn't want to work for The Firm, but they'd got me by the nuts and never let go. They just gripped harder now and then. The Firm is something that happens to you when you've got nowhere left to go. I didn't even know what The Firm really was – it didn't have a website, it wasn't in the telephone directory and I'd never even met Harry. To contact us you had to know someone who knew someone. And that person needed to know someone too. I walked along Curzon Street. "I know the score," I said. My job, after all, was to make money for The Firm. I think.

"Yes," Harry replied, "and where there's muck there's brass. Just don't mess it up, OK? No cash, only electronic transfer and we're using the new bank, the one in Zurich."

"Zurich, I know the one."

"And I want to know the objectives ASAP."

"Yes Harry," I sighed, "why didn't you just meet Belov?"

Harry's laugh was a machinegun bark. "I don't meet people like him, far too risky."

I'd looked Sergei Belov up on the Internet the night before; an ex-Communist Party economist. He'd worked for the Soviet nuclear power program before ending up as an energy industry Baron. Belov made his name when the Soviet-neglected reactors started melting, managing disasters and whistle-blowing on corruption. After the wall came down in 1989 he, like so many others, made his money in the Cowboy Capitalism years of Yeltsin before falling out with the new guard. High-tailed it to London and became a patron of arts, charities and lost anti-Kremlin causes. Every six months the Russians asked the UK to extradite him and, because there was no treaty between us and them, Her Majesty's Government refused.

Belov lived in a private mews off Curzon Street, one of those secret places London does so well. The disgraced international rich flock to The Smoke like those little fish that follow sharks. Hidden in plain sight, the bone-white townhouse lurked behind baroque gates. Turreted CCTV cameras panned towards me as I approached. A stocky guy in a black North Face jacket and fleece beanie hat stood outside, a radio clipped to his belt. He looked me up and down, took in my smart woollen suit, black trench coat and Brigade of Guards tie. It was my funeral, job interview and court appearance outfit. And I'd never served in the Guards. I nodded at the bodyguard, "I've got an appointment. My name's Adrian Clay." My name wasn't Adrian Clay either, but it would do.

The guard looked at his clipboard like it was a lie detector. "You're early," he said in a Geordie accent. A police car cruised past the top of the mews. He pulled a face.

I shrugged, like it was my problem. "Sorry."

He got on his radio and announced my arrival. A heavily-accented Russian voice said it was OK for me to go through. "They're all a bit jumpy in there at the moment," said the Geordie, patting me down, "no sudden moves, OK?" He motioned at me to open my coat.

I assumed the position as he expertly checked all the places you might hide a pistol or a knife, "you kidding me?"

"Wish I was."

"Thanks for that. I'll keep my hands where they can see them."

Belov's place had a dimly-lit hallway the size of my apartment. Dark wooden floors, taupe walls, an Old Master hanging here and there. Two shaven-headed lumps wearing black suits stood watching, arms crossed. I checked them out, noting the bulges of weapons under their jackets. I don't carry when I'm in the UK, unless it's completely unavoidable. It's too much of a drama. A young woman in a neat grey business suit stepped out from a wooden door in a cloud of Chanel No. 5. "Mister Winter?" she said in a cut glass English accent. She wore her blonde hair short, like her skirt.

"That's me," I said, offering my hand, "I prefer to use the name Adrian Clay. I thought that was made clear before the appointment?"

She took my hand and gave it a squeeze. "I'm so sorry," she smiled. "I'm Melissa Compton, Mister Belov's executive assistant."

She was pretty enough for me to forgive her immediately.

One of the Russians produced a metal-detector wand and waved it over me, discovering my Zippo lighter, keys and Blackberry. The other held out a brushed steel tray. "No metal objects or electronic devices, sir," he said politely in heavily-accented English.

"Of course," I replied, "do I get an aisle or window seat?"

Melissa smiled politely and opened a door, "please come through."

The office was like the reading room of a London gentlemen's club. Stylish leather armchairs were arranged around a fireplace. Rows of rare books lined the walls, a brushed steel desk positioned by the window. Scented candles burned here and there, smelling of incense. Dark oil paintings completed the look, Old Masters and icons. A large triptych of medieval depictions of heaven, hell and purgatory hung over the fire. A black monster, demonic and glaring, dined hungrily on sinners.

Sergei Belov posed by his desk, a study in casual hyper-wealth. He smoked a cigar big enough to play softball with, shod head to toe in black. I recognised him from his numerous appearances on TV, where he was usually stood outside a courtroom as he won his latest legal skirmish, berating the Russian government's mendacity and cunning. He was burly, with a big beaky nose and close set eyes. He said nothing but offered me a top-end Montecristo. OK, I thought, you know I like cigars. Melissa wrinkled her pretty little nose in disapproval as I lit up and exhaled a happy smoke ring. "This weather," he barked, performing a mock shiver, "it comes from Russia." His accent was less pronounced than it was on the TV, his English precise.

"Not your best export, sir," I replied.

"It is good to meet you, Mister Winter," said Belov, a warm smile breaking his craggy face. His voice was deep and raspy, "you are a difficult man to track down." He offered me his paw, which I shook.

"That's a relief, Mister Belov," I said. "I try to be as difficult to track down as possible."

Belov smiled and motioned for me to sit down in front of the fire. Melissa opened a hidden wooden panel, revealing a fridge. She pulled out a near-frozen bottle of *Zyr* vodka and two glasses. It was just before ten in the morning, but I was expecting it. I threw the gloopy vodka down my neck and waited for the next. Russians consider it rude to leave the bottle empty, and Zyr is good stuff. "Here's to long-life" said Belov, refilling my glass "if such a thing is possible!"

"To a long-life," I agreed. I downed the second glass of Zyr and enjoyed the burn.

"I am told you have worked in Russia" said Belov, "and you speak our language. This was important to me." He motioned for Melissa to leave. She nodded and walked towards the door. "So you might *understand* these things, as a Russian might."

I raised an eyebrow as Melissa sashayed out of the room.

13

"She's very efficient and nice to look at," chuckled the Russian, "but my wife keeps a close eye on her."

"Really, all the way from the Cayman Islands?" I said drily. The papers mentioned that Belov's family were spending the winter there, in the Oligarch's mansion.

"Quite."

"How can I help you, Mister Belov?"

"Let's drink first," he insisted, cooing and fussing as he refilled my tumbler.

"Thanks, that's very kind."

The Russian swallowed his vodka and smiled. "If two men cannot discuss business on a cold January morning over a bottle of vodka then we might as well all give up."

It was difficult to disagree. I took my glass, drank and said nothing, enjoying the heat of the fire. It was as if Belov simply wanted to sit and make small-talk. We enjoyed a companionable silence for a minute, smoking our cigars and drinking vodka. As I've said, I like Russians. I gazed at the fire again, the one illuminating that devilish triptych. Flames danced across cherry wood, hissing and popping. Charred corners of envelopes and other papers lay in the grate. I let myself wonder what secrets had gone up in smoke for a moment but thought better of it. "I'm going to tell you a story, Mister Winter," said the Russian finally.

"Please, call me Cal."

"Of course, Cal, and you will call me Sergei Nikolayevich."

I nodded at the compliment.

Sergei Nikolayevich exhaled deeply and opened the humidor. He plucked another cigar and lit it with a Dunhill lighter that functioned like a small flamethrower. Then, after he'd topped up our glasses again, he told me his story.

A month previously, Belov had been in his holiday home in Grand Cayman with his family. A Russian he knew from opposition politics arrived on Christmas Eve, told him he'd important news. Apparently this guy was a bit of a pain, always trying to tap Belov up for money. "He told me that he had been approached by officers of the SVR, as an intermediary."

"Why would Russian intelligence choose him?" I said. The *Sluzhba*

Vneshney Razvedki, or SVR, is Russia's version of MI6, and is meant to do the foreign intelligence stuff. The old-school KGB is now called the *Federal'naya sluzhba bezopasnosti Rossiyskoy Federatsii.* This is the notorious FSB, which is like the mafia with cop badges and heavy-duty top cover from The Kremlin. The two organisations don't enjoy good relations, especially as the FSB thinks it can do whatever it wants, wherever it wants.

Belov waved his hand, "my contact's brother's best friend is in the SVR. Cal this is Russia, everybody knows somebody, I'm sure you understand."

I understood. Russians loved rumours, the more complicated the better, and there was always an 'impeccable' source. Anyhow, this guy claimed the SVR knew of an FSB plot to assassinate Belov. Furthermore, the operation was unprecedented in its scope and professionalism. Belov was told that he should expect to be dead very soon. "And you believe this rumour?"

"Yes, absolutely," Belov shrugged. "I have made my own enquiries and corroborated the information to my satisfaction."

The tip of my cigar glowed happily. "Sergei Nikolayevich, if someone's trying to murder you, wouldn't you be better off with a private detective? Or police? Better bodyguards, perhaps? This isn't quite my area of... expertise. I'm not a protection officer."

The Russian shook his head then hurled his vodka down his throat. "Bodyguards? I have dozens of them, ex-*Spetsnaz,* 22 SAS, former Paratroopers and Ghurkhas – the very best. Call in the Police? Perhaps... but it would only be as a last resort. But if I am being hunted by the FSB, an organisation that has assassins like my football team has world-class strikers then I want my own assassin: a professional like you, Mister Winter."

I lowered my voice, "I'm not an assassin." Belov could have wired the room for sound for all I knew.

"Of course not!" he replied warmly, "and I am not a thief. You are a highly experienced private military consultant and I am a successful businessman. Now we have positioned our fig leaves *just so,* is that better?"

I looked at the painting above the fire. Heaven and Hell. Purgatory didn't look that bad, "how much is this job worth to you?"

Sergei smiled, now we were no longer flirting and moved straight to Third Base. "When my contacts in Moscow tell me that my would-be murderers are dead, I will pay The Firm fifteen million US dollars. Untraceable bearer bonds, naturally, unless you prefer some other equally discreet method of payment. All expenses up front in cash. You will also enjoy all the material assistance my business can covertly provide."

I tried not to cough. My share of a fee like that might be enough to buy me out of The Life, get The Firm off my back. Maybe.

"Mister Winter?" said Belov impatiently.

"I'm sorry, I was thinking about your offer. It's acceptable, of course. Tell me, I know you're no friend of the Kremlin… but why you specifically, and why now?" My attention kept being drawn back to that damn triptych, the ancient scabs of cracked oil paint almost three-dimensional in the shadows cast by the fire. My eyes followed Sergei's, to the furthest panel where the devil was chomping merrily through a plateful of sinners. Heaven still looked safe but dull.

Belov's eyes followed mine. He smiled, "reasons for the FSB to murder me? Take your pick. Have you not heard of the Shakuvo incident? My involvement in the affair after the accident helped bring down a number of powerful ex-Communists now back in positions of influence. Russians have long memories. Or my opposition politics, I help fund most of the main parties."

Shakuvo had been the scene of a nuclear power station meltdown in the early 1990s. It was legendary in energy security circles: Mismanagement, corruption and cover-ups led to a major scandal in the immediate post-Communist regime. Belov, who worked in the industry, was credited with whistle-blowing on the affair. He came out of it a heroic figure, a man to be trusted to make policy on Russia's oil and gas assets.

The Oligarch ran a hand across his shiny scalp, like he was looking for some hair. "There is no shortage of reasons, but I suspect this latest attempt by the FSB on my life might be connected to Pieter Van Basten."

"He's the internet guy, right?" I said. Pieter Van Basten was the geeky hacker genius behind a whistle-blowing website called *forbiddenfacts.net*. Anybody with a grudge and access to classified material could securely upload it to the site, Van Basten delighting in his notoriety. He'd leaked stuff on Afghanistan and Iraq, on US foreign policy, on the activities of naughty multinationals and snouts-in-the-trough politicians. He was currently living in the UK awaiting extradition to the US on hacking charges. The location of the *forbiddenfacts.net* server was a closely guarded secret, one every intelligence agency would kill to find out. The US National Security Agency couldn't trace it, or GCHQ. Van Basten had made a monkey out of all of them, and they weren't happy.

Sergei chuckled, "yes, you could say he's 'the internet guy' in the same way Leonardo Da Vinci was 'that painter.' I fund his legal campaign, and for the past three years I've funded his online operation. I am, I suppose, the hidden hand behind *forbiddenfacts.net*."

"Ah" I said, "who knows this?" I was glad that Belov understood the need to be candid.

"Clearly the FSB does," the Russian replied. "I know this because two months ago one of their agents emailed Pieter almost a terabyte of classified data, addressed to me personally. This is too much of a coincidence. It is a plot of some description."

"What sort of data?"

Sergei waved his hand, trailing sweet smoke around his face, "much of it is still encrypted, but the gist of the recoverable material is internal KGB / FSB intelligence on senior Russian government figures and their entirely predictable proclivities; corruption, sexual depravity, murder, sponsorship of terrorist activity, identities of overseas agents and proxies, the supply of weapons of mass destruction to failed states…"

"And there's only a terabyte?" I said.

"There's probably more," he laughed, "there must be, there's stuff I know about the bastards that we haven't decrypted yet."

I nodded as Sergei re-filled my glass, "If I agreed to help you, where would I start?"

"Here," said the Oligarch, pushing a cream-coloured envelope towards me. "Here are the details of the undeclared SVR *rezident* in London. This officer is aware of the operation to kill me. She is actively unsympathetic to the FSB and their plot. There is a clique within SVR who feel this way, and I am happy for us to make allies."

"And?" I said, looking at my watch, a battered army-issue G10. "Like I said, Sergei Nikolayevich, I'm not a detective."

"Find this SVR officer, help her discover who the FSB has sent to London" said Belov. "It is that simple, for a man like you Mister Winter. The hard work has already been done."

I looked at the end of my cigar then stubbed it out in a square steel ashtray. "Please be more specific." I like to make clients spell it out. Just so there are no misunderstandings later.

"I don't want you to ask them to go home nicely over coffee and fucking cake!" the Russian bawled. "Locate and kidnap these bastards. Torture them until they tell you what you need to know then execute them. Make these degenerates fuck off back under their stones, teach them to leave me alone."

"With respect, I'm not so sure…"

"There's something else in that file – details of crimes committed by CIA deniable operatives called NEOPHYTES," said Belov, a smile splitting his waxy face, "dirty business, eliminating human obstacles to the American anti-missile programme in Eastern Europe, all forgotten now, of course. Ancient history. Would that be of interest to you?"

"Perhaps" I said, making my poker face.

"Should I wish it, much of this material will end up in the newspapers and pored over by international law enforcement. Maybe you will find yourself on an FSB targeting list, or at your Old Bailey facing multiple murder charges or extradition to Ukraine perhaps? Yes, that would be fun. Luckily Pieter is pragmatic enough to publish only what I tell him, lest he finds himself spending the next thirty years in an American Supermax prison."

I looked back at the painting of the devil, the vodka and heat of the room making me sweat. "You did say fifteen million US, right?"

The fire crackled as a grinning Sergei tossed a fresh log onto it. He pulled another bottle of Zyr from the refrigerator to celebrate our deal. "*Durakam zakon ne pisan!*" he roared, emptying his glass.

I knew the Russian saying. *There is no law written for fools.*

I wasn't sure who he meant, but I drank anyway.

TWO

I looked at the envelope Belov had provided. My head was fuzzy from the vodka we'd put away, stomach queasy from the burger I'd eaten on my way back to my apartment to soak it up. Keeping my eye on the envelope, as if it would crawl away of its own volition, I switched on my pointlessly expensive coffee machine.

It was early afternoon, snow-laden clouds loitering over the Thames. My apartment looked out over Hammersmith Bridge, a queue of traffic inching across as it headed into town. The place had a flat screen TV the size of a cinema, and a kitchen that cost as much as a new BMW. It had gadgets I still hadn't worked out how to switch on. You couldn't hope for a more luxurious or well-appointed cell.

Putting the letter to one side, I took off my tie and mooched up to my office, a domed mezzanine overlooking the river like the turret on a Lancaster bomber. I sat at my desk and tapped the password into my laptop, finding an email from Sam. Sam's husband, Clarkie, was my best friend in the army. He was my platoon sergeant when he died in Iraq. Every month I sent money, no questions asked. For Christmas it was eight grand in cash. She seemed happy enough about it, seeing as Sam blames me for Clarkie's death. Being British, she's too polite to tell me, but I can see it in her eyes.

Personally I think Tony Blair owes her an apology too, but that's by-the-by.

The email from Sam contained a message from the kids, saying thanks for their presents. There was picture of them in their small back garden, making a snowman. Jack and Lucy. It seemed wrong that they'd never know their father, but that's war.

19

I smiled. They were good kids. I didn't see them much, it was awkward and I didn't want The Firm to know about my private life. They might view it as another weakness, something to exploit. Sam and the kids lived down in Kent, the Medway bad-lands where Clarkie grew up, one of the places where our regiment recruited. I'd offered to buy them somewhere bigger in a nicer area, but Sam politely said no. She wanted to be near her family.

After coffee and a hot shower I opened the concealed safe in my bedroom. Inside was a secure satellite phone, ID papers and passports in three different identities, a vacuum-packed bundle of used twenty pound notes and a suppressed .40 Walther PPS handgun. There was also the battered cardboard box where I kept my medals and medication. I pulled out the phone and called Harry. He answered on the third ring. This meant it was OK to talk.

"OK, I'm out of the meeting with The Russian," I said.

"What's the job?"

"A Tier One; unknown number of targets. He's prepared to pay fifteen million US in bearer bonds."

Harry grunted. "That's stupid money, even for an oligarch. Bearer bonds are acceptable, though, if he insists."

"Yes, but it's carnage he wants, Harry. On the FSB." Outside, fat flakes of snow began to fall. I outlined Belov's orders and told him about the sealed envelope.

"Leave it to me, Cal," said Harry, "I'll explain to his people that this sort of request is…"

"He knows about NEOPHYTE. He threatened to leak it if I didn't cooperate."

"How?"

"It's the internet whistle-blower, Van Basten. It's been leaked to him, along with a load of other stuff. So I don't see where I've much choice, unless of course I remove Belov for the FSB, let them send their goons home. Looks like you're not the only one with some dirt on me. It must be a growth industry."

"Don't even think about it. Belov has friends up in the stratosphere, plus a small army of bodyguards. He donates to all the big political parties."

I was no stranger to blackmail. I only joined The Firm because they know about something I did, something that would put me in prison for life.

And the only reason they know is because I got drunk and told someone a secret. The Firm promises not to let slip my misdemeanour as long as I play ball, and when they think it's time they'll let me go. Well, that's what the guy who 'recruited' me said.

Harry was moaning about the job as I opened the fridge and thought about making a sandwich, then rifled through some pizza menus instead. I interrupted him. "Why doesn't he get his stratospheric buddies to sort this drama out for him then?"

I could almost hear Harry's brain-box chugging away. "They won't want to get their hands dirty with Russian house-keeping. Who d'you want with you on this?"

"So we're doing it?" I said.

"Looks like it," he grumbled.

"Andy and Oz."

"Agreed," my handler replied. "They're both in rotation, send me the number you'll be using. I'll get them to contact you within twenty-four hours."

"Roger," I replied, stuck between the proletarian hot meaty pizza and the sophisticated roasted veggie and pesto one. "Can you speak to some contacts and find out the score with Pieter Van Basten?"

Harry sounded cagey. "Perhaps, but depending how this pans out there are people I'd prefer didn't know The Firm was making itself busy 'round this."

"Fair enough, but anything the intelligence fairy could leave under my pillow would be appreciated."

"Sure. Keep your head down, Cal."

"I always do," I said, putting the satellite phone down. I'd decided that I'd go for both pizzas and dialled the order on my Blackberry. I made another coffee, sat on the sofa, and put the Rolling Stones' *Tattoo You* on the stereo. Feeling an early hangover I looked at the wine-rack. This was the part of my cell I'd furnished personally, and it was well-stocked. My drinking is a bit like the questions on *Mastermind* – I've started so I'll finish. Draining my coffee I chose a bottle of Margaux. Then I pulled on a pair of surgical gloves and opened the envelope.

Inside was a folded sheet of high quality foolscap. The note was hand-written in spidery writing. Pulling out a digital camera I took a picture of the text before I'd even read it, and scanned it onto my laptop. E-mailing it on an encrypted account to Harry I sat back down and found a notepad and pen. Then I read the note. There was a Russian name, with a telephone number, email address, vehicle registration index and postcodes. Somebody had done their homework and I wondered if I could find out who Belov used for surveillance. I read the note, committing as many details as I could to memory before putting it back in its envelope and locking it in the safe in a clean plastic zip-lock bag. My pizza arrived. I ate it and felt sick, and crawled into bed.

I slept badly, tormented by a recurring dream where an old NEOPHYTE target, Colonel Petrovych, was with me in Iraq. Petrovych was dead, of course, his frozen corpse sitting next to me in my Land Rover. Clarkie was in the back. I'd done basic training with Clarkie, before I became an officer, and the pair of us were thick as thieves. Petrovych's corpse was still wearing his snow-dusted jacket, despite the desert heat. It started laughing. Petrovych's dead eyes bore into mine as more American bombs fell into the desert around us.

Friendly fire.

That was what really happened. Clarkie died in a friendly fire incident when a Yank warplane dropped a two-thousand pound bomb on us.

Groaning, I woke up bathed in booze-scented sweat. Fighting the urge to drink, I stood in my wet-room, turning the shower hot-then-cold, letting the water pummel me sober. It was just gone 04:00, the witching hour where I've sometimes sat looking at my gun, thought seriously about putting the barrel in my mouth and pulling the trigger. I shaved, took my pills and made too-sugary coffee. I fixed eggs, bacon and fried bread, shovelling it in my mouth. Carbs and fat and sugar and antidepressants. A murderer's breakfast.

Switching on my laptop, I waited for the encrypted connection to access the internet. Via a proxy server I searched for *forbiddenfacts.net*. The website looked trendily low-tech, black courier typewriter font on a plain white background. There was an appeal for funds to run the site and pay for Van Basten's legal war chest, then file upon file of stolen Government data to search through. Today's special feature on the homepage included a document claiming to name every foreign agent working for Pakistani

ISI in Europe, proving that Van Basten's interests didn't include making friends and influencing people. No mention of NEOPHYTE. Well, not yet.

Opening a link about the man, it revealed he was idling his time away in a Wiltshire mansion owned by Sir Evan Sands while fighting extradition to the USA. I'd heard of Sands, a famous tech-industry figure who'd made a fortune from e-commerce. He was now a successful financier, his private equity companies snapping up and turning over what was left of the European public sector for PFI deals. A quick search revealed that Sands' group of companies were co-owned, vicariously, by Sergei Nikolayevich Belov via a Caymans based hedge-fund.

I re-read the note inside the envelope Belov had given me. The name was Colonel Alisa Turov, allegedly of the SVR. There were two addresses for her, one a serviced office in St. John's Wood, the other a flat in Battersea. The author of the note had written: *TUROV'S role in London is to disrupt FSB operations and build relationships with British intelligence personnel. She represents a faction within SVR especially hostile to the FSB. Her professional skills include special operations, agent-running and sabotage. She has operated successfully in Chechnya, Asia and Europe.*

I pulled on a pair of jeans, well-worn boots and a zip-up sweater. From the safe I took the wallet containing ID for Adrian Clay, my alter ego. Adrian works is an energy security consultant in High-Risk, Low-Infrastructure environments. I like him: he's nothing like me and has a great credit rating. He even has five hundred quid cash, folded neatly inside his Mulberry wallet.

My Blackberry chirruped. It was 06:30. I answered it on the third ring.

"Mister Winter?" said a clipped female voice.

"How can I help?"

"It's Melissa Compton from Mister Belov's office. We met yesterday."

"Of course, Melissa, how are you?"

"I'm fine. Sergei asked me if there was anything else you needed."

"I need an advance for equipment and stuff," I said, chancing my arm, "fifty grand should see me right for now."

"Of course," Melissa replied. "Cash or electronic transfer?"

I gave her details for my personal Swiss account. It's the one The Firm knows nothing about. She agreed to get it paid immediately, via three holding companies in Belize.

"OK thanks," I said. It meant I could send Sam and the kids a bit more next month.

Next up on my phone were messages from Andy and Oz, the other two operators I'd be working with. I'm the cell leader, mainly because I'm the only ex-commissioned officer on The Firm's roster of field operators, and The Firm is nothing if it isn't a private army. My commission also helps balance out the fact that I'm also the only non-Special Forces man on the list. Andy and Oz are both twenty-two carat, referenced ex-UKSF. Andy served as an airborne combat engineer, then with 22 SAS before joining the Special Reconnaissance Regiment, the SRR. Andy once told me over a beer that The Firm has evidence linking him to five armed robberies in Manchester and Liverpool. He didn't sound as bothered as he should've been.

Oz is an ex-Royal Marine who made Colour Sergeant in the SBS, the Special Boat Service. This, I like to tease him, is like a poor man's SAS but with dinghies. He's a sneaky bastard, and we have a few issues, but we get on more than we fall out. Ex-SF operators are like that with those of us who never made the grades for The Blades. Oz wouldn't tell me what The Firm had on him, and I'd been unable to find out.

The ribbing gets old after a while, that I'm not ex-Special Forces, but generally the guys go along with what I suggest. I'm glad they're on my side. The rest of our team, Guy, Eddie and Al, were out of the UK. I didn't know where and didn't want to. They were even gnarlier than Oz and Andy.

I messaged them to meet me in a cafe in Bermondsey at eleven. Before I collected my car I pulled on my old waxed jacket and went for a walk by the river. The world was shades of silver and white, frozen slush and mud. I enjoyed a cigar, a Romeo Y Julietta No. 2, and watched some head-cases row upstream towards Putney in the gloom. The things people do for a hobby.

Then, heading for my crappy old Volvo, I got ready to go out and plan a kidnapping.

THREE

Oz pushed a piece of bacon around his plate and shook his head. "This job is shit, Cal. I can't believe Harry signed off on it."

"'You gonna eat that bacon?" said Andy, constructing a sandwich with our leftovers.

I watched Oz drop the scrap of food onto Andy's plate. "Look," I said, "Belov has dirt on me. Stuff I did when I first joined The Firm. So I'm in whatever happens. The pay's good and it's a London-based gig."

"Everybody's got some dirt on you," Oz replied, looking out of the cafe window. Snow was falling on black, slush-coated streets. Opposite the cafe some drunks were sat outside a betting shop, shivering as they tanked cans of Special Brew. "Call me ungrateful, but I'd prefer an out-of-London based job right now." He took off his fleece hat, revealing a cropped head tanned from his last job somewhere sunny.

"I'm easy," said Andy, "improvise, adapt, overcome and all that bollocks." He stuffed the sandwich into his mouth and grinned as he chomped on it. He brushed crumbs from his gingery moustache.

"That's the spirit" I said, taking a sip of his tea.

"So you're being blackmailed, what for this time?" said Oz.

Andy coughed theatrically then slurped some tea, "I don't want to know."

"You really don't," I agreed, "but the money is rock-star."

"No offence Cal, I'm only in because Harry ordered me." Oz stirred sugar into his tea and fixed me with narrow green eyes.

"None taken." I said. "I asked for you specifically."

The ex-SBS man's smile was tight, "don't add insult to injury Captain Winter."

"Fair enough, Colour Sergeant Osborne."

Andy looked around. The cafe was in a side street off Jamaica Road, and apart from us there was only a bored-looking Eastern European waitress and two bin men having a late breakfast. "So, where's this Russian bird live?" he said.

"Battersea," I replied, "not far from Chelsea Bridge."

"Right," said Andy. "So she's going to help us?"

"That's the plan."

Andy's specialities were murder, technical surveillance to facilitate murder and disguising murders as accidents. He was the best I'd ever met at all three. A lanky Mancunian, he was easy-going and professional. I handed him Turov's addresses on a post-it note. "Andy, could you plot up on these addresses ASAP please mate? The St. John's Wood one is her office apparently."

"Roger," he nodded, tucking the note into the pocket of his black wind-proof jacket.

"What d'you want me to do?" said Oz.

"Come with me to sort out some tools."

Oz, on top of his other skills, was our team armourer. He's a small arms expert and marksman, used to teach Marines how to stalk. "That's why I hate UK work," he grunted, "moving metalwork around London, when it's crawling with Old Bill…"

"For fuck's sake Oz," Andy replied. "I've just got back from the Pakistani border, mate. I caught dysentery. There was an IED every fifty yards and no booze. This job's fucking mustard, sitting in an obbo van in fucking Battersea drinking tea and eating fucking biscuits?"

"You're an ex-Para," Oz sniffed, "you'd be happy if they gave you a sack of spuds to peel." If there's one thing Oz took away from his time in the Royal Marines and never lost, it was geeing-up Paras.

"I was in the Royal Engineers first," said Andy breezily. "Last time I checked you had to be brainier to become a sapper than a boot-neck."

I let them get on with their banter and checked my Blackberry. A confirmation email from my bank, *Tete Noire*, had dropped into my inbox.

Belov's people had paid in the fifty grand. "Right" I said, "you two get fifteen grand up front for expenses and materiel. Each. Just don't tell Harry." I didn't mention the ten for me and another ten for Sam and the kids. She must have thought I was a drug dealer, although I claimed to be on the private military circuit.

Oz nodded approvingly. "OK, this job just got slightly better."

"What did I tell you?" said Andy, "I've got my season ticket to renew for City, that's 'urgent materiel' as far as I'm concerned."

"Do I look like an accountant?" I shrugged. I was paid a salary through the Adrian Clay legend. As far as the Inland Revenue was concerned, Cal Winter was non-domiciled and working abroad via a moody address in Geneva. The rest of the time I lived a virtual cash existence.

"Right, I'd better get on with it," said Andy cheerily, slapping down a tenner for breakfast. We shook hands. "I'll text you when I'm ground assigned," he said.

Oz shook his head as Andy trudged away through the snow. "He genuinely loves sitting around for hours watching a front door."

"You can't teach it," I said. "It's like a gift."

We drove east, through traffic-choked London streets. Two hours later we were in Epping Forest. Snow flurries whipped through the trees, settling on the frozen slush carpeting the woods. "What a winter wonderland," said Oz glumly, pulling a shovel from the boot of the Volvo. I followed him past a deserted snack van, and across the Earl's Path, into the forest. Oz stopped and looked around, sniffing the air like a dog figuring out where it had buried a bone. Finally he sank a shovel into the earth. "Keep an eye out," he said conspiratorially.

Sitting on a log, I kept an eye on the return path. I was halfway through my cigar when I heard Oz's shovel hit metal. Ankle deep in snow, I helped him drag an old metal dustbin free. Inside was a parcel made of heavy duty rubber sheeting sealed with duct-tape. Oz took the parcel, laying it on the ground. He threw me the shovel, "your turn."

Pulling on my gloves I filled the hole in, brambles and frost-covered foliage catching at my clothes. Finally I was done, thinking at least I wasn't burying bodies.

Oz scattered leaves and kicked snow over the disturbed earth. He hefted the parcel on his shoulder. "How did you end up hiding guns in woods for a living Cal?"

We tried not to talk about life before The Firm, and when we gave away something about our past we usually expected something back. The more we knew, the more vulnerable we were if we ever got caught. "If only it was just guns" I laughed. "That would be the least of my worries."

"I heard a story about you, from a mate of mine" said Oz casually, like it was no big deal.

"Go on then," I said. "My fame precedes me."

"He said you got binned off SAS selection in week two for decking one of the instructors." Oz wiped his nose with his free hand as he traipsed back towards the car.

"That's a strange version of the tale," I sniffed, "because it's more or less true. I've heard that I stabbed and shot the fucker too."

"No, the way I heard it the other instructors kicked seven shades of shit out of you. You ended up getting RTU'd then cashiered."

"That's true, Oz. It was the worst kicking I ever took in my life. The only reason I didn't get court-martialled was on account on my gong."

"I knew about the Military Cross. Good drills. Why d'you hit the bloke?"

"I was mentally ill and had some full-on substance abuse issues," I shrugged. "Besides, he was a big-timing SAS twat and he deserved it."

"Oh, the usual," he replied, "were you just slightly loony tunes or bat-shit crazy?"

"Bat-shit crazy," I said, fumbling in my pocket for the car keys. "What about you then?"

"None of your business," he grinned. "Go and find someone who knows me and ask them yourself." He put the plastic-wrapped bundle in the boot and threw the shovel in after it.

"I'll ask Andy," I said defensively.

"He thinks he knows about me, but most of it is stuff I made up," shrugged the ex-SBS man.

My Blackberry rang. It was Andy.

"I'm eyes-on," he whispered from the back of his converted builder's van, "it's a townhouse, no movement and no lights on. No trace of her car."

"Received," I said, "thanks for that, I'll be in touch. Don't stand down until she comes back."

"Roger."

We drove to Oz's place, out on the coast near Harwich. He keeps a lonely cottage there, looking over the North Sea. It was dusk. The world was white and grey as we parked, axle-deep in undisturbed snow. Inside Oz picked up a pile of mail and headed for the kettle. Leaving him to it, I took the bundle we'd recovered from the forest into the workshop at the side of the house. Pulling on surgical gloves, I sliced it open with my Gerber.

Ninety per cent of The Firm's work was overseas, so we usually picked up our kit in-theatre. But in the UK we had to be ultra-careful – no heavy weapons, nothing traceable and nothing that's ever been used before. Otherwise we'd give the police ballistics experts who turned up to examine our handiwork proper hard-ons. Anyhow, Oz was good at his job, so I wasn't surprised to see the contents of the parcel weren't too shabby.

First up were two stubby HK 416 assault rifles with ten-inch barrels and Trijicon sights, then a silenced MP5SD sub-machinegun. For close work there was a compact Kel-Tec KSG twelve gauge combat shotgun and three pistols, SIG P250s. Another bag contained suppressors, peripherals and ammunition. Oz arrived and gave me a mug of tea. "Where do you get these tools?" I said admiringly.

"Father Gun-mas leaves them in my stocking if I've been a good boy," he replied. "Right, now we've got enough tools for fifty years in Belmarsh," I said, "let's make a plan."

Oz put the rifle with the other weapons and put another log on the wood-burner. "We need somewhere quiet for a chat with the Russian woman," he said quietly.

"Agreed, any ideas?"

Oz poked at the burning wood with a piece of metal. "Let's try something different and take her for breakfast."

"Let's hope she's not on a New Year diet," I said, loading a P250 and making it ready.

FOUR

I checked my watch. 05:30. "Contact," crackled Andy's voice in my earpiece, "subject's out and towards her car, she's slim, about five foot-seven. Grey coat, black boots."

"Roger," I whispered into my mic. I walked around the corner towards Alisa Turov's dark blue One Series BMW. Oz, driving my Volvo on cloned number plates, cruised behind. The street was dark and quiet, only a few commuters navigating the icy streets, eyes down and striding for their buses and trains. "Alisa!" I called, "it's me!"

Alisa Turov had short bobbed hair and dark, catlike eyes. She bristled and went for her car keys. I jogged over with my arms open in front of me, a smile on my face.

"She's in my sights" whispered Andy. He had one of the HKs in the back of his van. "Say the word if you need her offed."

"Who are you?" she the woman in faintly-accented English.

I pulled back my jacket and flashed the handgun on my belt. "Get in the car behind me, Alisa. Just to talk. There's a rifle trained on you, by the way."

She was weighing up her options, glancing around the street.

"I know" I said, "no back-up? Ain't working natural cover a bastard?"

Turov glowered and stepped towards me. I stepped back, hand hovering by my belt as I pointed at the rear door of the Volvo. She pushed me aside and got in the car, Oz looking up and down the road. "Go" I said calmly, the suppressed pistol in my lap aimed at the SVR officer's belly.

"Who are you?" she replied, opening her coat slowly to show me she was unarmed, "this isn't the type of approach I'd expect from MI5 or MI6."

"We're the new lot, MI7," said Oz. "We're the poor man's agency. We get all the shit jobs."

"He's funny," she sneered, "where are you taking me?"

"For breakfast." I replied, "I hope you're hungry."

She swore in Russian. She called me a fat bastard and offered the view that my mother worked in a bordello, where she was routinely made airtight by syphilitic sailors.

"Such a sweet face, but such a dirty mouth," I laughed in the same language.

Alisa Turov's eyes were so brown they looked black. "You don't look smart enough to learn more than one language," she said in English.

I nudged my pistol gently into her kneecap, "Colonel Turov, my understanding is that traditional counter-interrogation training involves ingratiating yourself with your captors."

"I must have missed the lesson," she shrugged. "There'll be hell to pay at the Embassy."

"The Embassy?" Oz snorted, "fucking hell, love, you haven't got a clue have you?"

"Are you FSB?" she said quietly, eyes darting around the car.

"If we were we'd have shot you by now," I said. Behind us I saw Andy's van tailing us, as per our plan. We were taking Alisa to an industrial estate out in west London. Breakfast would be courtesy of a greasy sandwich van popular with builders.

Driving against the traffic, and in silence, we made it within the hour. We parked behind an empty workshop. I'd sat up here before on other jobs and knew that the CCTV was broken. Andy ambled off to get sandwiches and coffee. "This is very, how do you say? *Classy*?" Said Turov.

"You're welcome, Colonel. Now, tell me about the FSB plan to kill Sergei Belov," I replied.

"If you'd have told me that earlier we could have gone somewhere better for breakfast. No need for guns and thuggery."

"Sorry about that," said Oz, "force of habit."

She relaxed in her seat a little, "You work for Belov?"

"Please, who we are doesn't matter," I said.

Andy came back and passed us bacon sandwiches wrapped in greaseproof paper. He nodded at Turov. "Alright pet," he winked.

"Thank you," she replied, "my coffee is black, three sugars." She sniffed the sandwich, shrugged, and began to eat.

"No worries," said Andy, retreating to his van with his breakfast and the newspaper.

Now she'd relaxed, I took a proper look at Alisa Turov. She had a runner's figure, wiry and slim. Her boots were black patent leather. Underneath her heavy grey woollen coat and scarf she wore a black business suit with a V-neck cashmere sweater. Her skin was sallow under a wisp of makeup. She looked, to me, like she was from southern Russia. "My information is that the FSB have sent a Major and five men from *Spetzgruppa 'A'* to eliminate Belov," she said. "There is to be no clever poisoning or subtlety, the intention is to send a brutal, unambiguous message to the rogue oligarchs."

I sipped my coffee. "Why?"

"I assume Belov has done something above and beyond his usual role as prime irritant to Putin. What that precisely entails, I do not know."

If she was lying she was good. I had to assume that she didn't know about Pieter Van Basten's link to Belov.

"Six bad guys operating abroad?" said Oz, "not the worst odds. What's their back-up and support like over here?"

"How do I know I can trust you?" she said. "Let us for a moment imagine I believe you do not want to kill me. Why should I cooperate?"

I smiled, pulling a sock-shaped plastic package from my inside coat pocket "You're correct, Alisa, I'd hate to kill you. But I'd happily knock you unconscious and dump you outside a police station with this nine-bar of cocaine planted in your pocket. You can tell the nice policemen a tall story about the men who kidnapped you at gunpoint. You might even have to admit being an undeclared intelligence officer."

Oz chuckled, "yeah, drugs and espionage. That's got to be at least an eight-to-ten stretch on a guilty plea. No extradition treaties. No diplomatic immunity. What a nightmare."

"We are on the same side," I said, "sort of."

Turov sighed. "The FSB have a deniable agent here, a man called Misha

Baburin. I've been working against him, building up a profile. He is arranging for all the services and equipment the FSB team will need to complete their mission."

"What's the SVR interest?" said Oz, "why are you protecting Belov?"

"There are reasons why Belov is of more use alive," she said, "but we are more interested in protecting Russia from the activities of the FSB. They are gangsters. They put our efforts to reform our country back ten years every time they launch one of these idiotic actions."

I raised my eyebrows, "so you're the good guys?"

"Predictably simplistic, but if you wish to see it that way, yes," she replied. "The FSB are an embarrassment. Every setback for them, as far as my superiors are concerned, is an achievement for us."

I looked through the window. The car park was empty, "I thought the FSB and the government were deeply connected."

Turov's eyes creased when she smiled. "They are. Perhaps weakening one weakens both. Things must change in Russia. SVR will be on the right side."

"We intend to take out this Baburin guy and the FSB team" I said quietly, "will you help?"

"*Take out*?" said Turov suspiciously.

"We're going to shoot them, blow them up and then incinerate whatever's left," said Oz patiently. "I'm sure in your country you just tickle them until they promise not to misbehave again."

"*Da*," Alisa Turov smiled, offering me a small, cool hand, "your intentions are sympathetic to mine, and it saves SVR a job."

I un-wrapped my sandwich and took a bite. "What will you tell your bosses?"

Turov thought about it a moment. "The best lies have a core of truth. I tell them that I have met rogue UK intelligence agents prepared to eliminate the FSB special action unit. They need a large sum of money, which we split fifty-fifty."

"Naughty," said Oz approvingly.

"I am a patriot," she said matter-of-factly, "but my salary is an insult to my abilities. Here, have this back." Turov passed me my P-250, which she'd somehow taken from its holster.

I laughed.

"What do I call you?" She said.

"Call me Cal."

"Call me Colonel Turov."

I laughed and Alisa Turov told us about Misha Baburin. The way she told it, Baburin was a career criminal who'd finally been arrested for extortion by the FSB serious crime unit. Facing twenty years hard labour in Butryka high security prison, he happily turned informant. Eventually given a new identity, generous funding and expunged of his criminal record, he was sent as an agent to the UK to set up a covert support network. Now in his fifth year in London, he ran a successful security company in Hackney. *Spartak Security*, named after his favourite football team, provided everything from burglar alarms, security systems, static guarding, bodyguards and nightclub doormen. Turov also hinted that he had dodgy ex-cops on the payroll too. "Baburin is ideally suited to support covert operations," said Turov. "His business gives him access to equipment, vehicles and information. We know he facilitated the killing of a Chechen in London two years ago."

I'd heard the story. A prominent Chechen dissident had been murdered in Kensington two Christmases previously, which had been put down to a violent robbery. I remembered the suspect, an illegal immigrant, was found dead in the Thames from an overdose. It felt dodgy because it was the type of stunt I'd look to pull if I'd have been given the mark.

"Baburin is also well known in criminal circles" continued Turov, "a leopard cannot change its spots."

"Unless you peel it," said Oz, "with a knife."

Baburin's criminality made him vulnerable. Criminals always grassed on each other eventually, even Russians. I pulled my notepad out of my pocket. "How long do you think the FSB team have been in the UK?"

"One month," said the Russian quietly. "Your country closes for the Christmas holidays, they could have driven here in an armoured car and nobody would notice. I would expect them to have completed initial reconnaissance and be ready to carry out their operation soon."

I opened the car door, felt cold air on my face. "I'll get Andy to take a look at Mikhail Baburin. Colonel Turov, I'm sorry for the inconvenience."

Turov's eyes narrowed. "May I ask how you found me?"

"You may not. We'll drop you back at your flat."

She slid across the back seat next to me and slid out of the car. She smelt of something expensive. "I will make my own way."

"How do I contact you?" I shrugged, pulling a cigar tube out of my jacket. I handed her my number, printed on a small card with no name or other details.

"I'm sure you'll figure something out," she smiled. She walked past Andy, gave him a wave, and was gone.

I watched her. I liked her attitude. Oz was tapping his Blackberry, "here it is, Spartak Security. Just off Dalston Lane."

The satellite phone was in the boot. I walked around the car and dialled Harry's number.

"What do you know?" he barked.

I explained what Turov had told me about Mikhail Baburin.

"I'll get on it, see what my contacts can come up with but I need to be careful."

"Sure Harry, but I don't think time is on our side."

"Never is," the Handler sniffed. "Leave it with me. Are you sending Andy over to take a look?"

"Yeah, I'll give him the details," I said. "Can you find out more about Pieter Van Basten? The SVR officer we had a friendly chat with doesn't seem to know that part of the story."

"I'll try my best" said Harry, "what's the SVR officer like?"

"Attractive, sharp as a tack, morally flexible…"

"Just my type," Harry replied.

Ending the call, I gave Andy the details of Spartak Security. He nodded and went back to the snack van to stock up on bacon sandwiches and coffee. Andy had a battery of large lens cameras in the back of his wagon, so I asked him to get some imagery of the building and people coming in and out. Getting back into the front of the Volvo, my mobile phone rang.

"Cal, Melissa Compton."

"Hi Melissa, how can I…"

"Somebody tried to kill Sergei ten minutes ago," she gasped.

"He's OK?"

"Fine, one of his bodyguards got there first."

"Who was it? Are the police involved?"

Melissa's voice was shaky. "No police, the bodyguards have taken the man away, I don't know where…"

"Tell them not to harm the prisoner," I ordered. "We're on our way."

FIVE

Sergei Belov held a white handkerchief to his blackened eye. "I cannot believe this was a professional attempt on my life," he laughed unconvincingly. With his free hand he shakily poured cognac into a glass until it was near full. He wore a dark suit and a blue open-necked shirt, stained with spots of blood.

Melissa fussed over him, a first aid box perched on her lap. Oz padded around the room, taking in details. He raised his eyebrows at the triptych over the fire. "Tell me what happened," I said.

"Every morning I walk my Husky, Vladimir, to the café. As a creature of habit, I buy fresh bagels, sour cream and smoked salmon. I like to have a moment of freedom in the morning, outside of this cage. I always have a bodyguard with me, this morning it was Gareth, an ex-Paratrooper. I owe him my life."

"Doesn't Gareth tell you to vary your routine as a security precaution?" I sniffed.

"Of course," the Russian chuckled, draining the glass and wincing. "All the time. But I am terrible at taking good advice. And the bagels there are excellent."

"You must listen, Sergei," pleaded Melissa.

"Please, Melissa, I do not pay you for fucking lectures. I have a wife for those."

Melissa reddened and put the first aid box on the desk. "Of course, Mister Belov," she pouted, "I'll be in my office if you need me."

"I am sorry Melissa," sighed the Russian, "I am not myself."

"No, I was out of turn." The personal assistant nodded at me and left.

"You were saying?" said Oz.

"This is Mister Osborne," I said.

Belov nodded and offered his hand, "many thanks for your assistance, this is a difficult time…"

"No drama," Oz replied.

"As I left the café a man attacked me. He looked like a tramp, like he lived on the street. He punched me first, babbling like a lunatic. He had a knife."

I sat on the edge of my desk, shaking my head at the offered cognac. "Who else saw this?"

"It was early, and it happened in an instant. I think we were alone, in fact. Gareth disarmed him, struck him and escorted me home. He radioed the other bodyguards, there is always a mobile team nearby. They found the assassin minutes later and picked him up," Belov said, pointing at his desk. "There is the knife this wild man attacked me with."

Oz examined it, "L85A2 bayonet, military issue."

"Not exactly the average mugger's first choice," I said.

"Where is this bloke?" said Oz quietly, studying the bayonet.

Belov looked gingerly at the weapon and re-filled his glass. "My men have taken him to one of my properties, an empty office. I am sure they will discover the truth."

"Sergei Nikolayevich, call them off," I said. "I'll speak with this man, and if necessary dispose of him. It's what you're paying us for."

"Of course," the Russian nodded, reaching for his mobile, "you are correct."

"Who heads up your security?" asked Oz.

Belov's fingers shook as he dialled a number. "Dmitri Aseyev is in charge. He has been with me for ten years, I trust him utterly."

"He's the only one who meets us then," said Oz. "Tell the rest of the security team to disappear. OK?"

Belov looked the ex-SBS man up and down, "you are used to giving orders, Mister Osborne?"

"Yes, sir, I am," said Oz easily.

"It's time to start taking advice Sergei Nikolayevich" I said in Russian, "if you want to live."

Belov smiled uneasily, his little brown eyes darting around the room. "I knew it was a good idea to employ your organisation."

We left my Volvo in the underground car park below Sergei's townhouse, among a fleet of Range Rovers and top-end German engineering. Melissa got into a 7-series BMW and drove us north through the early morning traffic. She looked excited at the drama of it all. "Where are we going?" I said.

"The office is in Paddington," she replied, weaving in and out of side streets and double-backs.

Oz nodded approvingly. "Where did you learn to drive?"

"When I joined the company Sergei he sent me on an anti-hijack course with BMW, in Munich," she said proudly.

I opened the mini-bar in the back of the Beemer. I looked at the cognac, gritted my teeth and helped myself to a Diet Coke. "How does a nice English girl like you end up getting involved in anti-hijack driving and kidnapping?"

She looked at me in the rear view mirror. "After I finished my degree in Russian at Cambridge I joined the Foreign Office. I was on the fast-track scheme, sent to Moscow, but it was rather dull. I met some of Sergei's people, had seen first-hand how rotten the Russian government was. So when I was offered a job with his organisation at ten times my civil service salary..."

"You decided to become a secretary with a sugar daddy?" I said.

"Fuck you, Mister Winter," she said airily. "Sergei and me? I don't think so."

"Fair enough," I pulled a cigar from my pocket. "Only asking. Mind if I have a cigar?"

"Yes, I do."

I lit the Montecristo and handed one to Oz. "I'd say, Melissa, given the company you're keeping passive smoking is the least of your worries." I looked out the window, at cheap hotels and careworn pedestrians.

"That's my business."

"Don't take it personally," said Oz, "but no it ain't. We don't know you, an' this is heavy shit. Understand?"

Melissa treated us to a throaty, crone-like chuckle. "I work for Sergei

Belov's inner circle. Don't worry yourself too much, Mister Osborne. I've got some dirt under my fingernails."

"They look pretty well-manicured to me," I said. "Can you tell me about Pieter Van Basten?"

Her eyes narrowed when I mentioned the internet genius. "He's incredible, not just at a technical level but in how he understands the culture of communications… *conceptually*. Sergei sees it too. Pieter isn't the easiest person to get on with, but he's certainly changed the way governments do business. D'you think that's a bad thing?"

So Belov hadn't mentioned his grip on Van Basten's online operation to his PA. I shrugged, "depends on whether it affects me or not."

Melissa sniffed haughtily. "As long as we know where you stand, Mister Winter."

Oz stretched like a cat in his upholstered seat. "We're about to do some medieval style interrogation on somebody. So it's OK for us to play Guantanamo Bay with some poor bastard because we're on the side of the angels?"

"Yes" she said easily, "absolutely."

"As long as we know where you stand," Oz replied.

Melissa dropped us outside a row of run-down regency townhouses houses near St. Mary's Hospital. "Dmitri's in number seven. The other men have been stood down."

"Thanks," I said.

"Oh, and sugar-daddies? Don't talk to me like that again," she glowered, pushing her blonde hair back under her sunglasses. "You're hired help, just like me. I don't care how many men you've killed."

"I'll try my best," I growled.

"I won't," said Oz, "I'm the nice one."

The door sprung open as we reached number seven. The building was divided into small offices and had a 'TO LET' sign outside. The few items of furniture left were covered with dust sheets, packing crates containing lonely computer parts lying here and there. "Mister Winter?" said a Russian-accented voice. It belonged to a bulky, crop-headed man in his forties, with a careworn face that looked like it was no stranger to fists and boots. He wore dark jeans, Chelsea boots and a black waxed jacket. "I am Dmitri Asayev. I run Mister Belov's security operation."

"Where's the prisoner?" I said, shaking his hand.

"Come with me" said Aseyev, leading us into an empty office, "I hope you have better luck than I."

A scrawny young man sat on an office chair, hands and feet bound with cable ties. Over his head was a hessian sand-bag, secured with duct tape. He sat erect, but still. He was wearing a dirty, blood-stained T-shirt and jogging trousers. A jumbled pile of tatty outer clothes lay by the door, along with a pair of filthy training shoes. I pointed at the sand-bag, "Your guys ex-HM Forces?" Good drills as far as I was concerned; the hood would stop the prisoner knowing where he was, stop him spitting on you and stop him identifying you. Admittedly, it would probably fuck up your invitation to the Amnesty International Winterval vegan buffet. But you can't have everything.

"Some of them," Aseyev nodded, "they said they used the sand-bags in Iraq as hoods. They always keep some in the car."

Oz walked carefully towards the prisoner, snapping on surgical gloves and a balaclava helmet. I did the same. He positioned himself behind the man's head. "Mate," he said gently, "I'm going to take this bag off, OK? If you move, or spit or try to bite me I'm going to hurt you. Stay still and everything will be good."

The sand bag moved as the prisoner gently nodded his head. I could smell the street on him from five feet away.

Oz pulled a small pocket knife and cut the duct tape, then pulled the sand-bag away. "There you go," said Oz, "now let's have a chat, eh?"

The man was in his twenties, with wild matted hair and a wispy beard. His face was pinched and pale, like he spent a lot of time outdoors. His arms were covered with intricate tattoos of stars and beasts and runes. My eyes were drawn to his upper arm, where his blood group and a distinctive glider design was inked. It was the Tactical Recognition Flash of the old Staffordshire regiment. "See that?" I said to Oz.

"Yeah, ex-Squaddie" he whispered. "Now the bayonet makes sense."

"Some of my men noticed the tattoo," said Dmitri. "He was infantry, right?"

"Yeah," Oz replied, crouching down in front of the prisoner. "What's your name?"

"Kill me. I've failed. Kill me."

"That can certainly be arranged," I said, "but first we need information."

"I've nothin' to say," he wept. His eyes reddened, tears dribbling down hollowed cheeks.

"Let's start with name, rank and serial number. You were a Mercian, right?" said Oz.

"That was before," said the prisoner. "Don't matter now."

"Let's burn him," I said. "Dmitri, get me some petrol."

"It might be the only way," Oz agreed.

"Huh?" said the Russian, "but what about the office?"

"No problem," I shrugged. "We'll make it look like rat-boy here was looking for somewhere to sleep. He started a fire to keep warm and whoosh!"

"Nice one," Oz agreed. "What do you think, mate? You want to die, right?"

The prisoner's eyes bulged as Dmitri nodded grimly and left the room. He fidgeted in his chair. "Are you fuckin' serious?"

I pulled out my Zippo and lit it. "Yeah" I said, "sadly. But on the positive side, there won't be much in the way of forensics to worry about after a nice big fire. Just some charred bones and your teeth. They'll probably ID you via those."

Oz put his hand on the man's shoulder. "Look, all this talk about death? What a load of bollocks. You're a veteran, you've probably seen worse. You tell us why you tried to kill Belov this morning and we'll have a brew, maybe a sandwich? Then you can fuck off. You have my word."

The prisoner's eyes narrowed as he tried to focus. He twitched and blinked. He reminded me of some of the guys on my ward when I was in hospital. "It's so fucking complicated," he said mournfully. "Serious, mate. It just is."

We sat with him for a bit, calming him down and being as sensitive as two guys wearing balaclavas can be with a bloke strapped to an office chair. Finally he told us his name was Alex, he'd fought in Afghanistan and he'd been homeless until six months ago. A Russian he'd met on the street had taken him into a squat, which sounded like a commune or something. The

Russian, who he refused to name or describe, was friendly. After a month or so Alex was supplied with free heroin, encouraged to have sex with girls from the commune and make promises about an exciting, alternative future. Alex was vague about this part of his story, and wouldn't elaborate.

He was vulnerable and homeless and he'd been groomed by an expert.

"He wanted me to kill a man called Belov," said Alex, sniffing back bloody snot. "Then my place in the group would be sorted."

"What's the score with this commune?" I asked.

"I can't tell you."

"Why were you asked specifically to kill Belov this morning?"

"No reason. I was asked to do a favour for a friend."

I shook my head, "what do you mean you were asked? Its murder we're talking about here, Alex, not popping out for a pint of milk."

He looked at me with dead eyes. "I was in the army. I followed orders to kill people there. And they weren't my friends."

Dmitri came back in with a jerry can of petrol. "How are things?" he said hopefully.

"We're making some progress, aren't we Alex?"

"Yes," he nodded, "I don't want to burn to death. This is doin' my head in."

Oz ruffled his hair and headed for the door. "Let's get you a brew and something to eat."

"Thanks," he mumbled, "you're not going to call the police?"

"No," Oz replied.

I motioned for Dmitri Aseyev to join me in the corridor. On the way out I picked up Alex's filthy green field jacket and battered trainers. "What now?" said Aseyev.

Tugging off my balaclava, I pulled out my phone, "we let the hare run and see where he goes."

I rang Andy. He answered on the third ring. "What's occurring?"

"I'm going to give you a postcode in Paddington," I said, "can you join me with a dog collar, if you've got one in the wagon?"

"Fucking typical, I've just got on the plot in Dalston. Been taking photos."

I updated him on the situation. "Get back here, mate. It's all part of the glamour and excitement of The Firm, Andrew. ETA?"

"Fair enough, Cal. I'll be there in an hour and a bit. I've got a dog collar in my tech bag, one of the new ones."

"How small is it?"

"Tiny. Oh, about the size of your dick," he dead-panned. Squaddie humour, how I missed it so.

"Just fucking get over here," I said.

Andy laughed and rang off.

"Dog collar?" said Dmitri, "what are you talking about?"

"We're English," I smiled. "We're going to have a bit of a wait and a chat, a cuppa then walk the dog." I offered the baffled Russian a cigar and waited for Oz to come back with the brews. From the office I could hear Alex howling and begging forgiveness, like he was praying or trying to cast a hex or curse. I didn't understand the words. They sounded a little like Latin, or perhaps something Middle Eastern.

Crazy.

Bat-shit crazy.

SIX

By the time Andy arrived Alex was clucking for his heroin. The ex-soldier showed us the track marks along his feet and legs. He whined that he needed half a dozen ten-quid bags of Brown a day to keep mellow. We promised to let him go so he could score. He shook and sweated and rolled into a ball, throwing up the food we'd given him earlier. Andy crouched in the corridor out of sight, a black ballistic bag at his feet. The bag was full of electronic odds and ends, tools, batteries and other technical stuff that only Andy knew how to work. "Here's the new dog collar," he said proudly, "all my own work."

Dog Collar is the name we give to concealable GPS tracking devices. It's not exactly top secret or James Bond; you can pick them up in any electronics store or online. This one looked like a small USB flash-drive, the type you'd plug into your laptop. We called it a dog collar because Andy used one to track his Jack Russell.

Andy picked up Alex's dirty green jacket, looking in the pockets first to see if there were any sharps or needles. They were stuffed full of bits and pieces – string, coins, bits of paper, some broken cigarettes, an Oyster Card, keys, candies and other junk. "This crap in his pockets adds some weight to his clothes, so he'll not notice the device," said Andy. "We should be OK." Picking a razor blade from his stuff, he gently made an incision in the inside lining of the jacket, on the hemline underneath the pocket. He activated the dog collar and slid it into the gap, sealing it with a small piece of tailor's adhesive tape. He heated the end of a metal ruler with his lighter, touching it to the tape. The heat sealed the incision and was invisible. "Voila," he said.

Dmitri stroked his chin, "very skilful."

Andy flipped open his laptop, a sand-painted Panasonic Toughbook. He synched the dog collar to the tracking software. "There you go - it's sited us at a GSM mast at 900 MHZ. I'd say it was a hundred metres from here. Let the fucker run, Cal."

I nodded and called Oz out to join us. He pulled up his balaclava and said hello to Andy.

"That suits you," chuckled Andy, pointing at the mask.

"You're still wearing yours, right?" said the ex-SBS man.

I zipped up my jacket. "OK, let's give Alex some cash. The first place he'll go is either back to his Russian mate or to his dealer. We follow him anyhow. He's only seen Dmitri's face."

Andy nodded and passed me the jacket. Back in the office we gave Alex his stuff back and cut him loose. I gave him a hundred quid from the shrink-wrapped bundle. "Now fuck off," I growled. "If we see you near Belov again you're dead. Tell your Russian mate the same thing."

"What's the money for?" he mumbled.

"The information you gave us," Oz grinned. "You dirty grass."

"I'm not a grass!" cried Alex, wide-eyed.

"Yes you are," Dmitri spat, pulling a suppressed Glock from his belt, "go before I kill you myself. Sergei Belov is like a father to me, a hero."

"Why?" I asked.

"Sergei Nikolayevich uncovered the Shakuvo scandal," he said. "He could have let it lie, like those other thieving bastards in the Government, but he risked everything to tell the truth. My family lived near the reactor. Four of them have cancers from the accident. Now they have compensation, and the truth."

"I can see why people respect him for that." I put the sandbag back over Alex's head and took him downstairs. Bundling him out of the back of the building, through a tiny courtyard, we put him in Andy's van. Ten minutes later we took the sandbag off and dumped him near Westbourne Grove. He limped off towards the tube station, leaving footprints in the snow.

"The signal won't work on the tube," said Andy over his shoulder, driving

towards Paddington station. "We'll just have to see where he ends up."
We parked in a back street near the empty office and chatted, the laptop
open on Andy's lap.

"What a dirty bastard," said Oz, "this mysterious Russian. Gets some
poor fucker hooked on gear and persuades him to nut a complete stranger."

"He must be very persuasive," I said.

"Fuck off," laughed Andy, eyes fixed on the laptop screen. "He offered
a homeless squaddie somewhere warm to put his head down, birds to get
his leg across and free drugs. Makes sense to me."

"Quite, when you put it like that," I agreed, "but it doesn't fit what we
were told by Turov about the FSB team. I'm expecting a professional hit
by *Spetzgruppa*, not… this."

Oz reached into the cold-box Andy kept in the back of the van and
pulled out an apple. "Exactly, I wouldn't be surprised if the Russian woman
doesn't know about this either."

Andy pointed at the laptop, "bingo! GPS activation on a mast in
Tottenham. Hold on, I'll do a mast look-up online." He tapped away on his
keyboard. "One of three possibles, near Tottenham marshes and the reservoir."

I checked my pistol and screwed a suppressor onto the barrel. Oz nodded
and readied his .45. Andy slid a magazine into his assault rifle. He didn't
like pistols, claiming they were for 'Cowboys and Officers'.

We drove through snow-slushy streets, the sun struggling behind a wall
of cloud. Andy could be a London taxi driver if he ever fancied an honest
living, weaving in and out of the rat-runs around the Harrow Road and up
onto the North Circular. I looked at the laptop, displaying the OFCOM
website that lists every mobile phone mast in the UK. There were three
little flags around the diamond-shaped icon that marked the dog collar.
"Has it moved?" said Andy from the driver's seat.

I squinted at the Toughbook. "Nope, he's gone firm, but it looks like
the signal keeps dropping in and out."

"That's normal."

"Yeah, normal for your level of technical ability," Oz sniffed.

It was early afternoon when we arrived in Tottenham. Andy hid his
rifle under his parka and we split up, patrolling the side streets near the

reservoir and Lee Valley Park. I didn't know what we were looking for, except that I imagined a squat wouldn't be too difficult to identify. We checked a couple of grubby-looking houses and an industrial estate. Then we sat in the van and drank tea, stamped our feet against the cold and bitched about our lack of success. All the while, the dog collar showed Alex where we'd originally tracked him.

On our second patrol run, Oz made the spot. "There's a bloke who looks like swampy sneaking into the back of a building, to the rear of the metal recycling plant."

"Meet you there in five," I replied, calling in Andy. It was getting dark now, which suited me just fine. We met on the corner of the road, near a junkyard and a residential street full of shabby houses. Cold black sleet splashed the pavement, keeping people indoors.

"Right, what's the plan?" said Andy. "I've got stun grenades, handcuffs, plastic explosives, det cord and a timer-power unit."

"Andy," Oz sighed, "we're roughing up some hippies in a London suburb, not assaulting the Maginot Line."

"Be prepared," Andy chuckled, "like a good boy scout." He dished out personal role radios with earpieces, which we switched on and checked.

I'd already walked around the perimeter of the recycling plant. The building at the back looked like a derelict Victorian pump house, dark brickwork covered in Ivy and graffiti. There was no obvious way in that didn't involve going through the chained front gate. "Andy, bring the van up to the junction in case we need to exfil, then cover the back where Oz saw the guy enter the building. We'll go in via that route."

"OK," he replied, jogging back round the corner.

Oz pulled a torch from his jacket pocket and led the way, pistol ready. I followed, the suppressed SIG P250 held loosely down by the side of my leg. The doorway was concealed with a length of corrugated iron, disguised to look like part of the fencing. It was locked. The door itself was made of wood laminate and rotten, so I put my size eleven against the base of it and rocked it with my bulk until it popped open. Oz covered me, his .45 aimed into the blackness. Then, switching on his torch, he washed the interior of the building with light.

We walked carefully along a piss-scented corridor, empty drinks cans crunching beneath our feet. At the end was an open doorway, a dim light flickering in the gloom. Pistol up, I made the best sight picture I could and edged forward. Oz looked at me and made a hand signal, telling me he was going ahead then to the right-hand side of the room.

The room was dark, the light coming from a guttering garden heater turned down low. The walls were covered with graffiti and heavy black drapes. It smelt dirty and sweet, the smell clogging my nose – unwashed bodies, skunk cannabis and takeaway food. Oz's torch, like a searchlight, darted around the room. I saw glimpses of trash, syringes, beer cans and used condoms.

Oz fired a fraction of a second before I did, suppressed pistol hissing, a flash of pale skin in the torchlight. Dropping to a knee, I snapped off a sense of direction shot at the same target. There was a moan, then the thud of something hitting the ground. I backed towards the wall as I heard more movement. The smell of cordite tickled my nose as my eyes focussed past the luminous tritium dots on the rear sight of the pistol. Again Oz's pistol hissed. Spent brass tinkled against the concrete floor.

Oz's torch illuminated the body of a young man in his early twenties. He wore scruffy work trousers and a donkey jacket. I saw one entry wound in his shoulder, the other in his right temple, a neat black puddle behind his head. His hair was matted, beads and pieces of braid knotted into it. At the corner of one eye was a tattoo of a tear – prison ink. "There," I said, pointing with my pistol. A long carving knife was gripped in the dead man's grimy hand, the blade dark with blood.

"Fuck," said Oz.

My eyes followed the beam of his Maglite. Alex, the ex-squaddie, sat with his back to the wall, facing the door. He was stripped to the waist, his chest and lap dark and sticky with blood. His throat had been cut from ear-to-ear in one quick, clean cut. "The room's clear," I whispered, pistol pushed out in front of me in a Weaver grip.

Oz held his torch next to his pistol and lit something in front of the corpse, "what's that?"

At Alex's feet lay a flattened cardboard box. There was a message scrawled on it in marker pen:

"That's freaky shit," said Oz.

I squatted down and had a look at the handwriting, as if there might be an answer there, "it's a message."

Oz stepped back towards the door. "Yeah, I agree. It means 'let's get out of here.'"

I dialled Harry's number. "Harry, we need Ops Support ASAP."

"How many punters?" Harry sighed.

"Two, both messy, three rounds fired. The only weapon for disposal is a knife."

"Some halfwit came to a gun-fight with you three armed with a *knife*?" Harry scoffed. "Sounds like natural selection to me. Can you wait to put the team in safely?"

"Roger," I replied. The Ops Support team was a polite term for The Firm's body-shifters and cover-up artists. They kept two ex-cops, retired murder detectives, on handsome retainers to clean up our mess. Using their counter-forensic expertise and criminal contacts, the bodies would be gone forever in twelve hours. Spent rounds and brass would be located with metal detectors and destroyed, all traces of blood eliminated. They were like *CSI Miami* in reverse.

"I'll call them now – wait out," said Harry.

I looked around and found the dead man's jacket. With gloved hands I went to retrieve Andy's tracking device. It was gone. "Whoever found that was switched on," I said.

"Shit," said Oz. "Let's go."

We left the room as we found it, tracing our route back to Andy's van, mindful of being spotted as murder suspects. Given the number of people I'd killed, it would be typical for me to get pinched for the murder I didn't commit. Andy was drinking tea from his flask, the heater chugging against the cold. "Have some of this," he said, offering us the flask.

I thanked him and told him about the body and the shooting. The tea was stewed, but milky and sweet. It hit the spot. We waited for the Ops Support guys.

"Fucking hell," said Andy, "dead tramps and weird messages. And now we've had to call out the Corpse Fairies. Maybe the Pakistan border wasn't so bad after all."

It took forty-five minutes for a white Transit van to arrive. It was liveried as belonging to a hazardous material cleaning company in Hertfordshire. Its headlights flashed. The portly ex-cops, who I knew only from sight, met me on the corner of the street and nodded politely as they lit roll-up cigarettes. I showed them the entrance, made sure it was all clear and watched them sneak in wearing overalls, face-masks and carrying plastic sacks full of industrial cleaning equipment.

Andy drove back towards the North Circular, shaking his shaggy head. "Freaky shit, Cal. Freaky."

"That's what I said," Oz nodded. "I knew this job was cursed."

"We need to speak with Turov," I said, "because this is more *Hammer House of Horror* than FSB special action team. I reckon we all stay at my place tonight."

"We can sit up and tell ghost stories," laughed Andy.

I wasn't going to tell Belov's people anything yet. In my line of work it's not unusual for the intelligence brief to be inaccurate, but this was something different. I was sold a search and destroy. I wasn't sure what to call this. Oz rubbed his closely-cropped head. "Poor bastards. That could've been me back there, living in a squat."

I said nothing. It was true. After rehab I had nothing. Home was friends' sofas until they kicked me out too. The Firm might have given me no choice but to join, but they did give me money and a five-star roof over my head. All I was expected to do in return I was kill people. When I thought about it, the only difference between me and Alex was the quality of our accommodation and our respective vices. But I was still alive.

For now.

We stopped near my flat and bought beer and pizza. Inside, Andy unrolled a sleeping bag on the sofa. We sat and watched the news, cleaned our weapons, chatted and ate. It was good. Andy told us some stories about

Afghanistan, somewhere I never served. Well, not with the British army, anyway. Andy's stories usually involved explosions, football and sex, but happily not at the same time.

My Blackberry trilled. The number was withheld. "Hello?"

"It is Turov," said the SVR officer. "I know somebody tried to kill Sergei Belov today."

"This isn't a secure line," I replied. "I don't know what you're talking about."

"We need to meet, as soon as possible."

"Tomorrow?"

"It's always tomorrow with you English."

"Funny," I replied, "with Russians I always find that you prefer yesterday."

"Meet me at the end of the road where you first picked me up, tomorrow at oh-ten-hundred. Come alone."

I exhaled cigar smoke. "I'll say I'm coming alone, but of course I won't."

"Of course, Winter. See you then." The Russian rang off.

Oz had my laptop in front of him. "*O Creatures foolish*," he said, Googling the phrase, "it's from *Dante's Inferno*. You were an officer Cal, what's that about?"

I laughed, "I remember a bit from Sandhurst, but not the lectures on Fourteenth Century Italian poetry."

"Ah, you *do* know what it is," said Andy accusingly.

"Bloke gets lost in some woods," I shrugged, "then goes to hell."

"We've all been there," said Oz.

SEVEN

I stood stamping my feet against the cold outside Turov's apartment. I wore boots and cargo trousers, my pistol in a pancake holster under my sweater, spare magazines in the pockets of my waxed jacket. Andy and Oz, parked halfway up the road, already had three parking tickets. London parking attendants are like monetized, moped-borne *Spetsnaz*, and they never sleep. An anonymous-looking Ford with privacy-glassed windows pulled up next to me. Turov nodded impatiently at the passenger door. I nodded and got in. "Where are we going?"

"St. John's Wood, to my office." Turov wore a smart charcoal business suit, heels and smelt of Chanel No. 5. Her hair was in a glossy bob, her lips painted some shade of plum.

I reckoned Alisa Turov's cheekbones were sharp enough to draw blood and she looked good enough to eat. I looked at my watch, "given London traffic that's enough time for you to tell me a bit about yourself."

"I am an intelligence officer," she said curtly. "I don't get paid to talk about myself." Alisa switched on Radio Three as we crossed the bridge into town. She smiled as mournful-sounding music flooded the car.

"Who do you get paid to talk about?"

"Men like you, Captain Calum Aloysius Winter. You were born in London to what you British would call a lower middle-class Catholic family. Your father was from Donegal in the Republic of Ireland. He moved to south London and sold used motor cars. Your mother was Italian. She was an emergency room nurse at St. Thomas' Hospital."

"I sound fascinating. Do tell me more."

53

"You grew up bilingual and seem to have a natural affinity for languages. In the army you were an enlisted infantryman, then a reconnaissance specialist. You won a Military Cross in Iraq for leading a bayonet charge against an insurgent compound in Maysan Province. There is also your Mention in Dispatches from the Balkans, something very heroic about negotiating with Serb militias to arrange safe passage for Bosnian children."

"Alisa," I interrupted, "the truth about those two incidents was lost in the fog of war."

"If you say so, Winter. You were commissioned as an officer after four years as a private soldier. You served for a total of eleven and a half years. You were unable to achieve promotion to Major due to an inability to impress your superior officers and a tendency to insubordination. However, you were selected for Special Forces training. SAS. You failed."

"No, I failed Special Forces *selection*. I didn't get as far as training," I replied, trying to sound like I didn't give a shit. In the wing mirror I saw Andy's van two cars behind us.

Turov waved a hand. "Military semantics? Not important. You completed operational tours of Bosnia, Northern Ireland, Sierra Leone and three in Iraq. After you were discharged from the British army for assault and substance abuse, you joined Longbow Group private military company and worked in Iraq, Jordan, Israel and Lebanon… then you vanish. You reappear as an operator on The Firm seven years ago, initially sub-contracted as a CIA deniable asset." Turov gave me a tight smile and accelerated along a bus lane. "You are described as *an accomplished and professional killer, more thoughtful than the average mercenary thug*."

"Flattery will get you nowhere. You forgot to mention rehab, my Open University degree and the wine-tasting course I took in Umbria," I shrugged, popping the top off of a cigar tube. "And my old man? He'd be feckin' furious if you described him as 'lower middle-class,' he was a working-class hero."

"He died eight years ago. We *know* about you," Turov sniffed. "We also know about your history of mental illness. I didn't say you were an ideal candidate for this job, Winter."

"Congratulations," I said. "It's a shame the SVR doesn't appear to know as much about the important stuff."

She arched an eyebrow, "such as?"

"Why it was a homeless army veteran that tried to murder Sergei Belov yesterday. When we followed him to a squat, another homeless bloke attacked us with a knife. The first guy we found, the one who attacked Belov, was dead with his throat cut."

She fixed me with dark, almond-shaped eyes, "was there anything else?"

"A sign by the body: It said *O creatures foolish, how great is that ignorance that harms you!*"

"*Govno!*" she spat, "Fyodor Volk! He is obsessed with Dante."

I lowered the electric window to let cigar smoke waft away. Outside, on Chelsea Embankment, police were carrying out an anti-terrorism check. An illuminated sign said TERRORISM: SORRY FOR THE INCONVENIENCE, like Al Qaeda were a problem akin to road works. Armed cops in baggy fatigues milled about, sniffer dogs darting excitedly in the cars chosen for searching. My handgun suddenly felt hot in its holster. Looking up I saw riflemen on the roofs of nearby buildings. A helicopter buzzed overhead. I smiled at a pretty cop directing traffic into a search area. She ignored me. "Fyodor who?" I said.

Alisa Turov eyed the armoured and helmeted firearms officers warily as we were waved on. She accelerated towards the Houses of Parliament, where fires burnt from a demonstration on College Green. "Volk? A madman. The FSB's most precious asset when it comes to strategic targeted killing. But this doesn't make sense…"

"*Strategic targeted killing?*" I laughed, "I've heard wet-work called lots of things, but that's a first."

"I am serious. Volk can arrange for any man to be killed. I think he could take a high value target like a US President, if he put his mind to it."

"Alisa, you're not making any sense. Who is this guy?"

"I will explain." And, as we crawled through the central London traffic, hail whipping across the streets like bullets, she told me about Fyodor Volk.

Volk was from a small town near Shakuvo, in the Tatarstan region of central Russia. This was near the power plant where Sergei Belov made his name uncovering the scandal after the reactor there went into meltdown. Russia had another mini-Chernobyl on its hands, and the incompetence and corruption of the staff at the plant had become the stuff of legend. Fyodor's father, an engineer, died in the initial accident and his mother died of radiation sickness a year later. Even now, Shakuvo was a forbidden hot zone, only accessible to scientists and the military. "You'd have thought that Belov's role in the Shakuvo affair might make Volk think twice about taking him as a mark," I said, "ungrateful bastard."

Turov shrugged. "He wouldn't care less. His file makes yours look like Mother Teresa's – Volk is a criminally-insane sociopath with an acute narcissistic personality disorder. Of course, these traits made him a sensation in the FSB."

"You've got a file on Mother Teresa?"

"We have a file on everybody. We were so busy with our files we forgot to notice we'd lost the Cold War." She went on to explain that Volk moved to Moscow to live with his aunt, the authorities losing track of him in the mid-1990's, "it was a chaotic time in Russia, some records were destroyed including what we suspect was Volk's criminal record. He reappeared at the FSB training academy where he was fast-tracked onto 'V' Department."

I'd heard about the FSB's 'V' Department, or *Vympel*. "Covert dirty tricks, right?"

"Correct. But Volk wasn't the usual commando type. He did a tour of Chechnya as a field interrogator and surveillance operative then disappeared again. The official story was that he was fired for discipline offences, but that was his cover. In fact he went to the Covert Psychological and Unorthodox Special Warfare School at Makhachkala where he was he was part of the *Petrushka* Programme."

I knew that *Petrushka* was a puppet, the Russian equivalent of Mister Punch, the ugly wife-beating mannequin beloved of small children. "How do you know all this stuff?" I said.

"It is my job. My official role is overseas agent development, but I am also involved in the FSB monitoring programme. One day we will see them all in court, or in their caskets. I am collecting material for that day. Trust me, studying the FSB is like watching scorpions in a jar," Turov smiled. "*Petrushka* is one of their dirtiest secrets."

I finished my cigar. "The suspense is killing me."

"It might yet," she replied.

Turov explained that in the 1960s the KGB trialled advanced interrogation techniques involving suggestion, hypnotism and coercive persuasion. They brought in Chinese experts who'd used the techniques during the Korean War. They went on to experiment with drugs, sexual grooming, hypnotism and extreme religious and cult activities as coercive tools to make the weak-willed do their bidding. The results were mixed, and the programme was almost cut at the end of the Cold War. But the FSB retained it and Fyodor Volk was their star recruit, showing uncanny powers of persuasion and manipulation. "Volk is apparently extremely physically attractive," said Turov. "He is bisexual and uses this to his advantage. He will fuck anyone if it is to his advantage."

"Nothing wrong with that," I shrugged.

"I didn't say there was. There are no photographs of him in existence, so I have to take this on trust."

Volk's first subject was an educationally subnormal military recruit of unnatural physical strength. Given to the FSB officer as a pet, the recruit murdered and cannibalized his family at Volk's direction before committing suicide when ordered. "Volk was eventually sent back to Chechnya," said Turov, face grim, "to groom young rebel prisoners to go back and kill their leaders. Then he went to the Baltic States and set up a religious cult that poisoned anti-Russian activists. Then he disappears somewhere in South Africa and goes freelance, possibly for white supremacists. The FSB retained him for special cases."

I shook my head, "it sounds incredible."

Turov nodded. "It is, but Volk is a glass cannon; his operations are clean, because there is always a scapegoat. The assassinations are usually attributed to stalkers or lunatics. But his operations are fragile. They take a long time to put into place, and can be easily disrupted until they reach critical mass. So, as I say, he is a strategic asset. The decision to use such a precious resource is a major one to take…"

"How much time does it take for Volk to plan a hit?"

"Up to two years?" she said. "Perhaps more, going by previous operations."

"So the FSB could have been planning the hit on Belov for two years?"

"It is difficult to say. But it is not a recent decision if Volk is at the stage where his killers are operational."

"So what's the deal with the other hit team, the *Spetzgruppa*?"

"Until fifteen minutes ago I thought they were the only unit deployed against Belov," she said, "and they are definitely here. Misha Baburin is real, the FSB's best deniable asset in the UK. Anyway, we now meet some people at my office, they can help."

"Who?" I said sharply.

Turov smiled, "contacts I have cultivated here in the UK. Please, Cal, we are partners now right? You must trust me."

My hand brushed the pancake holster against my kidney where the SIG was tucked away. I couldn't see Andy's van behind me and hoped he hadn't lost us in the traffic. In any case, the spare GPS dog collar sewn into my jacket would help him. Turov and I spent the rest of the journey in silence, listening to classical music. I'm more of a Rolling Stones man, but I picked up some Mahler and I think Strauss. "I used to play the violin," said Alisa suddenly.

"Ah, a classic Russian over-achiever I suppose?" I teased. "Ballet, athletics, marksmanship, top marks at University, off to the SVR academy, best recruit of your syndicate and groomed for overseas operations…"

"How did you know?" she said, face reddening.

"Just a guess."

Turov's office was in a small block near the American School. We parked and went inside, stamping snow from our boots on a coconut mat. A bored receptionist sat by a fan heater, drinking tea and reading a Russian fashion magazine. Opposite her, trying not to look at me was a dangerous-looking little bloke wearing jeans and a windproof jacket. He was wearing a clear gel earpiece and leather gloves. Definitely an operator of some description. "Are you setting me up?" I whispered to Turov.

"Grow up, Winter."

I followed the SVR officer up two flights of stairs and into her office. A sign on the door read *Inter-Russia IT Solutions*. The office was set up as a conference room with an open-plan workspace near the window. The walls were decorated with tourist-style posters of Russian attractions, the Onion Domes of the Kremlin and the *Peterhof* in Saint Petersburg.

Two men sat at a table. The first was in his fifties, fat and wearing a dark woollen suit. His deep-set eyes, encased in grey bags, were watery behind thick tortoiseshell glasses. He had a face like a man with three ex-wives and a bad divorce lawyer. The second guy was an ex-army officer. I was one so I know. In his late thirties, he radiated confidence like a power station and wore red corduroys, suede brogues and a gingham checked shirt. The pinky ring and G10 watch with a claret-and-navy Brigade of Guards strap completed the look. "This is the one I was telling you about," said Turov, pouring coffee. In front of them was a plate of biscuits, which neither had touched.

I helped myself to a chocolate cookie and smiled. The older man coughed politely. His accent was a gentle Edinburgh burr. "I'm not sure we should be meeting Captain Winter," he said, looking at Turov.

"Yes," brayed the ex-army officer, whose accent was exactly what you'd expect, "there's a… conduit for dealing with his organisation. And it isn't us." Neither of them had acknowledged me.

"Hi, I'm Cal and I'm an alcoholic," I said.

Turov rolled her eyes as she spooned sugar into her brew. "MI6 and your protocols and 'conduits.' Is bullshit. This is the situation we are in – Belov has hired this man to protect him by killing the FSB team, he is talking to me, he has information… what else matters? What else do you want?"

When Belov said *MI6* both men bristled. The army-looking bloke hissed, stood up and strode around the room. And it wasn't because the correct term is 'SIS' either. "We're from the FCO," he said lamely, "and we aren't exactly in a position to negotiate with… this sort of *asset*."

"FCO?" I laughed, "sure, and I'm the Avon Lady." I helped myself to another biscuit. My Blackberry buzzed in my pocket. I checked the message, which was from Oz: HOSTILES ON THE PLOT. EX-SF. The spooks had brought back-up, which was to be expected.

I sent a reply: NO PROBLEM, SIS INCREMENTS.

The lardy intelligence officer looked into his coffee, then sadly at the biscuits. He was either pondering my status as an occasional MI6 deniable, or his waistline. "Well now we're here," he said, "it's probably best we have a preliminary discussion, download him then take advice as to the way forward."

"Yes," agreed ex-army guy, running a hand through his thin sandy hair. He treated me to a smile, revealing a couple of sharp yellow teeth.

The Scotsman finally looked at me. "I'm Marcus," he lied, offering a pudgy hand.

"I'm Chris," nodded the ex-army officer, blushing.

"Alisa, what are these gentlemen from the, er, FCO doing here?" I said, taking off my coat. Chris looked at the handgun strapped to my belt warily.

"I am liaising with them on the Belov operation," she replied. "They want him alive as much as you do. We all have the same objective; ensuring Sergei Belov lives and the FSB plot fails."

I sat down and sipped coffee. "OK then, show me yours and I'll show you mine."

Marcus chuckled, his shoulders gently rocking. "Fair enough, Captain Winter."

"Call me Cal, please" I said easily. "The army was a long time ago."

"Of course. Alisa contacted us six weeks ago. It clearly isn't in HMG's interest to have Russian commandos topping people, especially in the UK, and it's not like we're in any position to declare war on them is it?"

"You've let them get away with it before," I shrugged. We all knew that.

"We are where we are," Marcus replied, "and they do own all the gas." I like a man who sees the world the way it is, rather than the way he'd like it to be.

"Besides," Chris added, "Belov has something we want. We won't get it if he's dead. So luckily for him, there are a number of reasons why we want to protect him."

I dunked a biscuit into my coffee and popped it into my mouth. "I've been to Sergei's house. It's not exactly crawling with police protection."

"Oh, it's been offered," Marcus sighed, "but he won't have it. He's not wanting for bodyguards. He can afford anything we could give him and more besides. No, we're protecting him the way we know best, by managing the opposition."

"Managing?" I laughed, "I love the euphemisms you lot use. And if you don't mind me asking, why isn't Box 500 involved? Mainland UK operations are MI5 and police property. Ain't you trespassing?"

The two spies looked at each other. Marcus finally took a biscuit and nibbled it. "There are some… inter-departmental issues."

"Is same in Russia" said Turov approvingly. "Never tell other agency jack-shit about your plans. They will fuck it up for you, to make themselves look good."

A ghost of a smile crossed Marcus's face. There was a tactical silence, which I chose to break to get things moving. Spies, after all, are just civil servants. If you don't kick them up the arse, they'll just keep on scheduling meetings until it's too late. "You want Pieter Van Basten's server full of dirt on the Russian government then?" I said, just to get a reaction.

"How on earth d'you know about that?" said Chris, eyebrows raised.

"Oh, Sergei told me over vodka and cigars."

The ex-army officer sat forward in his chair, "go on…"

"I suspect we've already over-stepped the mark," said Marcus gently. "Chris, we're not in a position to task Captain Winter. We need to take advice on this matter."

"What do you mean?" I said. All this talk of conduits and tasking was new to me. I took my orders from Harry, who told me very little. I saw a rare chance to find out more about how The Firm worked. If I knew how it worked, then maybe I could escape.

"I'm sure you appreciate the need for discretion," said Marcus, suddenly sounding like a kindly highland GP, "for both your benefit and ours."

Turov gave a dirty laugh. "Is obvious, Cal. These guys are not responsible for using your organisation. They have different responsibilities and they don't want to tread on toes. There will be a sterile corridor between you and these two, MI6 will have a deniable officer who tasks your boss. So they are worried about contaminating your deniability, and theirs."

"For Christ's sake," spat Chris, "Alisa…"

"A secret is something a spy tells one person at a time," the Russian chuckled, "and I'm in a hurry. My organisation is impatient. I only tell Winter what is obvious, he is not completely stupid."

"Thanks for the vote of confidence," I said, "but why should I help MI6? Belov has offered me more money than you'll ever be authorised to pay."

"Really, Winter?" said Alisa, "he offers you a king's ransom?"

"It's a lot of money."

The Russian's eyes narrowed. "Where is the only place you find free cheese?"

"I don't know," I shrugged.

"A mousetrap."

"Exactly, Winter. And without our help you might never find the FSB team," said Marcus. "You might never have top-cover for any illegality you might need to indulge in. Leaving the country could be difficult too. The Firm might even find itself off of our independent covert assets list…"

"I get it," I said, "the usual."

"Exactly" Marcus smiled. "In the meantime, I'll talk to the relevant people in our organisation. We'll be in touch."

"There is something else," said Turov.

Chris glanced at his watch. "What is it?"

"Something happened yesterday, something that convinces me Belov has been targeted by another asset. A man called Fyodor Volk." She told them the whole story, except the bit about us killing and tidying up our attackers in the Tottenham squat. I was grateful.

"I thought the Petrushka program was a Cold War Relic," said Marcus.

Alisa spread her hands in front of her on the table, like it was a piano keyboard. "If only it was. Now, we should assume Volk has been in the UK for a considerable period of time. He will have a number of people groomed to kill Belov. He will have thoroughly prepared them and will have made it a priority to have detailed knowledge of Belov's movements, businesses and associates."

"And there's the *Spetzgruppa* to deal with too" I said, drawing a cigar tube from my jacket. "Can I smoke in here?"

"Shit," Chris moaned. I suppose his lunch plans were ruined. "We don't need this, we really don't."

Marcus took off his glasses and smiled queasily. He wiped them slowly with a small yellow cloth. "Alisa, do you have any more of those biscuits?" he said.

EIGHT

I gave the spooks' gnarly little bodyguard a wave as we left. He waved back and treated me to a death's-head grin. "What now?" I asked Turov as we walked to her car.

The Russian thought for a moment. "I think you don't tell Belov anything about this meeting. The plan is as good as it can be, given the circumstances."

The spooks agreed to do some work on Volk, promising to negotiate with the mysterious conduit between them and The Firm, channelling instructions via Harry. They also said they'd do some snooping on Misha Baburin, feeding any useful intelligence to us via Alisa. I guessed Harry wouldn't be impressed when he discovered I'd spoken directly to SIS. In the meantime our role was to concentrate on Baburin and the *Spetzgruppa* team.

We got in the Ford. "And what are you going to do?" I said. "Maybe we can grab something to eat?" A weak winter sun was breaking through the clouds. It was almost good weather for the first time in weeks and I was hungry. An afternoon chatting up Alisa over a bottle or two of claret appealed. I like Russians, sure, and I really liked Russian women.

"You haven't got time, Winter," she snapped. "You have work to do. Plus, you eat too many cookies. You will get fat."

"Russian women like their men big," I offered.

"This one doesn't. You are lazy and fat."

"I must warn you," I said in Russian, "I find rude, arrogant women irresistible."

Alisa Turov cocked her head as she pulled into the traffic. "Then you are even more stupid than you look."

We drove in silence after that. I looked around the car, which was spotless and smelt of vanilla air freshener. On the back seat were Turov's black leather shoulder bag and her coat. In the console behind the gearstick was some loose change and key fob. Under her coat was a magazine. "May I?" I said, pulling it out.

"Sure," she shrugged.

It was a London listings magazine. I flicked through it, noticing that the corner of a page near the back had been folded over. It was the eating out review section, and three top-end French restaurants were circled. "You like French food?" I said.

"Yes," she replied. "I worked in France for three years. If SVR is paying the bill I take contacts to the best French restaurants in town if I can. And you?"

"I prefer Italian," I replied. "Like mama used to make."

"Peasant food," she sniffed.

"Fucking hell, what happened to solidarity with the Proletariat, comrade?"

"Grow up." She dropped me near Swiss Cottage and gave me her business card. "I will talk to Moscow and contact you later. In the meantime you will conduct close target reconnaissance on Misha Baburin, twenty-four hour coverage."

"You're not my boss, love," I said casually.

"No, this is true," she smiled, "as I would never employ someone like you. But in this case I have little choice in the matter. And neither do you." She pulled the door shut and drove off.

I checked my gun, remembering Alisa's pick-pocketing the last time I was in the car with her. It was still there. But there was another cookie in my pocket, wrapped in a yellow Post-It note. On the note was a drawing of a pig. I wondered where she learnt to pick-pocket, even if it was in reverse. I dialled Oz.

He answered on the third ring. "That plot had at least four ex-SF operators cutting about on it," he said.

"Yeah, there was one inside too. It was OK."

"Who were they? They didn't look Russian," said Oz. "I reckon one of 'em was ex-SBS. He didn't see me."

"Our friends from Vauxhall Cross were there," I sighed.

"Harry will be proper pissed off. You know we're not meant to meet the brains."

"I'm not sure I did," I laughed. "Perhaps, can you ring him and tell him the good news?"

"That's fucking typical, you oxygen-thief. Me? What do I tell him?" asked Oz.

"That SIS will be in touch and that they've an interest in this operation. Tell him the meeting was an ambush and I didn't know anything about it. I'm off to see Belov now."

"OK, what do you want me and Andy to do?"

"Go and plot up on this Baburin bloke, Spartak security," I said. "Updates on the hour, please."

"What's your plan after you've met Belov?"

"Intelligence-gathering," I said guardedly.

"You're going to the pub aren't you?"

"No, wouldn't dream of it," I laughed. "I'll pull tomorrow night's shift, OK?"

"Roger," said Oz, ringing off.

I took a cab to Sergei Belov's townhouse, the guy on the gate letting me in with a nod. The bodyguards inside even spared me the metal detector once I'd opened my coat and showed them I was carrying, but I had to leave the pistol in a safe. My stubby Walther remained undetected in an ankle holster.

"Cal!" said Sergei Belov, giving me a hug. "Tell me, is there progress?" The fire blazed, and truth be told the office was too hot. The Russian oligarch busied himself fixing drinks, but to his disappointment I stuck to iced water.

I sipped my drink. "The young vagrant who attacked you said a Russian put him up to it. The Russian was supplying him with drugs and girls. We followed the guy who attacked you to his squat, but when we got there he was dead. His throat was slit." I didn't mention Volk, the guy we'd killed or my meeting with MI6.

"Yes, Dmitri was impressed with your techniques," said Sergei approvingly, "do you think the FSB put this tramp up to it?"

"It's possible. I've also spoken with some contacts. There is a Russian in East London who we know is providing the FSB team with equipment and shelter. We're going to work on him next."

"What is this Russian's name?"

"Sergei, it doesn't matter. You must trust me."

The Russian downed his vodka and smiled. "You are telling me to take good advice again, eh?"

"Yes Sergei. You pay us to take the risks – leave your people out of it, OK? When dead FSB men start turning up everywhere, d'you want Scotland Yard knocking on your door?"

"No, you are right. But what if they knock on *your* door?"

I smiled. "I assume you can afford the best lawyers in the country?"

"Naturally," he replied, "is there anything else you need?"

I shifted uneasily in my chair. "Is there any chance you could leave the UK until this dies down?"

"Impossible. I have court cases to fight, Pieter's case to look after and business matters that require my personal attention. My family are safe in Grand Cayman but I must remain. This is why I hired you."

I pulled a face. "OK, but I'll need your diary for the next month."

"This is no problem. I will ask Melissa to arrange it."

He pressed a button and the PA walked in wearing jeans, riding boots and a black sweater instead of her usual smart business suit. She gave me a dirty look, sat down next to Belov's computer and typed in a password. Belov asked for his diary to be copied for me. "Hi Melissa, is it dress-down Thursday?" I said.

"Good afternoon Mister Winter," she replied primly. She slipped a memory stick into the computer, tapped away at the keyboard and gave me the thumb-drive. "This is Mister Belov's diary until the end of February, password protected," she said.

I took the memory stick, "which is?"

"The password is *chauvinist pig*," Melissa smiled. "I trust you can spell *chauvinist*?" She stood up, nodded at Sergei and left.

Sergei grinned. "She really hates you."

"You need an expensive English education to be that rude," I chuckled, "but I like to think it's just the early stages of infatuation. It's easy to get the two mixed up."

Sergei shook his head and emptied his glass. "No, I have been married enough times to know real hatred when I see it. She told me that you suggested I was her sugar daddy."

"Aren't you?"

"Never screw your secretary, Cal. Not only is it a cliché, but why ruin such an important relationship?" He reached for the fridge and pulled out another bottle. "I like to screw my lawyers if I can though, after all enough of them have screwed me."

I laughed. "Fair enough, if I ever get a lawyer I'll remember that."

Sergei patted my back like he was my favourite uncle, not that I've ever had one. "Besides, Pieter and Melissa are close, she manages him for me when he gets… difficult."

I suppressed a smile. "Ah, but she doesn't know that you pull the strings with *Forbiddenfacts.net*, does she?"

The Russian shot me a look. "No, and I'd prefer it if she didn't. Sometimes I talk too much over a glass of vodka. She's young and idealistic, who can blame her?"

"So how close is she to Van Basten?"

"Close." Sergei raised his hairy eyebrows, "but not *that* close. Pieter isn't interested in women. He is a homosexual."

"We say *Gay* nowadays," I said.

"Trust me, there is nothing 'Gay' about Pieter Van Basten. He is a miserable bastard. But he and Melissa, they are like brother and sister. Did you know Pieter's only sister died of Leukaemia when she was seven?"

"No."

The Russian nodded sagely, "when he first started hacking he exposed the pharmaceutical companies working on Leukaemia drugs, he calls it 'big pharma.'" Sergei struggled with the word *pharma*, stressing each syllable carefully in his otherwise excellent English.

"I'd like to meet him," I said.

"Pieter? Ah, now you are beginning to sound like a cop!" laughed Sergei.

I stood up. "Maybe he's at risk too. If you'll excuse me Sergei Nikolayevich…"

"Of course, keep me updated and if you need anything then ask."

"Actually Sergei, there is something."

"Just ask."

"Can you get me a table at short notice at *La Minoterie*? A good one?" It was a three-starred French restaurant in Mayfair. The waiting list for a table was six months.

"One of my favourites, of course. You may take my usual table. What time?" he said with a wave of his hand.

"Eight-thirty?"

"Of course, now go. Dinner is on me," said the Russian. "Melissa will book it."

Picking up my SIG from the safe, I went down to the basement car park and got in the Volvo. In the boot I keep a small but powerful frequency scanner, hidden in a bracket under the spare tyre. I switched on the hand-sized console and put it in on the dashboard. Driving to the surface, it started warbling. I'd expected Belov to have my car bugged, and he didn't disappoint. I found the wiring and disconnected it. When I got back to my apartment in Hammersmith I put my weapons in the safe and phoned Alisa Turov.

"Are you watching Baburin?" she snapped.

"No, I'm deciding what to wear when I take you out for dinner later. My elite team of seasoned operatives are watching the target for me."

"Idiot," she said, although her voice was less harsh than usual.

I looked out over the river. The afternoon sun was setting behind the green-painted bridge. "I've got us the best table at La Minoterie for eighty-thirty. You like French food, right?"

"La Minoterie? How?" she said suspiciously.

"I'm a man about town. I know someone," I explained, although I wasn't going to say who. "We can talk this operation over properly."

Alisa was uncharacteristically quiet for a moment. "OK" she said finally, "no need to pick me up. I will meet you there."

"Good," I said, pulling a chilled bottle of beer from the fridge. Bohemia Regent Pilsner, flash stuff I get off the internet. "See you at eight-thirty." After I finished my beer, I had a nap. I showered before putting on a dark woollen suit and overcoat. I checked my Walther then decided to leave it in the flat. The counter-surveillance route I prefer to the taxi rank took me another fifteen minutes, during which I enjoyed a smoke: a Romeo Y Julietta No.2.

I took a black cab to Mayfair. We were only stopped once by the police counter-terrorism patrols, but there were more helicopters, searchlight beams picking out tall buildings as they thundered overhead. "You'd have thought there was a war on," I said to the driver.

"Ain't been a bomb for a while," he replied, "but I still get turned over three times a day."

"Are there are no bombs because of all the patrols?" I wondered out loud.

"I doubt it" said the driver, a lardy east Londoner wearing a West Ham shirt, "more like they want to scare the shit out of those fucking rioters." Ever since Greece went up in smoke, groups of anarchists had been sending letter bombs and attacking bankers in the streets. Public sympathy was conspicuous by its absence.

An hour early, I got the driver to drop me at a pub opposite the restaurant. The boozer was full of after-work city types and couples dressed for a night at the theatre. I got myself a pint of London Pride and sat by the window, watching the comings and goings from the restaurant, which had a small frontage clad in honey-coloured stone. Perfectly manicured pot plants stood outside, along with a sharp-suited doorman in black tie who looked impervious to the cold. Black-uniformed security guards, who the rich now employed to protect them from the rest of us, lurked nearby.

I spotted the first surveillance operator shortly afterwards. He was in his fifties, wearing jeans and a dark zip-up jacket. I noticed him mumbling into a hidden mic as he settled into his bar stool and unfolded a newspaper. Again, Sergei hadn't let me down and clearly trusted me about as much as I trusted him. Across the road a glamorous couple walked towards the restaurant. He wore a dark suit and a turtle-neck sweater, the woman a shimmering silver dress. They dipped their heads as they spoke into something the woman tucked in her clutch bag. The man discretely performed a three-sixty look around as he neared the doorway. I had no doubt they'd be at a table near mine.

I waited for another forty-five minutes, enjoying another beer and spotting two more operators loitering around and taking up positions. I was hoping that my meeting tonight would be enough of a trigger for Sergei to tell me what he knew, if anything, about Alisa Turov. I hate to generalise, but in my experience Russians love secrets and plots, but sometimes need a gentle push to cough them up. Finally I crossed the road and waited for a few minutes. Alisa was five minutes early, wearing a little black dress and knee-boots under a grey double-breasted greatcoat. "Good evening" I said, kissing her on both cheeks.

"*Zdravstvujtye*," she said, almost shyly, using the formal 'vih' term for good evening.

I held my hands up. "It's going to be like that, is it?"

"No, of course not," she said in English, "shall we?"

The weather-resistant doorman gave us a brilliant smile and a *bonsoir* and we walked through the door, into La Minoterie. I had a table at the best restaurant in town, a beautiful dinner companion and somebody else footing the bill. If it wasn't for the hostile surveillance it had all the ingredients of a good night out.

NINE

The room at La Minoterie was formal and dimly lit, with impeccable service from guardsman-smart waiters. I ate lobster tails in Norman cider, then venison with pears and *foie gras*. To finish I wolfed down a chocolate tart, along with a bottle of an eye-wateringly expensive 1977 vintage Chateau d'Yquem Sauterne. The sommelier was thrilled. Along with the two bottles of 1993 Margaux we'd drunk beforehand, I hoped Sergei would notice my good taste when he settled the bill. I patted my stomach and ordered cheese, coffee, brandy and petit fours.

"As I said," Alisa smiled, "you are a greedy pig."

"I spent years eating army rations or boarding-school stodge in the officer's mess. Then, on the Firm, it's all Third World street food. I discovered fine dining relatively late in life – I've got some catching up to do."

Belov's surveillance operators were sat two tables away. They were good, paying each other lots of attention and only occasionally snatching a glance at us. They drank little, the woman in the silver dress tapping away at her phone now and then. Eventually, satisfied they couldn't hear our conversation, I began to ignore them.

Alisa Romanovna Turov, to use the patronymic she offered, was good company. She ate scallops; a fillet of beef cooked *bleu* with steamed vegetables, skipped pudding but polished off a bottle of the Margaux. She told me about herself in fast, slang-laden Russian. I had to assume it was all a carefully-constructed lie, but I was interested anyway and nodded politely at the salient parts.

She said she was born near Rostov-on-Don in southern Russia, growing up in a pleasant suburb near the Sea of Azov. Her parents worked in the university – her father, a lapsed Jew, was a lecturer at the law school. Her mother, his second wife, was an administrative assistant. Her step-brother Ivan died during the soviet withdrawal from Afghanistan aged eighteen, when she was a baby. "He'd been conscripted six months before" she said matter-of-factly, "his armoured vehicle was blown up by a bomb planted by the mujahedeen."

"Some things never change," I said. "I'm sorry."

"We should never have been in Afghanistan," she replied.

"Like I said, some things never change."

"Quite. The Government killed him as far as I'm concerned. My father had contacts in the intelligence agencies through his work in the university, when I was approached to join SVR he was very supportive. He knew that I would be with a group of people who wanted a better Russia, people who were against gangsterism and the FSB."

"You don't strike me as the revolutionary type, Alisa."

"Good," she said, "it's not something I wish to advertise."

"And the SVR is crawling with anti-government types too?"

She reddened slightly. "Of course not. We have many pro-government officers. But there is a cadre within SVR that feels the way I do – we support each other and use our influence when we can. It includes very senior people, we can achieve much."

"So tell me," I smiled, changing the subject, "where did you learn to pick pockets? I've never had a gun taken like that from me before."

"Or had a cookie planted on you?" she laughed. "My father loved tricks and magic. He taught me. Then, when I went to the academy the instructors thought it might come in useful, as tradecraft."

"The SVR trained you to pickpocket?"

"Sure," she said, sipping her drink, "but I prefer the term sleight-of-hand. They brought out this old guy, a thief. He'd spent ten years in a Gulag in the old days. He taught me misdirection, pick-pocketing and lock-picking."

I looked at her long, slender fingers. Her nails were cut short and she wore no rings or bracelets. "There's nothing up your sleeve then?"

"I imagine that the only rabbit in this place is in the kitchen," she laughed.

I sat closer, so our conversation wouldn't be overheard. "What happens if the FSB get Belov?"

"Crushing opposition can embolden it," she said quietly, her voice almost a whisper over the jazz playing in the background. "In Russia there is a growing protest movement. But if the FSB can show that the most heavily-protected exiles can still be slaughtered with impunity? In the UK? Men like Belov are still important in Russia. Their fortunes help fund the opposition."

I speared a piece of artisan *Brie de Melun* with a knife. "Even though Belov's a thief? He told me as much."

"So? Everyone was a thief in the 90s," she shrugged. "The victor writes the history book, no? The only the ones labelled thieves were the oligarchs who fell out of favour with the government. It makes no difference to me. My enemy's enemy is my friend."

We sipped cognac and coffee, the couple watching us taking their time over their meal.

"We are being watched. They aren't bad," whispered Alisa, "especially the woman. But he is too obvious."

"Maybe he's just checking you out. You look great."

She ignored the compliment, "did you know?"

"Sure," I shrugged, "I spotted one of them in the pub opposite here an hour before our date."

"This isn't a date."

"Yes it is, a platonic date."

"That might work," she replied.

The waiter refilled my coffee cup and I nodded my thanks. "It's Belov's people, he thinks I don't know."

Alisa's face clouded over. "He doesn't trust you."

"I'd be worried if he did. He's a Russian oligarch. I'm a British mercenary. The FSB is trying to kill him. What do you think?"

"I think that sometimes having your enemy's enemy as your friend is a pain in the ass," she looked at the cheese and pulled a face, ordering another cognac instead. "You told me your family are dead. How is that?"

I finished my coffee. "My Old Man? Died of a heart attack. Fifty-a-day smoker and drank like a fish. My mother died of cancer just after I left the army. She went home to Parma and passed away in her sleep with her sisters sitting with her. I was there too. I never had any brothers or sisters. Mum had me late in life, I think they call it a 'happy accident.' That's it, nothing overly dramatic or tragic. I loved them, they were good parents."

"*Happy Accident*, I like that," she smiled. "So there's nobody else?"

I don't know why, but I told her about Sam and the kids, and Clarkie. I didn't give up any names, just that there was a family I had to look after. Alisa Turov nodded approvingly. "It is good, that you send money to a dead comrade's family. It is the proper thing to do."

I shrugged, "I've got to do something right. It balances out all the things I've done wrong."

"This is true, although wouldn't you say that most of your targets deserve their fate?"

I scratched my head at that one. "I think it's probably a seventy-thirty per cent split, thirty per cent are just poor bastards who chose the wrong side."

"That is like war, no? Maybe you should look after their families too," she said playfully.

"If I earned enough? I probably would."

We finished our meal. I left the waiter a tip big enough not to embarrass Sergei Belov. The surveillance couple smooched as we walked by to collect our coats. "I'll walk you to the taxi rank," I said gallantly.

"Thank you Cal, I'm sure I'd never make it by myself," she laughed. She wasn't drunk, after all she was a Russian intelligence officer, but she was flushed from the booze.

"Anyway," I whispered in her ear, "let's lose these watchers. It should be easy after a bottle and a half of good wine and two cognacs."

She laughed and touched my arm. It had stopped snowing, the pavements gritted and slushy as we walked through Mount Street Gardens, cooing at the grand apartment blocks. It was after eleven, and quiet apart from the distant buzz of traffic. We walked towards Park Lane. I satisfied myself that the surveillance operatives had either been called off or had lost us.

As we neared the exit from the park, Alisa groaned and fell. I turned, head fuzzy from drink, and saw two men in dark clothing on top of her. I felt a sharp pain in my ribs as another man jumped me. My flank burnt as he stabbed me. I fell to one knee and grabbed him, fingers clawing at his throat. Behind me I heard grunts and groans. Alisa was swearing in Russian as she fought. My attacker was a scruffy, lanky kid in his late teens, wearing a dark hoodie. Facial piercings glimmered in the street lights. The whites of his eyes were large and round, the zombie-stare of the crack-head on his pale pinched face. He looked at the sharpened screwdriver in his hands, amazed that it hadn't killed me. I hit him in the face with an old-fashioned uppercut, breaking his nose and pushing him backwards. He was trying to get up when I planted my size eleven into his crotch like I was taking a football penalty.

I turned around to see one of Alisa's attackers on the floor unconscious, the other guy wrestling with her. A machete lay on the floor. She broke his grip expertly and pivoted on one leg, delivering a round-house kick to his throat. Gurgling, the man fell to the ground, clutching at his neck. She grabbed the back of his head by his ears and drove his face into her knee. Catching his head in the crook of her elbow, she twisted her body and wrenched the man's head through one-hundred eighty degrees. There was a snapping noise and he fell silently to the ground. "Cal!" she called.

I turned around to see the kid I'd kicked in the nuts stagger towards me, the screwdriver in his hand. I slipped on the snow-slick grass as he tried to stab me again. The puncture wound in my side was starting to throb, my shirt slick with blood. He hesitated as he thought about how he was going to stab someone who was lying down.

Alisa stalked around the kid, sizing him up. Realising something terrible was going to happen, he went to run, but the Russian caught him with a kick to his shin. He stumbled to the ground. She pulled him up by an arm then delivered a series of strikes to his face and head. It was high-level mixed martial arts, the kid collapsing in a bloodied heap on the wet grass. Blood bubbled from his nose like cappuccino froth as she stamped on his throat. "Let's go!" she hissed, grabbing my arm, "before the police arrive." Behind us our three attackers lay still, one moaning gently. Alisa's coat and shoes were streaked with mud, her stockings torn.

"Sure," I said, hauling myself up, "thanks for that."

"You've been stabbed," she said, pushing her hand against my ribs. I felt her finger probe the wound and I howled in pain.

"Shut up cry-baby! It's a shallow wound. You'll be fine."

We made it to South Audley Street, where she hailed a black taxi. "Battersea," she barked at the driver, giving her address.

The cabbie nodded, "what happened to you?"

"My husband has drunk too much," she laughed, "he fell over in the park!" Her accent was now cut-glass English. It was like she'd just walked out of Cheltenham Ladies' College.

"As long as he ain't sick in the back," the cabbie grumbled.

She flashed him a brilliant smile. "If he does he'll be in even more trouble!"

Outside her apartment she gave the cabbie a handful of cash, and he drove off happy. "Hope the hangover ain't too bad!" he chirruped.

Turov's place was spartanly-furnished, the white-painted sitting room almost empty apart from a TV and two angular cream sofas. Blood dripped onto the cushions as I collapsed onto one of the sofas. "Wait there, I'll the get first aid kit" she said, sounding Russian again. She took off her muddy high-heeled boots and looked at them sadly.

"I'd rather have a drink" I replied, examining my injury. It was a ragged puncture two inches above my belt, just below my ribcage. I'd suffered worse. I'd been stabbed twice before, working for a PMC in Iraq, although one of those was during a bar-fight at the Marhaban hotel in the Baghdad Green Zone. I'd been shot once in the calf with a .22 pistol, on a job in Trieste two years earlier. And in the army I'd been injured by shrapnel in Basra and Bosnia. Sierra Leone was all about gonorrhoea. The screw-driver wound sustained in Mayfair joined my CV of interesting injuries.

Alisa came back in with a green plastic first aid box. She cleaned the wound and fussed about dressing it, a frown on her face. "How did they know where we were? I thought that was Belov's surveillance."

I winced. "It was – he's got a leak. He knew where I was having dinner this evening."

She put my hand on the dressing and cut a length of surgical tape. "So it was Volk's followers? I don't understand."

"Neither do I," I grimaced. "Sergei and I are going to have a chat."

She finished, nodded and put a bottle of vodka, one of my favourite pain-killers, in front of me with two shot glasses. Mahler wafted from hidden speakers. "Have a drink, I won't be a minute." When she came back she was wearing sweatpants and a vest. She put a Beretta PX4 compact handgun on the table in front of me. "That one is spare, just in case."

"Thanks," I said, checking the weapon and putting it down next to the bottle of *Stolichnaya*. "Where did you learn to fight like that?"

"Ballet school," she smirked, pouring a slug of vodka. "Tomorrow I am scheduled to speak with my controller in Moscow on a secure line, I will see if we can get support. I think you are right, Volk must have somebody close to Belov, but not close enough to kill him."

Alisa gave me a glass of water and a duvet. "Stay here tonight," she pointed at the dressing on my gut. "Let me know if that starts bleeding again."

I nodded and tossed my vodka down my throat, then kicked my shoes off. Alisa walked over to the window, a Glock-19 pistol held loosely in her hand. She screwed a suppressor onto the barrel and closed the curtains. She picked up one of the shot glasses and drank, then poured another. She could drink like a Soviet tank driver, I gave her that. "I'm going to get some sleep," she said. "You get some too."

I yawned and took off my jacket. "Agreed, but there was one more thing I wanted to ask you though?"

"Of course, what is it?"

"Fyodor Volk. What's the deal with Dante? And why the quotes from The Inferno?"

She looked at the shot glass and smiled. "I don't know. All I know is that his file mentions an interest in Dante. But you know Cal? Before I kill him, I'll make sure I ask." She turned on her heel and went to bed.

TEN

"Why meet here?" asked Belov, nodding his thanks as he took the offered cigar. I'd called the meeting as soon as I woke up at Alisa's apartment. Before I left she gave me a memory stick with Misha Baburin's prison photographs on it. She told me she'd be in touch after she'd spoken to her boss in Moscow. I'd gone home and showered and dressed. I had my Walther strapped to my shin and the SIG in a shoulder holster, my covert body armour rubbing against the field dressing on my side.

We sat on a bench in a frost-white Richmond Park. Out of earshot bodyguards stood drinking tea from the cafe, occasionally talking into their hidden microphones. I'd given Belov a selective update about the operation. "You've got a leak in your organisation," I said matter-of-factly, "three men tried to kill me and my Russian contact last night. Same as before – they looked like homeless men."

"Impossible," Sergei replied. "I spy on all of my employees. I would know if there was a traitor."

"Well I'm out of ideas then," I said, watching the joggers trudge by, "but I was stabbed last night by some eighteen-year old junkie."

"You didn't tell me that you were having dinner with the SVR officer," he said, changing the subject. He pulled a pewter hipflask from inside his coat and took a swig. He offered it to me and I happily took a gulp.

"What do you expect? You gave me her name, Sergei," I shrugged. "She's been very helpful."

"This man you tell me about, the FSB asset Baburin? Maybe this is his work."

"Perhaps," I agreed, not mentioning Fyodor Volk, "but that still doesn't explain how they knew about my dinner date last night. In fact the only people about were your surveillance team."

"Ah," he chuckled, holding his hands up in mock surrender, "mea culpa. I will have words with them. They should have followed you home, so you would have had protection."

"Don't worry about it," I replied. "Alisa Turov doesn't need protection. She saved my life last night."

"I will review my security and have my office re-swept for bugs."

"Thanks," I replied, getting to my feet. "We're out looking at Baburin tonight, I'll keep you updated. In the meanwhile don't discuss this with anyone."

The Russian offered a gloved hand, his breath making a cigar-and-booze smelling cloud, "OK, but next time don't drag me to a park in the suburbs!" As unobtrusive as ever, Sergei stalked off to his armoured Maybach limo with his bodyguards. A Range Rover with four more goons in it cleared the way.

Once they'd gone I looked at my phone and the three missed calls from Harry. I'd never actually met the Handler. I didn't know what Harry looked like or where he lived. My pay was always on time and operations ran smoothly. So I wasn't complaining. Pulling a face, I decided there was no point putting it off. I rang him and sat back down on the bench. "On operations in high-risk low-infrastructure environments," said the Handler calmly, "I don't expect you to call me every five minutes. But in London…"

"Sorry Harry."

"Oz told me you've met with SIS. Why?"

"It was an ambush," I said apologetically. "The Russian contact we made pulled me onto a meeting and they were there. There wasn't a lot I could do." I told him about my conversation with 'Marcus' and 'Chris.'

Harry's voice was quiet and measured. "Cal, if you meet intelligence officers I have to brief upwards and explain. It arcs established relationships for me and jeopardizes operational security for you, The Firm and the intelligence officers. What's one of the cardinal rules of The Firm?"

"*There's need-to-know and then there's nice-to-know. We don't need-to-know*," I recited like a school kid doing five times table.

"Exactly, and if you keep on accidentally having these sorts of meetings then it's entirely fucking possible that somebody will plant a fifty-fucking-calibre round in your thick fucking head. Do you understand?"

"Yes."

"Good. Now give me an update."

I filled him in, including the attempt on our lives. "I've just met Belov and told him he's got a mole in his office."

I could hear Harry slurping his coffee, "I wish we could fold this job, but now SIS is involved. Stabbings in the middle of town, slotting murderous tramps, next thing you know the Old Bill is involved…"

"I know," I said, "which is why we need to crack on and sort out this Baburin character and the FSB team. That's fifty per cent of this operation resolved right there."

"Get on with it then. Stop fucking about in flash restaurants."

"Roger." I got in the Volvo, brushing snow off the windscreen with my sleeve. Oz, accusing me of slacking, was expecting me over in Hackney later to take over observation duties. He and Andy had spent over twenty-four hours watching the Spartak Security office and come up with nothing. They'd not seen Misha Baburin or anybody else of interest. And I'd heard nothing from Alisa, Sergei sounded unconvinced and Harry was pissed off. This operation felt like it was going nowhere, that all the cards were held by Fyodor Volk.

I arrived in Hackney just after thirteen-hundred. Andy's van was parked up on a junction looking towards the front of Spartak Security's low-rise office building. A squat building made of grey concrete slabs, it had a yard next door where three liveried vans were parked. Opening the van's back door, I climbed inside. Andy, wearing a black field jacket and a fleece hat, was crouched behind a camera with a Canon 600mm lens. The camera body was mounted on a black Manfrotto tripod and aimed forward through the cab. A small hatch had been cut in the cab wall between the front passenger seats to give a forward view. There was a similar arrangement at the back which allowed for a view depending on which way the vehicle was parked. Next to him was a personal role radio, a book of crossword puzzles, a flask and a lemonade bottle full of piss. I'd suggested a chemical toilet for the van but he was having none of it. "Where's Oz?" I whispered. I was carrying supplies – Mars Bars, another flask, sandwiches and a spare lemonade bottle.

"Went to get some scoff, he's OK."

I sat down on the vinyl-covered bench opposite him and helped myself to coffee, "anything happening?"

The ex-SRR operator sighed. "Assorted meatheads come and go, there's a bloke with a burglar alarm van who spends all day smoking in the car park, I've seen two cars get screwed by local kids and that's about it mate."

"So, nobody who looks like the boss?"

"Nope." We chatted for a bit, and told him about the men who'd attacked us last night. "The Russian has a grass in the camp," was Andy's blunt assessment.

"Yeah, my thoughts exactly," I replied. "OK, get some sleep, the Volvo's around the corner." I tossed him the keys to my car.

"Good stuff Cal," said Andy, "I'm as stiff as a board." He'd spent twenty-four hours in the van.

I took off my body armour and settled in behind the camera. I hate surveillance. Although soldiers are used to spending hours sitting around waiting for stuff to happen, it was my least favourite part of the job. On surveillance this is magnified to the power of ten. You can sit on a dead plot for weeks. Men like Andy, surveillance specialists, had a level of patience that I'd never developed. Jack, Sam and Clarkie's boy, started sending me text messages on my spare phone. He's ten and knows I was in the army with his dad, so he's always asking me stupid questions about guns, fighting and action movies. *No*, I texted him back, *you can't fire two machine guns, one in each hand.* And a few minutes later, *No I've never used a flame thrower and the army don't use plasma rifles last time I checked.*

Oz returned with food and newspapers. He stretched out on the opposite bench with the Toughbook. The idea was that he'd run comms back to Harry on a secure satellite phone, or do some open-source research on the internet if I saw anything interesting. In reality, he played chess against the computer and ate fast food.

It was almost dusk when a gleaming white Range Rover Sport pulled up outside the Spartak Security office. I started taking photos of the lump who climbed out and stood on the pavement, talking on his phone. He was easily six and a half feet tall, broad as a barn, wearing a white tracksuit and a black padded jacket with a fur-trimmed hood. He was joined by another track-suited gorilla. "Did you get the registration of the vehicle?" Oz half-whispered.

"Roger. It's Sierra-Papa-Tango-Kilo-One. Cherish transfer number plate."

"Very low-key," said Oz, "is it him?"

"Dunno," I whispered, "possibly. Phone it into Harry and see if he can get it checked." I patted my pocket and found the memory stick Alisa had given me. "There's an old prison mug shot of him on that, check it out."

Oz picked up the satellite phone and called Harry, repeating the registration number. I don't know how Harry gets vehicles checked. Maybe it's a government thing via the Old Bill, or blagged through the DVLA or an insurance database. But he can get it done fairly quickly.

"Look at this," said Oz, swivelling the laptop around so the screen faced me. The black and white image showed the head-and-shoulders of a big guy in his twenties with short dark hair and a flat boxer's nose. I could see the edges of Russian gang tattoos creeping up his neck. I peered back at the man on the pavement through the camera. Magnified, he had the same broken nose, was older and his hair was shorter. His winter parka covered any ink. "I'd say that was a positive identification."

"Good drills," said Oz. "Andy will be gutted you made the spot only half an hour after he left."

Misha Baburin finished his telephone call and went inside his office. The other track-suited gorilla lit a cigarette and stood outside, oblivious to the cold. A lonely traffic warden looked at the Range Rover and hefted his little computer. The goon went up, said something and the traffic warden walked quickly away.

The satellite phone chirruped and Oz answered. He wrote something down and rang off. "Cal, that motor is registered to an English name at an address in Essex. *Black Hall Farm, Southminster*."

"Where?"

"It's on the Essex coast I think, up from Southend. The middle of nowhere." It made sense that Baburin would never register a car in his own name.

"OK, see if Harry can get anything on that address from the spooks. We'll let Andy get some sleep, then get him over there tomorrow." If there's anything Andy liked more than hiding in the back of vans and spying on people, it was hiding in holes in the countryside and spying on people.

We sat in silence and waited. After an hour a fat guy wearing overalls started locking the yard at the side of the office and Baburin appeared. Another car pulled up, a blue BMW on Polish number plates. The driver, an older guy wearing a smart suit, got out and gave him a hug. They spoke for a few minutes and then both got in the BMW and drove away. The second goon got in the Range Rover and followed them. "Do you think Harry can check Polish number plates?" I thought out loud.

"We can ask I suppose," Oz replied. "How about Alisa?"

I tapped Alisa's number into my Blackberry. She answered immediately. "I said I'd phone you after I'd spoken to Moscow."

"I'm at Misha Baburin's, I need a check run on a Polish number plate, owner details."

I heard the rustling of a notepad. "Go on." I repeated the BMW's registration. "That's a Krakow number plate" she said. "Leave it with me, we have people who can check that."

I motioned at Oz to get ready to bug-out. "Baburin's in that vehicle now, I want to know who he's with. I've also got an address for him in Essex."

Her voice brightened, "can you give it to me?"

"Yes, but can you promise not to do anything without discussing it with us?"

"Of course," she huffed, "we have a deal."

I gave her the address of Black Hall farm and rang off. Oz climbed into the front of the van and drove off in the direction we'd last seen the BMW, north towards Stoke Newington. Stuck in traffic, we waited patiently for a call.

It was twenty long minutes before my phone went. We'd made it as far as Stamford Hill, red tail lights stacked up in front of us as far as I could see. "The car is a 2009 Five-Series BMW" said Alisa, "it used to belong to a man called Bolek Sobczak, from Krakow. He told the authorities that it was sold it last year but there is no record of who bought it. Sobczak is linked to people-smuggling and prostitution."

"Is there any criminal intelligence linking him to the UK?" I asked hopefully.

"Nothing specific. His record suggests he was smuggling girls from the Baltic States and Poland to mainland Europe, to work in saunas and brothels. This is a big problem in UK, no?"

"Yeah, it makes sense that he might be knocking about with Baburin."

Alisa sounded calm, but interested, "it is good to see progress. I will see if there is anything else about him, or this Black Hall farm. OK?"

"Great, speak later."

"Where to?" said Oz.

"I don't want to go out to the farm tonight, not without the right kit and we need Andy. Let's park up and wait, in case Alisa or Harry find something for us."

We found a supermarket car park and sat in the van with the heater on full blast. On the news there was a story about internet rebel Pieter Van Basten's forthcoming appearance at the High Court. He was fighting extradition to the US, where I suspected it would be even more difficult for the FSB to get at him. Van Basten's gentle voice, with only a trace of an Afrikaans accent in it, came on the radio:

Ahead of the hearing next week, and whatever the outcome, and I would like to thank my legal team, all the loyal activists on Forbiddenfacts.net and of course my friend and mentor Sergei Belov, a man who genuinely understands the meaning of freedom. As long as I draw breath I will not hesitate to shine a light in places where the powerful would prefer there to be darkness.

I laughed so hard I choked on my coffee. "He only puts out the stuff Sergei allows him to, the fucking hypocrite."

"The Yanks have seriously got it in for him," Oz replied. "After he posted all that stuff about The President." Van Basten had famously got leaked a report from the US State Department, outlining an invective-fuelled rant the President of the United States had made about Israel. He'd posted it next to an equally invective-fuelled rant the Prime Minister of Israel had made about the United States. It would have been funny if it wasn't for the state of the Middle East, which was even more screwed-up than usual. But I guessed this was chickenfeed compared to what Van Basten had stored on his top secret server, the FSB's treasure trove of dirt on the top echelons of the Russian government.

An hour later my phone went. It was Alisa. "I have spent the last hour pulling in favours. My boss has too. We have an address in the UK loosely connected to Bolek Sobczak. His telephone number was registered to this address using an international telephone card a month ago. This is the best we can do."

I grabbed my notepad, "go ahead." She read out an address in Holloway, not far from the infamous women's prison.

"Are you going there now?" she said guardedly.

"We'll take a look."

"I will join you," she announced, "meet me at the Shopping Centre on Holloway Road."

There was no arguing with her. Oz pulled a face, then laughed and pulled out into the traffic.

ELEVEN

The address in Holloway was an Edwardian house on a quiet back street. It had seen better days, with four un-emptied bins outside and a rusty bicycle lying in the garden. A sickly pink bulb lit the drapes in the upstairs window. "There," said Oz as we did a drive-by. The Polish-registered BMW was parked several doors down.

"Only recently parked," said Alisa, squeezed next to me in the front of the van, "the snow hasn't settled on the bonnet." She checked her Glock 19 and screwed on the suppressor with surgically-gloved hands.

Oz did the same with his .45, sliding the pistol from its shoulder-holster "I'll take the back." He pulled a balaclava from his pocket and tugged it over his head, disappearing along the side of the house.

Alisa and I went to the front door. The sitting room was dimly lit behind loose orange curtains. I could hear the bass thump-thump-thump of dance music as we stepped closer. The front door was locked with a Yale mortise and two sturdy bolts. There was no burglar alarm and no CCTV. "I've got it," Alisa whispered. Then she knocked loudly on the door.

"Who is it?" said a heavily accented male voice in English.

"I am Natasha," she said in Russian, "Alexei asked me to come over."

"Fuck off. I don't know anybody called Alexei," said the voice.

Alisa sighed. "Fuck off yourself. It's about a job, you know?"

"Ah," said the voice, "look, hold on for a moment…"

I heard the noise of the latch on the Yale lock. I pulled down my balaclava over my face. Nodding at Alisa, I sprang around the corner and barrelled into it with all my weight, the door flying open and knocking the man behind it to the ground. Alisa stepped in behind me, pistol pushed out in front of her. The music was some sort of awful European dance shit. "It's the police!" coughed the man on the floor. He was a fat bloke in his forties, wearing jeans and a black muscle-vest. He was also drunk. The hallway was warm, the central heating turned up high.

Misha Baburin stepped out of a doorway, a black handgun in his meaty fist. Alisa fired, the silenced bullet splintering the doorframe by his head. Eyes wide, he went to duck back into the sitting room. I took aim with my SIG and fired twice, deliberately kneecapping him in the right leg. Baburin dropped the pistol and crashed to the ground, pawing at his shattered knee and groaning.

Alisa closed the door behind her, shooting the drunken man who'd answered it twice in the chest. "I'm not the police," she said casually. "Baburin, where's Bolek Sobczak?"

"Upstairs," he grunted through gritted teeth. "Who the fuck are you?"

"Let's talk," I said, gesturing with my pistol for him to crawl into the sitting room. He slithered past me, trailing blood. I tossed him an ampoule of Morphine. "Take that. It's for the pain. And turn that music off, please."

Oz walked in with the guy in the suit we'd seen picking up Baburin earlier. The suited guy's hands were up, Oz's .45 plugged into the side of his head. "This dickhead was upstairs" said Oz, "there are five bedrooms and eight young girls. The girls are locked up and sedated, I'd be surprised if the oldest was fifteen. The usual shit's up there, condoms, bondage gear, drugs... It's a sex factory."

"Oh dear," I said to Baburin in Russian. "I take a dim view of that sort of thing. I really do."

Baburin injected the Morphine and glowered at me, his face pale and sweaty. The room had a couple of dilapidated leather sofas, a giant flat screen TV and a drinks cabinet. A glass coffee table was scattered with the usual detritus of criminal relaxation – oversized cigarette papers, small bags of cannabis, beer cans, wraps of cocaine and cash. Alisa pointed at Baburin. "We interrogate this one first. Oz, please take the other one somewhere else for now. Find out what he knows."

Oz nodded and led the terrified Polish guy out of the room.

I sat on the sofa, pistol in my lap. Noticing the remote control for the stereo, I switched on Radio Three. "Thank you" said Alisa gratefully as gentle music filled the room. "That's better. Ah, it's Prokofiev. *Peter and the Wolf*. It was my favourite as a little girl."

Baburin grinned, revealing a row of gold-capped teeth. "When I find out who you are, bitch, I'm going to be the last one to ass-fuck you before you die. But only after I ass-fuck your mother dead while you watch."

"Really?" she spat, pistol-whipping the giant Russian, splitting his brow. "You will answer my questions or pray for a quick death. Macho bullshit like that will only make it worse." She stamped on Baburin's injured knee, the pain making him squeal and roll into a ball. The narrator of *Peter and the Wolf* warbled away in the background, telling his tale of a little boy lost in the woods.

"Look, I'm only here for the girls," Baburin groaned. "This is Sobczak's business. If you want to fuck-up every man who gets himself an *Amazonka* you might as well drop a bomb on London!"

Amazonka, or *Amazon*, was criminal Russian slang for a prostitute. I laughed, "don't give me Amazonka, Misha! Trafficked kids? With your money you could pay for a proper girl."

"Fuck you too. What do you want?"

"When are the team from *Spetzgruppa 'A'* going to kill Sergei Belov?" said Alisa.

He caught a laugh in his throat, despite the pain. "Fuck off. I'm more scared of them than you."

I shook my head, "a pervert *and* stupid."

Turov pulled a pair of chain-link handcuffs from her jacket and tossed them over to me. "'Cuff him, he will need to be persuaded."

"What are you going to do?" said Baburin, eyes wide.

The SVR officer looked him in the eye, a smile twitching at the corner of her mouth. "Cut your dick off, you piece of shit. For the girls upstairs and for every other woman you've gone near. I'm going to watch you give yourself a blow-job, Baburin, while you bleed to death."

"What?" he gasped.

"Cut. Your. Dick. Off. This will be the third dick I've cut off in my career. I'm sure I'll find it, even if it is tiny."

Baburin looked at me, as if male fraternal sympathy might save him. I shrugged as Alisa pulled a black-bladed knife. I slipped the cuffs over Baburin's wrists and locked them tight. Alisa pulled down the Russian's tracksuit bottoms. He wore black briefs, her hand hovering by the waistband. "I want to know when the operation is planned against Belov and where the *Spetzgruppa* are now!"

Baburin glanced, wide-eyed, down towards his crotch as Alisa rested the blade on his groin. She heated the tip of the knife with a cheap plastic lighter.

"Do it," I said, "he's too stupid to talk. Anyway, you wouldn't want him to breed."

Baburin looked at us both, teeth gritted, "you'll both die watching your families raped, this I promise!"

Alisa shook her head and held the red-hot tip of the knife to Barburin's scrotum, gently puncturing the skin. I smelt burning hair and flesh. He yelped and writhed in agony, his eyes white and round like a cornered dog. I found a tracksuit top and jammed it in his mouth. "What is this, little Misha? No more threats? I'm only getting started."

I gave the gangster a sympathetic smile. "Baburin you might walk away from this. Well, hobble. And you might still have a cock at the end of it too."

The torture and morphine finally hit him. And he gave up. Everybody does eventually. I know I have. He nodded, and I took the gag out of his mouth. "Don't," gasped Baburin, head bowed, "but please, I don't understand."

"Go on," said Alisa, moving the knife away from his balls.

"The Spetzgruppa is here, OK? They have been here six weeks. But why are you going on about Sergei Belov?"

"He's the target," I said.

"I don't know of any plan to kill Sergei Belov," Baburin replied, his eyes glazed from the opiates and the pain of the gunshot wound, "you must believe me!"

I sat on my haunches, near his head, "who is the target?"

Baburin gulped then fell back onto the threadbare carpet. "The target is the South African internet guy, Van Basten."

Alisa Turov's eyes narrowed, "where and when?"

"Some big English house in the countryside," he coughed, "in two or three days, maybe?"

The SVR officer sheathed her knife. "Tell us everything, Misha."

Baburin told us that a team of six undeclared Russian FSB men had arrived before Christmas. His orders were to provide them with accommodation, vehicles and cover. They'd been dropped off on the coast by a rigid inflatable, launched from an Estonian freighter coming into Harwich. Baburin picked them up and took them to his farm on the coast nearby.

"Black Hall farm is clean," said Baburin, "I bought it five years ago. I used it as a cannabis farm for a while, but the *Musors* started sniffing around. Now I just party there at weekends, use it as my home when I'm not in London. It's nice and quiet. I've built myself a gym, a place to keep my cars."

He wisely decided to have as little to do with the FSB *Spetzgruppa* as possible. Their leader was a man who called himself Ruslan. "Ruslan is a hard guy, you can tell. From his accent I would say he was from the South, maybe Kharkov. He would spend all day either training or going out into the countryside looking at the target. The other men worship him. I've looked after a few FSB jobs, but this is the heaviest – top secret. These guys are like ghosts – they don't exist, no papers, no records…"

"Weapons?" said Alisa.

Baburin swooned, as if he was going to faint. I passed him another ampoule of Morphine and he nodded his thanks. He expertly pricked his arm and sighed as the ultra-powerful dose entered his blood-stream. Stress, shock, and morphine would screw with a prisoner, disorient him. Misha Baburin would feel fear and pain, ecstasy and comfort in equal measure. "They brought tools with them" he said woozily, "on their little boat. Serious tools, AKs, sniper rifles, RPGs, grenades and explosives. Shit like that. It was like they were going to start a war. I told them my life here was good and they should be careful. They just laughed, like I was joking. Everybody would think it was terrorists, they told me."

Then, finally, he passed out. I looked at the torn muscle and cartilage on what was left of his knee and shook my head at Alisa. "He's never going to walk out of here, or anywhere else for that matter," I shrugged.

"No problem," she said. Grunting, she hauled him over so he lay face-down. Pulling the suppressed Glock she shot him in the back of the head twice. She checked his pockets and retrieved his iPhone and keys. Then she pulled a small card from a clear plastic bag in her pocket and left it by Baburin's corpse.

"What's that?" I asked, pointing at the card. Printed on it was a grinning skull surrounded by four small black crosses. I started picking up spent bullet casings. I suspected the Ops Support body-shifters were likely to refuse this one. Three corpses, multiple firearms and eight trafficked prostitutes wasn't my idea of an ideal night's cleaning work either.

"This is the calling card of a Mafia group from Georgia. When he was in prison, Baburin knifed one of this group's members and killed him. They have always promised revenge. It was on Baburin's file." The SVR officer looked at the body and shook her head, "we might as well give your police something to investigate, even though I doubt Moscow will be doing much to help Scotland Yard investigate an FSB covert asset."

I picked up the pistol Baburin had dropped, a 9mm Browning Hi-Power. I called up the stairs. "Oz, have you finished with that creature?"

"Yeah," he said, pushing the terrified pimp in front of him, "he's got nothing to say. He just begs for his life and keeps pissing himself. Apparently the girls are happy to be chained up all day and screwed by complete strangers. He's the misunderstood kindly uncle type, y'know?"

"Alisa, turn the music up." I motioned for Oz to get out of the way. Picking up a cushion from the sofa I pushed it against the pimp's head, feeling him shiver and sob. Sometimes, at moments like these, I can almost feel the karma. When I was in hospital, after Iraq, my shrink hated this admission the most. But I can't help but think that if you want to avoid being murdered by a gunman in a balaclava, don't traffic teenaged sex slaves.

I stuffed Baburin's pistol as far as I could into the fabric of the cushion, pinning the pimp's head to the wall and pulling the trigger. The bang was muffled, his body collapsing in the doorway to the sitting room. A trail of dark red goo dripped from the back of the cushion. I tossed the Browning onto the sofa.

"Good," said Alisa. "Release the girls. Don't let them see your faces."

I stepped over Baburin's carcass "Turov, how many dicks have you really cut off?"

She stopped to think for a moment. "Three," she said.

"I thought that was just to scare him."

She shrugged and headed for the door.

On the radio the narrator of *Peter and the Wolf* was still at it. *But Peter tied the other end of rope to the tree, and the wolf's jumping only made the rope round his tail tighter.*

TWELVE

We left the house and split up. Oz took the van, Alisa headed off to her car and I hailed a cab a safe distance away on the Holloway Road. We agreed to speak the next morning, after I'd spoken to Harry. The cabbie dropped me at Paddington, where I jumped on the tube home.

I got back to my apartment just after ten. I showered, scrubbing myself raw with a nail brush to get rid of firearms residue. Then I put on the 24 hour news. There was nothing about the shooting yet, but there would be soon. The terrified Eastern European girls, still drugged, had wandered off like zombies into the night and would be found sooner rather than later. Baburin's story, about Van Basten being the real FSB target, rang true. As I sat in front of the TV nursing a beer, I reasoned that meant that Volk's target must be Belov: two targets and two teams. It made some sort of sense.

But why not get Fyodor Volk to eliminate both?

In any case, we had to travel to Black Hall farm and take out the FSB team. Harry answered the phone on the third ring. "SITREP please," he barked. I heard the sound of a keyboard rattling in the background.

"We found Baburin," I yawned, still knackered from my night on Alisa's sofa. My ribcage ached. "He was in a brothel. He's dead. We also got two other collateral targets."

"Who are the collaterals?"

"Pimps," I said, "they were trafficking young girls."

"No dramas. God's work is God's work, even by accident. What about the clean-up?"

"I think the scene was too risky for Ops Support," I replied, "it's forensically sound and we weren't identified."

The Handler sucked his teeth as he thought about it. "Dump your weapons."

"Sure, but we need suppressed kit for the job on the farm Harry. I want it to be low-key."

"Roger" he said, "anything else?"

I explained Alisa's trick with the calling card, linking the shooting to the Georgian mafia.

"Good" he said, "I like the cut of her jib, for a Russian."

"What's the problem with Russians?" I said.

"I fought the fuckers in the 'Stan in 1981, with the Muj" he replied, "but I didn't tell you that, OK?"

"Sure." I updated him about Baburin's story, that Van Basten was the target of the FSB commando cell.

"Shit," said Harry. "D'you believe him?"

I sipped my beer and sighed, "yes. The attempts on my life and Sergei's were made by vagrants of one type or another, not Special Forces."

"OK, hit the farm first. Then we move onto Volk."

"Why, in case Baburin was lying about who the target is?"

Harry lowered his voice. "Partly, but mainly because the men from the FCO have been back in touch. Our orders have changed, and now we're working for two masters. Belov is to be kept alive at all costs, as is Pieter Van Basten. They especially want to know where Van Basten keeps his servers and hard drives. So he's my priority."

I walked over to the fridge and popped open another beer. "Harry, this is going to get heavy. The police are going to be sniffing around the shooting tonight. What sort of top-cover are we getting?"

Harry laughed. "Don't get all fucking soft on me Cal. Apparently some spook has signed a bit of paper that covers your arse."

"Bollocks to that. What's the point of having the Regiment?" The SAS had a team specifically set up for this sort of drama, specifically counter-terrorism support to the civil power. "There's me, Andy and Oz to deal with this and we've got to worry about getting nicked too?"

"I'm sure the regiment are more than up for it," said Harry defensively, "but you know how it works. It's politics."

"It might be to you Harry, but to me it's forty years in Belmarsh."

"You're going to get surveillance and intelligence support, imagery of the plot, equipment, safe exfil and decompression facilities abroad," he said. "So it's not all bad. Our instructions are to take out the FSB team within twenty-four hours from midnight tonight."

"Shit."

"Think about the money," said Harry. "I always do."

I sighed. "I'll be back in touch when we're on the start line. Let me know about weapons and stores."

"Sure. Oz will deal with it, I'll contact him direct. Wait out." And with that, Harry ended the call.

I sent a coded text message to Oz and Andy, asking them to meet me at Oz's cottage the following morning. They both messaged back within the minute confirming the meet.

I went to bed and slept badly.

The US warplanes were strafing my platoon, the Iraqi desert burning like a vision of hell. As my men died, they morphed into the homeless servants of Fyodor Volk, and I had to kill them too. When I ran out of ammunition I clubbed them to death with the butt of my rifle. Colonel Petrovych, who I'd murdered in 2008, sat huddled and frozen in his greatcoat. His dead face was frozen, and he laughed at me, worms wriggling from his empty eye sockets…

I woke up, soaked with cold sweat, panting. The bed-sheets were sodden. Stumbling into my living room, I pulled a clean blanket from the airing cupboard. Then I took some tranquilizers and collapsed on the sofa. Anything, even unconsciousness, was better than this.

The buzzer to my front door rang. The tritium dial on my watch read 04:00. Pulling myself to my feet, I pulled on my dressing gown and picked up my Walther, "Yeah?" I groaned into the entry-phone.

The tinny voice had an unmistakable Scottish accent. "Winter? It's Marcus."

"Marcus?"

"From the… *FCO*. It's bloody freezing out here! Can I come in?"

"I thought you weren't authorised to speak with me."

"I'm bloody well not laddie, so just open the door before somebody sees me."

I pressed the buzzer and let him in. Marcus appeared, his doughy face obscured by a silly waxed hat, sleet dripping from the brim. He smiled gently, looking me up and down. "Having a bad night, Calum?"

"I don't sleep well," I shrugged.

He looked at my pistol and raised an eyebrow. "Yes, it says that in your file." He squeezed past me and stood in my sitting room, water pooling around his sturdy black shoes.

Everybody had a file on me. Why wasn't I flattered? I went to the fridge and opened a can of Coke, emptying it into a beaker of ice, "drink?"

"Yes please, coffee if you have it," he said, looking at my gleaming coffee machine approvingly. Espresso, perhaps?" the intelligence officer took off his hat and coat, dark eyes roaming the apartment. I fixed coffee. He nodded happily and drained it.

"Go on then," I said, "what is it? I've a busy day ahead, slotting Russians for you lot."

Marcus glanced back at the Gaggia and I made him another brew. We stood in silence for a moment. The MI6 man sipped his second cup, "your handler doesn't know I'm here. Is that a problem for you, Cal?"

"Only if he finds out," I replied, draining my cola. I crunched an ice cube between my teeth, spat it into my palm and rubbed it on my clammy forehead, "where's your partner, the ex-army bloke?"

"Chris? He hasn't a clue I'm here either. He's a good sort, but he's a military attachment. He'll be going back to his regiment in the spring, he'll be happier marching about and riding horses or whatever it is they do up at Windsor Castle."

"What do you want, then? The suspense is killing me."

"There are things you need to know about this operation," he said quietly. "Is this apartment swept regularly?"

"Weekly" I nodded, "for bugs at least. I only hoover monthly."

"Can I sit down?"

"No," I said. "I'd be grateful if you spat out whatever it is you want to say, then fuck off."

A baggy pouch of flesh twitched at the corner of Marcus' mouth, making a smile as thin as he was fat. "It's the way of things, in my experience, that men like you don't have much time for men like me. You do the wet-work. I sit in an office, get a pension and an MBE. It's entirely understandable."

I grunted my agreement. I wanted to get on the road to Oz's place.

"That's good espresso," said Marcus. "In any case, I shall get to the point. The material the FSB sent to Pieter Van Basten must never see the light of day. Not by SIS, the Security Service, Police, Media… absolutely nobody. Do you understand?"

"Not really."

Marcus allowed a gentle sigh to escape his lips. "Suffice it to say the rogue Russian official who leaked it was sufficiently highly-placed to release historic agent details going back to the late 1950's and up to 1991. I really must sit down, Cal, my leg is killing me."

"If you must," I replied.

He winced and half-collapsed onto my sofa. "Thanks. We know that hidden amongst the data sent to Forbiddenfacts.net was a series of off-the-record archives called *Zamok*. We know that the original copies of Zamok were destroyed in Moscow in the early nineties."

I knew that *zamok* was Russian for castle. Opening another soda I sat opposite Marcus. "How do you know they were destroyed?"

"Because, Calum, I was the SIS officer who put the hard copy files in an industrial shredder. I took them to an office in Saganka and did the deed in 1991. The UK Government paid two-and-a half million dollars for them."

I laughed. "So some sly bastard must've copied them first, right?"

"Yes, that's precisely what happened," the spy chuckled. "Zamok was the ultra-secret KGB and, later, FSB index of off-the-book European agents. If you saw the names on it, the famous political and cultural figures that spied, agitated and sympathised for the Soviets, or after the collapse of Communism went on to pull financial tricks for the Kremlin… and now I have to assume that Zamok has been updated to the present day."

"I thought all that Cold War stuff was out in the open?"

The spy rubbed his knee and winced, "no, not by half! This isn't guff like the Cambridge Spy Ring? Anthony Blunt? What, some doddery old queen, preaching Communism in his Pall Mall club? No. This is about people still up there in the Establishment stratosphere. There's a serving Major-General, twelve MPs, some surprising elements of the Labour Party, a Tory ex-Minister of State, a couple of High Court judges, a retired Chief Constable or two…"

I sipped Cola. "I'm still not managing to work up enough energy to give a shit. Sergei Belov, on the other hand, is offering me a shed load of cash."

Marcus smiled. "I'm sure he is. Of course, there's other peripheral material in there since 1991, reports separate from Zamok – stuff relating to The Firm, possibly your adventures for the Yanks. We know about NEOPHYTE. Suffice it to say, Cal, almost everybody in our world has an interest in not allowing these archives to see light of day. Try to enjoy your riches in prison. We'll make sure it's the secure unit, with the paedos, terrorists and bent cops…"

I yawned. The early morning visit was starting to make sense. "I suppose there's dirty secrets about you in that file too, Marcus. Which is why you're here, right?"

The spy looked at his watch. "Indeed. I wasn't always sat in an office. But I'm vain enough to want my MBE and Scottish enough to covet my pension."

Snow drifted by the window past the bridge. "Tell me, why isn't this juicy stuff on the forbiddenfacts.com website? And why are sharing this with me?"

"The answer to the first question, courtesy of my man at Cheltenham, is the encryption on the files is top notch. The person who sent the file had a protected version with nine levels of security. He had only cracked the first two. Even Van Basten's technical experts will take time to crack it, but crack it they certainly will."

"Go on."

"And the second is that Alisa Turov wants Zamok for the SVR to play with." The spook spoke slowly, eyes roaming my face. "That's her primary mission. We are very much an alliance of limited convenience, I suspect."

I shifted uneasily. "So she isn't the anti-FSB crusader she makes out she is?"

"Oh yes. She's a zealot when it comes to her hatred of the FSB, and then some. But she'd happily take down our government and national business infrastructure in order to achieve her mission. My view is she can still achieve her objectives without getting her hands on Zamok, there's enough FSB dirt to go round without that specific file."

"And you want me to make sure that she doesn't get hold of it?"

Marcus nodded slowly, a contented smile on his moon-shaped face. "Indeed I do Cal, not her or anyone else. It needs to be destroyed. In return you'll have a friend inside of SIS. You never know when The Firm might have no need of you anymore. And if that happens… you can call Uncle Marcus, day or night."

Opening the fridge, I pulled out bacon and eggs. "Do you want some breakfast Uncle Marcus?"

Marcus patted his gut lovingly, "given my blood pressure I shouldn't, but you can take the boy out of Glasgow…"

"I want out of The Firm," I said.

"That makes sense," he purred, "in your shoes, so would I. Maybe a job with us, something secure."

I pulled out the frying pan and began cooking. "Can you help me do that?"

Marcus smiled like a TV quizmaster with all the answers on a card in his pocket. I made him breakfast as he offered to be my guardian angel, in exchange for guaranteeing the destruction of the Zamok archive. If Harry found out he'd have me killed. I told Marcus that.

The spook methodically dissected his fried egg, balanced it on top three rashers of bacon and slid the lot onto a slice of heavily buttered bread. He sighed happily. "When we met, Alisa explained quite adequately what the situation is."

"Yes," I said, "you don't deal with the likes of me. In which case how can you help?"

He chewed on a mouthful of food as he thought about it. "The service codename of the officer that looks after contact with The Firm is DIADEM. The identity of the DIADEM is a closely-guarded secret within SIS but I knew who the last one was."

"How?"

"I was married to her," he said. "Margaret was a wonderful woman, died of MS Christmas before last." He reached across and took more bread, "of course, Maggie broke service confidentiality when she showed me the files, but only when she genuinely needed my advice. I've been a case officer for over twenty-five years. I've served in Moscow, Riyadh, Brussels, Baghdad, Berlin… she valued my opinion."

"I'm sorry about your wife," I said, and I was.

"That's very kind of you Cal. When she passed away I copied her paperwork. So I had your details, and those of your colleagues. I even know who Harry is."

I shot him a look. "Can you help me get out? To walk away from The Firm?"

The intelligence officer smiled and looked out of the window. It was dawn. "Perhaps. One day, if you're good, I might tell you more. But right now is there any chance of some more of that excellent bacon?" Marcus shambled over to the open-plan kitchen and cracked some eggs. "We're making a big omelette!" he laughed. "Yes, I can help you, but it depends what they have on you, to coerce you to stay and keep quiet. You'll need to tell me about your sins. How bad is your story?"

"Pretty bad."

"Precisely, we'll see. But before you send my hair white with shock at your moral depravity, tell me what you've discovered about the FSB."

I told him about Misha Baburin. "Will the police be all over his farm in Essex?"

"Not yet – I checked with my man at Thames House. They've only got him officially linked to a flat in East London. He kept the farm off the grid for obvious reasons, although I'm sure the police will trace it eventually. I'd be quick."

I left the SIS officer cooking and got ready. After I showered I strapped on my body armour and slid the Walther into the pancake holster on my belt. I made sure I was carrying no ID.

"I'll let myself out when I'm finished," said Marcus. The smell of fried food and the sound of Radio 4 drifted from the kitchen.

I padded towards the front door, dry-swallowing three painkillers. "How do I contact you?"

"Here," Marcus replied, tossing me a padded envelope. "That mobile phone has one number programmed into it. Mine. Only use it in emergencies."

"I will," I said, putting it in my pocket.

"Thank you."

"It's a bit early for that. Let's see how it goes when someone turns the heat up a little."

"Indeed," said Marcus, his pudgy face softening. He walked over and put his hand on my shoulder, a piece of egg stuck to his chin. His voice was low and gentle, like you'd get at a confession. "Tell me what it is you did? This terrible thing The Firm has on you?"

So I told him, as I stood in my apartment with my head pounding. Outside snow tumbled from the sky, blocking out the sun.

THIRTEEN

Maysan Province, Iraq, 2006

The Commanding Officer for my final Iraq tour was called Lieutenant-Colonel Justin Powell. Since his last trip to Staff College he'd morphed into a complete tool, heart set on red staff tabs and a general's pension. The chatter in the officer's mess was that on previous Op. TELIC tours, as a Major on Brigade Staff, he'd taken unnecessary risks with the boys to impress the brass. His promotion to Colonel was a given, but delayed due to operations, and he was pissed off about it – he was in a hurry to make Brigadier. And we all knew our battalion suffered more casualties since his appointment. Nor did it help that our last CO had been a brilliant leader and universally popular.

'Colonel Justin' thought I was too informal with my soldiers, and we both knew that as long as he was in the chair my chances of making Major were zero. He'd also been a platoon commander when I was a lance corporal, and I don't think he liked me then either. He called me into the battalion CP, set up in an old house in the crumbling, fly-blown shithole that was Amara. The place was held together with bullet holes and dried blood. I knew he was on the radio to Brigade HQ from the puppyish expression on his ruddy, handsome face. He ran a beefy hand through his mop of golden hair and motioned for me to sit down. "Yes sir," he said smoothly into the handset, "but we've got some problems up there with IED attacks, I'd rather…"

I sat down and took off my helmet, working clumps of sand out of my greasy scalp with filthy fingers. One of the HQ Company signallers gave me a "hallo sir," and offered me a brew. I nodded gratefully and emptied four sugars into it, giving the signaller a fag from a bashed-up pack of Marlboro Red. Funny how in scorching weather all I wanted was a hot, sweet brew and a cigarette.

"I understand, Sir. What, their three-star is jumping up and down?" said the CO, "Yes, I know what the Yanks are like. I'll get right onto it." He put the handset down and sighed. "Cal, I want you to take Recce Platoon up to Al Halfayah. We've got more reports of sabotage on the oil pipeline up there, Brigade want eyes on ASAP. We'll O-Group in…"

"With respect, Colonel Justin" I replied, offering him the packet of Marlboro, "I've got two wagons out of action, three of my men are injured and Harris was killed the day before yesterday up on the MSR. My snipers are attached to 'C' Company, so I'm down three guys there. That part of Maysan is crawling with insurgents. I'll need support. Maybe 'A' Coy can lend us a half a platoon?"

'A' Company was bolstered by a platoon of Gurkhas on attachment, and was shit-hot. As a result, Powell had taken to wearing a Nepalese *Kukri* fighting knife on his webbing, an affectation that made us all think he was an even bigger wanker.

"Are you saying you won't do it, Cal?" Powell replied, head cocked as he took a cigarette. He almost smiled. I knew he was pissed off about my medal citation because it had been personally OK'd and pushed up the line by a Colonel from Brigade who'd witnessed my alleged act of heroism. We both knew it gave me unofficial traction.

"No, Sir. I'm just letting you know we're not best placed to do it," I replied. "Not until I get my wagons back. Just so you can make an informed decision."

"That's not the attitude I've imbued in this battalion Cal. I expect can-do. Everyone has been run ragged, not just Recce Platoon."

"By 'can-do' do you mean getting the fuck blown out of us in unarmoured Land Rovers?" I said quietly. I stood up so I was face-to-face with the Colonel. We were still waiting for the long-promised Mastiff armoured cars, so still had to rely on flimsy, WMIK-fitted Land Rovers.

"Look Cal" he said finally in a treacly voice, a hand resting on my shoulder, "I know your guys have had a tough time, and you've been operating at full capacity, so I'll let that one go. But remember, you get the tough jobs because you're good," he treated me to a flinty-eyed gaze. "Our battle group is one of the best-performing in theatre, and I'm the forward-facing guy with Brigade. I know your job is tough, but dealing with all the bullshit up the chain of command has its moments too."

Behind him the Ops Officer, a major, attempted a sympathetic smile. Then he disappeared, busying himself with maps and reports when he saw I was up for a ruck.

"Sir, we get a dozen reports of insurgent activity up on that pipeline a week. You know it's usually just bait for another bloody IED." I shrugged and sat down again, "they must be laughing their beards off that we always fall for it."

"It's the business we're in. We're infantry soldiers, not shelf-stackers at Tesco. This is a big deal for Brigade for some reason. The Americans need us up there, and the Poles have their hands full to the North." He looked at his watch and lowered his voice. "I want you to leave ASAP. The Yanks are running fast air if you need it. This is important." His missions for Brigade were always bloody important because he was camped so far up the Brigadier's rectum he needed a flashlight to read his watch.

"Of course, Colonel," I said wearily, picking up my rifle and helmet. "I take it that's a direct order despite my representations?"

"*Representations*, Winter? I know it's a bit of a cliché, but I'm paid to give orders," he said, studying the tip of his cigarette, "and you're paid to follow them."

"Yessir," I barked like a Day One recruit.

Powell's eyes narrowed, his voice barely a whisper, "and if you ever question me in front of the men again, you chippy little cunt, I'll have you court-martialled. Now fuck off and never barrack-room lawyer me again. It might have worked when you were a lance corporal but not now."

Ah, the days when I followed orders. I sloped out of Battalion HQ and made my way back to the platoon.

Clarkie and the others didn't make a girly fuss like I did. They rolled their eyes, sorted out their kit and told sick jokes as they brewed up tea. After the O-Group we loaded up the dusty, shrapnel-pocked WMIKs, checked that our laughably crap radios weren't working and drove up the dusty, pot-holed road east towards Al Halfayah.

The next morning we got into a contact with some insurgents cutting about in an old Toyota pickup. We were advancing to contact when one of our wagons was predictably fucked by shrapnel from an IED. As we went to help them out of their WMIK, skilfully hidden insurgents with MGs and mortars opened up on us. We were pinned down, tracer bouncing across the pancake-flat landscape and mortar bombs exploding around us. We returned the serve with AT4, GPMG and .50 cal machineguns but it wasn't enough. Two men were injured and we took cover in a fold in the ground. Some five hundred metres away, hidden snipers engaged us with their long-range Dragunov rifles.

I got on the radio and called in the Yank fast air for urgent support, Danger Close. The F15E dropped a pair of 2000lb JDAMs. One shredded Clarkie's Land Rover with shrapnel. It killed him instantly and critically injured his driver.

It was my airstrike. My call.

It killed Clarkie. If I hadn't called in the fast air he'd be alive. Fact.

Later on, an inquiry would decide that it was one of those things, not my fault or the pilot's. It didn't feel like it then and it doesn't feel like it now. I must have got the grid wrong, or the drills. There was no Forward Air Controller available.

It was down to me.

Clarkie was blown into pieces, as was the Toyota full of insurgents. They stopped shooting, and I took the opportunity to look for my friend. Clarkie's torso was a chunk of roasted meat, both his legs severed at the knee and his innards trailing behind him like putrid sausage. We found his head a hundred metres away, but never located his right arm. I'll never forget the stench, explosives and petrol and burning guts and shit. I shovelled him into his sleeping bag and put him in my vehicle. His dog-tags were in the foot well of his Land Rover, and I tucked them away in my body armour. In his wallet was a photo of Sam and the kids, which I kept. I've still got it at my flat, the corner charred and black. I feel guilty about the photograph, just like I feel guilty about everything else.

We pulled back as the RAF CASEVAC landed and took away the wounded. Vultures circled overhead. The Yank F-15s finally returned and blew up the dug-in mortars, MGs and two adjacent villages. We drove back to Amara, the engine of Clarkie's smouldering WMIK still burning by the side of the road. Our mission, whatever the fuck it was meant to be, was accomplished. We made it back to Battalion HQ the next morning. It turned out that my patrol had been ordered to act as a distraction for some American SF naughtiness going on a few miles north. Another success for the battalion. Hoo-fucking-rah!

Colonel Justin was up at Brigade HQ so I didn't get to deliver the angry speech I'd prepared. The Ops Officer told me Powell even made an entry in his ops log stating that I'd taken the patrol out under-strength without asking for extra resources, to cover his arse for the inevitable Steward's Inquiry. He also me put on a charge for insubordination.

By that point I couldn't care less about the lying bastard, as I'd received my joining instructions for Special Forces selection. I knew my future in The Battalion was finished. By the time of Clarkie's funeral Justin Powell was already a full colonel. When they lowered Clarkie into the earth, Powell didn't look me in the eye, and never did again.

Well, that's not strictly true.

He looked me straight in the eye, with surprise, after I was fresh out of rehab. He was enjoying a solitary morning's fly-fishing in the Borders. Brigadier Powell almost said "hello," before I double-tapped him with .45 hollow-point rounds, which blew his handsome golden head clean off his shoulders. His corpse slipped into the misty waters of the Teviot, his surprised looking dog howling in indignation. Re-holstering my pistol, I patted the mutt on the head and took a salmon for later.

As far as I was concerned it was karma. Powell rolled the dice when he sent us out on that patrol and put his ambition before us.

The next day I drove down to Kent, to put fresh flowers on Clarkie's grave and threw the acid-cleansed gun in the Medway. I took Sam and the kids out to lunch afterwards. "You look happier, Cal," said Sam brightly as she fussed over the kids in the restaurant, "I think that place you went to has worked wonders." She didn't want to say 'rehab' or 'mental hospital' in front of the kids. She was wearing a short red dress, hair worn in a trendy bob. She looked great. Her mum called her *The Merry Widow*, but you only had to look in her eyes to see the truth. "Thanks" I smiled, "I feel better. Hey, this burger's good."

"This place was Jason's favourite," she said. "They give you too much food, the beer is dead cheap and he fancied the waitresses." It was funny. I knew Clarkie for eleven years and never called him Jason.

Brigadier Powell's murder hit the newspapers and was *mystery du jour* for a couple of months. Then some nutty fringe Irish terrorists claimed responsibility, the first time I'd ever been grateful to Republicans. I was working back out in Iraq by then, for a PMC called Longbow. I was on leave in Amman, drinking too much again and trying not to develop a rock-star level cocaine habit.

In Amman I met a bloke in a noisy hotel bar who'd been a sergeant in my old Battalion before joining Special Forces. I vaguely remembered him, a guy called Bishop who'd left about the time I went to Sandhurst. One night, after too much booze, cocaine and exaggerated reminiscences, the subject got onto Justin Powell. Bishop was a good listener, and I'd already told him about my language training, recce experience and my medal. I'd even told him about getting kicked off SAS selection, but he knew that already. "I remember Powell," said Bishop, offering me another drink. "He was my Company Commander just before I went for selection for the Regiment. What a wanker." He told me an anecdote about Powell behaving like a dick in South Armagh.

"Tell me about it," I said. For some reason we were drinking Japanese whisky, *Suntory*. Bishop poured me another slug, so big it would have made Ollie Reed blush. I drank it, itching to go to the bog so I could hoover up more Gak. At the other end of the bar a shoal of Hookers circled. I hadn't had an erection for a year but was willing to try.

Then I did it.

"I shot the fucker, y'know," I slurred drunkenly, literally shouting in his ear over the pounding pop music.

"Good drills," Bishop laughed.

"I'm not joking."

"What?"

I told him the story. Keeping the secret was like having a bottle of fizzy soda you've shaken too much – the top has to come off eventually. I felt warm and happy as I got it off my chest.

Bishop smiled and looked in his glass. "Your secret's safe with me," he lied.

I'm still sure it was an unfortunate coincidence that Bishop was a talent scout for The Firm. His brief was to look for suitable operators on the private military circuit, people who were vulnerable and could be persuaded to give it all up for a monastic life of ultra-secret wet-work.

Bishop gave me the good news over lunch in London soon afterwards. I was off to Ukraine, as a NEOPHYTE. He apologized as he showed me the statement he'd give the police if I played up, and the mobile telephone data linked to my mobile. It put me near Powell on the Borders on the day he was murdered. He also explained that they'd accessed my medical records. "Nobody will believe you if you want to return the serve, make allegations about us. You've been sectioned once under the Mental Health Act. You've been in rehab, you're damaged goods. It's a shame, the way things have panned out."

"Fuck you," I growled.

Bishop's smile was almost sympathetic. He'd heard it all before. "For what it's worth, Cal" he said, jabbing his fork into a gobbet of rare, bloody beef, "by and large, The Firm is on the side of the angels and the money is good. You might even enjoy it."

Like I said, Bishop was a liar. And I was a murderer. We've all got feet of clay.

"So now you know who you've hired," I shrugged, finishing the story. I left Marcus standing in my flat, face grim. There was nothing else left to say.

FOURTEEN

Oz picked me up near Hammersmith station and headed east, out of town and towards the Essex coast. Despite my lack of sleep I was feeling OK, the prospect of action firing adrenalin around my body. My phone bleeped. Harry had sent me some intelligence on Black Hall Farm, on an encrypted email account. I skimmed them and decided they could wait until the briefing. I sipped the cup of coffee Oz had got me, "I asked for suppressed weapons. Any luck?"

Oz nodded. "We've got three MP5 SD4s and a suppressed M6 rifle with all the toys on."

"Pistols?"

"Only the ones at my place, two of them are clean."

"That'll have to do."

The Holloway incident had made the news. The BBC reported a shooting at a brothel linked to people-traffickers and someone had leaked the details of the Georgian mafia connection to the press. The police had arrested two men linked to Eastern European crime in Enfield. Baburin's name wasn't mentioned, only that three males were found murdered from gunshot wounds. Luckily a Premiership footballer had been arrested for rape, which kept the story languishing on page seven of the papers. "That should keep them busy for a bit," said Oz gratefully.

We got to Oz's cottage late morning. Andy's battered Ford Transit was parked outside, the ex-SRR man sitting in the front reading the newspaper. "Morning," he said, getting out of the cab. "It's fucking snowing for a change."

"It's a weather front from Russia," I said.

"Like everything else in this cake-and-arse party," Oz grumbled, traipsing through the snow to the back of the van. Inside, under the hardboard floor panels, was a tarpaulin-wrapped bundle containing weapons and equipment. We were unloading the van when a black VW Golf bumped down the track towards the cottage. My hand went to my holster, Andy sliding an assault rifle from his tool bag.

"It's OK" said Oz, "it's Turov."

Alisa parked next to my Volvo. I saw the sticker for a hire car company in the window of her VW. "*Privet*," she said brightly, like we were going on a family day out. She wore black Gore-Tex leggings, walking boots and a green hooded North Face jacket. "I looked at the map," she said, "why have we travelled north to go back south again?"

"Our equipment is in there," I said pointing to the cottage. Beyond was the sea, flat and grey, the horizon merging with the sky.

"Plus its lovely this time of year," Andy laughed.

We went inside and sat in the small kitchen and Oz built a fire. Andy whistled tunelessly while he made sandwiches and tea. Alisa nodded her approval, pulling chocolate and a flask from her rucksack.

I opened up an Ordnance Survey map of Essex. My plan was to put in an assault in the early hours, late enough to ensure they'd be tucked up in bed and early enough to give us a few hours of darkness to exfil. The farm was east of Southminster, on the coast. The landscape was flat – frozen fields and muddy farmland interspersed with hedgerows and copses of trees. I cleared my throat and tapped the map. "The nearest inhabited buildings to Black Hall Farm are two kilometres away in every direction. There's a tiny local police station, the nearest armed cops would have to motor down from Colchester I'd imagine."

"I'll dial in some moody 999 bollocks or a bomb threat before we go in," said Andy. "It'll keep the Boys in Blue busy."

"I like it," Oz dead-panned. "I mean, Essex must be the number one terrorist target in the UK."

Alisa ignored them, pulling a tablet computer from her rucksack and opening a file of high-resolution images on the screen. "Courtesy of your excellent GCHQ," she smiled, "taken yesterday morning." The farm was a ramshackle pile surrounded by a cluster of barns, out-buildings and a mobile home. The back of the farmhouse had clearly been up-dated with a smart red-brick extension. "Baburin used this new part of the building to live in," said Alisa, tracing a finger across the screen, "the barns and shacks have three vehicles parked outside, and on the imagery you can see two men by the mobile home."

The detail on the satellite photos was crystal clear. Two men wearing hooded winter field jackets stood in the snow by the trailer. One was holding something to his ear, the other clearly smoking. "One road in, one road out," said Andy happily. "Why don't we lay up an ambush on it and flush them out, set up a kill zone here and a cut-off there?" He pointed to the rutted farm track, some half a kilometre long that met the single-track road leading to Southminster.

"It's not a bad idea" Oz agreed, "but if we want to contain the fire-fight, make sure we don't attract attention, then maybe we need to take them out in the buildings."

"I agree with Oz," said Alisa, "let us take them inside."

"Yeah," I said, "but Andy's got a point. We leave one shooter to cover the road in any case. Anything trying to leave the plot gets slotted."

"Sure," said Oz, "who do you want in there?"

"Andy," I said. We were all good rifle shots, and Oz had been a sniper's course instructor in the Marines, but Andy was the most patient and skilled surveillance monkey I'd met. The farmland was like anywhere in Antrim or Armagh, where he'd learnt his trade in 'The Det', the secretive army surveillance unit.

"OK" Andy sighed, disappointed he wouldn't be in on the assault.

"Andy, I've got you a suppressed M6, box-fresh," said Oz.

"Really?" said the ex-SRR man, cheering up now there were toys to play with.

We talked through the plan. We were the expecting six FSB *Spetzgruppa* commandos and maybe some of Baburin's lackeys. There were four of us, well-armed with the element of surprise. Finally, we waited for Andy to say something. He looked alternatively at the satellite imagery and my map. Then he drank his tea and rolled a cigarette.

"Go on then" said Oz, "as you can imagine, I'm on the edge of my seat."

"He is like my uncle, back home," said Turov.

"What, a silent-but-deadly hunter?" said Andy with a lop-sided grin.

"No, he has dementia," she laughed.

"I love being abused and humiliated," Andy replied. "Marry me!"

"Tell me your plan, crazy person, I then think about it."

"I've got night vision kit and PRRs in the van," said Andy, his grimy finger pointing at the map. "See this copse of bushes and pine trees? It runs parallel to the end of the track and it's on high ground. So it gives me a good view over the farm and the road in both directions. I'll go in as soon as I can and CTR from there at dusk."

"Are you sure you can Close Target Recce that close?" I said. Andy was talking about sneaking right into the farm and taking a look.

The lanky Mancunian looked offended. "It's me, Cal, for fuck's sake! When I'm done I'll take my post with the rifle at the cut-off as per your plan."

Oz held his hands up. "Andy's right, he can do it. Remember that job in Estonia?"

Last year we'd cut the brakes on some Mafia kingpin's car near Maardu. Andy had snuck into the target's compound, picked the lock on the garage door and done the reverse-engineering on his BMW while two guards sat outside smoking. I'd sat in our control vehicle, arse-clenched, ready to dash out with my AK. "If he is confident he can do it then he should go," said Alisa, slamming her small hand on the table, "is a good, simple plan."

"Hey, who's in charge here?" I said.

"I am a full Colonel, you *were* a Captain," said the SVR officer, raising an eyebrow.

"Spy ranks don't count," said Oz, "sneaking about and writing reports and eating Ferrero Rocher at the ambassador's reception…"

Alisa Turov's eyes narrowed. "I led a special action unit in Chechnya, Mister Osborne," she purred. "I do not recall any diplomatic parties in Grozny during that time."

"OK, point taken," said Oz, "even if you were on the wrong side."

"Right," I said sharply, glancing at my watch, "let's get on with it. Andy, get ready for your CTR and set up comms. Oz prep weapons, we'll zero them as soon as possible. Alisa, can you check for any last minute intelligence updates please?"

I went outside and lit a cigar as they busied themselves with their tasks. It had stopped snowing, but the ground was still covered in a couple of inches of powder, higher ground topped with frozen slush. I called Harry. "We're good," I said, "we go in at 03:00."

"OK," the handler replied. "For some reason SIS are very happy, they're convinced that the risk to Belov from this Fyodor Volk character is a fantasy. Their sources in Russia have never heard of him."

"SIS also confidently predicted Saddam had doomsday weapons," I said, exhaling smoke. "You'll forgive me if I keep an open mind."

"As helpful as ever," Harry grumbled, "after this is done you need to speak with Pieter Van Basten and persuade him to give up the location of his server. If Belov feels he's safe he might help."

"Whoa, let's rewind there Harry," I spluttered, "I'm a shooter, not a negotiator. How am I meant to do that?"

"You have Turov with you to assist, and you've developed a relationship with Belov. You know that we only want a portion of the data, not all of it. So crack on."

I wasn't in the mood for Harry's bullshit. He'd forgotten who the client was in his rush to suck up to SIS. But he didn't have to ride four horses – Belov, SIS, SVR and Pieter Van Basten. "I'll let you know as soon as we're finished here."

"Good. I'll update you if I hear anything from SIS." Harry rang off.

Back in the cottage, Oz was playing quartermaster. He had neatly laid out a weapon, night-vision goggles, ammunition, flash-bangs, radio and a winter camouflage suit for each of us. "Do you have body armour, Alisa?" he said.

"No," she shrugged, checking the suppressed Heckler & Koch SD4. The submachinegun had a thick suppressed barrel, four-position trigger group and custom grips. Trijicon night-sights completed the package.

Oz had camouflaged the submachineguns with white tape, breaking up the shape of the solid black gunmetal. "Take this, level 3A Fortis covert armour, not bad," he said. "It's male, I'm afraid but it's small."

"That will be fine, Oz, thank you," she said. She stripped down to her sports bra. Glowering as I enjoyed the view, she strapped on the armour.

"I'm only human," I said innocently.

"This is a matter of opinion," she hissed.

Andy walked in, wearing white camouflage overalls over his clothing. On his head he wore a balaclava rolled into a hat. Over his shoulder was slung the M6 suppressed rifle with a custom bipod and Trijicon ACOG scope. "Right, I'm off," he said.

"Good luck Andrew," said Oz.

"Luck? Nah, luck is for amateurs," he grinned, "I'll call you as soon as I've got eyes on." He zipped a blue windcheater over his winter whites and climbed into the van. The engine coughed into life and he drove off, southwest towards Colchester.

Behind the cottage was a field flanked by trees and blackthorn bushes, overlooking the sea. We traipsed through the snow and set up some Figure Eleven targets, the one with the black-and-ochre charging squaddie on it. Oz gave range orders and we spent forty-five minutes zeroing our MP5s and pistols. The suppressed MP5SD4 was virtually silent, the only noise a hiss and the metallic snap of the bolt. We were using sub-sonic hollow-point 9mm ammunition, designed to cause maximum damage with minimum noise. "That'll do," said Oz. "We're good."

We picked up the spent brass and went back to the cottage, where we brewed more tea. "You look tired, Cal" said Alisa, "we have time to kill, get some sleep."

Oz patted my back, "she's right, you look like shit."

"I slept badly last night." I hadn't mentioned my early morning visit from MI6 and didn't plan to either. I nodded and took off my Altberg boots, kneading warmth into my toes. Upstairs was Oz's spare bedroom, where I stripped off my sweater and flopped down onto the bed. I fell quickly into a dreamless, happy sleep.

FIFTEEN

"There are at least three subjects, Andy whispered over the secure net. "Big fellas – cropped hair, proper gym bunnies by the look of 'em."

"Are they commando-types?" I asked.

"Not unless Russian special forces go in for day-glow orange tans and hair gel."

We'd parked my car in a lay-by behind a roadside barn a mile from Black Hall Farm. I'd smeared mud on the frozen number plates to obscure the registration mark. We sat quietly as Andy called in updates from his hide. He'd identified no CCTV or burglar alarms. Even the barrier by the front gate, an old scaffolding pole mounted on a bracket, was unlocked.

"I've had a good look around the farm" he continued, "three vehicles – people carrier, Land Rover and a BMW. No sign of weapons. Not even a dog. The extension at the rear of the farm has the lights on. Entry is via two UPVC-type doors. They're a bastard to break into: I'd go in via the side door, it's a crappy old wooden thing."

It was just after 23:00. "Let me know when the lights go out," I said "then we move."

"Roger," he replied.

We waited another hour when Andy called back in, reporting that the farm was now dark.

"Give 'em an hour to fall asleep," Oz half-yawned, stretching his legs across the back seat.

Turov sipped her coffee and nodded her agreement. Our weapons were stashed in the boot, along with our night vision kit, body armour and radios.

I held my hands to the chugging in-car heater, "I expected six. Where are the rest of them?"

"There's a gym in there, no?" said Turov, "Spetzgruppa? They will be working out, or drunk. Trust me."

We saw headlights across the field as a car drove slowly through the snow. We ducked down as it passed, a battered estate driven by an elderly man. It was the first vehicle we'd seen in two hours. It was nearly 02:00 when I called Andy. "We're going to park just by the junction with the road, then on foot down the track. I'm gonna put a flash-bang in so expect noise."

"Roger," he whispered. "Still no movement. I can take anything coming up or down the track, and have eyes on the farmhouse."

We put on body armour and NVGs, pulling the baggy snow-suits over our winter clothes. Then Oz handed out the suppressed submachine guns and six spare magazines each. I tapped the end of the clip against my boot heel to settle the rounds, slid it into the housing on the underside of the weapon and pulled back the stubby bolt on top of the receiver. My thumb slid the safety off and onto single-shot. I drove the mile to the top of the drive-way and found another lay-by by the junction. I tucked the car behind some trees, a sheet of snow falling onto the windscreen as I disturbed the branches. We got out and hit the start line for the operation. Oz gave a thumbs-up. Alisa nodded, the stubby black SMG tucked into her shoulder as we patrolled along the track.

Oz took the lead. I followed him, scanning arcs with my SMG. My boots crunched in the snow as we passed the metal gate, the low roof of the farmhouse thirty metres to my left. Turov stalked to my right, peering through her NVGs. Standing still, I took a look at the out-buildings and the mobile home, mounted on breeze-blocks. Black Hill Farm was unremarkable in every way. The cars were covered with an even half inch of snow. Oz walked slowly to the wooden front door. Pushing his NVGs onto the top of his head, he examined the lock. He motioned for us to go firm and take cover. I knelt by the workshop door opposite him and Turov took position by the mobile home, weapon shouldered. "I'm going to drill the lock," whispered Oz into the mic of his PRR. "Come closer. Get in like shit off a shovel when I'm done."

"Roger, entry as planned," I replied. I pulled the M84 stun grenade from my chest rig and clutched it tightly. There was a technical term for the extreme disorientation an M84 going off causes, but as Andy preferred to say, *it just really fucks you up.*

Oz crouched down and slipped the bit of a battery-powered drill into the lock. Turov stood behind him. I walked slowly over to the door and stood opposite, MP5 slung across my chest.

The screech of the drill ripped through the night-time silence. Oz drilled out the lock in seconds, pushed the door open and brought his MP5 to bear. I pulled the pin on the stun grenade and tossed it as far into the corridor as I could. With no neighbours for miles, I was gambling that one bang contained inside a building would go unnoticed, unlike an exchange of automatic weapon fire.

I covered my ears and waited, anticipation not dulling the boom of the M84 detonating. The million-candlelight flash flared in my peripheral vision. I ducked into the doorway, weapon first and darted in. The corridor smelt of smoke and gunpowder, a flight of stairs to my left and a doorway straight ahead leading towards the back of the farmhouse where the extension was located. "Go" I barked, covering the stairway.

Oz passed me, MP5 scanning the corridor like an extension of his body.

Tchk! Tchk! went a suppressed MP5 behind me, the distinctive metallic snap of the bolt. I felt the rounds whistle past my ear. "Clear!" said Turov. In front of me I saw a body sprawled in the doorway. I hadn't even seen him. Oz stepped over the corpse, which was clad only in tracksuit trousers, and into the next room. Oz took the left side, I took the right. It was a large kitchen. I saw movement in the corner of the room and I fired two sense-of-direction shots. A window shattered as it was struck by a bullet, and I heard a grunt.

Then, the buzz-saw stammer of an automatic weapon filled my ears, the room a maelstrom of incoming rounds, plasterboard and debris. We all instinctively ducked, Oz firing as he hugged the floor. Someone on the other side of the thin partition wall had fired straight through it, leaving a crazy trail of ragged bullet holes. It was still pitch black. "I'm hit," Oz groaned.

I thumbed the MP5 onto three-round bursts and opened fire, working backwards to mirror the bullet holes in the wall. Turov, seeing what I was doing, nodded and fired on automatic. Her stream of bullets joined mine as they raked across the wall. The only sounds were the bolts of our weapons, spent shell casings hitting the floor and the thud of rounds splintering flimsy MDF like tissue paper. I ejected the empty magazine and reloaded.

The intensity of return fire suggested multiple assailants, and through the gashes in the ruined wall I could see muzzle flashes. The men were aiming high, their fire unfocussed. This wasn't the work of professionals.

I didn't see the guy who barrelled into me, knocking me flat. I tried to twist to bring my SMG around, but a bony fist crashed into my face, a hand scrabbling at the MP5. Turov was grunting with effort as she, too wrestled with a dark shape. Again I heard the familiar hiss of a suppressed weapon and my attacker shuddered. I pulled my pistol, stuffed it against his ribs and squeezed the trigger twice. Rolling off of the body of an athletic, Asiatic-looking man I saw Turov pinned to the ground by a bigger combatant, the dull gleam of a combat knife in his grip. I brought my Walther up and fired, catching the knifeman in the back of the head. His body crashed forwards on top of the SVR officer. The automatic fire stopped, and I heard swearing in Russian and the metallic scrape of magazines being taken out of weapons.

"Alisa?" I hissed.

"It's OK," she whispered.

Readying my SMG, I crawled towards the door for a better look, pulling down my NVGs. Two semi-clothed muscle-men were huddled in the darkness, behind a pile of crazily upturned furniture. They were reloading their AK assault rifles and whispering in low voices. In front of them was a body, a neat trail of red bullet wounds stitched across his torso. "Hands up!" I bellowed in Russian.

One of the men spun towards me, blinking in the dark. His hand snatched at the cocking lever on his AK. I fired a three round bust, the bullets finding their mark. He flopped forward, the wall behind him painted with gore.

"HANDS UP, YOU FUCKING IDIOT" I bawled. The second guy dropped his AK, looking around in the darkness. I stood up and rushed him, smashing his jaw with the butt of my SMG and kicking his rifle across the floor "ROOM CLEAR! How's Oz?" I said. The Russian curled into a groaning ball of muscle as I aimed my weapon at his head.

I heard Alisa's voice. "He's OK, it's an in-and-out shot. Upper arm."

"No, I'm not fucking OK," the ex-SBS man coughed. "I'll never play the violin again."

"That bastard who jumped us actually stabbed me," she laughed. "Thanks for the body armour." I could see her motioning to her mid-riff, her white camouflage coveralls slashed open.

I switched on a light, revealing the carnage. Blood-streaked furniture, weapons and bodies littered the corridor and sitting room. I could see the remnants of a heavy drinking session – empty vodka bottles, opened bags of white powder, sleeves of boot-legged cigarettes and a pile of porno DVDs. The wide-screen TV, big enough for a small cinema, was splintered with bullet holes. I keyed the mic of my PRR. "Andy, what did that sound like?"

"World War fucking Three" he groaned, "they'd have heard that in Belgium."

"We're good, will exfil in five."

"Make it two."

"You," I barked in Russian at the muscle-man, glaring at me as he spat out a tooth, "where are the FSB men? *The Spetzgruppa?*" He looked around at the corpses, then at the nearest weapon. "Don't even think about it," I said quietly, pressing the muzzle of my SMG against his forehead. "Where are they?"

Turov and Oz joined me. Oz's face was screwed up in pain. He was clutching a field dressing against his bloody arm, pieces of gristle and muscle bulging from the wound. The sleeve of his white coverall was soaked red. And his DNA was now all over the plot. "Tell him what he wants to know, idiot," said Alisa, her SMG pointed at the Russian gangster.

"They have gone," he croaked, blood running down his chin, "on their fucking mission, like good soldier boys."

"Where?" I said.

"I don't know, they don't tell me. I just babysit their stuff. The commander's room is upstairs, they are coming back, tomorrow or maybe the day after. Then they go home."

"When did they leave?" I said.

"This morning," he said, "just after breakfast."

Alisa pointed with her SMG "And who are you?"

"Me? Nobody. I work for Misha, for his security team. We were looking after the boys for him, that's all."

"Then you have failed." Alisa stepped back and shot him with a three round burst to the chest, the Russian collapsing like a sack of meat. "I'll search upstairs," she said.

"We don't have time," I replied. "They've gone to find Van Basten, right?"

Alisa said nothing, just hurried out of the room. I heard her boots thumping on the stairs. "We've gotta go," Oz groaned. His face was pale and shiny with sweat.

I was worried he'd go into shock. I pulled another field dressing from my pocket and un-wrapped it, placing it gently over the first. Then I passed him an inhaler dose of nasal Ketamine, a better and faster-painkiller than morphine. "You good?"

"Fuck," whistled Oz, "that actually hurts." He took the plastic bottle and took a sniff.

"Never been shot before?" I chided.

"Only the once, in the 'Stan," he winced.

"Where?"

Oz rolled his eyes, "Helmand, you daft bastard."

"No, where on your body?" I said, wanting to keep him talking.

Oz staggered as he tried not to laugh. "In my arse, Terry Taliban plinked me in the jacksie with a 5.45 round from three hundred metres. I was taking a dump at the time."

Turov skipped down the stairs, a laptop computer cradled in her arms. "I have also found mobile telephones and a map. They were hidden inside a mattress. The map is a military one of Wiltshire."

I put Oz's arm around my shoulder and helped him towards the door. "That's great, but we need to think about this place, it's a forensic nightmare."

Then I heard sirens.

SIXTEEN

"I can see blue lights, headed north" said Andy calmly over our PRR net, "one cop car." From his hide he could see the main road in either direction. "It's OK, he's heading the wrong way, but I expect him to turn around when he gets to the next farm."

"Get out of there," I ordered.

"With respect, Captain, no," he replied, "I've got tricks in the wagon, plus that plot needs cleaning up."

Alisa helped me with Oz as we hobbled up the drive. I'd covered his arm with a carrier bag I'd found in the kitchen so his blood wouldn't drip in the snow, leaving more DNA for the cops. I heard the whine of Andy's van, wheels spinning in the snow as he pulled up next to us. "Get in" Andy ordered. "I'll be one minute."

"Oz, Alisa, in the van," I said. "I'll get the car and meet you at Oz's place. Andy can come with me. Go!" Oz nodded and fell gratefully into the side door of the van. I slid it shut and tapped on it. Alisa climbed in the driver's seat and gunned the engine. "We don't shoot cops, OK?" I said to the SVR officer "it's one of our rules."

"OK," she laughed, "is there a rule about shooting the engine blocks out of their cars?"

"No, that's allowed."

"Good." She fast-reversed the van back up the drive, the Transit sliding and bumping on the icy track. Then she was gone.

"Right," said Andy, shrugging an old-fashioned canvas rucksack off his back. He pulled out three matt green canisters duct-taped together with plastic soda bottles. Andy grinned. "My special cleaning kit, two M14 incendiary grenades, one white phosphorous grenade and two litres of four-star petrol."

We jogged across the farmyard and into the shattered kitchen. "This is where it kicked off" I said, "hurry."

Andy took in the bodies, weapons and blood-splashes. With a bottle of petrol in each hand he carefully ran a trail through both rooms. He paid special attention to the curtains and furniture, putting the bottles back in his rucksack when he was finished. We dashed out of the door as he pulled the pin on the bundle of phosphorous and incendiary grenades. "Fire in the hole!" he hollered, tossing them into the kitchen. Then he giggled. "I've always wanted to say that." There was a dull thump as the grenades and petrol ignited, then the smoky, fizzing flash of the white phosphorous. Flames licked out of the door, and a window popped. Black Hall Farm, without urgent fire brigade attention, would be a smoking ruin in twenty minutes.

We reached my Volvo, tucked in the lay-by, as a police car careered towards the farm track. It slowed down as the driver spotted me, the police turret lights washing us with angry blue light. "Get that fucker started" said Andy, pointing at the car. He shouldered the M6 rifle and fired a burst along the radiator and bonnet of the marked police Ford. It groaned to a halt, the cop scrabbling at his radio. Andy shot out the tyres nearest us, two rounds in each. "Out of the car!" the ex-SRR man barked, smoke curling from the barrel of the M6. "On your belly! NOW! Look away from me!" The startled policeman, a young, complied immediately. Andy ripped the Airwave radio from the cop's body-armour and tossed it into the snow-topped blackthorns running along the drive. "Sorry, mate, about your car" he said.

"Fuck off," the cop spat.

I pulled forward, Andy jumping in the front of the car. I motored away, throwing the Volvo right and fish-tailing along the icy main road. I was confident this early in the morning in rural Essex there wouldn't be too many cops about, but I was worried about their helicopter. There's no escaping police helis in a rural area. "I love this job," said Andy. "I really feel like I'm contributing to society in a special way."

"Really?" I replied, "there was me thinking it was because you're a pyro-maniac with a firearms fetish." I drove along lonely back-roads, skirting around Southminster then north towards Maldon. In the distance I saw a heli, the tell-tale searchlight making it look like a UFO as it swept towards the farm. Andy pulled a ski jacket over his winter camouflage and helped me wriggle out of mine as I drove. We cleaned up with wet-wipes, Andy stashing our weapons and kit in a large vinyl ski-bag. By then I was on the back roads that ran northeast to Colchester, then onto the main road to Harwich. Cop cars sped by in the other direction, sirens howling.

"That was too close for my liking" said Andy, offering me coffee from his flask, "reckon there'll be a roadblock?"

"Possibly," I nodded, "get on the phone to Harry. Tell him Oz took one in the arm."

Andy took the offered satellite phone and punched in the number. Harry answered on the third ring. I tucked my Walther under my thigh, just in case.

Harry's conversation with Andy was short. "Harry says to send Oz to an RV and he'll send the doctor, but he's out of the game. They'll take him abroad for treatment." The Firm had a tame trauma doctor. If operatives were injured he'd stabilise them, then the casualty was flown to a private hospital in Spain for treatment. That way we never appeared on any UK medical records. I don't know what happened to our bodies if we didn't make it, but I guessed it involved holding up flyovers or feeding pigs.

I slowed right down as ambulances and fire engines rushed by. Switching on the radio news, the reporter was already announcing 'a major incident' on the Essex coast. Another heli clattered overhead, then another. Andy and I looked at each other and said nothing for the rest of the journey.

At the cottage there was no sign of the van, but Alisa was waiting by the kitchen window and waved. We emptied our kit inside and went into the small sitting room, where a fire was blazing. Oz was sat on the sofa, sweaty and pale, arm elevated. Alisa had found our trauma kit, an IV line snaking from Oz's arm.

"Where's the van?" I asked.

"I have parked it behind the cottage, out of view," said Turov, passing out mugs of steaming coffee. "What do we do about Oz?"

I explained that we had a doctor on standby. "You're off to Spain, Oz" I said cheerily.

"Thank fuck for that," he groaned, "I could murder a Sangria."

"Can I come too?" said Andy. "I'm suffering trauma after all that."

"There is no time for jokes," said Alisa, "we must get to Van Basten – if he dies we will never find the location of his server."

Andy looked out of the window. "It's crawling with Old Bill out there."

"Alisa's right," I said. "The FSB team won't hang about. For all we know, they might already be at their target." I pulled out my Blackberry and phoned Melissa Compton's number.

"What time is it?" she groaned sleepily.

"It's Cal Winter, where are Sergei and Pieter Van Basten right now?"

"We're all down in Wiltshire, at Evan's place."

Wiltshire. Fuck. "Near Salisbury Plain?" I said.

"Yes," she replied, "right next to it, actually." I could hear Melissa starting to wake up. "We're at Sir Evan Sands' house. He's Sergei's business partner. Pieter's living here while he waits for the appeal. Why, what's wrong?"

"Tell Sergei you're all in danger, the FSB are on their way, if they haven't arrived already. Get the security team to lock the house down and get Aseyev to call me as soon as possible."

"Got it," she said. "I'll send the address right now."

"Good. Tell Sergei I'll be there soon as I can. Put Pieter somewhere safe, with a guard."

"Why Pieter?"

"Because I think he's the target, Melissa. Under no circumstances do you call the police."

"Calling the police has never been on of Sergei's priorities," she said, and put the phone down.

I called Harry and explained the situation, "I need to be in Wiltshire, ASAP."

"This is going tits-up," he said sourly, "it's not like I can summon a heli out of thin air."

"Okay, but Sort out Oz. We'll head there in the car."

"Sure" the handler replied. "I'll send the medical team to Oz's place, but keep me updated. I'll bat off SIS when they phone up and ask what's going on."

The next call I made was on the cheap throwaway phone the freelancing SIS officer, Marcus, had given me. He picked up immediately. "I'm watching the news Calum," he said brightly, "my but you're a ruthless bastard!

"I need a heli" I said. "Else Pieter Van Basten is going to get slotted along with Sergei Belov. We missed the FSB team. If we don't get to Wiltshire then there's no file."

"If you didn't get the FSB operators, who are the unfortunate bastards incinerated in a farm in Essex I'm watching on the BBC right now?"

"Russian gangsters. Misha Baburin's boys, they were looking after the FSB unit."

"Where are you?" said Marcus wearily, "because I'm about to take the biggest bloody risk of my career doing this."

"Think of that pension and the MBE," I said, "I'm still in Essex."

"A gong is of little use in prison," he sighed. He gave me the address of a private airfield ten miles north of Colchester. "We have an arrangement with the owner. I'll have a heli there in the hour, how many passengers?"

"Three. I'm leaving now."

"After this you're on your own."

"Good to see some SIS traditions never change," I laughed, and rang off.

Oz was asleep, the combination of fatigue, pain and Ketamine finally knocking him out. Andy checked him and pronounced him stable. "It's a fairly clean wound but I can't tell if the median nerve has been damaged. It's missed the bone anyhow."

"He needs surgery" said Alisa, checking the IV, "he's lost much blood."

We checked and re-loaded our weapons, stowing them in ballistic bags. Andy readied spare ammunition, flash-bangs and medical kits. Alisa found Evan Sands' house on her laptop, feeding in the coordinates Mellissa had emailed. "It is a mansion" she said, "*Croll House*, very remote. It's eight miles from the nearest town, a place called Market Laverick."

"I know Market Laverick," said Andy. "It's not far from Warminster, right?"

We all knew Warminster, slap-bang in the middle of army training country. I took a look at the online map, "yeah, on the edge of Salisbury

Plain." Market Laverick wouldn't even qualify as a half-a-horse town, a quiet Wiltshire backwater popular with retirees.

I checked Oz, who opened his blood-shot eyes. "Fuck off" he said, "I'll be OK."

I laughed, and checked his IV drip, "I'll leave you some more Ketamine. The medical team are on their way."

"Cheers Cal," he said, "just promise me you'll nail the bastards and take care. OK?"

I hefted the ballistic bag onto my shoulder. "Since when did I start making promises like that?"

Oz chuckled then coughed. I left a pistol on his lap and the door on the latch. We made it to the airfield in under an hour, Andy driving like a demon and Alisa laughing throatily every time we almost skidded off the road. It was almost dawn as we arrived, weak grey light bleeding across the horizon. A sign read FOXBRIDGE FLYING CLUB – MEMBERS ONLY.

A stocky guy in his fifties stood by the gate. He wore a parka over a flying suit, stamping his feet against the cold. "Come on," he grunted, striding off towards the out buildings. "And please, for the love of God, don't talk to me."

The heli squatted on the snowy airfield, where four light aircraft were parked by a small control tower. It was a white Augusta 109 with no livery, but a VP-G registration mark painted on the fuselage. "This heli's registered in Gibraltar?" I asked.

"I said don't talk to me," the pilot huffed. "Just get in."

"This is just like flying with the RAF," said Andy, "but friendlier."

"Develop some manners," said Alisa coolly, pulling her pistol "or I will shoot you. You are just a taxi driver as far as I'm concerned. I will fly the helicopter myself if necessary."

"Listen to the lady" I said, telling him where we were going, "and you might just get a tip."

The pilot shook his head and went through his pre-flight checks. "I'll drop you in the grounds of the house if you want."

"No" I replied, pointing at the map. "It might not be a friendly LZ. Put us down on the other side of this road if you can? We'll walk in."

"OK," said the pilot. "It'll take about forty-five minutes to get there." The Augusta lifted off, turning one-hundred and eighty degrees and thundering west. Inside, the heli was kitted out like a military transport aircraft, with removable canvass seats and an RAF-issue first aid kit. The deck looked like it had brackets welded on, the sort you could use to mount weapons. The pilot took us up above the low-lying cloud, and for the first time in weeks I saw brilliant blue skies and sunshine. Whoever or whatever the pilot was, he didn't need to speak to any ATC or use a call-sign. He flew in silence, face blank behind his sunglasses.

"That taxi driver comment must have hurt," shouted Andy over the engine noise.

"It is true," Alisa shrugged.

"You can fly a helicopter?" I said.

"No," she smiled.

I closed my eyes for a few moments, my stomach heaving as the helicopter pitched and yawed. Then I feel asleep. Andy nudged me awake, shouting. Below us, snowdrifts had divided the fields like silver-white dunes. The pilot's voice crackled in my headphones, "don't expect me to pick you up: there's a fresh dump of snow forecast for tonight, a Red weather warning. Nothing will be flying for the next day or two I'd imagine."

I nodded and took the offered water bottle from Andy. He showed me his smart-phone. "It's Oz, he's with the doctor."

"Good," I said, happy that the MEDEVAC system worked. I tapped Melissa's number into my phone and told her to pick us up. We were two miles from Croll House, out of view of any surveillance operators dug into hides.

"Sergei has his best bodyguards here," she said darkly. "The house is full of guns."

I laughed as the heli descended. "Melissa, that's the first good news I've heard all day."

SEVENTEEN

The heli took off as soon as we'd unloaded our last kit bag, its rotor-wash blasting us with tiny shards of ice. Laden with equipment, we trudged through the snow towards the road. I sighed, putting on a black fleece hat and lighting a cigar, half-expecting the smoke to freeze as I exhaled. A Mercedes four-wheel drive SUV approached, side windows tinted and snow chains churning up ice. Melissa Compton sat in the front passenger seat, a big man wearing a black coat behind the wheel. Melissa jumped out and opened the side doors, "let's go." She wore a fur *ushanka* hat and a padded jacket.

We loaded our stuff and climbed in. Dmitri Aseyev, Sergei's security chief, was driving. He grunted hello in heavily-accented English as he spun the Merc around towards the road. After a short drive I noticed a solid brick wall, some eight feet high, running alongside the road. Fine motion-sensitive security monitors ran along the top, the occasional black dome of a security camera visible here and there. The Mercedes turned right, through a natural break in the wall and along a tree-lined drive.

"This is it" said Melissa, "Croll House. We should be safe, we're in the middle of nowhere. I've told Sergei that we should go back to London, or even out of the UK, but he's in a foul mood. He says if they want him they can come and get him."

"I'm not so sure it's Sergei they want. And they are probably watching us now," said Turov.

"Who are you?" said Melissa coolly.

"Her name's Alisa. She's working with me," I said.

"No," said Alisa, "he's working *for* me."

I was too tired to argue. I shrugged and puffed on my cigar.

"Well, Alisa, good luck with that," said Melissa.

"You can say what you like about Sergei Nikolayevich, but he has balls," said Dmitri, "I wouldn't run from these FSB shit-heads either."

"What use are balls if you are dead?" replied Alisa in Russian.

He laughed, "You have a point, sweetheart." Under his coat he wore a MP5K on a shoulder sling, his sweater bulky over body armour.

"You've met Dmitri," said Melissa. "He's security director for Mister Belov."

"I'm still not sure if this is all a joke played on us by the FSB," the big Russian spat. "If I hadn't seen that place burning on the news this morning, the farm full of mafia…" his big yellow teeth filled the rear view mirror as he grinned.

I pulled a notepad from the cargo pocket of my trousers and started making a rough map of the drive and main road. Andy saw what I was doing. He nodded approvingly and rummaged in his day-sack for the Tough-book. "Remember Brecon? *Defence from a fixed position?*"

"Yeah, but I don't think we're gonna have machineguns and mortars on this one."

"We're not far off," Dmitri chuckled.

Melissa shot Dmitri a look. "This is Sir Evan Sands' house. Evan is pretty shaken by all this, so is Pieter. Can you play down the…"

"…Heavy weapons and threat of imminent death?" said Alisa.

"Quite. I was hoping your plan was evacuation. Why stay here?"

"Because I've got all the bait I need sat in that house," I said quietly, "let them come to us."

"And look at the weather Miss Compton," said Dmitri. "It almost reminds me of springtime at home. Trust me when I say none of us are going anywhere when that snowstorm hits." Above us the sky swirled with strange oyster-coloured clouds, pulses of white flakes already cutting by, as if on a recce for the big snow-dump.

"Hopefully they'll freeze to death out there, whoever they are," said Melissa.

Dmitri shrugged. "If they are FSB Spetsnaz, and they are likely to be, then this weather is just another day at work for the bastards."

"Dmitri is correct," said Alisa, "these men will be from FSB *Spetzgruppa A*, a sub-unit called *Grob*."

"*Grob*? Like coffin?" I laughed, "how subtle."

Turov smiled, "FSB isn't known for subtlety, but these men will be trained to operate in hostile conditions, at the Winter Warfare School."

"I lost a toe there myself," Dmitri laughed. "In 1996, I was a paratrooper."

Alisa nodded, "the are called 'coffin' teams because they are meant to be buried, hidden, left behind. When the enemy pass them they climb from their graves and strike."

I guessed the drive was a mile long, a straight metalled road flanked by dense, twisted bushes and trees. As we pulled up to the house the sky finally began dumping snow. Croll House was a fortified manor from the pages of a history book, with mock-battlements, a Belvedere tower and defensive loopholes. Gargoyles leered at us hungrily. As my eyes tracked across the building, I could see where, over the years, the house had been renovated in different styles and materials. It was like a timeline of ownership. Eventually, to the south-westerly side of the house, I saw an ultra-modern glass-and-timber extension running into the woods that surrounded the property. A white and silver communications array towered over it, a clutch of satellite dishes pointing into the sky. Parked outside was Sergei Belov's black Maybach 62S, the armoured limo like a beached whale in the snow.

"The house used to belong to a rock star, in the 1970's" said Melissa. She sounded like a tour guide. "Sir Evan bought it in the mid-eighties, when *SandsSoft* took off."

SandsSoft was one of Britain's most well-known tech companies, a baby version of *Apple* that had diversified into everything from cable TV, banking, e-readers and holidays. Sir Evan Sands, the founder, was everyone's favourite counter-cultural capitalist. He was often seen at demonstrations and student sit-ins. Most memorably, he had once been arrested for offering the Prime Minister a spliff at a press conference. I'd seen him interviewed often on the TV – he always came across as a decent bloke and his staff adored him. I knew from the army that a good way to gauge a leader is to check morale, and by that standard, Sands wasn't doing too badly. He gave away millions to charities, even if he was a vicious bastard in the boardroom.

"Yeah," said Andy "wasn't this mansion Kenny Moody's place?"

"I think so," said Melissa lightly, "a bit before my time, though."

Andy nodded, "thought so, he was the drummer with *Diamond Cult*."

"Who? I've never heard of them," I said.

"That's because you don't have a secret but slightly embarrassing interest in progressive rock," smiled the ex-SRR man. "They were great, like early *Genesis* meets *Rush*."

"Who were they?" Melissa asked.

"What happened to this musician?" said Alisa.

"Kenny drowned in the swimming pool after a drug-fuelled orgy, like a proper seventies rock star," Andy replied. "Although there's a rumour he was murdered by his missus, who spiked his drink."

"Sounds like my kind of party, *tovarich*," laughed Dmitri, stopping the Merc. He pulled a radio from his coat pocket. "Everything's OK," he said in Russian into the mic and wooden, castle-thick, gates rumbled open. A burly man stepped out armed with a Kalashnikov. He covered us, aiming into the trees. Looking up, I saw another man wearing a white snowsuit armed with a long rifle, prowling the battlements. "Go" said Dmitri, pulling the MP5K out from under his coat, "I've got you covered."

We jogged from the Mercedes into the house, through a small ante-chamber that led into a long stone hall. I gazed up at the barrel-vaulted ceiling, the smell of incense tickling my nose. "Wow" said Andy, dumping his kitbags.

The hall was painted stark white, lit by row after row of church candles mounted on metal chandeliers. A red Persian rug ran the length of the flag-stoned floor. In the centre of the room was an oak dining table big enough to sit thirty people. The medieval effect jarred with the works of modern art mounted on the walls. I noticed some of the more famous ones – a Jackson Pollock, an Andy Warhol and a brace of Roy Lichtensteins. The pieces were illuminated by cleverly hidden lights. "A vulgar juxtaposition," Alisa sniffed.

"Sir Evan has one of the largest collections of modern and pop art in the UK," said Melissa.

"Fascinating," I said flatly. "Where are Sergei and Van Basten?"

"In Sir Evans' office, come on," she said. "The guards will look after your equipment.

"No they won't love," said Andy gently, "it stays with us OK?" He pulled his M6 out of the bag and loaded it. The snap of the action echoed in the room.

"Of course," said Melissa, eyeing the firearm, "follow me."

Dmitri followed us as we walked through the hall into a spacious sitting room, then along a deeply carpeted corridor. Everything was new and old, from the paintings to the furniture. Eventually we were ushered into a large pine-panelled office, the window overlooking a sunken garden. Three men were waiting for us. "Close the blinds please," I said. Andy nodded and padded over, pressing a switch. The blinds glided down. Soft lighting automatically flooded the room.

"The glass is armoured. Let the bastards see me!" Sergei was sat by the fire nursing a tumbler of vodka. He wore a turtle-neck sweater and corduroys, face grim.

Melissa scowled, "Sergei, if you need me I'll be upstairs."

"Of course," Belov replied.

"I'll speak to you in a bit," said Pieter Van Basten as Melissa left the room. I recognised the internet maverick from his photos in the newspaper. He stood next to Sergei, slightly-built, in his thirties with short sandy hair and amused-looking blue eyes. He smiled sheepishly, taking in our guns and equipment. "Hello," he said, voice reedy but friendly "I'm so sorry about all of… this."

Sergei drained his glass. "He's such a polite boy."

Sir Evan Sands was a tall, lean man with shoulder length grey hair and designer stubble. He wore faded jeans, snow boots and a sleeveless gilet over a fisherman's jumper. His craggy face looked tired and pale, his nose red with cold. "I don't want to appear rude," he said, "but what in the name of fuck is going on?" His voice was public-school posh, but with the glottal stop the well-to-do affect when they're trying to slum it.

"My name's Winter" I said, "I'm Sergei's UK security consultant. This is my team. How much has Mister Belov told you?"

I offered my hand to Sands, who looked at it and eventually squeezed it lightly. "Not enough," he croaked, blowing his nose and walking over to the drinks cabinet. He pulled out a carton of orange juice and poured a glass.

"I have told them there is an extraordinary security situation," said Belov, "but that you had the latest information, Cal."

Sands ran a hand through his silvery mop of hair. "Why the guns? Why no police?"

Pieter Van Basten raised an eyebrow, the slightest trace of a smile on his face.

"Cal, please explain," said Sergei.

"OK, but first my colleague is going to check the security arrangements and alarm system." I gave Andy a look. He nodded and led Dmitri to one side.

"I will take a look around too, I think," said Alisa Turov. Then, in Russian, she addressed Sergei Belov. "Both you and Van Basten are in danger, even if it is from different directions. Listen to Winter, he is a blunt instrument but he will do the job."

"You are from the SVR?" replied Belov in the same language.

Alisa headed for the door, her MP5 slung across her chest, "it is in my interest that you and Van Basten survive, will that do for now?"

"I suppose it will have to," smiled the oligarch as he eyed her up and down, "would you like a drink?"

"Not when I'm working," she said. "Maybe later, old man."

"Old man?" Sergei chuckled, settling back in his chair, "I like her. Does she need a job?"

"Why didn't you leave the UK?" I said to him as Alisa stalked out of the room.

"I have been running from these bastards for fifteen years," he said angrily, "and that is enough."

Van Basten warmed his hands by the fire and shivered, "besides, I'm fairly sure they'd find us wherever we went."

"Why do you think that?" I said.

Van Basten laughed. "Mister Winter, for the past five years I've been reading and publishing thousands of leaked intelligence reports. I'm *au fait* with how government agencies of every stripe conduct business in scenarios like this, especially the Russians. If it were the Americans, I suspect a Predator drone might be circling overhead right now."

"Sir Evan," I said, "there are matters I'd like to discuss with Sergei and Peter alone? Would you mind?"

"Yes I bloody well would," he said gloomily, "my house is full of men with illegally-held firearms and I understand that the grounds might be full of assassins. So I'll be staying right here."

"It might be better, in the long-run, if you weren't exposed to this, Evan," said Belov, his gravelly voice low. He stood up and put his hand on the Englishman's shoulder, "but if you want to stay then I understand. What happens to me is my affair, but *SandSoft* is too important to be brought down by my hobby-horses."

Sands looked at me, then into the fire. "Maybe you're right, Sergei. Look, I need some time to think. I'll be in the sitting room. If you need anything, ring Anna. She's in her quarters."

"Anna?" I said.

"Anna is the housekeeper here. I sent all of the other staff away. My family are on their winter break in the Bahamas, I wished I'd gone myself."

I raised an eyebrow, "might it be better if Anna left too?"

Sir Evan Sands cackled, "I don't think so. The old battle-axe has been with me for twenty years! You'd need dynamite to get her out of here."

"The weather is closing in," said Sergei, "we are here for the duration."

"Anna makes an excellent breakfast too," said Pieter Van Basten. "May I thank you again for your hospitality, Sir Evan?" His eyes looked straight through his host as he spoke.

"It was a pleasure, Pieter," Sands replied, gripping Van Basten's hand and shaking it "I might have sold out, but I still love it when somebody socks it to The Man. Promise me you'll never give up on *Forbiddenfacts.*"

"That's a promise that's easy to make," said Van Basten dreamily.

"And just as easy to break," Belov grunted. "Let's see where we are at daybreak tomorrow before we make statements like that?"

"I'll leave you to it then," said Sands. "Mister Winter, good luck, I shall see you for dinner later I hope?"

"I look forward to it sir," I said. "Before you go, may I ask a question?"

"Of course."

"Do you have anywhere to store the art collection?"

"I suppose so, yes," said Sands, "the cellar. Why?"

"There might be bullet holes," I said.

"Bollocks," he grumbled over his shoulder as he stomped out of the room, "it would take a team of art removal specialists. It's all fucking insured."

Van Basten chuckled. "I hate pop art. Wouldn't it be an ironic act of artistic expression to shoot a gun at that collection?"

"Rubbish or not, there's still ten million pounds worth out there," said Belov.

"I'll get straight to the point" I said, putting my submachinegun on the floor next to my chair. "This is all about the FSB file sent to *Forbiddenfacts. net*. As Turov said, both of you are in danger. Specifically, the FSB are after you, Pieter. Somebody else is after Sergei and we're still working on identifying who." I was still wary of telling Sergei, or Van Basten for that matter, about Fyodor Volk.

"What do you mean?" said Sergei sharply. "This is a new development. Who is trying to kill me if it isn't the FSB?"

"Hold on," I said, "Pieter, where is the data the FSB sent you? What server is it on?"

Pieter Van Basten looked at his feet, then into the flames of the fire. He cleared his throat and hugged himself. "I can't tell you" he said, sounding more South African than before, "and even I did you wouldn't believe me."

His back to Sergei Belov, he almost smiled.

I cut the end off of a cigar with my combat knife. If Uncle Marcus from SIS was correct, then the file might be my escape route off of The Firm. That was my Holy Grail, something I wasn't going to let slip away any time soon. "Try me," I said.

EIGHTEEN

"I'll spare you the technical details" said Van Basten, tossing a log onto the fire, "but the FSB file came to me untitled. *Forbiddenfacts.net* has a unique routing system, not unlike TOR but even more deniable, and it processes data faster." I knew that TOR was an online proxy set up to safeguard online privacy. Even the military used it. Van Basten sat back down, watching the fire blaze. "It ensures that both the recipient and sender don't know the other's IP address, so I couldn't tell you anything about the sender even if I wanted to."

"How did you know it was for Sergei?" I said. I offered Belov a cigar, which he took.

"Oh, it came with an email. It said *A PRESENT FOR THE HERO OF SHAKUVO! ENJOY,* hardly a mystery, Mister Winter. There's only one hero of Shakuvo," he said tartly. "And it wasn't the firemen who went in after the reactor blew."

Sergei Belov waved his hands. "Yes, quite Pieter. If the truth were told, I am embarrassed by the plaudits. But I do not know how they made the link between Pieter and me. My funding of the website has been extraordinarily discreet."

Van Basten nodded, "but somehow the FSB knew. In any case, the file itself was encrypted with a symmetric-key algorithm, like Rijndael. Once we cracked that there was another, and then another. The core files suggest there are nine in total. I like to think it's like a Russian Doll – we can tell that the outer files are bigger and they get smaller and harder to crack."

136

I leant forward in my chair, "who's working on the file from your organisation?"

"At the moment, nobody," said Van Basten, "Forbiddenfacts.net has been subjected to repeated and increasingly sophisticated hacking attempts. My sources tell me the cryptographers at both Fort Meade and GCHQ are putting in the overtime with no luck."

"Do you think it can be fully cracked?" I said.

"In time I would think so, yes. But since the Americans are trying to extradite me, I've decided to protect the activist base on the site by winding things down for a while. The FSB file isn't connected to anything. It's on a hard drive, locked away somewhere safe. When my legal battle is won then we will proceed and get to that ninth layer. I call the file Matryoshka, after the doll."

"How much of it did you crack?" I said "before you had to stop?"

"We'd opened the first four levels," said Van Basten, "level five is pretty challenging. We're almost there, actually. It's almost like the creators of the encryption know how long each one will take us. It's an agreeable puzzle, for sure."

"It is very strange," intoned Belov solemnly.

Van Basten smiled, colour finally spreading across his cheeks. "In any case, the material we've unearthed so far would keep the site in the news for a couple of years, not to mention bring down several governments."

We sat in silence for a moment. "Where is it Pieter?" I said, "the hard drive?"

The South African examined his fingernails, which were long and manicured. "It is in the safest place I can imagine. Only two people know of its location and that's how it's going to stay."

"Who is the other person?" I said.

"Tell us," Belov growled, slamming down his glass.

Van Basten stood up and walked to the window, slipping the blind open and looking outside. "No."

"He's too stubborn" spat Sergei, "he will not tell."

I stood up and threw the stub of my cigar into the fire. Then I picked up my SMG. "If he's still alive tomorrow morning we can discuss it further. I'll do everything in my power to make sure that happens. OK?"

"You have my thanks Mister Winter," said Van Basten, "but I think I'll be OK."

"Why?"

His eyes creased as he smiled, "I must have an angel on my shoulder, I think."

"And a devil on mine," said Belov, reaching for the bottle.

I went and found Andy. He was with Turov and Dmitri in an office next to the great hall. The room was a security suite, with a bank of CCTV monitors and alarm system controls. Andy sat in front of a console, a notepad in front of him. "Right, Cal, here's the SITREP. The central station alarm has been disabled, I don't know how. The landlines are cut too, but this place has a hard-wired internet connection so we have comms. The cameras are all OK. There are twenty in total, five of which are motion-sensitive."

"Thanks," I said. "Dmitri?"

The big Russian slurped from a mug of coffee. "I have five men here, the best on the team – three Russians, one Brit and a Serbian. We have two long rifles, four AKs, grenades and pistols. There's also enough food and ammunition to last six months if we needed to. The Brit is an advanced combat medical technician. We have trauma kits and a good supply of plasma, blood, IVs and Ketamine. We also have night vision optics and body armour. I have one rifleman on the roof and another positioned at the back of the extension where Mister Belov is staying. The rest of the guys are a quick-reaction force in the main building."

"Are you patrolling outside?" said Alisa.

Dmitri shrugged. "Yes, but only a sweep of the tree-line. Since I heard who the bad guys are we've stopped. Do you want that done again now?"

"I'll think on it, what you're doing now is fine," I said, "best draw them to us."

"Perhaps, but I will go and take a look myself," said Alisa.

"If you want," I replied, knowing that she was going to do what she liked whatever I said.

"Let me know when and I'll radio the riflemen," said Dmitri, "they might be a little trigger-happy."

"I will cover one circuit of the perimeter on foot," she said, pulling on her padded jacket and snowsuit. "I'm OK on my own."

"Hold on, there's something else," said Andy, folding a map out on his knee. "Look here."

The map was a protective survey prepared by the security company that had installed the alarm system, dated six months previously. It was detailed and covered the entire estate, noting the positions of cameras, motion sensors and alarms. Andy's finger traced a path through the woods south of the extension, past a detached garage and villa marked *Staff Quarters*. A kilometre south of that there was a collection of small outbuildings marked *Guest Camp*. "What's that?" I asked.

Dmitri looked at it, "yeah that's like you say... a hippy commune. The crazy English guy, Sands, lets them camp there."

"In this weather?" said Turov. "I'll take a look."

I put my hand on her shoulder, "no, Alisa, just do the perimeter please."

She looked at me, then nodded. "Perhaps you are right. I'll be back in an hour or so I think."

"Stay near the treeline and we track you on the cameras," said Dmitri, "take this." He handed her a personal role radio of a type I'd not seen before. It had to be better than our British army-issue ones.

I took Andy to the sitting room and knocked on the door. "Come," said Sir Evan Sands. He sat on a pile of cushions, an e-reader in his hands. The room was furnished like a futuristic Bedouin tent, with colourful drapes and carpets. Giant monitors showed pictures of a camel train crossing a desert, then I realised he was playing the movie *Lawrence of Arabia*. He smiled, "can I help?"

Andy cleared his throat. "Sir, can you tell us about the commune on the estate? They might be in danger if they're still on site."

"Oh, my ragged guests?" Sands chuckled, "although I'm sure they'd prefer the term anarcho syndicalists. I wouldn't be surprised if a couple of them are toughing it out, I leave them to get on with it."

"Why are they here?" I said.

"About eighteen months ago they pitched up. They were protesting about something or another, a few of them are hoary old veterans of the rave and protest scene, back in the nineties. Ah, happy days, those were. I dropped more acid than William Burroughs back then. Anyway, the police sent them packing from a squat they'd settled in London, so they'd nowhere to go. So when they pitched up and asked me if they could stay, of course I said yes." He smiled sadly. "I feel guilty about my wealth. In my heart I'm with them, but in my head I'm in my mansion."

"That was very generous," I said, "are there any problems?"

Sir Evan smiled and sipped his tea. "Not really, only the occasional noisy party, but I tend to get invited to those. The army makes more noise with their helicopters and manoeuvres out on the Plain. I have more land than I know what to do with, and they're a decent bunch. You wouldn't know they were there most of the time. There's no rubbish, they grow their own food and recycle everything. A lot of them are even ex-military types like you. They know Salisbury Plain like the back of their hands."

"When did you last see any of them?"

"Only last week," he said. "One of the guys, he calls himself Bones, asked for some firewood. They have caravans and yurts down there, run power off a diesel generator. I said sure, that they could help themselves. I offered up the staff quarters but they said no."

"How do they get onto the estate?" said Andy, looking at the map.

"There's an access track, but it won't be on that map. It's bumpy, but you can get four-wheel drive vehicles up it. It runs south onto the other side of the estate and takes you onto the army training area. The nearest town south of there is Larkhill."

"Thanks for that," I said.

On the screens Peter O'Toole was leading a camel charge. Sir Evan switched it off. "Look, I'm sure those chaps can look after themselves, but can we see if they're OK? Some of them have girlfriends, but there are no kids that I know of."

"Absolutely," said Andy, "we'll check it out."

"I'm grateful," he replied, pulling himself to his feet and stretching theatrically. An olive-skinned woman in her fifties entered the room with a tray and started tidying up. She wore a long skirt and a shapeless black jumper, her hair in plaits. "Anna, these gentlemen are from Mister Belov's security team," said Sands. "Anna is my housekeeper."

Anna looked at our clothes and weapons and scowled. "I'm sure they are," she said drily. Her accent was Eastern European, but I couldn't place where. "Excuse me," she said, and left the room.

"She's Hungarian," said Sir Evan. "She doesn't like Russians and she absolutely hates guns."

"No problem." We left him and returned to the security office.

"What do you think?" said Andy.

"The commune needs checking out. They could all be dead by now, unless they're connected.

Andy checked his watch. "We've got about three hours of daylight left, but Jesus I'm tired."

We'd been awake for twenty-four hours. I had Amphetamines in my pack, but only planned on taking them as a last resort. "OK, we join Alisa and go down there in one of the vehicles. We check it out, come back and get some zeds and let Dmitri's guys look after things."

"Sounds like a plan," said Andy, "but where are the bad guys?"

"No plan survives first contact with the enemy," I laughed, "they're probably dug in but weren't expecting riflemen on the roof and a load of crusties in the back garden."

Andy nodded. "You're right Cal. If I was them I'd be taking my time and making a new plan. They're SF operators, not Kamikazes."

I found Dmitri in the great hall, where he'd laid out an armoury on the oak table. He was loading magazines, thumbing bullets expertly into the curved AK clips. Another bodyguard stood with him doing the same. "This is Eduard," he said, jerking an oily thumb at the other guy.

"Hello" grunted Eduard. He wore a smart black suit and a Kevlar vest. He had cropped hair, a pock-marked face and looked like a killer.

I nodded. "We're going to check out the commune with Alisa, are you OK here?"

"We were OK before you got here, Winter," smiled Dmitri, "I guess we'll have to struggle on for a bit longer."

"OK," I said. "Can you track us on the cameras?"

"No problem. Eduard?"

Eduard nodded and marched towards the security office. "Here, take these radios. They are very good," said Dmitri.

I thanked him and zipped up my snowsuit, taking one of the offered AK74 rifles. I strapped on a chest-rig full of spare magazines and checked my pistol. Andy nodded that he was ready and we stepped outside. "Alisa?" I said into my mic, "this is Cal."

The SVR officer's voice crackled in my ear. "I'm over by the staff quarters."

"Wait there, we're going to join you."

"Received," she said, "I've found a blood trail."

The drive had been gritted and was easy to walk on, but as soon as we reached the gardens the snow was calf-deep. We trudged along the tree line, weapons shouldered as the wind drove fresh powder at us. I pulled my fleece hat down, Andy pulling a full-face balaclava over his head. He'd taken the suppressor off his M6, the stubby assault rifle almost toy-like in his hands. I saw the extension to my left as we approached the staff quarters. On the roof a man in a white camouflage suit waved, a rifle on a bipod in front of him. "I've got you. No movement apart from the woman," crackled an accented voice in my ear, as the rooftop sniper spoke to me over the radio net.

"Roger," I replied, waving back.

The staff quarter was a modern, brick-built, two-storey villa attached to a garage. Lights burnt in the front window, footprints leading from the front door to the main house. Only Anna, the housekeeper, was in residence. I squinted past the villa towards the wooded estate, some fifty metres away. Through the flurries of snow I could just make out Alisa in her white camouflage over suit, SMG cradled in her arms. She was crouched down, examining something. "Alisa, we're behind you," I said, keying my mic. We walked slowly towards her, weapons trained into the trees. Alisa raised her hand as she saw us, pointing to a dark patch in the snow near the tree line.

"Blood," she said. "I found the trail there and followed it into the woods for about a hundred metres."

"And?" said Andy.

"I found this," she said, pointing to something lying in the snow, something pale and bluish-pink.

"What is it?" I said.

The SVR officer looked at me over her shoulder, clearing away the snow so I could see. "It's a human tongue."

NINETEEN

"*But first each one had his tongue tight between his teeth toward their leader, as a signal* – The Inferno, Canto 21" said Alisa. "This is Volk's work."

"What do you mean?" said Andy. "That poor bastard's tongue ain't tight between anybody's teeth."

"In the Eighth Circle of Hell, Dante meets a company of devils who escort him to a bridge. Of course, the devils end up chasing him."

"We should follow the blood trail," I said, "can you see? The snow's been disturbed." Beyond the trees there were signs of a struggle, dark stains dotting the virgin snow. We headed into the trees, finding the snow was less deep on the forest floor. Before long we'd found scraps of bloody clothing and a black fleece hat. The hat had semi-frozen blood on it.

"No sign of spent cartridges," Alisa noted, shining her flashlight into the trees.

"Look right twenty metres," said Andy sharply, like he was giving a fire control order. "Over there. See that tree with the U-shaped branch?"

"Seen," I replied.

"Three O' Clock, by the holly bush."

"Got it," I said. There was a something in the snow, a shade darker than the snow and only semi-covered in powder.

We patrolled towards it, weapons making arcs. I took a knee and squinted through the optics on my AK. It was clear. I motioned for us to move forward with the chop of my hand. "It's a body" said Alisa.

The corpse was an athletically-built male in his late thirties, wearing a *klyaksa*-style Russian military snowsuit. On his hands were padded gloves.

His face was smashed in from his forehead to chin, the front of the skull eviscerated by blunt trauma. There was no trace of his eyes or nose, the corpse's tooth-studded lower jaw lolling obscenely. The tongue was missing. The freezing air had chilled the blood into a crust, making his head look like a side of cold-store offal. Blood stained the front of his white over-suit like a dark apron. "That looks like it was done with a hammer," said Andy, who would know.

"No weapon or personal equipment," Alisa added.

Crouching over the body, I unzipped the gore-stained snowsuit. Underneath he wore civilian outdoor clothing and body armour. He had no wallet or identity papers. I tried to move his arm, but the freezing weather and rigor mortis meant that the body was iron-hard. "Are you trying to see if he's tattooed?" said Alisa, reading my mind. She passed me her knife.

I took the blade and slashed the sleeve open from shoulder to elbow. I'd never met a Russian Special Forces soldier who didn't have ink. "There you go," I said. The pale, muscled upper arm had a death's head tattoo, superimposed in front of a parachute. Monstrous bat-wings grew from the skull, under which Cyrillic lettering was etched into a scroll.

"That reads *67 Detached Special Purpose Brigade,*" said Alisa, "the second scroll says *Grozny 2007* and *South Ossetia 2008*. This man must have served in the old GRU Spetsnaz before joining FSB."

"Is that significant?" I asked.

She shrugged. "Maybe – the 67th were based in the Siberian military district. I would expect them to be winter warfare and survival specialists."

"Well, Sherlock, as far as I'm concerned that's our Spetzgruppa alright," said Andy.

I turned away from the body. "I wonder how many there are left?"

"Volk's followers got to him before we did," Alisa shrugged Alisa. "I think they're all dead."

I shook my head. "You think the Spetzgruppa and Volk's people are at war out here?"

"I think so. Who else would have killed this man?"

"But why?"

"I don't know. But we do know Belov and Volk are both targets, and there are two groups of assassins."

"Is this a blue-on-blue, perhaps?" I said, using the military term for when friendly forces clash by accident.

Alisa pulled a face, "unlikely."

"Whatever the score, we've got to check the commune," said Andy, "and mob-handed. Crusty ex-squaddies trying to kill us? It's sounding familiar."

"How long did Sands say these travellers had been here?" said Turov.

"About eighteen months," I replied, remembering Alisa's estimate on the time it took Fyodor Volk to plan a hit.

"It's got to be Volk," said the Russian, "do you have grenades?"

"Does a bear coil one down in an area with an abundance of trees?" Andy chuckled. He probably took grenades in the shower with him.

"We need to get back to the house" I said, "now."

"Shit!" Andy hissed, "get down." He fell to one knee then rolled as a second suppressed round hit a tree next to his head. He scrambled backwards on his elbows and knees, rifle cradled clear of the ground.

Alisa leapt over a fallen tree and took cover, MP5 pointed into the woods. Half-guessing the direction of the incoming rounds, I opened fire with my AK. The bark of automatic fire crushed the quiet, scattering birds in every direction. Turov squeezed off a burst then ducked down behind a tree as incoming rounds stitched along the ground in front of her. I looked over at Andy. He was checking his body armour, his face twisted in pain. "It's OK," he said, "I took one in the vest." He opened the bipod on his M6 and settled it in front of him.

"I can't see anything," I said, peering into the falling snow.

"He's dug in," said Andy, "but if it was a high-calibre round I'd be in trouble, I think that's a 9mm or thereabouts."

That meant that the shooter had an SMG. He could only be forty or fifty or so metres away at most. "Dmitri from Cal," I hissed into my PRR, "contact in the woods behind the staff quarters."

"I heard," said the Russian calmly, "we're on our way."

I keyed my mic, "wait by the tree line: don't get drawn in. We're going to exfil, cover us."

"OK, on your signal," he said. "We've got the tree line covered."

"Let's stir this bastard up," said Andy. He fired a long burst into the woods, left to right. The 5.56mm rounds kicked up spumes of chewed-up bark, foliage and snow across the trees to our front. He slid a fresh magazine into the M6 and repeated the exercise. Turov lay quietly in cover, scanning the woods with her sights.

I joined in, the rattle of the AK ringing in my ears as the stock bit into my shoulder. "Dmitri, we're ready."

"Go!" he barked.

I signalled for Andy and Alisa to pull back. As they passed by, I slid a frag grenade from my ammo pouch. I pulled the pin on the black, apple-sized grenade and hurled it as far as I could into the trees. It exploded, white hot shrapnel zipping through the trees, and I ducked back behind the others. Andy tossed another grenade as he ran, the metal sphere knocking snow from tree branches before exploding in the air, showering shrapnel onto the forest floor. Dmitri crouched by the staff quarters, AK pointing into the woods. Two more men wearing black padded winter jackets lay in the snow, covering us. We sprinted past them, panting, and re-grouped behind the garage. The three security men opened fire, raking the woods with their assault rifles. "You OK?" I said to Andy as the sound of gunfire died down.

"It stings like fuck," he gasped, ripping the Velcro flaps on his armour. There was a small hole in the Kevlar panel that hadn't penetrated, and Andy's stomach had a livid bruise where the impact had been spread around his body. "That was a good shot, slap-bang in the middle of the target." Andy rubbed his pasty-white face and winced while he laughed.

"You were lucky," said Alisa, examining the wound. She passed him some painkillers and a bottle of water, "I'd have aimed for your head."

I took off my glove and rooted around in the vest until I found the squashed lead of the bullet. It was a 9mm, as Andy suspected. I guessed it was from a submachinegun of some description, the shooter professional enough not to fire on automatic at long range.

"Could it be a silenced 9mm rifle? Spetsnaz use them" Alisa asked.

"No," I replied. I'd used the VSS silenced rifle myself, "the 9mm ammo it uses is sixteen-grams and armoured piercing. Andy would've been dead, a sniper would have head-shot him from the VSS' effective range anyway."

"I feel so much better now," said Andy, gingerly pressing his ribcage around the bruise.

Dmitri walked over, Kalashnikov ready. "What happened?"

I told him that we found the mutilated body of a Russian commando and shot at by an unseen gunman. "This is like Chechnya, but with central heating and a swimming pool," the big Russian grinned. "We must speak with the boss."

"Hold the perimeter, Dmitri" said Alisa, slapping his back. "We will speak with Sergei Nikolayevich."

"*Da,*" he replied, turning on his heel, "although I say this weather is the best defence we could hope for."

"Napoleon and Hitler both found that out," Andy chuckled. "Thank fuck for the awful Russian weather front."

I walked to the doorway of the garage, brushing wet snow from my face. I checked my phone, which had a weak signal. I called Harry. "How did you get down there so fast?" he said suspiciously.

"I blagged a heli" I said.

"How?"

Mentioning my off-policy contact with Marcus would have been suicidal. "Colonel Turov had contacts, she made it happen. I didn't ask too many questions."

"OK," he replied, "as long as you got there. Update please."

I gave him a SITREP.

"Jesus. There's no way we can cover that up," Harry sighed, "although the fire in Essex seems to have done the trick, there's untold cops and media there. There's a Russian gangster hunt going on, I don't think sleepy Wiltshire will be a priority."

"I agree. We're snowed in and stuck on Salisbury Plain."

"I'm sure that's a familiar feeling, Captain Winter. After this is all over you're off abroad for decompression leave."

"Harry, we've got two sets of assassins and two targets. The thing is, the assassins look like they're killing each other. We don't know why."

The Handler chuckled. "The whole thing sounds like a fucked-up version of Cluedo to me, was it Colonel Mustard in the woods with the Kalashnikov?"

"I'm glad this is amusing you."

The Handler lowered his voice. "I've got SIS providing me with a communications intelligence package later – all the known SIGINT around FSB operations in the UK and material on Sergei Belov. I'll call you after I've had a look at it, perhaps it might help."

"OK," I said, wondering if they'd hand over anything useful.

"I'll call you later on the satellite phone. By the way, London officially ground to a halt this morning. The storm is headed west. The weather where you are is just for starters."

"Is there any good news?" I said, "how's Oz?"

"He's OK, but out of the game for five or six months. With good physio he'll recover. He's in a private clinic in London right now, but we'll fly him to Spain as soon as the weather clears. Don't worry, he'll be looked after."

"Good," I said, signing off.

We returned to the house, into the great hall. Belov, Van Basten and Sands stood inside, staring at the weapons arranged on the big oak table. Melissa was stood by the door to the security office. "Is everybody OK?" said Sands, "I heard shooting."

"There is fighting in the woods," said Alisa, "your guests, the ones you call New Age Travellers? They are part of this I think."

We explained that we'd found a body, and that in London we'd been attacked by homeless veterans who claimed they were groomed by a mysterious Russian. "It's incredible," said Sands, "why would they do that?"

"To kill these two," I said, pointing at Belov and Van Basten. "Your association with Sergei is hardly a secret and he's a regular visitor here." I put my AK on the table and rubbed my frozen hands together. "I need answers. There are two groups of killers out there, and they're fighting each other. Why?"

Belov glowered and walked around the table. "This is ridiculous! The FSB want me, not Pieter. Why kill him?"

"To get access to the file I hold in trust from the FSB whistle-blower." Van Basten stepped forward, making that creepy smile of his. "also, to set an example to other online activists. If even an FSB agent thinks he can leak with impunity, where does that leave the regime? What other choice do they have?"

Alisa rubbed her forehead, face drawn. "Sergei, you weren't told before, for your own protection, but we suspect this is the work of a man called Fyodor Volk."

"Who?" said Belov. "Why wasn't I told before?"

"Indeed," said Van Basten sharply.

"You've hardly been candid Pieter," I said quietly. What about the location of the server? Besides, operational security, Sergei. In case you had a leak in your organisation," I sat on the edge of the table, scratched from the weapons we'd laid on it. "Volk used to work for the FSB, their most feared killer. Now he wants you dead."

Belov pointed at his assistant, "Melissa, find out about this man, Volk..."

"No," said Alisa, "don't do anything that might tip off the FSB we know about him, not that you'd find anything anyway."

"Excuse me, but is there another possibility?" said Sands clearing his throat, "from what Pieter tells me from his research, intelligence services often compartmentalise their operations. Couldn't it simply be a blunder? Perhaps the two groups out there don't know about the other? In that case, the advantage is ours."

Alisa looked at Sands and smiled, "you understand these things, Sir Evan. And if it were anyone other than Fyodor Volk I would be inclined to agree. No, for whatever twisted reason Volk has, this is his plan."

"He could be right," I said. "Maybe we've looked for a deeper explanation when the simpler one will do."

"Hanlon's Razor," said Sands brightly, "*never attribute to malice that which is adequately explained by stupidity.*"

"In the absence of any other explanation, I think that might have to do for now," said Van Basten quietly, "but I have never heard of this person."

"Balls," spat Belov, "there is more to this than meets the fucking eye, I swear it!"

Alisa smiled. "I understand Sergei, a Russian could never have written *Hanlon's Razor.*"

The British bodyguard, a tall guy with short fair hair and a goatee beard, walked in. He wore black foul-weather gear, a Kalashnikov slung over his shoulder. "Mister Belov," he said, "Dmitri says the perimeter is clear. The men on the roof see nothing. But the weather's closing in. I can't see them trying anything in this."

"Thank you, Carl. What is the temperature outside?"

"The thermometer says minus twelve, sir. Forecast is for minus eighteen to twenty tonight." The bodyguard turned on his heel and left, nodding at me as he went.

"Minus eighteen?" said Sands, "I think we're OK."

"The men out there are trained in arctic warfare," Alisa chuckled. "I would advise against complacency."

"I agree" I nodded. "We must prepare to defend against an assault. In the morning we go to the camp in force and settle this thing, one way or another. Then we clean up and move on."

"Well" said Sir Evan, pushing his long grey hair back on his head, "blood on the carpet? Although this time it's more literal. I'm going to plan dinner. Its rabbit tonight, I'm pleased to report."

"Dinner? I love the English," said Sergei, craggy face creasing into a grin. He patted Sands on the back, "you always get your priorities right. Evan, may I raid your wine cellar?"

"My wine cellar is yours, *tovarich*," the businessman replied. "A noble beast such as the rabbit demands a fine wine to see it on its way."

"Crazy bastards," said Alisa.

"I wouldn't mind a look down there too," I said, lighting a cigar, "it's not often you get to see a multi-millionaire's wine cellar."

"It would be a pleasure Captain Winter," said Sir Evan Sands, grinning. "I would hate to disappoint."

TWENTY

In the end I skipped dinner with Sir Evan, but did liberate a couple of bottles of *Chateau Lafleur Pomerol* from his cellar. Andy scrounged bread, cheese, goulash and cold meat from Anna. We sat in the great hall and ate, the sound of classical music drifting from the dining room. Occasionally I could hear Belov's booming laugh. The wind whistled and creaked in the ancient manor house, mixed with the murmur of radio static and the clatter of weapons being assembled.

Dmitri's men padded about nervously, checking and double-checking windows and locks. The riflemen on the roof grumbled about the cold and the guys began to do an hour about. Carl, the British bodyguard, sat watching monitors as cameras silently scanned the estate. The drifting snow made it difficult to see anything, the images on the monitors a crazy kaleidoscope of white blobs.

The three of us agreed a guard rota and checked our preparations – non-armoured windows had been taped to prevent shattering and non-essential doors barricaded. Andy laid down three more motion-sensitive cameras inside, from his bag of tricks. He linked them to his laptop and tested them. "Anybody who tries to sneak into the hall, front or rear doors will pop up on this," he said through a mouthful of bread and stew, pointing a cheese knife at the monitor.

"Good," said Alisa, "do you have any audio devices in that bag? This wine is excellent, by the way."

"I might have some bits and pieces," said Andy coyly. He was possessive of his toys, "why?"

"I am a spy. I thought I would listen in on Belov and Van Basten's conversation later," she said innocently.

"Ah," said Andy.

"Makes sense," I shrugged, helping myself to some excellent Brie. The doctor advises me to avoid cheese and red wine, but I've usually more urgent threats to my health to worry about. "I don't trust any of them."

Andy stroked his chin. "In which case, if she's a super-spook, why ain't she got her own equipment?"

"I have some tricks up my sleeve, but there is a time and a place. This isn't it," the SVR officer replied tartly.

Andy pulled the battered ballistic bag onto his lap and rifled around inside. "I've got a bog-standard GSM audio bug here," he whispered, pulling out a slim plastic box the size of a bar of chocolate. He called us closer.

"You can monitor that over a mobile telephone, yes?" she said, examining the device. It had an adhesive pad on one side, for sticking under a table or desk.

"Bingo," said Andy, "just whack a spare SIM in it and off you go. It really is corner electronics shop stuff, and it'll ping even basic detection equipment. But if you need a quick and dirty solution…"

"I've only got a weak signal here," I said, "but I'm quick and dirty."

"There's very Gucci hard-wired internet in this place," said Andy. "I can run this one over a Wi-Fi network instead." He tapped the device and pressed some buttons, "yep, it's picked up the Wi-Fi. Carl gave me the password for the cameras. I'll just show it as a spare webcam on the network."

"Do it," I said.

"Good," smiled Alisa, taking a fresh mobile telephone from her rucksack. She slipped the SIM card into the audio bug, winked and left the room.

Andy and I poured another glass of the wine. "Delicious," he said, sniffing the Pomerol, "I'm picking up notes of wine, wine and wine."

He often took the piss out of my wine-tasting course, which I'd argue is equally as important a skill as technical surveillance, "bugger off, Philistine" I laughed.

"But I'm from Manchester," he protested, finishing the glass.

"Andy, there's something I need to tell you."

"Now's not the time to declare your undying love, although I've suspected for a while."

I put my hand on Andy's arm and gripped it, "listen to me and stop fucking about for five seconds. I think I've found a way out of The Firm."

Andy shook his head, "Cal, they'll kill you. Leave it, eventually they'll let you go, when they've finished with you. I know two guys who've retired. They're fit and well and got a decent bung at the end of it. That's my plan, a villa in Spain with City on the satellite telly twice a week. End of."

"I want out," I said flatly.

"And do what? What the fuck are we qualified for except for *this*?" he said, pointing at the weapons and equipment.

"I don't know if you've noticed, but *this* isn't a healthy way to make a living."

Andy snorted, "and neither was earning peanuts as IED bait in the 'Stan or Iraq or whatever shithole they sent us to next. I'm sat here, with you, drinking five-hundred quid a bottle vino in a mansion and that's good enough for now."

"Think about it, Andy."

"About what? About the evidence they've got of the armed robbery I did on a cash-in-transit van in Hyde six years ago? Then there's the ballistic evidence and a pistol with my prints on. They took it from my flat when they press-ganged me. I killed a man for that, for selling gear to my little brother. Trust me I've thought about it a lot."

I poured him another glass of wine. "Andy, the file Van Basten has? If I can get it I know somebody who can get us off The Firm. Maybe give us a better gig than this, more legit. Make that stuff go away."

"Bollocks. And who is this mystery saviour?"

I leant closer to Andy, "MI6. One of their senior spooks came to see me at the flat. His wife used to be the officer who liaised with The Firm – she knew Harry. There's enough information for us to get out, do a deal."

Andy's laugh was hollow, "Listen to yourself? M-I-fucking-Six? Fuck off Cal. I'll take my chances with The Firm. After I left the army I swore I'd never work for the Government again."

"So that's a no then?"

"Good luck to you if that's what you want. I like working with you,

you're a good operator. But don't involve me in this. And I'm going to forget this conversation."

"OK," I said, "I'm sorry I mentioned it."

Andy shook his head, "look let's get this drama sorted, OK? Then maybe we can talk about it."

We both knew we wouldn't. I stood up and looked down the corridor. Alisa was padding back along it, looking at the framed movie prints and mementoes of Sir Evan Sands' business career. She was still wearing her body armour, the MP5SD in her hands. "It's done," she said. "I asked if I could borrow a memory stick and Sergei waved me into the office. It's been attached under the desk, about one-and-a-half metres from the armchairs by the fireplace. The girl, Melissa, wanted to help me but I put her in her place. She is suspicious of me."

"Don't blame her" said Andy. "The audio should be fine as long as they don't sit their phones on that desk. You can get feedback if you're unlucky."

"If that happens we just deny all knowledge," I said, "have they finished dinner?"

Turov smiled. "Yes. Wine loosens tongues and there are four empty bottles on the table. Sir Evan looks tired, Pieter is sober but Sergei has just started drinking cognac. Melissa was going to bed, she looks terrified."

"I think Sands is alright," said Andy, "for a posh bloke."

"He is a rich fool," sniffed Alisa, "but on the less detestable end of the spectrum."

I yawned. "Let's get some sleep, first stag is in two hours."

Alisa nodded. "I will monitor the listening device."

"We all can, under the blankets with a comic and a torch," Andy sniggered.

"Idiot," she smiled, rolling her eyes.

We left the hall. I told Carl that we'd be down to start our shifts stagging on at midnight, and he waved his approval. Upstairs we settled in one of the guest rooms, which had white goose-feather duvets, central heating and a mini-bar. I flopped down on the bed, my head light from the lack of sleep and three glasses of decent wine.

Alisa sat on the bed next to me and switched on the mobile telephone

Andy had slaved to the listening device, "Andy what is the battery life on your bug?" she asked.

"About six hours juice," he said, "plenty."

She switched the mobile to loudspeaker and propped it up on the bedside table. We sat listening to static for ten minutes. Then we heard voices over the phone.

"Pieter, you can't go on like this," said Sergei. "We need to know where you keep the server, in case anything happens to you."

"I have a safeguard," Van Basten replied. "A close friend knows the location. Believe me, it is safe."

"Tell me, Pieter before I lose my temper."

"Then lose your temper, Sergei! I'm tired of your games and bullying. When I agreed to your support I said there could be no conditions. You agreed. Now I'm a puppet. I disgust myself, I'm no better than the people I expose."

"Please, there are always conditions when you do a deal," Sergei sighed. "Don't be naive, you've had three-and-a-half million dollars from me, plus the best legal team money can buy. I'm the only thing between you and a Yankee prison." I heard the clink of a decanter on glass and the glug-glug-glug of liquid being poured into a schooner.

"I told you the sound was good," Andy beamed.

Van Basten's voice sounded pained. "I share your concerns about the government in Russia. I support the focus *Forbiddenfacts* has put on your interests in the opposition and dissident activity, but it's become all-consuming."

"Precisely my point," Sergei sighed, "to the extent that both our lives are at risk now. We need to use the file to our advantage before this thing gets even more out of control. We can do a deal."

"That can only mean the FSB," Van Basten replied. "It won't work."

There was a paused and the clink of glass-on-glass, "agreed, but we could offer it to the British or the Americans," said Sergei. "They would move heaven and earth for that material."

"No. That archive needs to be online and open for the world to see. It will be *Forbiddenfacts*' defining moment. I've been working towards this for ten years. Selling it out doesn't feel right."

"Feel right? Neither does a bullet in the head, I suspect."

"What about Winter?" said Van Basten, "and the other mercenaries?"

"Winter comes highly recommended. He is a professional, I'm sure he will understand. I will pay compensation to him and his employers for their trouble, and their protection."

"What a gentleman," Andy gasped in mock surprise. "I'm on his side."

Alisa shook her head. "*Nyet,* Andy. Belov just has enough enemies without making another out of your organisation."

"Quiet please," I said.

"Pay off Winter for all I care," Van Basten continued, "but it doesn't solve this nightmare we're in now. And it doesn't change the fact that I feel used and betrayed. By you."

"I hear this phrase used a lot on the internet," said Sergei quietly, "it is *stop being such a Drama Queen.* You can be used and betrayed and live, or noble and admirable and die. Your choice, I tire of your theatrics. And if the FSB don't kill you, then I might. It is certainly an option right now."

"You? Kill me? Then I have another choice!" snapped Van Basten angrily, his voice high-pitched. I think he was crying.

"Which is..?"

"For you to find out, Sergei Nikolayevich. My work trumps your threats. *Without fame, he who spends his time on earth leaves only such a mark upon the world as smoke does on air or foam on water.*"

"Poetry?" laughed Sergei, "you'll need more than poetry to get out of this. I'll leave you to think about it, Pieter. After tonight I think you'll see sense."

"As might we all," said Van Basten. Then there was silence.

"What was that all about?" said Andy.

I recognised the tone of the verse. I looked at Alisa and shook my head. The SVR Colonel's eyes were wide as she reached for her SMG. "*The Inferno:* Canto XXIV," she said.

I stood and looked out of the window, across at the woods. The snow fell against the glass, then into the dark. I squinted.

And in the trees, something moved.

TWENTY ONE

"Give me your rifle" I said to Andy. I walked towards the window, "and turn the lights out." Tapping the trigger group to show me the safety was off, Andy passed the M6. The assault rifle was fitted with a night scope, which I used to track the tree line for movement.

Alisa spoke into her radio, telling the riflemen on the roof to switch on, radio traffic crackling into life as our tiny guard force stood to. "What is it?" she whispered, hand on my shoulder.

"There's something out there, it looks like a cross." I made out the angular shape emerging from the trees, drifting snow making it difficult to focus. Suddenly I winced, the sights filled with light as sodium floodlights snapped into life. They were aimed straight at us.

"What the fuck?" said Andy. "Who drags lights and generators through a wood at minus twenty?"

My eyes focussed on the floodlit grounds behind the mansion. "It's a crucifixion," I said. A man was tied to a cross made from scaffolding poles lashed together. I flipped the daytime optics on the M6 and squinted through them, zooming in on the figure on the cross. He was stripped to the waist, wearing black fatigue trousers and heavy boots. I could see him shivering like he was being electrocuted, bloodied face streaked with filth. He arched his back, mouth agape as he screamed."

"It would be a good idea to rescue him if we can," said Alisa.

"He's almost certainly an FSB commando," I said. "Since when does rescuing them become a priority? Those woods will be crawling with Volk's pet loonies."

"He needs interrogating," she said flatly, "although I would have thought that was obvious."

Andy looked at his watch, "make your mind up. I'd say he's got five minutes before he hits severe hypothermia. He might even be there now."

"Let's go," I growled, keying the mic on my PRR. "Dmitri from Winter – meet me in the Grand Hall, over?" I could understand, even sympathise, with the FSB operators. Their job was in the same grid square as mine. What I couldn't get were the crazies out there following Fyodor Volk.

"Received," said Dmitri groggily, "do you want us to open fire? The men can see movement."

"Not yet, but on my signal I want them to shoot out those lights."

"What are you going to do?"

"Rescue that poor bastard," I said, "now move."

Dmitri was zipping up his big winter jacket as we strode in, a black polymer AK rifle on the table next to him. He wore a ballistic helmet and body armour. "You have a plan, Winter?"

"He does," said Alisa, "but we need those lights extinguished first."

I nodded. "And we're going to drive out there in our very own APC. Dmitri, what's the security package like on Sergei's Maybach?"

The Russian smiled even as he shook his head. "The limousine? That baby has the full works – a *Gunther and Voss* presidential-grade custom security fit. B6 armour, a ramming bar, escape hatch in the roof, run-flat tyre system, engine fire suppressants, armoured radiator grilles and STANAG II NATO standard armoured glass. Unless they have .50 Cal or light anti-armour weapons we're OK."

"And a mini-bar," said Andy. "Right?"

"Fire it up, Dmitri," I said, "we're gonna drive out there. On my signal your guys shoot the lights out, we advance to contact. After that your guys slot anything they see that isn't us or the bloke strapped up on that cross, OK?"

"Good. Carl?" Dmitri barked at the British bodyguard, "you heard Winter, pass on those orders."

"Sure boss," he nodded, tossing the keys for the armoured limousine to the Russian. "Your man will have hypothermia – bring him straight here,

I'll prep warm saline and dextrose. We'll put him on an IV immediately." He pulled a medical kit from under his desk and began unpacking it.

"Good, now follow me," said Dmitri, leading us outside, "it's about time that car paid for its keep."

"It's going to get shot to fuck," I laughed.

"I know," Dmitri boomed. "Sergei will be hopping mad. I'm almost jealous." It doesn't matter what nationality you are, ex-squaddies love seeing expensive stuff getting shot to pieces. Outside there was a respite from the snow, only light flurries skimming the top of the knee-deep white desert around us. The Maybach squatted next to the Range Rover outside the manor house. Dmitri slid into the driver's seat. The inside of the luxury limo smelt of leather, aftershave and cigars. Dmitri passed me his AK and Kevlar helmet, "take this. If you're getting out you'll need it more than me." He pulled his stubby MP5K and put it on his lap.

"Thanks," I said, taking the helmet and putting it on.

In the back Alisa and Andy readied weapons and adjusted body armour. Alisa had swapped her MP5 for one of the Kalashnikov rifles. Both wore Kevlar helmets. Andy checked his M6 and readied it. Three black frag-grenades were taped to his chest rig.

"Let's go," I said. The Maybach's engines purred into life as the V12 twin-turbo engines fired. Dmitri pulled out gently, building the acceleration as the snow-tyres bit into the ice. He turned left and following the service road towards the staff quarters. We broke the building line, the Maybach powering through the snow. Inside the armoured cocoon of the limousine it was eerily quiet. The armoured belly-plate scraped against the ground as we powered towards the trees.

"Incoming," said Andy. Bullets began bouncing off of the armoured windscreen, a high-pitched wail that spider-webbed the glass. In front of us the trees, twisted and black against the lights, grew closer. And the crucified man lolled on his cross.

"Ten seconds," said Dmitri, feeding the steering wheel through his meaty hands. The heavy limousine fish-tailed, waves of powder breaking across the bonnet.

"I'll grab him," I said, readying my knife.

"I'll take left," said Andy. He touched Alisa's shoulder, "you take right, OK?"

"*Da*," she said, snapping the folding stock on her assault rifle into position.

Andy nodded. "Just put as many rounds down as you can. Win the fire fight."

I put my gloved hand on the door handle, the other keying my PRR mic. "Take out the lights."

I couldn't hear the crack of the rifles, but in front of us floodlights shattered, darkness enveloping the tree line. Now I saw muzzle flashes as unseen shooters returned fire. "Go," said Dmitri, paddling the steering wheel crazily. He slid the car sideways in front of the scaffolding pole crucifix, offside facing the enemy. Incoming rounds thudded against the armoured car as we de-bussed, Andy's M6 booming as he fired into the woods. Alisa took cover behind the boot and opened fire with her AK74. Ropes of tracer raked the treeline from the roof of Croll house as Dmitri's men provided covering fire.

"I'm out!" I hollered, cordite stinging my nose as I loped towards the man on the cross. Bullets churned the snow in front of me as I advanced.

"Winter, get down!" crackled a heavily-accented voice urgently in my earpiece. It was the Serbian bodyguard, on the roof behind me.

I ducked, falling into the snow. I felt the marksman's bullet sail over my shoulder into the trees, silencing another automatic weapon. "Tango down," said the voice. "Move!"

I staggered forwards, the snow like quicksand dragging at my feet. Andy had one-in-three tracer in his rifle, green fireflies bouncing into the trees as he put down more covering fire. The crucifix was less than three metres away, stray bullets whistling by. "Jesus Christ save me!" chattered the man on the cross in Russian, his face crazy with fear and pain.

"Hold on," I bellowed, firing my AK into the woods. As I got closer I saw the crucifix was a box-like structure built from metal poles, the cross sticking up from a tangled base that held it aloft. The Russian was attached at the ankles by a thick sheath of black duct tape. I sawed through it with my knife, feet thrashing like a man in a noose. I saw Dmitri edge the car forward, flashing its headlights and trying to attract fire towards the Maybach. Sparks flew off the bodywork as bullets peppered the chassis, ugly scabs of silver metal stitching along the vehicle.

"Two tangos toward you," said the Serbian marksman into my earpiece. "You're in the way of my line of fire."

"Roger," I replied, two dark shapes looming out of the dark. They were hooded, swathed in layers of tattered winter clothing, hair long and matted. Their pinched, filthy faces were grinning as they ran through the snow. One had a shotgun, the other a long-handled wood-chopping axe. I could smell the sweet stink of unwashed bodies and stale booze as they drew closer.

The man with the shotgun shouldered the weapon in time for Andy's tracer to hit him in the chest, shoulder and head, twisting him around as blood spattered the snow. Grunting, eyes white as they rolled lifelessly into his skull, he collapsed to the ground. The man with the axe ducked low and swung at me crazily, the blade biting into a scaffolding pole with a dull clanging noise. The man on the crucifix lurched as the blow dislodged one of the supports. I dropped my knife and snatched my AK. I levelled it at the axe-man and squeezed the trigger.

Click. Empty.

I scrabbled for my pistol. My attacker locked his dark, shining eyes on mine and stepped forward, hefting his axe. The Russian on the crucifix groaned as he swung his body, using his legs to pivot on the scaffolding. He kicked the axe man in the face with the full force of his booted feet. My attacker staggered and I hurtled into him, hands reaching for his throat. We fell into the snow as the gunfire around us intensified, the sound of metal-on-metal as the Maybach absorbed yet more fire.

The ragged man coughed blood, hands pummelling my armoured torso. I rammed my elbow into his shattered nose with a crunch. Finally I tugged my pistol from its holster and stuffed it into his head, pulling the trigger until he was still. The heat of the blood on my face stung against the cold. "*Get…me…down…*" came a voice from the cross. The Russian's eyes were closed, his face contorted in agony. I climbed up onto the scaffolding and slid the knife into the jumble of ropes and tape holding his wrists to the cross. I cut his arm as I slashed at his bonds, and he grunted in pain. "Don't stop" he yelled, "please."

I looked down. Dmitri was driving forwards, Andy and Alisa scurrying behind the car for cover. Both opened fire, muzzle flash marking incoming rounds from the woods. Finally the man collapsed into the snow, shivering and sobbing. Alisa appeared and grabbed him, helping me bundle him into the car. "Let's go," I said to Dmitri. I pulled a fleece blanket from Andy's bag and wrapped it around the Russian.

"Let's go," Andy hollered, bowling a grenade into the trees and ducking back into the car. The incoming fire was more ragged as our rooftop marksmen found more targets for their rifles. Dmitri threw the limo in a circle and powered towards the garage. The windscreen was pocked with bullet strikes, but the armoured glass remained intact. Warm air from the heater flooded the vehicle, the Russian convulsing in pain.

"Carl from Winter" I said into the radio, "We've got the casualty, be with you in two minutes."

"Roger," the bodyguard replied. "I'm ready."

Dmitri keyed his mic. "Keep Mister Belov and the others away from the hall for now, hopefully it's safer now."

"I'm glad you think so Dmitri," I panted. "I think this is just the start." I opened the window as we careered towards the house. From the woods I heard the sound of whooping and grunting and jeering, like animals baying for blood.

TWENTY TWO

Andy and I burst into the great hall, dragging the freezing Russian into the security office. Carl wrapped a survival blanket around him then inserted an IV. Studying the Russian's eyes, he took his pulse. "Do you speak English, mate?" He spoke in that slow but friendly voice medics use with patients.

"Yes," the Russian stuttered, teeth chattering like those wind-up toys kids get.

"How long were you out there?" said Carl, "stripped?"

"Maybe thirty minutes?" the Russian said, "then they put me up on that cross."

Carl shook his head. "You should be dead. Do you feel the need to strip, or to get into an enclosed space?"

"Don't be stupid," the Russian replied slowly, "I understand hypothermia; there'll be no *paradoxical undressing* with me. That is a warm saline drip, no? That is good, *tovarich*. After that coffee and hot food would be excellent."

The British bodyguard looked at me. "This is one hard bastard, Winter."

"What is your name?" I said.

"Fuck you" the Russian replied. "I'm grateful for the rescue, but that doesn't mean I'll tell you anything."

Alisa Turov pulled her pistol. "Kick this cretin back out into the snow," she spat.

"Sure," I said. "Carl, take the IV out."

The Russian commando shrugged, "you're bluffing."

I slid the drip out of his arm and took the blanket. "No, I'm not. If you can't tell us about those crazy bastards out there then you might as well go back and join them."

"Your mission is over," said Turov, "I imagine the rest of your *Spetzgruppa* are dead. Pieter Van Basten is safe. Sergei Belov is safe. The only issue now is survival, and I could get you home to Russia if I chose. So, tell me, are you proud or just stupid?"

The Russian looked at the survival blanket, grim-faced. The colour was returning to his cheeks. The Serbian bodyguard walked in carrying a coffee pot, rifle slung over his shoulder. The Russian sniffed the air, the aroma of coffee clearly irresistible after the cold. He touched his battered face and winced. His arms had the familiar military tattoos running from his deltoid to his wrists. He had close-set blue eyes and cropped hair, numerous scars marking his face and chest. "And who are you?" he said to Alisa, voice gravelly.

"Colonel Alisa Romanova Turov of the SVR, Directorate 'S'", she said coolly, "we know about Misha Baburin, about the farmhouse you stayed at."

"What happened to Baburin?" grunted the Russian.

"He's dead," I said.

"No great loss. He was an arsehole."

"Those tattoos are a giveaway," she said, "why do you send agents into the field so easily identifiable? I see you served in the 45th Detached Airborne Reconnaissance Regiment. Ah, and you saw action in South Ossetia." She shook her head, "superb tradecraft soldier."

"Jesus, darling, you want to be careful," the Russian replied, shaking his head, "if you get any more pleased with yourself you might disappear up that cute little arse of yours. I am Major Ruslan Ivanovich Dudko, FSB Spetzgruppa Five, Special Group *Grob*. I'm a soldier, not a fucking spy. Go and fuck yourself with your tradecraft. Now can I have a cup of coffee?"

I poured him a brew. Dudko took a sugar bowl and emptied it into his coffee, stirred it with a finger and slurped hungrily. He wiped his mouth with the back of his hand. "Another" he said.

"Here," said Dmitri, "have some of this." He slid a pewter flask from his pocket and emptied a slug of vodka into the coffee.

"*O, Klasno*" said Dudko, holding out his cup, "this is more like it." His English was fluent, and like many Russians had a hint of an American accent. I pulled out a chair and lit a cigar, offering the FSB Major one too. He took it and smiled, "you see, why pull my fingernails out or wire my nuts to the electricity? Coffee and a good *Cubano*? I'm all yours."

"I'm Cal," I nodded, sitting down. "I work for Mister Belov."

"That wily old prick, I've been watching him for twenty-four hours. I could have shot him twice."

"Why didn't you?" said Turov.

"Belov? The man isn't my objective," he replied. "I'm old-fashioned about following orders. I'm sure he won't die in his bed, but now isn't his time."

I poured more coffee, "who is then?"

"Pieter Van Basten. He doesn't go outside as far as I can tell. I was going to assault the building and take him tonight on my own, but we were attacked."

"Tell me about that, Dudko. And what was with the craziness, you up on that cross?"

Dudko explained that when his team arrived he ordered them to conduct a close target recce, based on satellite imagery of the estate. One of his men dug a covert observation post and watched the house whilst the rest of the patrol headed south to check out the New Age traveller's camp on the southern perimeter. "It's near a military training area," said Dudko, "there were signs warning us about tanks. Not that we saw any."

"Tanks? I think we sold them all" said Andy, "defence cuts."

"Their camp is in a lightly wooded area," Dudko continued, "they have these tents, some caravans and a couple of shacks. It looked deserted, so we patrolled into it. That's when we lost Sasha."

"How?" I said.

"He was shot in the neck with as crossbow. We had silenced weapons so we shot up the tents and shacks. We headed back into the woods, but they'd prepared traps. One of the men fell into a pit, an old-fashioned hole full of sharpened sticks. There were only four of us left. We returned to our OP, but our man was dead. They'd smashed his face in."

"We found his body" said Alisa, "they'd cut out his tongue."

"Yes, that was Lev. A good man," said Dudko quietly. "I thought we'd been set up, that it was some strange Psyops shit. Then we wondered if the British had led us into a trap and that their SAS were ambushing us.

That was when we were surrounded by the bastards. They crept up on us like ghosts. Some of them were dug into OPs like ours, those guys were definitely trained. They looked like tramps, but some of them had that feral look, you know? That look you see in guys who've been there but lost it along the way back."

I nodded and helped myself to more coffee, "they took you prisoner?"

"Yes, and here's the crazy bit, the guy in charge? He was Russian."

"Tell me about him," said Turov, her eyes wide. "You are one of the few people to have ever met Fyodor Volk."

"Volk? He never mentioned his name. He lived in one of the tents, which looked clean and tidy. The men were completely obedient to him. He was tall and slim, almost two metres I guess. He had black hair and a beard, pale skin. Very striking looks and his accent was strange, like he'd lived abroad."

I pulled my chair forward. "Did he question you?"

"Sort of, although he liked the sound of his own voice if you ask me. He gave sermons, like a religious nut, describing us as evil servants of a discredited regime. Banged on about Capitalism, it was like being back at junior school in the old days."

By Dudko's account, the strange Russian said that they were being tormented as punishment for their sins, for planning to murder Van Basten. "He kept talking about treachery and betrayal, and the devil would gnaw on us for eternity. His friends lapped all this shit up, kept talking about banking and greed and war. Of course, the place was full of drugs. When I was tied up in one of the caravans I saw LSD, Mescaline, Ketamine and the rest, like a pharmacy. While I was there they were all smoking this very strong skunk, all of them sucking on big fat reefers and drinking. These guys didn't give a fuck, seriously."

"What did he say about Van Basten?" I said.

"He described Van Basten as a man who could shine a light into something he called the *Ninth Circle* and show the betrayers for what they were. He gave this speech where he said protecting him was a duty that would always be remembered, more meaningful than the false wars they'd been sent to fight. It was a load of horse-shit in my opinion, but they were hanging on every word. There were at least twenty-five of them that I saw."

I refilled the Russian's mug with steaming coffee. "But why are they here, they couldn't have known about you?"

"Oh, that's easy," Dudko smiled, exhaling cigar smoke. "They're here to kill Sergei Belov. They were upfront about it. I heard them talking, I didn't let on I knew any English. They were going to assault the house, kill everybody except Van Basten then burn it down. They've stockpiled incendiary grenades and petrol, the crazy sons-of-bitches."

"But they'd go to prison for life" I said.

"Those guys don't care. They were talking about how easy it is in prison, how they'd be heroes in there."

"This man is definitely Fyodor Volk," said Alisa, folding her arms across her chest. "But there's something I don't understand, because he works for the FSB too. I'm tracking him."

"Like I say, I've never heard of him," Dudko shrugged, pulling a face. "If I see him again I'm going to rip his arms and legs off while he watches."

"Maybe he's gone freelance?" said Andy, "can you find out Alisa?"

"I will send a message to Moscow," she replied. "After I've interrogated Pieter Van Basten."

Dmitri coughed politely, "sweetheart, if you think Sergei is going to let you do that…"

"Dmitri," the SVR officer snapped, "let's not ruin what is turning into a useful friendship, *sweetheart*. I eavesdropped on a conversation of his earlier – I think he's linked in some way to Volk."

Dmitri let out a booming laugh, "Pieter? He's a geek. He spends all day on the internet. Really, Alisa Romanova, you've let your suspicions get the better of you."

I stood up, "Andy, play the recording to Dmitri, will you?"

Andy nodded and pulled the recording device from his bag. "It's true," he said.

"I'd hurry up, whatever it is you intend to do" Dudko said, wrapping the blankets around him, "because those crazies are going to attack this place as soon as they've re-grouped. I'd do it just before daybreak if I were them."

"I agree," I said, "We're going to their camp to return the serve." My phone chirruped in my pocket. It was a message from Harry, a document attached to an email. "Excuse me for a moment."

"I'll go and speak to Sergei," said Dmitri.

Alisa nodded. "I'll come with you."

"Wait" I said, "Belov is paying me to look after him. Let me explain the situation, tell him that we need to speak with Van Basten."

Dmitri looked me up and down. "That makes sense," he said.

Alisa shrugged, poured herself a coffee and glowered at Ruslan Dudko. The big Russian commando blew her a kiss and helped himself to more vodka. I went into the corridor and checked the message from Harry. Harry's message was short and to the point:

GET THE JOB DONE AND RV @ HEATHROW. FLIGHTS ARRANGED. I WILL MANAGE POST-OP ADMIN WITH CLIENT.

The attached report contained analysis of internet traffic and mobile telephone data for phones attributed to Sergei Belov and Pieter Van Basten. It was marked SECRET and my phone wasn't encrypted to that level. I guessed it was the fruits of the decades-long relationship with the Americans and their technical wizards at Fort Meade. Harry would only send it if it were vital. I scanned the document, ignoring the pages of numbers and association charts, scrolling to the analyst's conclusion at the end:

Comms traffic between BELOV and VAN BASTEN is what one would expect given the nature of their relationship: a high volume of routine communication. On average the two men communicated 8.9 times a week over an eighteen-month period. VAN BASTEN habitually uses encrypted devices for online communication using proprietary military-grade security software that to date has defied attempts to access. However, sensitive techniques have allowed us to 'ghost track' parallel data attributed to known associates linked to Forbiddenfacts. net. The use of these techniques has led us to conclude that:

VAN BASTEN possibly communicates using Voice Over Internet Protocol (VOIP) to a satellite telephone at least twice a day, we have given this communications device the codename PLINTH. More detailed call data is not currently available;

Russian mobile telephone service provider data shows that PLINTH was called by a number attributed to a radical Russian hacking collective known as TROIKA. This was on one occasion last year, assessed as being a lapse in operational security;

Members of TROIKA were subsequently arrested for an occult-linked murder in Moscow, open-source research reveals a wealth of lurid tabloid material about how members murdered a person they believed reported them to the authorities;

TROIKA were vociferous supporters of Forbiddenfacts.net;

PLINTH has been used in Africa, Central Russia and most recently in the United Kingdom;

PLINTH is still active, last call data was forty-five minutes prior to the time of writing in the Central / Western part of the United Kingdom;

Russian intelligence services are believed to also be attempting to intercept data from both VAN BASTEN and PLINTH;

+++ REPORT ENDS +++

I called Alisa over and showed her the report. "The gist of this is that Van Basten has been on the phone to Volk all the time" I said.

She nodded. "We need that phone."

Sergei was with Evan Sands and Melissa in the office. Melissa sat in a chair, head in hands. "Is it over?" said Sergei.

"It's just getting started," I replied. "Where's Van Basten?"

"Why?" Melissa asked.

"You don't need to know, but we need to speak with him," said Turov.

"We had an argument earlier, over the website," said Sergei apologetically, "he is upset. Leave him be."

"Sergei," I said stonily, "the men out there, the ones trying to kill you? We think Pieter's in telephone contact with them."

"Ridiculous."

"Total bollocks," said Sands. "Pieter is a peaceful man."

"We haven't time for your disappointment," said Alisa. "Sergei, I bugged the room. Van Basten used a trigger phrase from Dante that I believe links him to Fyodor Volk. Volk is trying to kill you."

"A phrase from Dante?" You expect me to…"

"Poetry aside," I said, raising a hand, "I've just received intelligence data from my organisation. Van Basten probably has a satellite phone in his room. It's linked to a number I think belongs to Fyodor Volk."

"If that is true, then I would like to see for myself," said Sergei.

"Listen to yourself, Sergei," said Melissa, standing up. She balled her trembling hands into fists. "We all know Pieter wouldn't harm a fly."

I brushed past them and headed for the stairs. "Show me to Van Basten's room," I ordered.

Sergei and Melissa sat back down. Sergei put him arm around Melissa and whispered to her, like she were a troubled child. Dmitri shook his head and poured a drink. "Follow me," said Sir Evan Sands.

"Don't hurt him, please," said Melissa.

"That will be Pieter's decision," said Alisa, picking up her rifle. "Not mine."

TWENTY THREE

Sands lead us up two flights of stairs and along a winding corridor. At the end was a light grey door. "He's in there," he said.

"Wait here," I replied. I handed my AK to Alisa and drew my pistol. She gave the rifle to Sands, who looked at it in horror as she pulled her own handgun. I nudged the door open with my toe and stepped into the freezing room, pistol in a Weaver grip. Alisa followed, her weapon drawing arcs. The double bed was strewn with clothes, the only other item a laptop computer on a desk. "Clear," I sighed. The full-length window was open, satin drapes billowing in the wind. Turning off the light, I followed the wall to the window and peered out. A trail of fresh footprints led to the trees. Outside the window was an ivy-covered Juliet balcony, below that a flat roof. There were more footprints. I could have jumped it too, if I'd lowered myself to my full height from the balcony. "Rapunzel, Rapunzel, let down your hair," I whispered.

The first bullet smashed into the window frame inches from my head, splinters stinging my cheek as I threw myself to the floor. The stammer of automatic fire jarred in my ears as a volley of incoming rounds hammered the walls surrounding the arched window.

"Got that," said a calm voice in Russian through my earpiece. I heard the crack-and-boom of a bullet piercing the sound barrier as one of Dmitri's men returned fire. From the tree line I saw more muzzle flashes as other shooters joined in. Tracer arced through the trees, as the buzz-saw rattle of a machinegun joined the chorus of firearms.

"Did you see anybody leave the house from my location?" I hissed into my mic.

"Negative, I've just taken this position," replied the marksman over the net, "there's movement in the tree line along the southwestern perimeter."

Alisa was on her belly, crawling towards the laptop. "No," I spat, my back to the thick manor house wall. More rounds smashed into and through the window, zipping around the room, gouging deep holes in plaster.

"Shit," spat the SVR officer as a ricochet hit her, splintering the screen of the computer. She clutched her hand, face twisted in pain.

"Casualty, upstairs bedroom," I said into my PRR. "Get Carl onto the second floor."

We scrambled out of the room, Sands lying on the floor and clutching my AK like a drowning man with a lifebelt. "Bloody hell," he said, pointing at the Kalashnikov, "how does this bastard thing work?"

I examined Alisa's hand. "It's a scratch," I grinned. The ricochet had caught the top of her left hand behind the knuckles, skimming it and leaving a livid cut from thumb to little finger. Blood ran freely from the injury, running down her wrist. I clasped my hand over it to staunch the bleeding.

"Bastard," she winced, returning the smile. "When you were grazed by that screwdriver in London I made a fuss over you."

"Grazed? Excuse me, that was a proper stab wound," I dead-panned. "Do they give you Purple Hearts in the SVR for being injured in action?"

"No, but your heart will be purple when I cut it out," she said, catching a sob in her throat. "That's actually very painful."

"Is Pieter alright?" said Sands.

"He's gone," I said, "into the trees with his friends." Sands and shook his head. I nudged his shoulder and smiled, "look on the bright side, Sir Evan, at least you live in a castle."

Carl jogged along the corridor, Kalashnikov in one hand and a trauma kit in the other. He knelt down and looked at Turov's hand. "You were lucky," he said, "that looks worse than it is, but there might be some nerve damage. Let's clean it up first."

"I am a pianist," said Alisa matter-of-factly.

"You were," Carl replied, "and if you do what I say you might be again in a couple of months."

I left Carl with Sands and Turov and headed back down the stairs. Sergei slouched in his office chair, face pale. Melissa was sitting staring into the fire, head in her hands. "Pieter?" said Sergei.

"He's gone, Sergei."

"Why?" said the Oligarch, hooded eyes locking onto mine.

"I don't know."

"He felt trapped," said Melissa coldly, "by you Sergei. He wanted to be free, but you were always in control."

"Watch your mouth," Sergei spat. "It was business. Without my support he'd be just another unemployed slacker, mouldering in a bedsit. Now he's a household name."

"Let's call the police," said Melissa, hands trembling in her lap. "We're going to die out here."

"No police," I said. "All of us are looking at thirty years if we're lucky – firearms possession, arson and murder for starters. In any case, how will the cops get here? There's three feet of snow on the roads. Their helis can't fly. Their radio network is probably down too. It's just us and those crazy bastards outside."

"He's right, Melissa," said Sergei, shaking his head. "It's the FSB file, Cal. He hasn't been the same since he received it."

"What other skeletons do you have in that cupboard?" I asked.

The Russian's smile was tight, a row of straight white teeth visible under his lip. "A few, perhaps, but no more than you, Captain Winter."

"I want you and Melissa to stay here." I passed Sergei the Kalashnikov, "you know how one of these works?"

"Of course," he replied, taking the weapon. "Although my days in the army were a long time ago. Ah, the new AK74… it feels just the same as the old one."

I nodded, "it never leaves you. The windows here are armoured, the doors are fireproof and it's in the centre of the house. You're safe, but we will be attacked. Lock the doors and don't let anybody in until I say so. I'll send Sir Evan down, he has a spare rifle."

"Good luck," said Sergei as I left. Sands stood in the corridor, rifle held loosely in his hands.

"Into your office and lock the doors," I said, "shoot anybody who comes in."

"I don't know if I can," the businessman replied.

"You can, trust me," I said, closing the door behind me. "Or you can die. Your choice." I hurried back to the great hall. Carl and Alisa had come back down and were readying weapons.

Dmitri was strapping Ruslan Dudko into a set of body armour. "My enemies' enemy is my friend," said the FSB commando.

"Yes, I think our differences can wait for tonight," Alisa replied.

"Carl," I said, double-checking my weapons. "Did you capture Van Basten on the security cameras."

"Hold on, I'll check," he said, heading for the adjacent security office.

"Zoran's hit," shouted a voice over the radio net, "they're on the roof."

"Calm down," said Dmitri into his mic, "where are you?"

We heard screaming, then silence. The static buzzed in my ear. Then I heard laughing. "You fuckers are next, hear that?" said a manic, high-pitched voice. "I'm cutting this bastard's heart out."

Carl walked in, rifle ready. "Boss, the power to the cameras is down."

"Right," Andy grinned. "Fix bayonets."

The other Russian bodyguard came over the net. "Dmitri, I have eyes on the house from the staff quarters. Anna, the housekeeper, is dead. They cut her throat. The enemy have split into two groups; one is climbing onto the roof with ladders via the rear of the house. The other is trying to break in via the rear dining room doors with sledgehammers. They've set fires along the building line."

"How many?" said Dmitri.

"I guess fifteen at least. They look like fucking tramps. They've got rifles, SMGs, shotguns and axes. I can see a light machinegun and one crazy fucker even has a chainsaw."

"OK," I said. "Dmitri, Ruslan and Carl – cover the dining room. Andy, Alisa and me will go upstairs and cover the roof."

Dmitri nodded and passed Ruslan, the FSB officer, a rifle. Carl readied his AK and put on a helmet equipped with night vision goggles. The three men filed into the corridor and headed to the back of the house.

"Here," said Andy, unzipping one of his ballistic bags. He handed me

175

the stubby Kel-Tec KSG shotgun, one of the weapons we'd retrieved in Epping Forest what seemed a lifetime ago. The black, evil-looking weapon felt good in my hands, a dual-purpose infrared and red-dot laser sight mounted on a rail. There were five boxes of shells, Twelve Gauge Number One Buckshot, our chosen ammo for close combat work. I slung the AK over my back, checked my pistol then headed for the stairs. Andy followed me, his M6 shouldered, Alisa at the rear. Carl had strapped her hand up with a field dressing. She'd pulled a black ski glove over it, suppressed SMG resting in her palm.

From upstairs we heard the sound of smashing glass and banging. Behind us we heard gunfire and shouting. "Contact, contact," said Carl over the net.

I quickly climbed the stairs. On the landing I crouched down and glanced around the corner. Three scruffily-dressed men, wearing army surplus fatigues stood by a door, armed with hunting rifles and shotguns. The guy who was meant to be covering my end of the corridor had waist-length dreadlocks, his face half-covered with a tribal tattoo. He was pissing on the carpet, a fat joint hanging out of the corner of his mouth. "Clear," came a gruff voice from one of the bedrooms.

The man finished urinating and turned towards me, reaching for the old 7.62 Self-Loading Rifle he'd propped against the wall. I fired the shotgun from my hip, the blast hitting him at the top of his leg, sending him crashing to the floor. I chambered another round and fired, the camouflaged figure behind him writhing as the shell blew open his chest. Behind me, Andy opened up with his M6, the harsh clatter of gunfire battering my ears. Another body fell, a crazy trail of bullet holes ripping across the blood-spattered walls. "Return fire!" yelled another voice over the groaning and swearing.

The lights went out. The white bursts of muzzle flash were the only source of illumination. I hit the deck, a fine spray of buckshot whistling overhead from a shotgun. I fired again, the gout of flame from the stubby barrel of the Kel-Tec lighting the corridor. "Grenade!" Andy barked, as I heard the tinny *ching* of the lever ejecting from the body of the weapon. Ahead of us there was swearing and the sound of men fighting to find cover. The spherical frag grenade made a noise as it bounced once on the carpeted floor.

I scurried back around the corner, chambering another round in my shotgun. The thump of the grenade going off in the enclosed space deafened me for a moment before I heard howling and screaming. Pulling my night vision goggles from their pouch, I fixed them in place, Alisa firing her SMG from the other side of the landing. In the grey-green light I saw at least four bodies on the floor, the carpets thick with debris, weapons and body parts.

Andy gingerly stepped forward, rifle in shoulder. His NVGs made him look like a bug-eyed alien as he stalked along the corridor. "Clear!" he shouted.

I checked the bodies. The men were in their thirties and forties. They had long, matted hair and weather-beaten faces. All smelt strongly of booze. Andy gestured he was going to the end of the corridor, where the windows were open. An icy blast of wind cut along the corridor. "Dmitri" I said quietly into my PRR, "you OK down there?"

"Yes," the Russian replied. "We've exchanged fire with them, killed two. They've fallen back into the garden. They're trying to get to the centre of the house, like they know where Sergei is."

"Van Basten," I spat, "he's told them."

"Shit. They're using incendiary grenades. They've started fires."

"Hold on," I said, "we're almost done up here."

Over the radio I heard gunshots and Dmitri barking orders. Then he keyed his mic off. At least I hoped it was him. I joined Andy by the open window. A long ladder was propped against it, which I tipped back down. Andy pulled the pin on a grenade and jammed it, safety lever down, under the sash window. He pulled the curtains across to cover his handiwork. If anybody opened it they'd be in for a nasty surprise.

We continued along the corridor, noticing boot-prints on the deeply carpeted floors. I lay down on my belly as we reached the next corner, shuffling forward to look. As soon as my helmeted head broke the line of the wall I heard shots, automatic fire passing over my head and chewing into the brickwork. "Shit" I hissed, pushing myself backwards with my elbows. Alisa pushed her weapon out into the corridor at arm's length and opened fire, emptying the magazine in one long burst. I could see the pain in her eyes as her damaged hand grasped the stubby grip of the weapon. Andy tossed me a flash-bang. I pulled the pin and threw it around the corner. After burst of white light, I pushed myself into the corridor with the enthusiasm of a man jumping off a cliff without a parachute. I saw a dark shape in my NVGs, a man crouching in a doorway to my left. My weapon panned towards him, the infrared dot sweeping across his body. I fired and fell to one knee as Andy dashed past me, firing bursts from his M6. The man fell backwards into a bedroom, scrabbling on his back like he was on fire. I shot him again, the blast taking off the side of his head like an over-ripe melon. I heard Andy's voice from the next room, "Cal, in here."

Alisa joined me in a guest room and switched on the light. One of Volk's followers was curled in a ball in the middle of the room, rocking and sobbing. His hands were bloodied, fingers missing where they'd caught part of my shotgun blast. An abandoned Uzi lay on the bed. "Where's Volk?" said Alisa gently, putting her hand on the man's head.

"He's watching," he hissed, face grey and twisted. His hair was cut short, beard hewn into a forked Mephistopheles, "he'll kill you all."

I looked into his yellowed eyes, pupils pinprick-small. I patted him down as he shivered, mangled hands fluttering. He wore an old army-surplus jacket over layers of jumpers. His pockets were full of empty brown medicine bottles, a dark canvass rucksack lying next to him. "Methadone" said Andy, "fuel for the New Age fighting man."

"Why aren't you trying to kill us?" said Alisa, stroking his filthy hair, "what is your name?"

"Tony," he groaned through chattering teeth. He was trying to smile, "I'm so cold. And I am meant to kill you."

"How?" I said.

Tony smiled, his eyes rolling woozily in his skull. He pointed a bloody finger at the rucksack by his feet and kicked it over. I saw the mobile telephone taped to a creamy-grey block of plastic explosive. "It's live," he giggled. "I can't set it off with my hands like this, but it's on a timer anyway. Run if you can."

"IED," said Andy coolly. "I'd say that's half a kilo of PE4." He plugged his M6 into the side of the wild man's head and pulled the trigger twice. He crouched down and looked at the device, "it's dialling in. Fucking MOVE."

We ran, dashing around the corner. We made it halfway towards the landing when the bomb exploded, the blast evaporating the brick wall as if it were made of cardboard. An invisible force, like a giant's fist, punched me into a window, heavy drapes curling around me like a Venus flytrap. The air was full of hot, sharp debris as I tumbled into the night. I landed on a flat-roof, in the snow. I tasted blood in my mouth as I coughed up smoke, dust and what felt like my guts. Thankful for my body armour and helmet I looked down at my shredded trousers, legs covered in scratches and cuts. I took a mouthful of fresh snow to clean out the inside of my rank-tasting mouth. Looking across the grounds of Croll House, I saw fires burning, chemical-smelling smoke drifting into the night. The gunfire was more sporadic now.

And from the tree line came more dark shapes, men with weapons shuffling through the snow.

TWENTY FOUR

I took aim at the figures moving slowly towards us, like an army of scarecrows. I fired aimed shots, two men collapsing as I found my mark. Incoming tracer spat from the tree line, forcing me to keep my head down. My radio had taken a thumb-sized piece of shrapnel and was broken. I felt like I was breathing blood. Below me fires crackled and flared, dirty smoke curling up the walls of Croll House. "Cal," called Andy from the ragged hole in the wall. "You OK?" He aimed his M6 and opened fire.

"Yeah," I lied, "where's Alisa?"

"Unconscious - she was thrown into the wall. I need to get her to Carl."

"Are you OK?"

Andy grinned. "I think you took most of that blast for me, you fat bastard."

"Cover me. I'm coming back inside." I crawled towards the window, disentangling myself from the curtains.

Andy helped me back into the corridor. Alisa was slumped on her side, in the recovery position. "Concussion," he said. "We can't leave her here."

We picked up Alisa and made for the stairs, gunfire close and to our left. "Carl?" I hollered.

Dmitri poked his head around the corner, his face shiny with sweat and blood. "I think Carl's dead."

"Dudko?" I said, shaking my head.

"The Devil looks after his own," said Dudko, striding into the hall and festooned with weapons and ammunition. He was reloading a rifle and grinning, "I must have taken at least five of those dirty bastards."

"We barricaded the corridor leading to the office," Dmitri added, "but after they shot Carl they threw fire bombs. They've retreated for now, but we can't get to Sergei."

"The doors are all fireproof, right?" said Andy.

"Sure," Dmitri replied, "but they can get to him from the other side of the house. If we go down that corridor we're exposed to more incendiaries. The bastards are waiting in the snow for us to try and get down there."

Alisa stirred, a trickle of blood rolling from her nose. "Where's Belov?"

"He's in the panic room, at the centre of the house," I said. "He's fine for now."

"Hey," said Dmitri, "my phone is ringing." He pulled the handset from a pocket on his body armour. "It's Pieter." The big Russian stabbed the speakerphone button so we could all hear.

"Dmitri," said Van Basten's voice, tinny and faint, "give us Sergei then you can all leave. He's the only one we want. There's been too much death tonight."

"Fuck you, you ungrateful piece of shit," Dmitri bawled, "I'm coming for you. I'm gonna pull your head out through your arsehole."

"So, you're on my side now?" smiled Ruslan Dudko, "maybe I get to finish this job after all."

"You don't understand, Dmitri," said Van Basten, his voice quiet but steady. "Sergei isn't the man you think he is. He is a betrayer."

"Pieter, its Cal Winter," I said into the phone, "what are you talking about?"

"Ah, the hired help," he scoffed. "I doubt it matters to you. I would simply ask that Dmitri meets hears me out. Belov isn't the man Dmitri thinks he serves."

"Tell Fyodor Volk we know he's out there," Alisa snapped. "We're coming for him. Did you know he works for Russia too, Van Basten? That he's FSB?"

"Fyodor has worked for many people," said Van Basten, "but not now. Come for him and you will die, like the others before you. This is his message to you, Colonel Turov."

The SVR officer winced, blood trickling from her nose. "Tell him I'm flattered. I'll bear it in mind when I've got him by the balls."

"Then you've made your choice," said Van Basten, *necessity brings him here, not pleasure.*" He ended the call.

"Don't tell me," I said, "Dante?"

Ruslan Dudko raised an eyebrow. "Canto XII, right?"

I swung around to face the FSB officer. "How d'you know that?"

"Hey, calm down. Anybody who went to the FSB Psych Warfare School at Makhachkala would have known it. The Commandant was Russia's biggest Dante freak. Every fucking lecture and every meal he'd read quotes – he said it was the ultimate treatise on treachery, that we should all learn it's lessons." Makhachkala – the FSB special warfare school where Fyodor Volk graduated as the star recruit.

"What did you study there?" Alisa asked.

"Apart from Dante?" he laughed, "I was a student on the special military services course, Covert Overseas Action Programme. Twelve months of my life I'll never get back. The Commandant could kiss my hairy arse."

Alisa shrugged. "That's one mystery solved."

"Okay, let's get our arses in gear," I said. "Alisa, Dudko and Dmitri; stay here and run defence. Andy and me will fetch Sergei. We RV back here. Any questions?"

"What's your phone number, Angel?" said Dudko, winking at Alisa.

"I'll tell you when hell freezes over," she sneered.

"I wouldn't speak too soon sweetheart," Dmitri grinned, "it's snowing even harder out there, it's just like home." From along the corridor came more noise – banging and crashing and shouting.

I left the Russians readying weapons and bickering. Andy picked up fresh ammunition and joined me at the front door. It was dark at the front of the house, with no fires. We followed the building line back towards Sir Evan's office, which was at the narrowest part of the mansion house, in the middle of the complex. The snow was knee deep, the powder sucking at my boots. Frozen moisture pierced every exposed part of my clothing. I saw movement in the trees flanking the drive. I lay down, AK ready. Andy, behind me, mirrored my movement. His weapon barked. "One down" he said, "get ready to move."

It took us five minutes to wade through the snow. The window to the office was made of armour plated glass, the anti-blast blinds lowered. I knocked on the window with my balled fist. "It's Winter," I yelled.

"There's no time Cal, let me blow the fucker." Andy pulled a strip of

PE4 plastic explosive from a pouch, moulding it like kid's modelling clay into strips. He ran them along the window frame and stuck a detonator cap into the end. "Leg it!" he grinned.

We waded through the snow and threw ourselves to the ground. The explosion was muffled, absorbed by the heavy brickwork and armoured glass. But the window was beginning to hang crazily out of its frame. Using our rifle butts we smashed at the armoured glass until it slid out, twisted and fractured from the explosion. "Sergei, its Cal," I yelled.

There was no reply from the darkened room.

I hopped up onto the windowsill and aimed my torch inside. The room was wrecked, dotted with smashed furniture. Melissa's body lay by the smouldering fireplace, bullet wounds running across her chest, hair was bloodied and singed. She looked like a broken doll. Andy covered me as I dropped down into the shattered room. "Sergei?" I called softly.

"Here," came a quiet voice from the corner of the room, by an upturned desk. I pulled the desk to one side. Sergei, face bloodied, was rolled into a ball. A rifle lay next to him. He smelt of smoke, blood and booze, his trousers stained where he'd soiled himself. "I've been a bad person," he jabbered, "a real bastard. But I swear, I don't deserve this."

"What happened?" I said softly, pulling his arm free.

Andy prowled into the room and checked the doorway. He signalled that it was clear and checked Melissa's body. He shook his head. "Poor cow."

"They got inside somehow, they broke down the door with sledgehammers," said Sergei, squinting as I switched on a table lamp. "I opened fire and hid behind the desk. Evan fired too, but he hit Melissa by mistake I think."

"Stay there," I said, stepping carefully towards the doorway. The corridor was pockmarked with bullet holes, the bodies of Volk's followers littering the place. The British bodyguard, Carl, was sprawled near the doorway riddled with bullets, head bashed in.

Sergei crawled towards me, "Carl saved our lives. When they came and took Evan, Carl appeared and shot many of them. They gave up looking for me and retreated, his attack was so determined."

"We thought he'd died earlier," I said, pointing at Carl's body.

Andy shrugged, "fog of war."

"They've got Sir Evan?" I said.

Sergei nodded. "Yes, I think they thought it was me. It was dark, very confusing."

Andy found a fire extinguisher and was putting out small blazes. "Cal, they've gone," he said. That's how battles end, not with trumpets and flags and victory, but with the slow realisation that the enemy fire has stopped, that you're alive.

And that's good enough.

Grabbing Sergei's arm I pulled him to his feet, the big man suddenly small, "Andy, get on the radio and call Dmitri's team forward."

Moments later we were all in the office. We covered Melissa's body with a curtain. Sergei, Dudko and Dmitri shook hands and drank vodka from chipped crystal glasses. "Ah, the FSB bastard," Sergei grunted, a sliver of his old arrogance returning. "Fuck you and your cock-sucking masters."

"Belov? You traitorous fucking parasite," said Ruslan Dudko, slapping Sergei on the back. "If you were my mark, you'd be roasting in hell by now."

"Who cares?" said Dmitri, "we are Russians in a strange land. That's all that matters. Fucking hell, with those savages outside I know what the Romans must have felt like."

I sat down and took my helmet off. Andy passed me a bottle of water, which I sipped then splashed on my face to wash off the smoke and blood, some of it my own.

"This is incredible" said Sergei, "who were those madmen?"

"Volk's followers, men he has groomed and manipulated," Alisa replied matter-of-factly.

The Oligarch poured more vodka, his eyes bloodshot. "Impossible."

Alisa looked out of the broken window and shrugged, snow drifting into the room. "Really? Tell that to the followers of *Aum Shinrikyo* who attacked the Tokyo subway with Sarin gas because their leader ordered them to. Seventy-four members of the Branch Davidian at Waco burned to death rather than abandon David Koresh. Charles Manson persuaded people to murder for a crazy ideology he based on the lyrics of a Beatles song."

"I take your point," said Sergei. "I suppose."

"He is like Rasputin," said Dudko glumly, "but we'll need more than pistols and poisoned cake to kill this one I think."

I pulled my jacket around me and zipped it up as far as it would go. I fastened my helmet and bombed-up a fresh magazine for my Kalashnikov. "Then let's go and do it," I said. "That's what I was paid to do."

"What do you mean?" said Dmitri, poking the embers of the fire.

"We counter-attack," I replied, "at their camp, when they least expect it. I'm not leaving Evan Sands at the mercy of those maniacs."

"I'm with you," said Alisa. "We find Volk and Van Basten and end this."

"Roger that," Andy nodded, his smile grim. "I'm out of grenades and plastic explosive. Lots of ammo, though."

Dudko stepped forward, the powerfully-built FSB commando picking up abandoned weapons and slinging them across his back. "We have laid down supplies in the woods. There's an RPG, light machinegun and explosives hidden out there."

"Dmitri," I said, "you are Sergei's bodyguard. Stay with him, find somewhere safe and wait."

"Thank you," said Sergei, "but what about the police?"

"Look at this weather. There'll be no police for hours, but there's no way we can clean this one up. My organisation will come up with a plan to divert the blame." I wished I was as confident as I sounded. Harry had got me out of scrapes before, but nothing like this. And I'd be flying out to the decompression facility – tidying this shit up was work for politicians, spooks and lawyers, not shooters.

"Come on Sergei Nikolayevich," said Dmitri, shouldering his rifle. "We will find somewhere safe until this thing is done." He led the shambling Belov out of the room, the oligarch hugging a bottle of vodka like a comfort blanket.

"Let's do this," said Dudko, "and please tell me I'm allowed to kill that bastard Van Basten and complete my mission."

"Not unless I get to him first," I said.

We strode through the shattered house. As they left, the savage followers of Fyodor Volk had left their mark: crazy graffiti, human shit, carnage and corpses. Lots of corpses. Spent cartridges and glass crunched under my booted feet as the cold wind whipped through broken windows. We stepped into the garden, weapons ready.

"Colonel Turov, can you think of a good Dante quote for this?" said Dudko.

Alisa grinned. "Not right now, but I remember a bumper sticker I saw in Texas once. *Kill 'em all, let God sort 'em out.*"

"Now you're speaking my language, sister," laughed the FSB commando. And with that, we hefted our weapons and headed into the woods.

TWENTY FIVE

I called a halt when we reached the tree line. The others took cover, weapons covering all arcs. My phone gently buzzed in my pocket – Harry. He wasn't pleased about a demolished country house and thirty dead bodies, but then again who would be? "This is going to have to go down as some sort of full-moon lunacy by these New-Age traveller types," he grumbled.

"I'm sure the tabloids will buy into it by the time you've cast some of your dirty magic over the situation," I said. I peered out into the woods, the black shapes of the trees broken up by drifts of dirty snow. Boot prints marked the ground where our attackers had been, along with blood trails and the occasional abandoned weapon.

"You sound like shit," said Harry.

"I've been stabbed, blown up and haven't slept for thirty-six hours," I said. "Apart from that? Everything is peachy."

"Personal problem, Winter. So Van Basten's on the other side?"

"Looks like it. What do you want me to do about him?"

I could hear Harry sipping a drink, an ice cube clinking in a tumbler. "As long as that FSB file is located and Belov lives, then what happens to Van Basten is neither here nor there. He's also a witness. Do you understand?"

"Yes," I said. "I understand."

"Good. Stay in touch. Do the job, get Belov to wire the funds upon completion then make your way to the RV. You're off for a holiday."

"Roger," I said, almost grateful that the handler sounded like he had a grip of things.

Dudko led us to his hide, some hundred metres into the tree line.

His kit was stuffed into a shallow, snow-topped hole, a kitbag containing grenades, explosives and an RPG launcher. The commando also pulled out a light machinegun, a compact RPK74M. He loaded it and slung it across his chest. We left the hide, switched to NVGs and crept deeper into the woods, the world turning green and grey. Andy took point, off the path but parallel to it, leading us like goggle-eyed snowmen crunching through the icy forest. It took us a paranoid hour of creeping about to make the clearing where the New Age traveller camp was meant to be. Above us the night was slowly turning from black to blue as dawn drew near.

Andy stopped, dropped to his knee and signalled for us to halt. I joined him and crouched in the snow, squinting into my night optics. I could make out dark shapes – tents – pitched next to a cluster of knackered-out vehicles and caravans. In the distance I could make out a dim light. There were no other heat sources I could see.

I crawled towards the light. There was no noise except for the wind and trees creaking under their covering of snow. Ahead of me was a black-painted removal van converted into a mobile home. White graffiti was daubed along the side, crude cartoons of skeletons and ghosts and anti-Capitalist slogans. From a side door in the vehicle I saw a thin slice of yellow light. I whispered into my throat mic, "Andy, cover the removal van. I'm going forward." He keyed the squelch button on his radio in acknowledgement. The door to the van was held in place with a loop of wire over a bolt screwed into the chassis, an open padlock dangling from it. I clicked my pencil torch on and ran it up the length of the door, looking for tripwires.

From inside I a creaking noise.

Slipping the wire from the bolt, I let the door swing open. I aimed my rifle into the vehicle, my thumb sliding onto the fire selector. I put my weight on my booted foot as I stepped up, into the belly of the big black van. The interior of the vehicle was empty apart from a couple of mattresses, sleeping bags and camping junk. It smelt like the residents – stale booze, unwashed bodies and marijuana. Sitting in the middle, under a naked bulb, was Sir Evan Sands. He was lashed to a folding chair with gardening twine, a cheap sports bag dumped at his feet. His face was bruised, blood seeping from his nose and a deep gash on his forehead. A filthy rag had been stuffed into his mouth and duct-taped in place. The millionaire businessman stared at me, then at the bag. He grunted. His eyes were wide with fear, his blood-matted hair sticking out at crazy angles. "Sir Evan is here, secure the area around the vehicle," I whispered into my mic. I put my finger to my lips and loosened the gag. "Quiet, Sir Evan."

"They've gone," he whispered. "Get out of here now, before it's too late. Call the bloody police."

"Why?"

"There's a bomb in that bag in front of me. One of them explained how it worked while he was wiring it up, laughing like a lunatic. There's a pressure pad under me, like a plastic cushion. If I get up then the bomb explodes, that's what the bastard said."

Switching my radio off to avoid setting off any radio-sensitive detonator, I got on my knees and switched on my torch. A snake of neatly bundled electrical wires ran from the sports bag up along the chair leg, into a small hole bored into the seat. The bag was zipped up. "Why?" I said, "did they say anything about the device?"

"It's to create a delay, to allow them to escape," he said, breathing ragged in the freezing van. "They were furious when they realised I wasn't Sergei. Pieter came to see me, said he was sorry, but that I'd chosen sides when I went into business with Sergei. To be honest I think Pieter was on an acid trip or something."

"Did you see the Russian guy in charge?" I said, checking the rest of the chair, "his name is Fyodor Volk."

"No," said Sir Evan, "but Pieter spoke about him. He said that he'd been rescued by a kindred spirit or some-such bollocks."

"Wait here," I said. "We're not leaving without you." I went outside and found Andy and told him what I'd found.

"I'll take a look," he said, shaking his head. "I might be able to sort it."

Alisa joined us, gesturing at the removal van. "And Volk?"

"We deal with Volk after we rescue the poor bastard they wired to an IED," I said firmly. "Understand?"

"Sure, but they could still be out there."

"Take Dudko. Search the rest of the camp," I replied, "get clear of here anyway, in case that bomb goes off."

"Thanks for the vote of confidence," said Andy. "It's all good, trust Uncle Andrew."

I slapped him on the back, "are you trained in bomb disposal?"

"Can you make an omelette Cal?"

"Yes"

"Did you go to catering college?"

"No"

"Well fuck off then," he grinned. He took off his day-sack and rummaged around, pulling out a black tool bag. He picked up a head torch and, removing his helmet, strapped it to his forehead. "I know," he sighed, "these things make you look like a prick."

Alisa laughed and kissed Andy on the mouth, clasping the back of his head with her injured hand. "Good luck," she said quietly.

"I should offer to defuse bombs more often," he joked.

I didn't get a kiss.

Dudko joined Turov. I saw them pad towards the tents, weapons ready. Inside the van Evan Sands was shivering in his chair. "I'm trying not to move," he said.

Andy crouched down and examined the bag and wiring, "OK, try to relax. If it's a pressure pad on a chair like that, I reckon it'll need significant movement to set it off. Let's have a look." His voice had the detached interest of a plumber looking at a blocked sink. He got on his belly as I shone his Maglite at the wiring running up the chair. "Did the guy who wired you up to this say anything else?"

"I can't remember much, I was too busy trying not to piss myself," said Sands, "he said something about the pressure pad on my seat and that the bomb was a 'clever one.' He took a long time fixing that wire up the chair leg. He said he learnt about bombs in the army, in Iraq."

"Funny that, so did I," said Andy. "So the this device has some sort of anti-tamper mechanism." He stared up at the bottom of the chair. He peered into the bag and carefully unzipped it a few inches, "yep, that's at least three kilos of P4. They've thoughtfully surrounded it with nuts, bolts and nails."

"Am I going to die?" said Sands matter-of-factly.

"Well, not if I can help it seeing as I'm lying next to you," Andy smiled. "Cal, you might as well leg it mate. Just leave the torch there."

"No, I'll stay in case you need my help."

Andy rolled onto his back, wriggling gently away from the bag full of explosives. "When you tell me what to do I get on with it, don't I? Now I'm telling you – fuck off. I don't like being watched while I work, it's like you're spying on me while I'm taking a dump."

"I'll hold that thought. OK, see you when you're done. Sir Evan, you're in good hands."

The businessman attempted to smile, face sickly-grey, "I'm sure I am, Mister Winter."

I left the caravan and jogged over to the trees. The snow had stopped, the wind skimming the top of white hillocks where it had drifted against the tents and vehicles. I joined Dudko and Alisa, who were crouched by one of the vehicles, an old ice cream van. "There are tracks leading south," said Dudko, sniffing the wind.

I rubbed my face, trying to knead warmth into it, "that leads to the army training area."

"Maybe they have vehicles there," said Turov. "We should check."

"I agree…" said Dudko.

The explosion ripped through the camp. A dull thump, then a flash of white light rippling across the clearing. We fell into the snow, the twisted carcass of the removal van blazing at the edge of camp. Smoke billowed from the wreckage, stinking of chemicals and charred meat. Alisa gripped my shoulder.

"Even in this weather I think that would be heard," said Dudko.

"Cal, Move," said Alisa, pushing me towards the clearing.

I said nothing, tucking my rifle into my shoulder as I stumbled forward. As we passed I saw body parts in the snow, soggy meaty things that used to be my friend. I felt something at the back of my head, my old demon. It came to taunt me, a coldness worse than any winter, gripping what was left of my soul. It gloated at my failure, my inability to protect my friends.

"What's that?" said Dudko, machinegun shouldered. "Do you hear it?"

We all stopped and listened to the sound being carried on the wind, through the trees.

It was laughing.

"We should go back to the house," said Dudko, machinegun aimed towards the camp. I tried to focus on him, my eyes glazing over as hot tears stung my cheeks.

"Cal," said Alisa. "You must move."

That was when I retched and emptied my guts, acidic puke burning a hole in the snow. The demon sat on my shoulder, whispering allegations as I pounded my fists on the ground. I hadn't taken my medication since I'd left my flat. It's easy to forget. I fumbled for my rifle, wailing as I looked at what was left of Andy. His booted foot was to my left, a blood-glistening chunk of his torso to my right. Apparently you can get used to friends, people you were drinking tea and joking with five seconds before, being reduced to meat in wartime.

I never could, and wouldn't want to either.

And in my mind I was in Maysan. I heard Clarkie's voice and the screaming after-burners of jets. I knew it wasn't real, but it was. Normally this happened at three in the morning, when I could drink half a bottle of Scotch, or snort a fat line of gack. "Leave me," I sobbed. I wanted to die. The laughter from the woods rang in my ears, swirling into my brain like sweet poison. Death would be a merciful release. No Firm. No guilt. No failure.

Dudko's machinegun barked, yellow flame spewing from the muzzle. Alisa began dragging me away, wiry arms straining under the dead weight of my body, armour and weapons. "You'll be OK, baby," she gasped into my ear in Russian, breath hot. She mashed her lips against the side of my head. "Come on, Cal, you're gonna be OK."

That's what medics are trained to say, when they know you're going to die. I tried to feel my feet, lead weights at the end of my legs. My heart was racing as I shook, freezing sweat bathing my carcass. I hadn't had a panic attack like this, a breakdown, for two years. You look down on your crazy self, lucid but detached as a CCTV camera as you freak out. Meanwhile the men in white prepare the syringe. "Alisa," I groaned, "Go. I'm fucked."

The SVR officer gripped me under the arms as she dragged me towards the trees, wincing as she flexed her mangled hand. "Screw you, Cal Winter," she panted. Bullets whipped at the snow around us.

I looked over my shoulder. Dudko had fallen. His eyes popped open and closed as he scrabbled in the bloody snow. His face turned towards me as he tried to point into the trees.

"Alisa?" I said. Then a blunt, crushing pain at the side of my head. Above me, dark shapes shimmered in my peripheral vision as heavy boots stomped on my face. And still, the laughing and giggling like a pack of hyenas.

Then, mercifully, the pain was gone.

TWENTY SIX

I don't know how long I dreamt. I had familiar flashbacks – Colonel Petrovych sitting in my shrapnel-scarred Land Rover, Clarkie's lifeless body gripping the steering wheel as he tried to drive towards Amara. I dreamt of Sergei performing a slow waltz with Melissa's bullet-riddled body, her gown trailing blood across a polished marble floor, slack-jawed face trembling as they swayed to the music. Peter and the Wolf. I had a picnic with Sam and the kids in Whitstable, looking over the sea on a summer's day. We laughed as we watched Brigadier Justin Powell's corpse bobbing in the sea. His head was blown into chunks, which I found especially funny. I saw a boiling, golden mushroom cloud over the nuclear reactor at Shakuvo. Children's flesh melted from their bones in a cloud of radioactive gas, others hobbling under hideous deformities. Men in gas masks, armed with flamethrowers, cleansed the city of its suffering.

Also watching my dreams, like a friend at the cinema, was a Demon. He was a friendly Demon, who understood all the bad things I'd done. He sympathised knowingly with my excuses and self-justification. He asked lots of questions. If it wasn't for his appearance I would have thought him an angel. He told me of his sins, and how the worst of them all was Treachery. I agreed, and felt warm and happy, like a kid on his birthday. I was thirsty and hungry, but the Demon told me that food and drink would be bad for me right now, because I was ill.

I believed him and I slept. When I awoke my head was woozy, my mouth dry and tasting of chemicals and bile. The Demon wore black, a neatly pressed boiler suit, gloves and close-fitting mask. Now I was shivering but hot, staked out in the desert. I could feel my brain pulse, waves of vivid colour splashing across my eyes. I tried to stare at my arm, catching sight of the IV tubes plugged into the veins. I wondered where I was and how long I'd been there, but couldn't make the words in my mouth.

"So you killed your best friend?" said the Demon. His voice was like a musical instrument, his accent difficult to place. "During the Iraq war."

"I blame myself for his death, yes," I said, feeling like I was sobering up. "Sergeant Clarke. Clarkie."

"He died when you panicked, called in an American bomber. Correct?"

"How d'you know that?"

The Demon cocked his head, "you told me. You told me a great deal. I like talking to you, Captain Winter. I think we shall be friends. And you killed your other friend, in the bomb near Croll House, didn't you?"

"No," I said. My voice was stereophonic, crashing waves of noise inside my head, "the person who set the IED killed Andy, not me."

The Demon stepped closer. "Perhaps, but Sands deserved to die. My people loathe his ilk, killing him was my gift to them. You made the decision to interfere but didn't have the skills to disarm the bomb. So you sent your friend, who thought he did. We all have to send others to do our dirty work sometimes, don't we?"

I felt a surge of anger at the masked Demon, tried to clench my fists but couldn't feel my hands, "fuck you."

"And now you look after Clarkie's family. How kind. Samantha, this is the widow's name isn't it? Samantha Clarke." He rolled the name around in his mouth, "I could... *find* her."

"Careful" I growled, "because I've never met anything that couldn't be killed."

The Demon walked towards me. I realised that I lay on some sort of table, the desert turning from orange to yellow to green as I tried to focus. He stroked my hair with neoprene-gloved fingers, his voice a whisper. "Anger's unhelpful, Captain Winter. There's a pattern developing here, isn't there? You kill your friends because you lack the qualities required of an effective leader. It's a form of treachery, and you know how I feel about that. Then you turn to anger. You told me about your fear of failure earlier. Do you remember?"

"No, I don't. What are those tubes in my arm for?"

"The tubes are for your medicine. I'm healing you. You have injuries, mainly in your subconscious, but also facial injuries from where my friends stamped on your head. You're lucky, they were about to kill you but I stopped them. You have a broken cheekbone, I think."

"So you're a shrink too?" I tried to turn my head. I became aware of a dull pain in my neck.

"Of a sort," the Demon chuckled, "I was trained in psychiatry at one point. I think it a bogus discipline, personally, but elements of the technique are useful. I prefer chemistry myself, like the medicine I am giving you now. It is more effective than the counselling I'm sure you've had, or the pathetically weak antidepressants you were probably prescribed."

"What's the medicine?"

The Demon shrugged, "a mixture of barbiturates – sodium pentothal if you wish to be precise, something wonderful called SP-117 which I doubt you've ever heard of, a little LSD and some other substances I like to use as part of the healing process. Oh, and heroin. I know you like it. What's not to like about heroin?"

"Why do you want to heal me?" I said, "when you could just kill me?"

"You have useful information. When you are well and you have told me what I wish to know, I will let you go on your way. We are professionals whose paths have crossed in unfortunate circumstances. Nothing more and nothing less."

I laughed, the sound booming like cannon fire in my head. "I don't believe you."

"You are the one who betrays his friends and sends them to die, not I. My friends enjoy my bounty, promises of comfort and justice and revenge."

"I thought I'd told you everything," I said.

"No, not everything Captain Winter," the Demon sighed. "The substances I've given you aren't fool-proof. They're wearing off right now, if I give you more you might go into a coma and never recover. And there's still more for us to discuss."

The colours began to fade, the desert slowly morphing into darkness, "what do you want to know?"

"I require information on Sergei Belov. Everything you know about him. His relationship with your Government? What he told you about Pieter Van Basten? The risk to Pieter from FSB? Where Belov is likely to flee next?"

"Why?" I said. A dull ache gnawed at the back of my head. My vision started to blur then focus, the room getting darker and colder.

"There are many reasons – self-preservation. Revenge. But primarily Love. A powerful trinity, I hope you agree. The circumstances under which I've led my life so far has precluded love, but now I have experienced it, I realise that there is nothing I will not do to feed it. And it needs to be fed. It is insatiable. Does that make any sense?"

"Can I have something to drink?" I said, trying to sit up. Then I realised that I was strapped to a hospital gurney, rough leather straps around my ankles and wrists. Someone had stripped me naked and dressed me in a surgical gown. My feet were freezing. I tried to focus on the rest of the room, but my eyes were drawn to the face in the tight black mask. Behind the eye-slits emerald-green eyes stared at me.

"Of course. Have some coffee. I am going to release your left hand, if you try to move I will have to kill you." The black-clothed figure undid the strap on my wrist and passed me a chipped mug.

I drank gratefully, noting the pistol in his hand. "I thought you were a demon, in my dream."

The voice was gentle and calm. "Yes, part of your hallucinations. I did nothing to disabuse you of it. You exited the Seventh Circle and entered the Eighth."

I gulped the hot coffee, warm liquid running down my chin. My face ached, a sharp pain in my teeth and jaw. "You are Fyodor Volk," I said, "and in Dante the Seventh Circle is Violence? The Eighth is Fraud."

"You are correct on all counts, and Sergei Belov is a fraud *and* a betrayer. Pieter told me that you and the SVR woman figured out my identity. This intrigues me. I am flattered that anybody remembers my antics, I thought I was a relic of a time when things were done… *differently*."

"The Commandant at the FSB school at Makhachkala was an aficio-nado of Dante," I said.

"Indeed he was," said Volk. "You see? What an intriguing footnote. How did you know that?"

"One of the FSB men, the man you tried to crucify, told me."

"Ah, so he went to the school too? Yes, I remember the knuckle-dragging morons of the *Spetzgruppa* trying to learn the art. Rescuing him was audacious and amusing, but pointless. My people bashed his head into a paste with their rifle butts when we captured you."

"He was brave."

"Perhaps he was. *The Inferno* has many lessons. Perhaps the best lesson I learnt at that place."

My eyes began to focus. I was in a dimly-lit hospital operating theatre. It was dirty, with mildewed walls, trash littering the floor. I looked at the radiators and plug sockets, which were of the sort you get in Britain. I was still in the UK. In the background I heard the chug of a solitary vehicle engine. "Colonel Turov knows of you. She thought you were working for the FSB."

"The FSB?" said Volk lightly. "We parted amicably, but they couldn't keep up with me, or my… techniques. Their tame psychiatrist deemed me insane, you see. Such a diagnosis is just an opinion which I took exception to, naturally. I still work for the FSB occasionally, if the mark suits my purpose and their fee is generous enough. I am their creation, after all."

"Can I ask a question?" I said.

"Of course, I am an open book. But then you will answer *my* questions, as a simple courtesy."

"What do you mean when you say this is all because of love? And how did you do it, get those people to fight for you?"

He laughed as he pulled off the mask, running a gloved hand through thick, raven-black hair. "That is two questions, Captain Winter." Fyodor Volk was beautiful. I was man enough to admit it. His face was like one of those tortured, alabaster angels from a Michelangelo. He smiled, green eyes burning into mine, "Love? I am in love with Pieter, of course."

"How did that happen?"

"We met in South Africa, when I was between operations. He'd heard rumours about me from his research, from leaked documents and the like.

Pieter is a genius, a natural detective if you will. He hired me to kill Sergei Belov, but we fell in love. This is why he has never leaked the truth about me. Later on, when a whistle-blower from the FSB leaked the file to Pieter I found out more about The Betrayer, Belov. It is something that justifies any action to destroy him."

"So Pieter gets to choose who gets exposed on his website and who doesn't? He's the judge?"

"Yes," Volk smiled, pleased with the simplicity of his answer. "Information is a weapon, you must realise that. It has taken me time to persuade Pieter of this, but now he accepts the truth. It's no different than a rifle or a knife – you use it against your enemy. Governments once had that monopoly, now they don't. I'm going to use that data to topple governments, create chaos. Information is a viral weapon, unstoppable once unleashed."

At least it confirmed who the leak in Sergei's camp was. "What about those crazy bastards fighting for you?"

Fyodor Volk gently slid the IV out of my arm, carefully dabbing at the bloody puncture marks with a piece of cotton wool. "I have simply shown them how to achieve what they always wanted – inchoate anger became something else. Some of them are simply human detritus, consumed by anger and hatred. Those are the veterans of your ridiculous wars. Some are political nihilists, sick of your society and its pointless obsession with wealth and celebrity. And some simply adore violence, they are always the easiest to turn. I have spent two years showing them the way. My techniques are very persuasive, but they are predicated on getting people to do things they already desire, unlocking inhibition."

"You'll get caught."

"No, I won't," he laughed, and I think he was genuinely amused by the remark. "Your excellent Scotland Yard experts will discover a fully-formed and plausible domestic terror group, the quintessence of political frustration with your system. I have seeded the evidence from day one, and your country now hates the rich in a way that puts twentieth century Russia to shame. Their targets? Shameless bordello capitalists like Belov and Sands. I am not linked to it. The mysterious Svengali they speak of, their leader, will be assumed to be one of the dead."

"Sounds too good to be true," I slurred, a wave of nausea washing over me.

Volk shrugged, face pale in the gloom. "It worked when I manipulated the Chechen mujahedeen into bombing the Moscow metro. It was successful when I persuaded a dozen homeless kids in Odessa that I was a vampire – I directed them to murder a government minister and drink his blood. In America I set up an extreme Evangelical sect that went on to bomb the Israeli consulate. My *piece de resistance* was the Nazi suicide bomber, the one that blew up the mosque in Amsterdam? So I would appreciate if you didn't lecture me on the feasibility of my operations. Captain Winter, you are an agreeable brute, but still a drooling primate staring at something of which you have no understanding."

There was a tap on the frosted-glass door. "Wait," said Volk impatiently. He fastened the strap on my wrist.

"The Russian, she's fitting again," said a young woman's voice. "she's choking."

"I'll be there in a moment," he called, picking up a leather bag. "Colonel Turov is struggling to tolerate her medicine, poor girl. She'll probably end up as a cabbage after the treatment. She is very stubborn, letting her SVR training trump common sense."

"You know, I think the FSB shrink was right, you are insane."

Volk's smile was serene. "You are probably correct, but I am quietly confident that love will cure me. But I cannot love fully until Pieter is free of Sergei Belov. On this point Pieter is very certain."

"And I thought I was nuts," I said quietly, as Volk glided out of the room.

TWENTY SEVEN

I managed to sit up. My head was groggy and my body covered in welts and bruises. I could hardly feel my face. I'd had some brutal comedowns from LSD in my bad old days, but this was something else. I tested the leather straps on the gurney, flexing my aching body and limbs. It creaked but I was held fast, except for some give in the strap holding my left ankle. I wriggled it, the leather bond straining on its rickety metal buckle.

And Alisa was nearby. She was alive.

"Stay still," said a voice. It was a scruffy, hard-faced young woman in her twenties. She wore a black field jacket over stained denim dungarees, feet stuffed into mud-caked boots. Slung over her shoulder was one of our suppressed Heckler-Koch submachineguns.

"I'm sorry" I coughed, "my leg hurts."

"You're lucky to be alive," she spat. Her accent was middle-class, English. Her eyes were painted with kohl, spots of blood on her cheek. "I'd have killed you already if it were down to me."

"That might be why you're not in charge, love," I replied. I tried not to sneer, but I think I failed.

"You're the mercenary?" she said walking towards me, "the hired thug. Not so hard now, are you? I suppose killing civilians in Iraq for the Americans was easier than this."

"You haven't got a clue, have you?"

"I've seen the truth," she replied, "watched the videos online, read the reports." The girl punched me, her fist dislodging a tooth in my battered jaw. I shouted out in pain and arched my back, my left foot straining against the strap. I felt the buckle give slightly. I spat out the tooth, a trail of mauve gloop dribbling onto my dirty hospital gown. "Aren't you meant to guard me, so I can't escape?" I snorted "so why not just shut the fuck up and do that?"

The girl's pale lips curled into a smile, eyes gleaming with hate, "I saw you in the woods, crying like a baby. I laughed when your fascist friend and the millionaire blew up. I laughed when I stamped on your head. I'm going to laugh when we cut you from throat to groin and watch you bleed to death."

"Try it, bitch," I laughed, my body coursing with adrenaline and drugs. "I bet you're from Surrey. I bet your dad's a stock-broker and bought you a pony. I bet you've never had an opinion you couldn't-fucking-afford."

"Really? I think I'll start now," she whispered, eyes wide. She pulled a black-bladed knife from her belt. Unslinging the MP5, she put it on the table behind her. Big mistake.

"Come on then," I goaded. "As for the 'fascist' you laughed at when the bomb went off? His name was Andrew Wright. He was born in a Manchester slum, voted Labour and read the Daily Mirror. He was a soldier. He served his country with distinction in a way you could never begin to understand. Sir Evan Sands? He gave ten million quid to charity last year. Seriously, fuck off, you bat-shit crazy witch."

She pushed the tip of the knife into my neck, drawing blood. She smelt of joss-sticks, booze and stale sweat as she got closer, her matted hair tickling my face. "I'm going to cut you," she hissed. Her smile was cold as she walked slowly towards the end of the gurney, the tip of the blade screeching along the surface. She held the knife loosely in one hand while the other lifted my robe. I was naked underneath. The girl sneered as she lifted the robe, "if I can find it, I'll cut it."

Wrenching my foot free of the strap, I kicked her in the head with all the force I could muster. I twisted my bulk on the gurney, flipping it over and onto the tiled floor. The bottom end of the metal table hit her ankle, making her shriek with pain. She scrambled for the knife.

Writhing like I was electrocuted, I lashed out again my foot. The strap securing my other ankle came undone, allowing me to wrap my legs around the girl's neck, pushing myself down the steel table and yanking my arms to weaken the bonds around my wrists. Grunting, she wriggled free, ramming her elbow into my groin, narrowly missing my balls. I howled in pain, doubling up, the force snapping my left hand free from the ageing leather strap. I pivoted, grunting as I punched her in the side of the head. She fell into me, making an obscene embrace, snarling as she scratched my cheeks. Her knee jabbed at my genitals, but I was too numbed by drugs and hate to care.

We wrestled and fought. It was my bulk and rage pitted against her fitness and speed. She slipped on the blood-stained tiles, her forehead connecting with my bruised nose, sharp spikes of pain filling my head. With my free hand I pushed her face to one side and sank my teeth into her neck, biting as hard as I could. She tried to pull away, hands clawing at my face, but I bit harder until my canines met, warm salty blood. I pushed her head towards my jaws, shaking like a dog to make the wound bigger. She shook, screeching in agony. "No" she groaned, "please."

But it was too late. She'd rolled the dice. Released the thing inside. I opened my mouth and bit again, my free hand sliding across the floor until I felt the knife. Grasping it, I pushed it into the back of her neck, near the base of her skull. Holding her head in place with my teeth, I sawed the serrated blade back and forth with all the strength I had left, mashing her cerebellum and spinal cord. I watched her eyes roll into her head as she died. Finally, her body limp, she rolled off of me. I was painted red, like a woad-covered savage. I slid the blood-wet knife under the last strap and slit it.

I staggered to my feet, grabbing the MP5 and checking the magazine. The girl had another clip in her pocket, which I picked up but had nowhere to put. I walked barefoot, across the freezing tiles, to the door. In the distance I could hear music, heavy bass thumping and banging. I staggered into a dingy corridor. Yellowing posters warned of the hazards posed by smoking and unprotected sex as I padded to the next set of doors, leaving bloody footprints behind me.

The music got louder, tribal drums and synthesisers bleeping and roaring. I thumbed the fire selector on the MP5 to automatic as I nudged the fire door open with my shoulder. Three men sat around an electric fire, drinking cider from plastic bottles and listening to music. Their weapons were by their feet as I gunned them down with the suppressed carbine, muzzle flash lighting up the room. They clawed at bullet wounds as they crashed to the ground, lifeless bodies staring at me as the music reached a hellish crescendo. Shivering, I found a filthy fleece jacket, which I zipped up as far as it would go. My stomach churned. I vomited, falling to my knees as the poisonous drugs spilled from my guts, black puke splashing onto a corpse.

A door on the other side of the room creaked open. "Winter?" said Pieter Van Basten. He was unarmed, face pale.

I scrambled for the MP5 as he stepped back from the door. I fired, a burst splintering the door and frosted glass windows. Then I heard the 'dead man's click,' the bolt snapping forward as I emptied the weapon. Van Basten darted back around the corner. I dropped the MP5 and grabbed at a pump-action shotgun half-tucked under a dead body. It was an old Remington 870, sawn-off at the stock and barrel. The weapon was coated with blood. I tried to find a clean part of my robe to wipe my hands on, but failed.

The next corridor split left and right. I saw the double-doors to my left still swinging where someone had barged through them. Shotgun pushed in front of me, I jogged bare-foot down the rubber-floored corridor and listened at the door. I heard groaning and whispering, the metallic snap of weapons being readied. Then Volk's voice, calm and measured, "her heart rate is racing."

"Has she told you enough?" said another voice. In the background I heard the crackle of personal radios and the sound of tinny voices over a net, "do we leave her?" said the voice urgently, in English. It wasn't Van Basten.

"No, I have more questions. Go and look after Pieter, can you do that for me?"

"Yes, of course," said the other voice.

"Thank you," Volk replied. "Your kindness is a source of great comfort to me. I will go and deal with the other one."

"Take care, while I get the truck ready."

"Don't worry, go to Pieter and find the others," said Volk, "I have planned for this. Move the woman. I will meet you outside."

I jogged back up the corridor, looking for a window. My feet left bloody footprints behind me as I flipped off the light switch. I found myself in a small ground floor office, the windows covered up with chipboard panelling. Candles flickered on the shelves, a sleeping bag unrolled on the floor next to opened food containers. Lying on a desk was a waxed jacket and a woollen hat. I put them on and began pulling at the board covering the window, my hands scrabbling for a handle or lock. The board slid off of rotting brackets, the handle on the window freezing cold. I opened it, cold air buffeting me as I climbed outside. I knew I would have only minutes before my bare feet would be frostbitten. I followed the building line to the front of the old hospital. A faded sign read:

Royal Army Medical Corps / Queen Alexandra's Royal Army
Nursing Corps
LAVERICK FIELD TRAINING AREA
MILITARY HOSPITAL - KEEP OUT

Other signs declared that the building was unsafe, prepared for demolition and patrolled by service dogs. I knew that Laverick Field, a transit camp, had been closed for at least five years as part of defence cuts. I guessed I was only five miles from Croll House.

Feet numb, I ran barefoot through the snow. At the front of the hospital I heard the sound of a vehicle idling. Parked outside was an old Bedford army truck, suspension jacked up high, tyres shod in heavy-duty snow chains. The engine throbbed and chugged, diesel smoke billowing from the exhaust. The canvass-top was colourfully painted with what looked like Aboriginal patterns and graffiti. A man in dark clothing sat in the cab, the amber light of a cigarette bobbing around in the dark. I crept along the side of the truck and stepped up on the metal foot-plate near the passenger door and knocked on it. As the door swung open, I pointed the sawn-off Remington into the cab and fired. Pulling myself into the blood-warm cab with ice-cold hands, I fell on the dead driver, his head chewed off by the blast of a twelve gauge shell. The inside of the cab behind him was painted dark red with the insides of his skull. The passenger door handle was slick as I opened it, and I pushed the driver's body into the snow.

The engine roared as I revved the accelerator and rumbled along the side of the building, back past where I'd jumped out of the window. The chain-clad tyres crunched as they bit into the deep snow. I fought with the steering wheel as I bellied around the corner, lining up the front of the van with the pebble-dashed wall of the room where I'd heard voices. Hissing and swearing at the pain, I mashed my frozen foot into the accelerator. The engine rattled, rear wheels spinning as I released the clutch, the four-ton truck lurching forwards, ramming the wall. The brickwork collapsed inwards, glass shattering as the cab rumbled from side to side. I gripped the steering wheel, revving the engine, forcing the Bedford onwards. Bricks bashed against the roof of the cab, the chassis shaking as rubble jammed into the axles of the truck. In the headlights I saw figures darting towards the door, dust and snow glittering against the single-bulb lighting the room. Bullets splintered the windscreen as I ducked down behind the dashboard, my gore-stained hands clutching for the sawn-off. My body shook uncontrollably as I huddled in the foot-well, hugging the shotgun. I waited for bullets to hose down the doors, levelling the weapon shakily in front of me.

I heard nothing except the dying engine.

I reached for the ignition and turned it off. The wheezing engine rattled, steam hissing from the shattered radiator. Sliding out of the cab, I took cover behind the door, even now fighting the urge to sleep. In the distance I heard the crunching gears of a heavy vehicle, the throaty chug of a diesel engine.

"They've gone," groaned Alisa Turov.

My eyes focussed in the gloom. The SVR officer was secured to a gurney similar to the one they'd used on me, an identical tangle of tubes plugged into her bare arm. Her blood-spattered hospital robe was torn and dirty. "How do you feel?" I said, slipping the tubes out of her arm.

"What do you think? Like shit. I've never taken LSD before," she wheezed.

"What did you tell them?"

"I'm not sure, Cal," she replied as I undid the straps on the gurney. "The dreams were crazy. I thought he was my brother."

"He's manipulating us," I said.

"Yes, I agree. He told me that they will return to Russia, prepare for another attempt on Belov's life. And in the meantime they will publish all of the FSB material they have online." She rubbed her wrists, which were purple and red. "Volk is obsessed with Sergei Belov."

"Lucky Sergei," I grunted, handing her a blanket, "do you know where Van Basten's server is?"

"I think I might be able to figure that out. But tell me, do you know a woman called Samantha?"

"Yes," I said, "she's a friend, the woman I told you about when we went for dinner that time. The nearest thing I've got to family. Volk threatened her when he spoke with me."

"Yes, he told me that she would be killed, as punishment for our sins. He said that Sergei had hurt his own, that we should feel the same pain. But I don't know how he's going to do that now. I presume this woman lives here in the UK."

I stretched, my fury at Volk's threat bubbling like lava in my head. "Yes, Sam lives in England. But I'm going to kill him first, Alisa. Where will the bastard go?"

She limped over to a chair, her clothes strewn across it. She picked up one of her boots and, sliding her hand into it, pulled out a slim black phone. "This is Fyodor Volk's cell phone," she smiled. "I hope the answer to that question is in here somewhere."

"How did you get it?"

"I picked his pocket when I was captured, when he first threw me into the truck that brought us here. Then I slipped it into my boot when they were too busy murdering Dudko to notice. They never checked my clothes when I was ordered to undress."

"OK, let's go," I said, "our stuff must be here somewhere."

Alisa winced in pain as she pulled on her clothes. I covered the door with the shotgun, wondering if the Bedford would get us as far as the nearest town. "Let's go" she said when she was done. "I must make arrangements with my organisation."

"What arrangements?"

"For our journey to Russia, of course," she said, slapping my back. "Now, let's find your clothes and get out of this dump."

TWENTY EIGHT

I found my stuff dumped next to the ward where I'd been questioned by Volk. There was no sign of my weapons or body armour, but my muddy clothes and boots were there. I patted down the pockets and found my Blackberry. The battery had been taken out and the device smashed. I found my chest-rig in the corner, where I'd tucked away the cheap mobile phone Marcus had given me. It was still there, along with spare magazines and other stuff. Checking that I had a signal, I dialled his number. The MI6 officer answered immediately. "Where are you?"

"We're at Laverick Field training area, near Salisbury Plain." I gave him an update on our capture, and Fyodor Volk's escape.

"How many dead?"

"At least thirty. It's Harry's problem, although Volk's done a pretty good job of making this look like a fucked-up terrorist incident. I'm off abroad for the duration after I've finished."

"I'm glad you understand the importance of completing the operation," Marcus replied. "But Belov is safe?"

"Yeah, well he was when we last saw him. He was with his head of security at Croll House."

"You and Turov need to get out of there."

"No shit. I'm pumped full of drugs, there's three feet of snow outside and we've got a bullet-riddled Bedford lorry for transport. Some help would be appreciated."

"Nothing's flying right now, maybe later today if the weather clears up. Get out of there before the police arrive and lie low. I'll call you in the hour with instructions."

"Make sure you do," I said. "We've got Volk's mobile phone. Alisa stole it."

Marcus's voice brightened. "At last, laddie, a scrap of positive news. I'll see if I can get someone to take a look at it." He rang off.

We limped back to the Bedford, holding each other for support. "Will that truck still work?" said Turov.

"I hope so." In my pockets I found a packet of ibuprofen, which I wolfed down with some snow to help me swallow. I passed the rest to Alisa. We climbed into the truck and teased the engine into life, reversing it out of the building. "This isn't going to get us far," I said. The snowfall was lighter now, the sky a sickly dark grey colour beyond the rotting wire fence of the camp.

"Where is the nearest town?" said Turov.

"About five miles. I've been here before, when I was in the army."

We drove slowly out of the barracks, following the tracks of another heavy vehicle. I guessed it was Volk's. We turned off before the main road, onto a rutted service track than ran through the woods on the edge of the training area. The heavy lorry rumbled from side to side. Turov stuck her head out of the window and puked. We drove for two more miles before the Bedford's engine died. We dropped down from the cab and walked through the snow, due east. The mapping app on my phone told me that we were only a short distance from a road. "I need to speak with Harry" I said, "he's gonna love this."

"We can't stay out here," said Alisa, shivering. The clouds were lighter now, weak sunlight filtering through. Light flurries of snow swirled about our feet. Finally we came to the end of the path, a gentle slope leading to a gate topped with coils of razor-wire. I poked around in the bushes for a few moments, finding a hole where kids had forced their way through, empty cigarette packets and beer cans lying in the snow. We wriggled through, finding ourselves by the main road. The only sign of life was an abandoned car, buried under a snow drift. We walked south for another hour, towards Netheravon, without seeing any traffic. The fat grey clouds thickened again, obliterating the sun.

Finally my telephone rang. "Where are you now?" said Marcus impatiently.

"I'd say we were due north of Netheravon, on the main road."

The MI6 officer thought for a moment, as if he were conjuring the map in his mind. "Carry on walking, but news of your little adventure last night is filtering through. The police are trying to get to Croll House, so get off the main road. They've enlisted the RAF to fly them in. I'm going to get you moved as soon as the weather allows, same pilot as before."

"Where will you take us then?" I said.

"A safe house," he replied. "That's all you need to know."

I held the cheap plastic handset to my frozen ear and laughed, "as long as it's got a bed and hot running water."

On the outskirts of Netheravon we passed a cluster of houses, smoke curling from chimneys. In the distance I could hear children laughing as they played in the snow. By my watch it was ten in the morning, as if it mattered. I could have fallen where I was and slept, in the snow. I knew that I was running the risk of hypothermia. Alisa nudged me, checking my face. "Cal, wake up." She pinched my ear, making me wince.

We carried on. In our filthy and blood-stained outdoor gear we looked like the survivors of a plane crash, and we'd attract attention. Alisa led me away from the houses, to a lock-up garage tucked away near some trees. She fiddled with a small multi-tool and picked the cheap padlock. Inside, the concrete-floored garage was empty apart from some gardening equipment. "Sit down," she ordered, covering me with a rough woollen blanket that smelt of petrol. "This place has power."

A painter's table held an electric kettle, which we switched on. Alisa found some instant coffee in a rusted tin and some ceramic camping mugs. We huddled underneath the blanket and sipped the hot drinks. The smell of the strong black coffee tickled my nose, the taste and warmth better than any medicine. I held the hot cup to my bruised face. Pulling off my boots I rolled the edge of the hot mug around my battered feet and toes. I sighed happily as warmth returned to my body. "You'll get chill-blains" Alisa chided.

"I don't care" I grunted. "I never thought I'd say this, but on balance I prefer fighting in the desert."

Alisa shook her head and rubbed my hands with hers. Then, despite ourselves, we slept. When I came too, the phone on my lap was bleeping. "Are you OK?" said Marcus, "where are you?"

"Just outside Netheravon, we've found a garage to hide in."

"Good, the pilot will pick you up and drive you to the airfield, there's one in Netheravon on the east side of the village." Marcus gave me an RV in Haxton, a neighbouring village.

"One more thing" I said. "It's important."

"Go on."

"When I was drugged by Volk, I mentioned a family friend. He's threatened her and her kids. I want to you to make sure she's OK. It's a deal-breaker, Marcus."

"What's her name and where does she live?"

I gave him Sam's name and address. "Marcus, she doesn't know about…"

Marcus sighed. "I understand. I'll put some people, watchers, on her address. OK?"

"Thanks," I said.

Marcus ended the call. Alisa and I washed with melted snow, tidied up as much as we could then left the lock-up. Avoiding the main roads we made our way past a farmhouse where a man wearing a woollen hat busied himself with a tractor. We crept past him as best we could. At the end of the road an old-fashioned Land Rover idled in a haze of grey smoke. The headlights flashed and we got in. The sullen pilot from earlier was behind the steering wheel, eyes hidden by sun glasses. The seats were covered with plastic sheeting. "Forensics," he shrugged. "Can't be too careful. Where's your mate?"

"Dead."

"I'm sorry," the pilot replied, face reddening. He reversed the Land Rover, snow-chained rear wheels sliding on the icy road. "There's a flask of tea in my flight bag, help yourself."

I rested my head on the seat, rubbing my hands under the car heater. "Thanks." We drove slowly to Netheravon airfield, the apron dotted with snow-bound light aircraft. They looked like abandoned toys. A man wearing an orange parka was trying to clear snow with a shovel. He gave the pilot a wave. In the distance I heard the sirens of emergency vehicles.

The pilot returned the wave, mumbling under his breath. "This is too risky."

"We have spent all night being shot at and tortured," snorted Alisa. "That is riskier."

The Augusta sat on the frozen runway. The pilot pulled himself into the cockpit and started the engine. Minutes later we took off, the helicopter powering through the clouds, heading east. "Where are we going?" I asked.

"Sussex" the pilot replied. "Near Chichester, so it won't take long. The weather's been a bastard, this snow just won't stop." Alisa was already asleep, curled across three seats. Yawning, I stretched out opposite her and crashed out. The pilot woke me, his gloved hand shaking my shoulder. "I can't believe you slept through that landing" he smiled, "it wasn't the best of my career." Through the window I could see that the heli had been put down on the edge of a brilliant white golf course, rotor blades still turning.

"It's no problem," I said. "I just need to sleep."

The pilot's voice was urgent. "I've got to take off again, while I've got a chance. You'll be picked up on the edge of those trees. Your man's name is Bailey, OK?"

"Sure" I said, trailing a finger over my face to find a piece that wasn't sore.

"*Spasibo*," said Alisa, slapping the pilot on the shoulder. She sported a black eye and bloody nose, hair matted with blood. We climbed out of the heli, ducking our heads as the rotor blades threw up a vicious white hurricane. As we waded through the snow the Augusta took off, heading towards London. We made for the trees, finding a track marked by boot prints.

"Oi! Over here," said a gruff voice. I looked up and saw a short, swarthy man smoking a roll-up cigarette. He wore a waxed jacket and tweed trousers tucked into green Wellington boots. A russet-coloured spaniel sat patiently at his feet. "I'm Bailey, this is Buster." The spaniel wagged its tail.

"What's the plan?" I said, Alisa eyeing Bailey suspiciously.

"The plan? We go back to my place. I'm an Increment, one of Marcus's regulars. I'm sure you know what that means?"

Increment was MI6 parlance for a part-time, often deniable auxiliary. "Sure," I said.

Bailey's dark eyes flashed. "This one's even more off the books than usual, I know that much. Marcus asked me to look after you for a couple of days. He tells me you've got a telephone that needs examining too."

"Yes," said Alisa, "it's an HTC Android phone."

Bailey chuckled and started walking thought the trees. "My love, you might as well be talking Mandarin. I don't do gadgets. I'm more of a shooting, stealing and hiding things type. I'm also a trained paramedic. Mister Rice will be coming later to have a look at the telephone."

"Mister Rice?" I said.

"Another increment, but a boffin."

"Is your house far?" Turov asked as we limped through the snow.

"Ten miles, but my car is around the corner. First things first, you two need medical attention, food and sleep. Let's get that sorted first." Bailey's ageing Toyota Land Cruiser was parked on the other side of the trees. We got in, Buster the spaniel sniffing around us, tail wagging. "He used to be a firearms search dog," said Bailey knowingly, "you two must have been around guns."

"Enough questions Mister Bailey," said Alisa, "please."

"Fair enough," he replied amiably, switching on the stereo. Country and Western music flooded the car as we drove. Finally we stopped at a neat bungalow at the end of a pot-holed private road. Inside the place was barrack-room tidy and warm, smelling of baking and beeswax. Bailey put the kettle on as we stood awkwardly in the kitchen. "Right, here's the score with the safe house. The guest bedrooms are at the back. Take your pick. Leave all of your clothes in the garden waste sacks on the beds and they'll be incinerated this afternoon. In the wardrobes you'll find clean clothes in a variety of sizes, wear those for the time being."

"Excuse me?" I said.

"Don't interrupt," the increment barked, sergeant-major sharp. "I'll buy new clothes in Chichester tomorrow, write down your measurements and any special requirements on the pad near the television. There's food and drink in the fridge, help yourself. First you shower, the bedrooms are en suite. After that I'll triage and treat any minor injuries. Then you sleep, you look like corpses. I'll wake you when Mister Rice arrives."

I took the offered cup of tea and nodded my thanks, "what happens then?"

"Marcus will be in touch. Until then, rest. If you want to watch the news you'll see that your adventures are on every television channel in Europe. So don't leave the house, for Christ's sake. And no telephone calls *whatsoever* unless I say so."

"Can we trust you?" said Alisa. I followed her eyes to a knife-rack near the hob.

Bailey laughed, his skinny little hand reaching into a drawer. He pulled out a black, well-oiled Browning 9mm, unloaded it, and passed the weapon and magazine to Turov. "Yes, you can trust me. But, let's be honest, do you have much choice?"

"No, *tovarich,*" she smiled, leaning forward and kissing Bailey on the cheek, "I would say we do not." She reloaded the pistol and handed it back to him.

"Thanks. Now bugger off and sort yourselves out."

TWENTY NINE

I took a shower, near-scalding water stinging my carcass. I looked at the puncture marks in my arm and the stab injury below my ribs, pink water dribbling from the wounds. I turned the temperature up to maximum. Anything to take my mind off of the strange buzzing sensation in my head, mental after-shocks from whatever narcotics Fyodor Volk had given me.

Bailey knocked on the door and handed me a dressing gown. Then, after serving coffee and sandwiches, he gently treated the cuts and bruises covering my body. "Right, that's you done. Get some sleep," he said curtly, picking up his medical kit and heading for Alisa's room.

I slipped under the clean, warm sheets of the bed and crashed, sleeping dreamlessly. What seemed like seconds later I felt a hand on my cheek. "Cal, wake up" said Alisa. She was wearing a baggy grey hooded top and sweat pants.

"What time is it?" I said, rubbing my eyes.

She smiled and passed me a cup of coffee. A cut ran down the side of her face, sutured with butterfly stitches, "it's almost twenty-hundred. You've been out for six hours."

"How do you feel?"

"Better than I thought I would," she said lightly. "The technical expert is here, to look at Volk's telephone."

I swung my legs out of bed. Alisa shook her head at my nakedness as I dressed in a clean but careworn blue tracksuit. I stuffed my feet in a pair of green army socks and stood up, taking the offered coffee and draining the mug. "OK, let's go and see him."

A tall, balding man in his fifties was sitting at the dining room table, chatting quietly with Bailey. He wore a checked shirt and neatly-pressed jeans, a diamond stud sparkling in his right ear. A laptop computer and cabling was laid out in front of him, next to Fyodor Volk's Android phone. "Good evening. I'm Mister Rice" he said.

Alisa sat opposite him, "can you get into the phone?"

"Well" said Rice drily, "I'm not noted for my facility with small-talk, but you really take the biscuit." He had a nasal, Midlands accent and a goatee beard, which he stroked with precisely manicured fingers. He pulled on a pair of surgical gloves and powered-up the laptop. "Happily, this device isn't an iPhone. The new ones are a bastard to hack, ditto Blackberry." We sat and watched as he opened up a suite of system tools on the laptop. He slid the phone in a padded transparent bag and sealed it around the cabling protruding from it. Humming tunelessly, he attached an external hard drive to a device attached to the cable. "I'm not used to spectators while I'm working," he said.

"Tough, Alisa replied. "People died in order to get that phone. I was tortured. It's not leaving my sight."

"The lady has a point," I said.

"Is the hired help always so precious in this country?" she said.

"Occasionally, now Keep quiet while I work," Rice grumbled, slipping another USB cable into the phone through the seal in the bag. His fingers click-clacked over the keyboard of his computer, beady eyes narrowing as he worked. "Oh, so you're playing that game, are you?" he hissed.

"What is it?" I said.

"Occasionally, Android phones get hacked and infected with malware if you're not careful. But this one has been reverse-hacked, by some sly bastard trying to fool an operator like me. It's full of clever little digital booby-traps, designed to wipe the memory if I'm not careful."

I looked at the phone. "Makes sense, given the people who've had access to it."

"And who would they be?" said Rice.

Bailey cleared his throat, "you know the rules, Mister Rice…"

Alisa cocked her head and smiled. "He needs to know, Bailey. Anyway, if he opens his mouth, I'll cut his throat."

Rice scratched his beaky nose with a latex-covered finger and chuckled. "Actually, that's pretty standard in this line of work."

"The phone belongs to a person close to Pieter Van Basten," I said.

Rice's eyes widened, "Van Basten? That sanctimonious prick? The pleasure will be mine, he hacked GCHQ when I worked there. Not that I'd have cared less if I hadn't coded the anti-virus myself. Let's see if I can return the serve…"

We sat and watched Rice work, the technician's fingers fluttering over the keyboard as the phone lit up and bleeped. "I don't think I've ever seen a smart phone over-clocked before," he giggled. "The memory's bigger than you'd expect, too. This device has been completely re-engineered. Hold on I'm just trying something."

"What've you got?" I said, impatient of his techno-babble.

"Bloody everything," Rice beamed. He reached into a bag and took out another hard drive. "What are you interested in? You'll have to do a keyword search this data because I've pulled 600 megabytes of text and email off here, some images too."

"Tell us where you think the owner of this phone has gone. That's all I need to know right now," I said.

"I can't start messing around with telecommunications enquiries, too risky," said Rice, "but let me check the meta-data on these images." On the laptop screen were several pictures of Pieter Van Basten by a flat, grey lake. In the distance was a wire fence. He wore a black roll neck jumper, baseball cap and a padded winter coat. A yellow device, about the size of a cigarette packet, was clipped to his breast pocket. "Meta-data is stripped off," mumbled Rice, "let's see if I can scrape it back from here…"

"What is that on Van Basten's coat?" said Alisa, peering at the screen.

I joined her and studied the device. It had buttons and a small LCD screen. "Maybe it's an MP3 player?"

Rice looked up from the smart phone and pushed his glasses back up his nose. "No, I don't think so. It looks like a Dosimeter to me."

"Like a Geiger counter?" Alisa asked.

"Hmmm. Sort of, but not quite. But yes, it measures radiation." He enlarged the picture, focussing on the device. "There you go it's an Ecotest.

Ukrainian company, they need them over there, what with Chernobyl and everything."

Bailey broke his silence, "how do you know all this stuff?"

"What can I say," the technician smiled. "I'm an underrated genius. You should see me at a pub quiz."

"Shakuvo," said Alisa. "Fyodor Volk is originally from Shakuvo, where the nuclear accident happened. Could it be that's where they've gone?"

"A radioactive hot zone seems like a good place to hide something," I said, "like a server. Especially if you're a crazy bastard like Volk."

"Quite," said Rice, tapping at the keyboard. "I've scraped the coordinates for this picture from a cache, very sloppy. Feed the coordinates through Google maps and voila! Eastern Tatarstan or thereabouts, I'd say. The image was taken almost a year ago. There are a dozen other deleted images that have the same coordinates, from the past six months to November last year."

"Is there anything else?" I asked, looking at the satellite map of central Russia.

Rice nodded, "Yes, encrypted email traffic to and from an office, let me see if I can lift the IP address. There it is… somewhere in Kazan. That's the capital of Tatarstan."

"I'm Russian, you dolt," Alisa snapped, "I know."

"Keep your hair on love," Rice chuckled, rolling his eyes. "There's also some email headers from an independent travel company in London, a bucket shop. Looks like a back-street place in Stratford. The text has been deleted, but the dates are in the last two weeks and the title relates to airline tickets from London to Istanbul."

I took it all in as I finished my coffee, "How do we know this information isn't there to mislead us?" I said finally. "Van Basten is a genius, these look like schoolboy errors."

"I take your point," Rice nodded, stroking his beard. He rifled about in a paper bag full of sweets and offered us humbugs, "but this isn't Van Basten's phone. And there was a Guttmann-level data shredder installed on this, ready to go. But I bypassed it."

"And?" said Turov.

"Well, I'm not a gambling man, but I'd say this was the real deal." Rice smiled and popped a candy in his mouth. "Let me have a look, say an hour or two, and I'll see if there's anything else on here that helps. OK?"

"Sure," I said, resting my hand on Alisa's shoulder, "I think we both need to make some calls, right?"

"Yes. Mister Bailey, we need un-attributable satellite phones as soon as possible," she narrowed her eyes as she spoke. "Mister Rice, can I trust you with that phone?"

The technician held his hands up and grinned, "the pay for this gig is good and I'm genuinely scared of you. Yes, you can trust me."

"That is excellent," Alisa replied. "And also the correct answer."

Bailey stood up, pulling a telephone from the pocket of his corduroys. "I can do secure comms but I need authorisation from Marcus first."

"Do it," I said.

Bailey left the room, his dog padding after him. I went back to my room and turned on the TV. A reporter stood in the snow. Behind her was a line of fluttering tape and a day-glow jacketed policeman. Black smoke rose from a row of trees, the sound of helis overhead.

The reporter spoke excitedly into her microphone.

I've just received information that a man claiming to be from the 'Black Banner,' a splinter-group of the Greek-based 'Global Army Front' anarchist terrorist network, has claimed responsibility for the incident at Sir Evan Sands' multi-million pound country mansion. Sir Evan is believed to have been killed by an explosive device. The statement given to Reuters says that Sands' was targeted because of his controlling interest in Bachmann Brothers, the private equity group that was responsible for the privatised takeover of Greek public sector assets.

We have also just learnt that the Russian Oligarch Sergei Belov, a house guest here, has been taken by helicopter to a private hospital suffering from smoke inhalation. His Russian head of security was also arrested for illegal firearms possession by detectives from Wiltshire Police. Counter-terrorism officers are now on the scene, with the Home Secretary expected to make a statement shortly…

I switched the TV off and lay on the bed, looking at the ceiling. I'd never been involved in an operation this big in the UK, and wondered if anyone would buy the cover story Volk had put in place. I was sure as I could be that Dmitri Aseyev would keep his mouth shut until Sergei sent a crack battalion of lawyers to spring him from the Paddington Green anti-terrorist nick. Bailey hovered in the open doorway. "Here's the satellite phone. Marcus says you can make one call, no more than five minutes. OK?"

"It'll have to be," I said, sitting up and taking the black rubberized phone from him. After he left I punched the emergency number for Harry into the keypad. This was a phone used specifically for tits-up emergencies.

"I thought you were dead," said Harry. I wondered if there was a hint of disappointment in his voice.

"Andy died. He was blown up with Evan Sands, trying to defuse an IED."

"Jesus, not Andy," he said sourly. "Where are you now?"

"I don't know," I lied. "All I do know is that it's an SVR safe house and I'm in this until the end."

"What do you mean *the end*? Sergei Belov is alive, his attackers are dead. I think that massacre sends a pretty clear message to the Russians. Let's take our money and get you out of there."

"You want the FSB file for SIS, right? Well, I'm going to get it. And I'm going to take out Fyodor Volk, for Andy." I wasn't going to say anything about Sam or the kids. That was my secret.

Harry's voice dropped to an urgent whisper. "Cal, that's not how we do business."

"You've got to let me do this."

"No, I'm calling you in. We need to reassess before we go for the FSB material."

"Bollocks, Harry. It'll be leaked online by the end of the week, right? That means your contract with SIS is buggered. I'm going off the grid for the time being, I'll be in touch when it's done."

"Cal…" spat Harry as I ended the call.

Alisa walked in and smiled, "sounds like that went well." She took the phone from me, winked and punched in a number, sitting on the end of the bed next to me. "It's me" she said in Russian, "I'm alive. I have the

Englishman, the mercenary, with me. The target is Fyodor Volk, and the FSB commando team failed in their mission. Belov lives." I listened in on the conversation, as she told her version of Harry the story. Then she switched the conversation to Serbo-Croat, which I don't speak. I pulled a face. She stuck her tongue out. Eventually she ended the call.

"So?" I said.

"We fly to Moscow tomorrow, if we can get to the general aviation field at Farnborough. We have a private charter booked. Oh, and I told them you want a fee of half a million US dollars, which they agreed. We split it fifty-fifty, OK?"

"Sure, all contributions to my retirement fund are gratefully accepted. But why are you so sure they've gone to Russia? Why not lie low here?"

"They have money and connections. With those, in Russia, anything is possible," she replied. "And SVR received signals intelligence in the past hour suggesting that Volk has contacted an old FSB colleague in Kazan - this cannot be a coincidence."

I stood up, "and what do you want, Alisa? Belov is safe and the FSB have failed."

"I want Volk alive for interrogation, and I want to know where Van Basten is hiding the FSB files, the same as you."

"Yes, but I want Volk dead."

"OK, I can live with that," she smiled. Then, leaning forward, she kissed me on the cheek.

Alisa smelt of shampoo and coffee, her lips soft on my swollen face. I smiled, "you know that SVR and MI6 won't share those files, don't you? I'm meant to be getting them too."

"You have a saying in English – *we cross that bridge when we come to it.* OK?" She nuzzled my ear, gently bit my neck.

I gently pushed her away, avoiding her gaze "nice try, Turov."

The SVR officer's shoulders shook as she laughed. "You are not so bad, Winter. It's been a long time since I've been with a man, and you did save my life. A girl has to try, no?"

"We'll cross that bridge when we come to it," I said. Then I pulled her to me, kissing her hard.

THIRTY

I re-read the webpage again before closing down the browser on my phone;

WebpediA - The Shakuvo Disaster

The disaster at the Shakuvo nuclear power facility occurred on January 30th 1991. It was subsequently graded as Level Six on the INES (International Nuclear and Radiological Event Scale) only one level less than the Chernobyl and Fukushima incidents

The town of Shakuvo is situated in the northeast of the Russian Republic of Tatarstan. It had a population of 50,521 in 1991, but is now abandoned. A 20KM exclusion zone around the town is guarded by Interior Ministry troops. Access to the site, unlike Chernobyl / Pripyat in the Ukraine, is strictly controlled due to the greater radiological risk from the reactor core. The concrete-shrouded RBMK Generation 1A reactor building is an extreme radiological hot zone, generating life-threatening levels of radiation (up to 30 Sv/hr). Radiation levels in the restricted zone vary, in some places reaching 6-10 uSv/hr.

The RBMK Generation 1A was a military-variant of the original AM-1 Soviet reactor. A critical failure of the cooling system of Reactor Three led to an explosion, damaging other systems and leading to the dispersal of radioactive material into the atmosphere. Luckily, environmental factors such as heavy snowfall and low winds localised the spread of contamination in the critical days after the initial event. However, inside the plant it is estimated that the initial level of radiation was up to 100-200 Sv/hr. All of the sixty staff inside the plant died instantly. Only rapid and heroic action by local emergency personnel, many of whom subsequently perished, stopped the radiation spreading. Infamously, the authorities had covered-up failings in critical maintenance programmes, a key factor in causing the initial explosion. The ensuing scandal rocked the government, with some arguing the incident lead to the installation of a new power bloc in the post-Soviet Kremlin...

Bailey said his goodbyes, Buster the Spaniel licking my hand as we jumped out of his 4x4. Sunshine reflected on the snow, making me squint. The combination of pain-killers and fatigue made the next thirty-six hours pass in a blur – I remembered avoiding police checkpoints, then a helicopter ride to a small, private airfield. There two ferret-faced men in leather jackets issued me a hastily-forged Russian passport, in the name of Alexander Kaverin. My dazed-looking photo stared at me from the dark red passport, which I stuffed in the pocket of the new winter jacket the two SVR men had brought me, along with some dark denim jeans, a woollen sweater and a pair of heavy black boots. We suffered a bumpy flight to Moscow on a Lear Jet leased to BASNEFT, a Russian oil company.

All the time Alisa was on her phone, ordering, persuading and cajoling people to get things done. The information Rice had sucked out of Volk's telephone, along with the comms data the SVR had intercepted all suggested the same thing, that Fyodor Volk and Pieter Van Basten were en route to Russia. The intelligence indicated that they'd flown to Turkey then used an established underground terrorist and drug-trafficking route used by Chechen separatists to make it to Tatarstan. We were ahead of them and would arrive in Kazan at least a day before. In the city Volk was linked to an ex-FSB freelancer called Arkady Vitsin. "I have Vitsin's details here" said Alisa, tapping the laptop computer the SVR *resident* had handed her at Farnborough. "He's a typical snitch and drug-dealer, reports on local separatists and Muslim groups. I think Volk might have picked him up as a source in Chechnya, he was a drug-runner there on the White Heroin route."

The leather seats of the Lear Jet were too comfortable, and I felt sleepy, "what use would he be to Fyodor Volk?"

"That's exactly the point, and what we need to establish. But he is local. He knows the region and is a smuggler. And there are urgent operational security issues to consider."

"Such as?"

"The OMON, the interior ministry guards at Shakuvo, are supported by FSB troops. We cannot include anybody from the interior ministry in this operation, so we will have to infiltrate the site independently."

For the first time since I left Bailey's house I laughed. "The FSB are guarding the site where we think their leaked files are kept?"

"Yes," said Alisa, wincing with pain as she smiled. "The irony isn't lost on me."

"So how does Volk get onto the base?"

Alisa tapped the screen of her laptop. "This is what I hope Arkady Vitsin might be able to tell me."

At Moscow we were hurried through the airport by plain-clothed security men and ushered into a minibus. We drove around the perimeter track in silence before stopping at a hangar. Outside men in parkas worked clearing ice from an air force Antonov AN26 transport plane, liquid dripping from the twin-propellers as they hosed de-icer on the engines. "Not as luxurious as the Lear Jet" said Alisa chirpily, "sorry."

I slid out of the minibus and stretched, cold air pricking my face, "I suppose this operation is off the books for SVR too?"

"My directorate head is reporting that I'm investigating the trade in radiological materials. It fits my pattern of travel."

Inside the Antonov I made myself as comfortable as I could. We were given ear-defenders, cold-weather flying suits with a Russian Federation flag on the sleeve and fur-lined boots. The loadmaster handed us blankets, bread rolls and flasks of coffee. I stretched out on the canvas benches and closed my eyes. The airframe shuddered as the engines coughed into life, the Antonov taxiing onto the runway. Minutes later we were powering through the low, black clouds and heading east. Alisa ate, wiping crumbs from her mouth, laptop perched on the bench next to her. I napped, rolling into a ball underneath the rough woollen blankets as the plane yawed and bumped. Eventually I woke up and sipped my coffee. The loadmaster, a cheerful-looking bloke wearing a fur hat, pointed at the NO SMOKING sign and offered me a cigarette. I took it, a disgusting menthol thing, and lit up gratefully. I'd have killed for a decent cigar.

We landed a place with the improbable name of Borisoglebskoye, which the loadmaster told me was an old experimental airfield in the suburbs of Kazan. He shook my hand as we left the plane, leaving our flight suits and hats with him. He gave me his soft-pack of cigarettes as a good-bye present. "I'm out of vodka," he said sadly.

"Now that is a tragedy," I agreed as we waved farewell. The airfield was surrounded by low-level industrial buildings, snow-ploughs parked by the apron.

"Here's our ride," said Alisa, waving at a man leaning against a grimy SUV.

He waved back, huddled in an army surplus parka and fur hat. "I am Pechkin, welcome to Kazan," he said in a high-pitched voice. He was tubby, with a five o clock shadow and rimless spectacles. He had a smouldering *Sobranie* stuck to his lip that moved up and down as he spoke, "you two look like you've been to a boxing match with a gorilla."

"I am *Colonel* Turov," said Alisa, looking him up and down disapprovingly. She jerked a thumb at me, "but don't worry about him."

"Hey no problems, Colonel," said Pechkin, "does *Don't Worry About Him* have any luggage?"

"Don't worry about me," I shrugged.

"The first time we met you kidnapped me at gunpoint," she laughed, pinching my cheek. "Don't expect any special treatment."

"Get a room," said Pechkin, rolling his eyes as he opened the SUV's doors.

"Are you always this rude?" said Alisa.

"Well, I'm stuck in a covert facilities posting in Tatarstan in January, Colonel," said the fat SVR man as he drove us away. "I must have done something wrong."

"Yes, I imagine you have," Alisa replied. "Do you have the equipment I asked for?"

Pechkin grimaced. "Some pencil-neck from 'X' Directorate phoned up in the middle of the fucking night and said there was a shipment of protective equipment waiting for me at the warehouse I rent, I don't know who delivered it. I haven't had time to check."

"Take us straight there. What have you found out about Arkady Vitsin?"

"I know of Vitsin," said Pechkin, brightening up. "An informant I was running last year, some madman from Kazakhstan, was running heroin for him. Vitsin's front company is a tourist operation in town, does adventure sports and stuff. Kazan is becoming the sports capital of Russia, which is typical of my luck. I prefer chess to soccer."

Alisa nodded approvingly, "what surveillance capability do you have, Pechkin?"

"Me, some binoculars and this car," he replied. "If the OMON or FSB knew I was here I'd be fucked. And the local cops out here make the pigs in Moscow look like ballerinas."

"OK, after you take us to see our equipment, we go to Vitsin's office," she replied.

Pechkin cheered up at the prospect of some action, "hey, that's no problem. He's a rancid little shit, he won't give you any trouble. I've got weapons at the warehouse."

"There's one more thing, Pechkin," said Alisa quietly. "If you can manage it, you'll be posted out of here by spring."

"Hey, you name it Colonel," he puffed, overtaking a lorry on a blind bend, "I'll even suck the dicks of Vladimir Putin *and* his bodyguard if you like."

"I want you to get us into the secure zone at the Shakuvo reactor site, Pechkin," she said coolly."

"I think it would be easier for me to persuade Putin to drop his trousers, Colonel," he laughed. "But I'll try if it gets me back to Moscow, or a nice overseas posting."

The outskirts of Kazan were like any other big city, but in the distance I could see Onion domes and the turquoise spires of a great mosque. I knew Kazan was a fifty-fifty split between Christians and Muslims, and was one of those lucky places where faiths lived side-by-side in relative peace. We drove past some Soviet-era housing projects, the streets lined with little market stalls selling household goods and food. Pechkin finally parked at a back-street warehouse sandwiched between a sad-looking auto repair shop and a bakery. Swarthy men wearing leather jackets and fur hats stood around, smoking and drinking steaming cups of coffee. I got out of the car and lit up a cigarette. I winced as the harsh tobacco ticked my lungs. "Anywhere I can get some cigars around here?" I said.

"I've got some in the warehouse, Chinese cigars."

Alisa shook her head as we stepped inside. The warehouse was full of tinned food, caviar, boxed electrical items, tobacco and booze. Pechkin found a box of Great Wall cigars and tossed them to me. "Present from the SVR," he said.

"I guess that'll be the only one I'll get."

Alisa raised an eyebrow and went over to a pile of boxes marked SURVEY EQUIPMENT: FRAGILE. Pechkin passed her a pallet-knife and she slashed open the packaging. Inside were CBRN protective suits made of a thick grey rubberized material, complete with protective helmets fitted with breathing equipment. Another sealed plastic bag contained over-boots and gloves. "We don't need to wear these all the time on-site" she said. "the radiation levels are variable."

"That's the problem with Shakuvo," Pechkin agreed. "You could be in a park in the old town and you wouldn't need to wear anything. The ambient rads would just be just slightly higher than normal, but go a hundred metres in another direction? You could be in a hot zone. But I'd wear that stuff anywhere near the reactor site, say a kilometre."

Alisa passed me a small yellow Dosimeter, like the one we saw in the photo of Van Basten. "In Iraq we did lots of drills for chemical warfare, but that was years ago," I said.

"We will wear the Dosimeters all the time in the zone, OK? We might have to wear the suits, but we carry the breathing apparatus until we need it."

"Sure," I said. I lit a Chinese cigar. It wasn't Cuban, but it would do. I exhaled happily. "What next?"

"Weapons, please," said Alisa to Pechkin.

He nodded and unlocked a steel cupboard. Inside were rifles, shotguns, SMGs and pistols. "Take your pick, Colonel."

"Nothing too big," she said. "Concealable weapons only."

I chose a Walther P22, loaded it and tucked it into the waistband of my heavy denim trousers. Pechkin nodded and passed me a brutal-looking wooden truncheon studded with steel rivets. I took it and slid it into the inside pocket of my jacket. Alisa loaded a handgun, a Makarov. "Am I coming?" said Pechkin.

"Yes you're coming," Alisa sighed. "I don't know where Vitsin's office is."

Pechkin grinned. "I hope the fucker puts up a fight," he said, his jowly face splitting into a grin. "I've got a baseball bat in the car, in case he needs some persuading."

We went outside and got into Pechkin's SUV. "Are you OK?" said Alisa, touching my arm.

"I've got a box of cigars and I'm sitting next to a beautiful, heavily-armed woman," I said, "perhaps I could be happier, but I'm not sure by how much."

"Like I said," Pechkin sneered, "go get a fucking room."

Alisa shot the SVR officer a look. "Shut up and drive, before I recommend a posting to the Arctic Circle."

"Yes Colonel!"

I laughed and puffed on my cigar as the SVR man drove into Kazan, the sun glinting on the distant Mosque's minarets.

THIRTY ONE

Vitsin's office was on the ground floor of a mint-coloured building. Apart from the children playing in the snow in a nearby park, it was quiet. "The office is the one with the yellow sign outside," said Pechkin. "That's his car, the black BMW."

Alisa checked her pistol again. "Pechkin, wait outside until I call you in. If anything goes wrong you head back to the warehouse and we meet you there."

"Yes, I understand," he said, looking around for cops.

We walked to the office. A faded sign read TATAR ADVENTURE SPORTS in Russian, Tatar and English. The blinds were down, amber light visible from the doorway. I went up and rang on the bell on the entry phone. "Hi," said a friendly voice in Russian.

"My name is Alex," I said, "I've got some Americans visiting the university, they want to go boating. Can you help?"

"Sure, come in." The door buzzed.

We walked into an unremarkable office. Pictures of outdoor sports covered the walls, a couple of sad potted plants wilting by a heavy steel radiator. Sitting behind a desk was a skinny weasel in his thirties, dressed in ripped jeans and a black sweater. He was lighting a cigarette. "Sit down," he said, "I'm Arkady." His oiled black hair swept back behind his ears, his eyes sunk into his pale, angular face. An ashtray full of cigarette butts sat in front of him, next to a can of soda.

Alisa stepped forward, her face grim. She whipped the handgun from her jacket and stuffed the barrel into Arkady Vitsin's forehead. "Where is Fyodor Volk?"

"Are you a cop?" he replied calmly.

"Keep your hands on the table, Arkady," I said, locking the door, "we're not cops, so that's the start of your problems."

"FSB?"

Alisa reversed the pistol in her hand and smashed the butt of the weapon into Arkady's cheek. "I ask the questions!"

"Are you sure you're not a cop?" Vitsin laughed, spitting out a tooth. "Besides, who on earth should I be more scared of than Fyodor Volk?"

"Is that a challenge?" I said, pulling the wooden cosh from my pocket.

Vitsin rolled his eyes as his fingers dabbed at the cut on his face. "Look, I haven't seen him for a year. Yes, I know him. No, I don't work for him. Just leave me alone. Leave a message for him if you like."

Grabbing his wrist, I slammed Vitsin's left hand on the desk and battered it with the cosh. I didn't stop until every finger and knuckle was broken. Then I started on his wrist. "That was for a friend of mine," I growled, "who Volk murdered." Andy would have done the same for me, I think, but with a knife.

Alisa stuffed a rolled up magazine from his desk into Vitsin's mouth to muffle the screams. "Now work on his feet," she said.

"Let's see if he wants to talk." Vitsin slid from his chair and curled into a ball, sobbing. Kicking him out of the way I opened the drawer of his desk, emptying paperwork onto the floor.

Alisa checked his computer, opening his email account. "Where is your cell phone?" she said.

Vitsin's face was grey as he pointed at his coat, which was hung over the back of a chair. I checked the pockets, pulling out an iPhone. "Arkady, open up whatever hidden email account you've got on here."

He nodded as I held the phone in front of him. He tapped something into the phone with his free hand, eyes streaming. "There, that's it," he sobbed. I scrolled through the Cyrillic script of the email he'd opened, sent from a disposable covert account. I read out the username, "Malebranche?"

"More Dante," said Alisa, "it's a type of devil."

I opened the email.

From: Malebranche@insurgentmail.com
To: Arkady1982@insurgentmail.com
Subject: Visit
Happy New Year, Arkady. We need to visit soon. Is Oleg available?

"Who's Oleg?" I asked.

"He's a tour guide I use," he sobbed, "fuck this hurts."

Alisa stamped on his shattered hand with her boot, "a tour guide for where?"

"Shakuvo," he screeched. "Oleg specialises in breaking into Shakuvo."

"Why?" I said.

"It's an extreme sport. Americans pay big money to get in and explore the town, especially the secure zone. Oleg did his military service in a radiological warfare unit. He served in Shakuvo, knows the place like his own backyard."

I leant down and waved the wrap of heroin I'd found with the iPhones in front of Arkady's face. "Why would Volk want to go to Shakuvo?"

"Fyodor Volk is from Shakuvo. He goes to lay fresh flowers for his family who died there, you must believe me! It's the anniversary of the accident this week. Oleg always takes him in, to avoid the guards, he figures out where the new hot zones are…"

"Thank you, Arkady," said Alisa, "I'm sorry for having to hurt you. Now, if you can tell us when Volk is coming, and how we contact Oleg, then we will leave."

"I don't know when, but it must be soon. I called Oleg, he is expecting Volk and they will make their own arrangements. Oleg trusts me to put him in touch with people, after that it's his business. His telephone number and address is in my phone."

Alisa nodded at me. I flipped through the phone and found the name, Oleg Danshov, and an address in a place called Menzelinsk. I pulled the suppressed Walther and shot Vitsin twice in the head. We smashed up the office and emptied his cash-box, then I scattered heroin on the corpse. "Looks like a robbery to me" she said approvingly, "or a visit from the FSB."

"What's the difference? Let's go." We left the office, closing the door behind us and got into the car.

"And?" said Pechkin.

"And nothing," said Alisa. "Take us to the warehouse, then the airfield."

"Where are you going?" said Pechkin, pulling into traffic.

"I need you to pull the army records for a man called Oleg Danshov. He will have served in a Nuclear, Biological and Chemical Warfare unit. I guess he's a Tatar."

"Hopefully he's in Kazan," I said, "can we trace his phone?"

"I don't see any other way."

"Leave it with me," said Pechkin, undertaking a taxi and pumping the horn on the SUV.

Back at the warehouse we loaded our CBRN equipment into Pechkin's car while he made some calls. "Alisa, hold on" I said. "Why don't I just call this Oleg guy?"

"What do you mean?"

"Give me your phone." I punched Oleg's number into it and waited. After a few moments a man with a gruff voice answered.

"Who is it?" he said.

"Hi, my name is Alex. Arkady gave me your number."

"Oh did he? Did he tell you I'm busy?"

"Yes, but he said that you might listen to my offer."

"Make it quick."

"I have some Americans staying with me, extreme sports guys," I said, "they want to do a tour of Shakuvo, under the noses of the guards. They will pay a thousand US dollars cash, each, and I've got six of them here. Can you do anything for me? Arkady says you're the best."

"When? I've got another client first thing tomorrow morning."

"OK, how about straight afterwards, maybe after lunch? These guys have plenty of cash. I can arrange a transfer to fly them out to Shakuvo."

"Maybe, but they won't have long before it gets dark," Oleg replied. "If you meet me at the crossroads on the road south of Shakuvo airfield, near the gas station. Tomorrow at one o'clock? I can get them near the reactor shroud, within three hundred metres, and back before dark. I know all the low radiation zones, if you don't you can catch something nasty."

I smiled at Alisa and nodded, "Oleg, you are awesome."

"Whatever," he said wearily, "if you want me to provide Dosimeters and masks I can do that, but I want another three hundred dollars per person. Cash."

"Great Oleg," I gushed. "That sounds perfect, these guys will be thrilled."

"As long as they tip," he grumbled.

I ended the call. "I think he's taking Volk in first, I said we'd meet at thirteen-hundred. Volk and Van Basten must be flying in tonight."

"We can't cover the airport. The interior ministry would figure out the SVR are looking for Volk. And they'll have good papers, I'm sure of that."

"Then we need to get out to Shakuvo now," I said, "and wait for Volk to meet Oleg."

Pechkin cleared his throat, "I'm getting a research package on Oleg Danshov. He's got a website advertising extreme wilderness tours, and I have his army record. There's a photo being emailed now."

Alisa smiled and slapped Pechkin on the back so hard he spat his cigarette out, "excellent, your escape from this place draws ever nearer."

"Thank fuck for that, Colonel," he laughed.

We helped ourselves to rifles and ammunition from Pechkin's warehouse and drove back out to the airfield. The Antonov still squatted on the concrete apron, the loadmaster checking the fuselage and talking to mechanics. Alisa went to speak with the pilot, who nodded and signalled to the ground crew to prepare for take-off. "Call me with anything you get back about Danshov" said Alisa, shaking Pechkin's hand.

"Of course, and put a good word in for me, eh, Colonel?" He shuffled back off to his SUV, lighting a cigarette.

Fifteen minutes later we were flying east over Tatarstan. I gave the loadmaster a bottle of vodka and some Chinese cigars, liberated from Pechkin's warehouse. He was delighted, and piped awful Russian pop music through my earphones while we smoked and poured vodka into our coffee. The cold went away quickly after that. Alisa joined us, coughing on the cigar smoke and smiling at the taste of the boozy, hot drink.

It took less than an hour before the pilot announced that we were on our final approach into Shakuvo, a cold war strategic bomber base. I looked through the window and saw the airfield, the two parallel runways like long grey scars in the snow. There were a few light aircraft and a rescue helicopter visible by the hangers. "Can you see the reactor?" said Alisa, pointing at the horizon.

In the darkness I saw a faint glow beyond a forest. As I focussed it morphed into a hazy line of buildings. Perched next to it was a teetering black plinth, many stories high. A crooked metal chimney protruded from the top like a periscope. A red light blinked lazily from the tip, steam and smoke pissing from unseen apertures in the structure. "I see it," I said.

"That's the concrete shroud around the reactor," said Alisa, "it was only completed five years ago."

"And Shakuvo, the town itself, is where?"

She shuffled a map. "It's to the south of the reactor, on the other side of the forest. We're just skimming the edge of the control zone now, I think."

"We'll be landing in ten minutes," said the loadmaster. "Damn, this place gives me the creeps. It's cursed."

"Do you fly this route often?" I said.

"Only to take technicians out to the reactor. Most of the time we carry out routine flights for the intelligence people, down to Kazakhstan or across to Chechnya." We landed at the military airfield at dusk. White lights marked the tiny control tower, a red and white windsock fluttering from the roof.

"OK, the air force guys have arranged a vehicle, they're going to get us off base," said Alisa. "This is a special services squadron plane, they know not to ask questions."

I looked at my watch. "I guess we've got less than twelve hours before Oleg meets with Volk and Van Basten to take them in."

"Let's arrange a reception," nodded Alisa.

"Good luck," said the loadmaster, looking at our bulky kit bags full of weapons and CBRN equipment.

"And to you too, *tovarich*," I said, giving him a hug.

Alisa kissed his cheeks and gave him another bottle of vodka. "I don't think we'll need this," she said mock-sadly.

We climbed into a green-painted military 4 x 4, driven by the co-pilot, and bumped across the runway. At the gate a sentry leant out of his box and waved. "Special services!" called the pilot, flashing a yellow laminated pass, "We're coming through."

"Yes sir," said the sentry, saluting as we drove by.

"OK," said the air force officer in excellent English, "the vehicle is yours, good luck. If you want to reach the controlled zone, follow the orange road signs. We're going to be here for twenty-four hours, if you aren't back by then the next shuttle is the day after tomorrow."

"Thanks," I said.

"It is a pleasure, sir," he said smoothly, hopping out of the driver's seat. "Good luck." He turned on his heel and walked along the lonely perimeter road. I slid behind the steering wheel and motored south towards Shakuvo. The orange road signs all showed the radioactivity symbol, a black circle with three wedges radiating from it. A rusting sign read in Russian and English:

DANGER!
MINISTRY OF THE INTERIOR
SHAKUVO RADIOLOGICAL CONTROL ZONE
15 KM - NO ENTRY WITHOUT PERMIT

"Let's find somewhere to wait," said Turov quietly, pulling out the slim yellow Dosimeter and switching it on.

"What's the radiation level?" I said.

"About twice the normal ambient level of London" she shrugged, "nothing to worry about."

"I feel much safer now," I said, lighting a cigar.

THIRTY TWO

Three kilometres short of the control zone, at the crossroads Oleg had mentioned, we found a petrol station. A beefy-armed *babushka* had had opened a gift and snack shop, serving soup, pancakes and plastic models of the Shakuvo reactor building. The only customers were young interior ministry troops, wearing distinctive blue and grey camouflage uniforms and fur winter hats. They ignored us as they smoked, drank coffee and stuffed their faces.

We sat in our jeep, heater turned up to its highest setting. Alisa drummed her fingers on the dashboard, "do we take them out here, or follow them inside?"

"If the server is in the complex, does that mean it's connected to the internet?" I said.

"Volk wants to get into the control zone, right? I can't believe there's a connection in there. The whole point would be that nobody could hack the server, that it's completely sterile."

"Sure, what if there was? One we didn't know about? They could put the file online before we reach them."

Alisa pulled a face. "Do you think you can follow them in this weather, into the site, without being detected?"

I shook my head, "I doubt it, but there's another option."

"Go on."

"Look at those meatheads," I said, jerking a thumb at the OMON troops stood by the petrol station. "Maybe we can tip them off that somebody called Oleg is going to try to break into the control zone."

"I see. We can get inside before we put out the alert," said Alisa. "By the time they make it into the site we'll be ahead of them, if they get caught then it's usually a fine or a bribe. It will only delay them."

"Get Pechkin to put in an anonymous call," I said. "Mention Oleg, but not Volk."

Alisa's eyes narrowed as she concentrated, "not a bad plan, but how do we get through the control zone?"

I opened the map in front of us. "Look at this area, it's huge. There's no way you can patrol all of it. We know that Oleg meets clients near this crossroads. We just need to figure out where he'll go when he sees a reception committee of soldiers waiting to detain him. Then we hide up at the point nearest to Shakuvo from there."

"It's risky."

"This job has been risky from day one," I shrugged. We talked it through and agreed to break into the control zone at dusk, then contact Pechkin. The map showed the outskirts of Shakuvo eight kilometres from our location. We drove back up the road, turning off along a smaller track, rutted with the marks of heavy vehicles. At the end of the road was a concrete guard post. I guessed the fence was three metres high, topped with barbed wire and marked with yet more warning signs. We took the jeep off-track, driving parallel to the fence across the fields. It was quiet, the glow of lights from guard towers the only source of light. Finally we parked on a hard-standing where a broken down truck languished, the rear tyres missing. "We wait here" said Alisa, "it must be minus fifteen out there."

I rifled through my kit and found a camping stove and brewed coffee. Turov called Pechkin and told him to make an anonymous tip-off to the authorities about Oleg, and about his rendezvous point near the petrol station. Eventually we dozed, our yellow Dosimeters still clipped to our pockets. It was 0500 when I was woken up by the sound of engines, the jeep's heater still chugging by my knee. I rubbed frost from inside the window and saw three white-painted troop carriers rumbling past us on the service road. Two trucks and a 4 x 4 followed.

"Well done Pechkin," mumbled Turov sleepily from under a blanket.

"I don't suppose the guard force here get much action," I said. "OK, let's go." When the interior ministry troops had passed by I pulled a pair of bolt-croppers from the boot of the jeep and jogged to the perimeter fence. I carefully snipped the wire to create a panel big enough for us to drive through then let drop back down behind us, making the gap look less obvious. Turov put her thumb up and nudged the air force GAZ jeep through the gap. I climbed back in and we drove slowly through a wood, reaching another gritted service road. A sign read:

CONTROLLED ZONE
Shakuvo (Town) 8 KM
Shakuvo (Reactor) 12 KM
Administrative Centre 3 KM
PROTECTIVE EQUIPMENT TO BE WORN
2 KM FROM REACTOR
By order of the Interior Ministry

"People work here, you know," said Turov as we headed for the town. "Mainly scientific specialists and researchers."

We passed abandoned buildings and warehouses. Two men, wearing boiler suits and driving a small tractor, waved at the air force jeep as we drove by. Finally we reached the outskirts of Shakuvo, weak sunlight filtering through the clouds. It was a ghost town. Grey-green vines and foliage snaked up the sides of buildings, rusting vehicles sitting where they'd been abandoned in 1991. A fox trotted past us and gave us a curious look as it padded away. There were trees everywhere, growing on the pavements and through the tops of buildings. "The wildlife does OK then?" I said.

"Only because there are no humans," replied Alisa. "Although new-born cattle were horribly mutated, and you can't eat the fish."

I opened a bar of chocolate and took a bite. "This is what the end of the world looks like?"

"Don't you think it's beautiful?" she said.

"No, I think it's spooky."

"It's so quiet."

We drove through town, the concrete sarcophagus of the reactor looming

238

in the distance. As we drew closer I could see it was constructed with slabs of dark grey stone, held in place with steel joists and scaffolding. Weather-stained and rotting, it oozed dark fluids from pipes and vents. It looked alien and wrong.

Then my Dosimeter bleeped.

"6.9uSv/hr" said Turov, "that's dangerous. Let's suit up." We reversed back a hundred yards and the reading dropped. I realised that the contamination was completely localised. A gentle breeze blew from behind us, scattering a few flakes of snow. We unloaded our CBRN equipment and I wriggled into the heavy grey over-suit. In the cold it was another welcome layer. Next were over-boots and a respirator hood. Alisa and I checked each other's kit and taped the joins at our wrists and ankles. A small box sewn into the suit allowed me to switch the air supply on or off, depending on the level of radiation.

We drove to the town centre, where there was a monument to the emergency workers and reactor staff who perished in the accident. Carved from a slab of black marble, it showed a man in a hard hat helping a fireman get to his feet. Underneath were carved the names of all of the victims, in Russian and Tatar. Around the plinth were scattered bouquets of shrivelled flowers. "Well, if he's laying flowers this is it," I said through my mask. I got out of the jeep and shouldered my AK-74. The town hall, built in the brutalist soviet style, had two angular concrete towers at either end. "Let's go up there," I said, pointing at the towers. We parked at the back of the building and stepped through an open doorway.

Alisa nodded and shouldered her rifle. Inside, the building was frozen in January 1991. Old books and papers littered the floor, mouldy furniture littering the rooms. I checked my Dosimeter. The radiation level had dropped to a safe level again, and I took off the uncomfortable respirator. "This is doing nothing for my hair," Alisa smiled as she slipped off her mask. We plodded up the stairs in our heavy over-boots. The staircase was covered in graffiti from explorers and adventure tourists. At the top was an office, picked clean by souvenir-hunters. It had a panoramic view of the town, the reactor behind us.

Pulling a pair of binoculars from my day-sack, I leant by the broken window. From the office I could see the main routes into and out of town, a line of trees on the horizon marking the entry to the controlled zone some eight kilometres away. In the distance, to my right, I could see a white low-rise building with vehicles parked outside.

"That's the OMON barracks," said Alisa. The OMON were the interior ministry guards. I found myself checking my Dosimeter every few seconds, but it remained constant. We waited for two hours, gazing over the ruined town and the black, fortress-like reactor building. "Look" said Alisa, pointing towards the trees.

We stood back from the window as three men trudged into view, wearing green protective suits and respirators. They all wore packs, one of the men armed with a rifle. "Is it them?" I whispered.

"Yes," she replied. "They're heading towards us."

At the monument, one of the men stepped forward and put a wreath on the plinth directly below us. I could hear voices on the wind, but couldn't make out words. I checked the safety on my weapon and took aim at the man who'd placed the wreath. "Wait" said Alisa. "See where they go – I want that server."

The men carried on slowly past us, towards the reactor building. Then they walked out of view, towards a gnarly, forested hill. Putting on our respirators, we headed back downstairs towards the plinth. I walked carefully towards it, rifle ready. The flowers were white lilies and Russian ivy, decorated with black ribbon. I nudged the piece of card tied to the wreath to look for the message. It was there, in Russian: *You shouldn't have followed me.*

"Alisa!" I shouted. My voice was muffled in the helmet, breath misting the visor. Alisa saw me and crouched in cover near a block of concrete stairs. Then automatic fire stitched crazily across the walls, the SVR officer disappearing in a cloud of brick dust and debris. I fell to my belly and scrambled towards her, more incoming fire sweeping the square. I glanced up and saw muzzle flashes in the trees. More bullets splashed about us, birds skittering out of the trees in protest at the commotion.

I breathed out gently and aimed, lining up the muzzle flash in the optics of the AK. Squeezing the trigger I fired three single shots, then hauled myself to my feet and sprinted towards Alisa, dragging her into cover.

The firing stopped.

Bullets had raked Alisa's body, dark red entry wounds staining the protective suit on her thighs, abdomen and chest. The inside of her helmet was spattered red. She groaned, her gloved hands fluttering by her sides. I ripped a field dressing from my pocket. She shook her head. "What is it?" I gasped, patting myself down to see if we'd packed morphine.

"I can't die in here," she sobbed, "take this helmet off, Cal. Please."

"The radiation..."

Alisa tried to laugh, but could only let out a hacking cough. "Cancer is the least of my worries. I want to die under the sky, not in... *here*."

My fingers fumbled at the catches on the respirator helmet as I pulled it clear of her head. Her eyes glazed over, breathing shallow. Dark red blood bubbled from her mouth, spraying my visor as she exhaled. "Cal..."

"It's OK baby," I said, holding her to me.

"Say my name, when you kill Volk," she said.

Then she was gone.

I waited for a few minutes, then dragged her body to the front of the plinth. I searched her for spare ammunition then, reloading my rifle, I made for the trees.

THIRTY THREE

I followed fresh prints left behind by heavy over-boots. Entering the trees I paused, spotting spent shell casings in the snow. In front of me birds wheeled into the sky, squawking and cawing. Rifle in my hand, I lowered myself to the ground and waited. Through my rifle optics I scanned the trees, spotting a low, flat-roofed building through the spindly branches. It, like the rest of Shakuvo, was made of stained grey concrete. At the edge of the building line I saw movement.

Slowly, hugging the ground, I edged forward to the next tree. Thick brambles barred my way, obscuring the view. I found a gap in the thick, twisted vegetation and aimed through it. The building was a school, a faded painting of a boy and a girl holding hands decorating the wall. In the playground, crouching behind a concrete slab was a tall man in protective equipment. His rifle was aimed into the trees, slightly to the right of where I was hiding. Inside the respirator it was stuffy, the visor steaming up. At least the protective suit kept me warm in the snow, on top of my cold-weather clothing. Alisa's blood stained my gloves and clothes, hot tears stinging my eyes.

I wanted to tear off the mask and attack.

The only thing stopping me was my plan for Fyodor Volk. That, and the voice at the back of my head, the one the therapist had persuaded me to cultivate. It reminded me that I'd not taken my pills for days. I needed to breathe deeply and think.

So I waited. My impatience with surveillance was gone. I wondered what Sam was doing right now. If she'd spotted the watchers Marcus had said would cover her. If the watchers weren't there, if I'd been betrayed, I'd kill Marcus too. Inside the helmet I could feel the blood pounding around my skull. Like war drums.

All the time Alisa's voice was in my head, like background music. I guessed that it was good that it hurt me when it happened. That freaky, numbing pain that hits you when somebody so alive, so vital, dies in front of you. At one point, after Clarkie was killed in Maysan, I stopped caring. The letters to bereaved families became impossible unless I'd drunk a bottle of vodka, and even then I'd laugh while I wrote them.

I wondered if I would die out here. I decided that I didn't mind if I did as long as Volk joined me, down into the Ninth Circle.

I checked the timer on my Dosimeter, the reading higher than before. I'd been lying in the snow for an hour, the guy in the playground losing his patience and walking about, stamping his feet. I know an impatient smoker when I see one, the guys hands sweeping across the visor of his respirator.

The other two men came out of a doorway. They joined the third and stood talking. I thumbed the fire selector on the AK to auto and pulled the stock tight into my shoulder, curling my other hand over the top of the hand-guard. Getting to my feet, I lined up the figure with the rifle at knee height, knowing that on automatic the weapon would fire high. I squeezed the trigger. The staccato of gunfire filled my ears as I swept the AK74 from right to left. Bullets sliced through the thighs and guts of the first target and clipped the second in the chest, the impact throwing him onto his back. The third guy bristled and disappeared back into the doorway, like a startled cat.

I slid a fresh magazine into the receiver of the AK and stepped forward. The man I'd shot in the chest was trying to get up. I fired a three round burst into his chest. He twitched and was still, the snow stained red. Training the rifle on the doorway, I walked slowly towards the bodies.

The first man I didn't recognise, but I guessed was the guide, Oleg. His rifle lay next to him in the snow. The second was Pieter Van Basten, dead eyes staring over my shoulder. I shot him again, in the head, just to be sure. I patted down the bodies, but found nothing.

I stepped into the school, debris crunching underneath my heavy boots.

The classroom in front of me was empty, apart from some upturned tables and a doorway. Covering the gap with my rifle, I crept through. Looking down I saw drops of blood on the floor, congealing between the cracks in the rotting linoleum. They led to a heavy fire door. A sign said EMERGENCY SHELTER in Russian, a cold war hangover from when they still thought a nuclear war was survivable. Beyond the door was a flight of stairs, leading down to the shelter. The blood trail stopped halfway down the stairs, my boots echoing on the raw concrete steps. "Volk," I called, "are you're injured?" I wondered where the server was, whether Volk could destroy it, or had a computer connected to the internet down here.

"Come in Winter," said Volk calmly, "come and join me." The shelter was a long, narrow room lit with guttering storm lamps, strange shadows dancing against the walls. Sat behind a school desk was Fyodor Volk, his helmet on the surface in front of him. He was nursing his hand where it had been struck by a bullet, blood stains on the sleeve of his protective suit.

"How did you know we were following you?" I said, weapon trained on his chest.

"That creature, Pechkin," Volk chuckled, "he crawled straight out of the ooze of the Ninth Circle. He's worked for me for a year now. All he wants is money and whores."

"He's a dead man," I shrugged.

"Good. You can take your helmet off in here, by the way," he said. "The radiation is very low. It's one of the reasons I chose it."

"And what's the other reason?" I said, I training my Kalashnikov on him. I undid the neck-clasp and pulled off the respirator cowl. The air was damp and cool. It smelt tangy and metallic in my nostrils, but was refreshing after the stuffiness of the respirator.

"This is my old school. Happy memories. Tell me, is Pieter dead?"

"Yes," I said.

Volk's head slumped to his chest, raven-black hair falling across his brow. His hand slipped under the desk. "Keep your hands…" I barked as a bullet whipped past me, the desk flying forward as Volk kicked it over.

I fell to a knee and returned fire, the muzzle flash like a dragon's breath. The desk splintered into shards of wood and plastic as gunfire chewed into it. Volk had rolled to one side, clawing at a bullet wound in his calf. A stubby black pistol lay next to him. He was laughing. I kicked the pistol towards the door. "This wasn't as I imagined it" he said, "I never thought you'd find Shakuvo."

"Where's Van Basten's server?" I said quietly. "Tell me and it will be quick."

"May I take some morphine?" he replied.

I grunted that he could.

Volk checked his pouch pockets and pulled out a medical kit. He injected a large bore needle into his arm and sighed. "Did Pieter die quickly?"

"Yes, I shot him in the heart and brain."

The Russian nodded sadly and dragged himself into a sitting position, back to the wall. "The server is behind me, under those boxes. Pieter figured out the ninth level of security, but the code was never written down. He'd memorized it."

"What was in it?" I said. I stepped back, as despite his injuries Volk looked strong. He rotated his handsome head on his neck, tensing his muscles. White teeth flashed in the torchlight.

"We'll never know. If it was worse than the previous eight, then even I fear for the future of Russia."

The pile of mildewed cardboard boxes covered a small metal hatch. I turned a wheel and it hissed as it opened. Inside was a compartment containing a black ballistic bag. "Have you rigged this to explode too?" I said, carefully examining the bag.

"Not at all," Volk replied. "There is a simple four terabyte hard drive and a small external drive. They are encrypted and the FSB files are copied to both. And there is no internet signal here, and no computer. They can't be hacked. They are sealed in lead-impregnated resin, so they aren't radioactive."

"Where's the encryption key?"

"Here," he said, passing a thumb drive from his pocket with bloodied fingers.

"Why so easy?" I replied.

"Because Pieter is dead," he whispered, "and because you are what you are, Winter. Information is like bird flu virus, or HIV. If you have the information, whoever you give it to, it will be leaked and spread. Even if it won't be as we planned. And there are things there I'd be happy to see on the web. It was Pieter's wish."

I took the thumb drive. "How can you be so sure?"

"It was leaked, wasn't it? Secrets are like water – they always find their own level."

"And you wanted Belov dead because he was stopping Pieter from controlling his own information?"

"Partly," smiled Volk, dark eyes boring into mine, "but there's something else. Something much, much… *worse*. It's all on the file. Take a look when you get out of here, maybe back to the seaside in England. I know you like it there."

Volk's eyes were like pools of churning black water, his smile warm and sweet. He reached forward and touched my face and I felt faint. In my mind I was back on the gurney, talking to the black-masked Demon.

He understood me so well.

"Give me your rifle," he said gently, like the weapon might hurt me, "you don't need it, Cal." Volk was my friend, it was making sense now. "You know Colonel Turov was going to betray you, don't you?" he said, the words musical and soft. "She told me when I gave her the medicine. She wanted the server for her SVR masters. She would have killed you for it, Winter. It was lucky for you, for all of us, that Oleg killed her back there. She was a lying, murdering bitch…"

Something snapped. It was if there was a camera on my shoulder showing the scene, Alisa and I together in the bedroom at Bailey's safe house in England. Warm. Safe, even. Woozy, I staggered forward. I saw Volk's snarling, ghostly-white face. I snatched the rifle back and smashed the steel-shod butt into his cheek. He feinted backwards, lashing out with his booted foot, hitting my ankle and sending me to my knee. Grabbing the black ballistic bag he darted to the stairs, snatching at the pistol as he went. He fired wildly, his face a bloody mask. The bullet hit the ground and bounced into my upper arm. It felt like I'd been kicked with someone wearing a knife on their boot. I rolled to the ground, grabbing the Kalashnikov and returning fire.

But Volk was gone, the servers with him.

I wriggled out of the suit sleeve and examined my arm. The low-calibre slug had penetrated the thick reinforced fabric of my protective suit. The lead blob was stuck in my arm, a livid welt marking where the ricochet had struck. Pulling the round out of the pulpy, black-and-mauve flesh I pulled the suit back on and found an adhesive repair pouch in the chest pocket. I stuck several on the hole and patted them down, fixing the patches in place with the sealant tape we'd used on our ankles and sleeves. The simplicity of the work concentrated my mind, bringing me down from the hypnosis. I took some more gulps of the cool underground air before tugging the respirator back on my head.

Volk's respirator was at my feet. Following the fresh blood-trail up the hard concrete steps, I reappeared under the shadow of the reactor. The towering black slab seemed bigger in the watery sunlight. The blood-spattered foot-prints leading towards it dragged me nearer. And the Dosimeter shrieked as I advanced, a high-pitched tattoo warning of danger. I switched it off.

I cleared the small copse of trees, where the tracks disappeared into a maze of warehouses on the outskirts of the reactor plant. A line of rusting trucks sat next to a security fence, signs warning of radiation and certain death. Inside the first warehouse I picked up the blood trail, hand prints suggesting that Volk was moving on all fours. Holes in the roof allowed light to flood through, winter-bare tree roots creeping along the edge of the interior. In the distance I saw a figure staggering out of a doorway. I aimed and fired a snap shot, my bullet hitting the metal-framed door.

The emergency repairs on my protective suit appeared to be holding, the pain in my arm getting no worse. I jogged along the side of the warehouse, panting now, my visor blurred by condensation and smeared blood. The two of us played cat-and-mouse, through the warehouses and goods yards. As I neared the reactor shroud I felt a throbbing noise in the earth, like a distant heartbeat. I knew that occasionally technicians had to visit the main reactor to carry out maintenance on the shroud, but I saw no sign of life.

Then, in the distance, I heard the pop of pistol shots.

Following the sound, I reached the edge of the security fence. A gate hung open, the padlocks shot out. Again, blood spatters in the snow led the way, towards a service road and then yet another fence.

247

More shots.

Fyodor Volk stood at the last gate, smoke curling from the barrel of his handgun. A flurry of dirty snowflakes swirled about him. He fell into the steel mesh door and was through, running for the sake of running. Shouldering the AK I went to fire a three round burst. The weapon jammed. I fell to a knee and tried to clear the blockage, a round stuck in the breech. I couldn't budge the bullet with my gloved fingers. I tried pulling the action backwards and forwards angrily, sitting in the snow. Dumping the rifle with disgust, I lumbered towards Volk, drunk with rage.

Fyodor Volk lay crumpled by the protective ditch surrounding the reactor core, a twenty metre drop into an ice-covered abyss. It was like the moat around a castle, except I saw it contained dead animals and sharp pieces of debris and scaffolding. A bloated dog carcass was half-submerged in the ice, dead black eyes staring at us. "This is it" he groaned, bloody hands scratching at the black ballistic bag. His pistol lay next to him, the slide snapped back telling me it was unloaded. His Dosimeter trilled constantly.

"Give me the bag," I panted.

"I can feel it, the radioactivity," he murmured, smiling, "it itches. It should have taken me when it took my family." I stepped towards him, but he was finished. His face was pale from blood loss, his shattered hand laying like a crippled bird on his chest. Behind us the dark concrete shroud buzzed with hidden, malevolent energy.

Shoving my boot into his ribcage, I shuffled him nearer the edge of the pit. "Alisa wanted me to say her name when I killed you."

"I told you, didn't I? About love?" Volk whispered. "Men like us are an aberration are we not, to kill so easily and yet flourish? We are monsters. I learnt too late… the only use for that power is to protect the ones you love."

"Or avenge them?" I said.

"Of course. Read the files. Remember Sergei Belov."

With one final shove, I kicked him over the side of the icy pit. "Alisa," I said as Volk fell into the Ninth Circle, his mouth open in a silent scream.

THIRTY FOUR

I staggered back to the abandoned school, the ballistic bag clutched to my chest. In the bomb shelter I found the dead men's rucksacks containing food, water and a satellite phone. Picking up the supplies, I returned to the town square and loaded Alisa's body into the jeep. The drive to the perimeter road took fifteen minutes, with no sign of the OMON guard force or anybody else. Checking the Dosimeter I took off my helmet and rubbed the cold, oily sweat from my face. I punched a number into the satellite phone.

"Where the Hell have you been?" said Marcus.

"I have the server," I said, "the FSB files, all of them."

"I want to destroy them myself. Are you sure there are no copies or duplicates?"

I slid the spare external drive into my map pocket. "No, Marcus. Just the main hard drive, it wasn't attached to a computer and it was the only piece of kit here. It's sterile."

"Are you OK?" asked the MI6 officer. He finally sounded satisfied.

"Minor injuries, but I've been exposed to some radiation. Alisa is dead."

"Where do you need picking up from?" he said quietly. "And for God's sake, get hosed-down as soon as possible. You need decontaminating."

"I will. I need to get out of Kazan, in Tatarstan."

"I'll call you on this line with extraction details, wait out."

I found the gap in the fence and drove onto the road, back to the petrol station where more interior ministry troops sat eating. Seeing a jeep with air force markings they just looked up from their food and waved. I waved back. I was ushered into the airfield by a guard, and drove up to the Antonov. The pilot and loadmaster were stood in a hut, warming their hands on a brazier and smoking my cigars.

"Colonel Turov is dead," I said, pointing at the jeep. "Our mission is complete. I need to return to Kazan, to inform her superiors."

"Of course," said the pilot sadly. "Our orders are to ask no questions. I will arrange for her body to be put on the plane."

"She's been exposed to radiation," I said.

"We have special body bags for that," said the loadmaster gently, "we'll get a decontamination unit on standby at Kazan." He put an arm around me and offered me a tin cup of vodka-laced coffee.

I nodded and took a sip. "Thanks" I said, "she was a good friend, and brave." I sat next to the lead-lined body-bag containing Alisa Turov's irradiated body on the flight back to Kazan. Even in death she carried the stain of Fyodor Volk and Shakuvo.

Pulling out a dog-eared notebook, I wrote a brief, fictional report in Russian for the SVR outlining what happened. I explained that the FSB files had been wiped by Volk in order to cover up details of his crimes. The only true part was where I highlighted Alisa's bravery and resourcefulness. When we landed near Kazan, a crew set up a decontamination arch. We all stripped in the snow and showered, men in protective equipment brushing us down with long hard brooms. I stood silently as hot, chemical-smelling water ran down my pale, bruised body. My eyes were fixed on the black ballistic bag.

"There is a Mister Pechkin here for you," said the Captain as I dressed in a spare Russian air force flight suit.

"Excellent" I said, "thanks for all your help."

The air force officer saluted smartly and left.

Pechkin was sat in his dirty 4x4, smoking a cigarette. "Where's the Colonel?" he said warily.

"She's dead."

"Well there goes my transfer. Did you find it?"

"Find what?" I said.

"Whatever it was you were looking for," he laughed. "I ask too many questions sometimes I guess. Where do you want to go?"

"The warehouse, please, Mister Pechkin. I need to write a report for your bosses. And Colonel Turov's body needs collecting from the airfield."

"Sure, no problem. A shame about the Colonel, eh?"

"Yes, a terrible shame, Pechkin."

Half an hour later, at the warehouse, I strangled Pechkin. I stared into his piggy eyes as he pissed himself with fear. I left my report for the SVR on his corpse, adding that he was a traitor who had leaked intelligence to Fyodor Volk. Amongst the booty in the warehouse I found warm civilian clothes, luggage and sturdy outdoor boots. I packed the hard drives carefully away, next to a new Japanese laptop I took from the stash of electrical goods. Then I ate a bar of chocolate and waited for the phone to ring.

When it did, Marcus told me to make my way to a cafe near the Turkish Consulate and wait for a man called Balsan. I took Pechkin's jeep and punched the details into the satellite navigation, pulling out into heavy traffic.

Balsan turned out to be a skinny man in his thirties, wearing a heavy black overcoat and a fur hat. As we smoked and drank strong black coffee he gave me a British Passport, credit card, a fat wad of Roubles, a driving licence and fresh mobile telephone. The photograph in the passport was identical to the one I had in my Adrian Clay pseudonym. "The e-tickets are booked," said Balsan, passing me a piece of paper. "You fly to Istanbul tonight, connecting flight to Heathrow. Fucking first class seat, geezer, you must be very important." His accent was straight out of London. He told me he was originally from Haringey.

"Thanks for your help, Balsan," I said.

"No problem. Well, best of British mate" he said as he got up to leave, "see you around."

I called Harry on my new phone. "At last" he said angrily, "I've been answering some very uncomfortable questions."

"The job's finished. Tell Belov that Volk is dead. The servers belonging to Pieter Van Basten are destroyed."

"And we're meant to take your word for that?"

"Yes."

"Belov has already released the funds to us," said Harry. "Job done."

"What's my cut?" I asked.

"Time or money?" said Harry carefully.

"What do you mean?"

"You owe us three more years on The Firm. You can halve that if you only take quarter of a million US, which you collect on termination of contract with interest. It's a good deal, Cal."

"Eighteen months and I'm out? I'll take the time off my sentence," I said coolly. "I'll be in touch." I ended the call. The cafe was warm. I lit a cigar, ordered cake and coffee. Then I watched the world go by.

EPILOGUE

London, England. Two weeks later.

Dmitri Aseyev and I sat in a pub in Shepherd's Market. All that was left of the mighty January storm was dirty slush on the pavements. "They got me off the firearms charges and bailed out of prison," said the Russian quietly, sipping a beer. "The rest is going to be self-defence, according to Sergei's lawyers. The anti-terrorist police have been OK, I think your government has my back. I'm just waiting for the prosecutors to make decision."

"That's good news, Dmitri," I said, handing him a piece of paper. "Now read this."

He studied the report slowly, shaking his meaty head as he took in the contents. "No, Cal. This is... *bullshit.*"

I put my hand on his shoulder. "I'm sorry, but it's true."

The scanned copy of the report was the first thing that popped up on screen when I attached the spare hard drive to my laptop, using the encryption key Volk had given me. The original drive had been handed to Marcus at Heathrow, who told me he was off to destroy it immediately. He thanked me, told me that I had a friend. He'd made sure that Sam and the kids were protected while I was gone, had kept his word.

Even if I hadn't kept mine.

He'd sent half a dozen increments, hard men, to watch her house. He showed me the surveillance photographs to prove it, Sam leaving the house. Sam getting into her car with a dark-haired man. Sam...

"So, what are you going to do?" said the Russian security man, looking around the half-empty pub.

I drained my beer and ordered another, "don't you mean what are *we* going to do?"

Dmitri's eyes filled with tears as he nodded. He stared into his drink and emptied a slug of vodka into his pint. Sergei knew about NEOPHYTE. He'd threatened me. And the evidence I'd put in front of Dmitri proved that, in his own way, Sergei had created Fyodor Volk. There was only one way this could end. It was justice, of sorts. The sort that a court could never provide.

And to hell with The Firm.

I'd just come back from a hell, of sorts, and the frozen Ninth Circle below Shakuvo scared me more than Harry ever could. "When do you want to do this?" said Dmitri.

"Tonight."

Just after ten that evening, Dmitri stood down the guards and let me into the side entrance of Sergei Belov's Mayfair townhouse. He disabled the alarms and CCTV, his big hands sheathed in leather gloves.

I stepped into the study, where the oligarch sat watching the fire, drinking. A big black book sat on his lap. "Good evening, Sergei" I said.

"Cal," he replied, surprised. The supressed Walther hissed as I shot him twice in the forehead. Sergei crashed sideways, onto the carpet, his glass rolling into the grate of the fire. The devil in the oil painting leered at me from the mantelpiece. From a pocket I pulled a sterile copy of the report I'd shown Dmitri. With surgically gloved fingers, I left it next to his body.

SECRET - KGB Regional Headquarters (Central)
Sixth Directorate – Economic Counterintelligence and Industrial Security

4th December 1990
Subject: Sergei Nikolayevich BELOV
Provenance: Personal / Delicate
Grade: Highly credible

Intelligence: BELOV is the Chairman of the industrial standards committee of the Shakuvo energy complex in Tatarstan. Last year he fraudulently transferred twelve million roubles offshore from the core maintenance budget for the Shakuvo reactor. BELOV has manipulated monthly maintenance reports to conceal the fraud. Two members of the committee who are aware of this theft and have warned of declining safety standards have been framed and murdered by persons suspected to be linked to mafia groups in Kazan. BELOV has political aspirations and is described as being well-thought of in Moscow.

Action: BELOV was a respected Party Member prior to 1989. This report should be filed and revisited when resources allow, pending fresh security structures established by the new government.

I pocketed my spent cartridges and left the house. Dmitri locked the door behind me, nodded and headed for his car. The ground was coated with frost beneath my feet. London still froze, but the snow had gone. I checked my fake passport and the airline tickets for Barcelona, quickened my step. Phoning Sam Clarke as I headed towards Berkeley Square, I asked if I could visit tomorrow. I told her I was heading off to Spain for a while and would like to catch up. She said yes, it would be good to see me before I left. Maybe we could go to the cinema with the kids. The conversation with Sam made the things that squirm and chatter at the back of my head go away for a while, better than any drug.

I decided to enjoy it while it lasted.